The Silent Touch of Shadows

ALSO BY CHRISTINA COURTENAY
FROM CLIPPER LARGE PRINT

Trade Winds
The Scarlet Kimono
Highland Storms

The Silent Touch of Shadows

Christina Courtenay

W F HOWES LTD

This large print edition published in 2012 by
W F Howes Ltd
Unit 4, Rearsby Business Park, Gaddesby Lane,
Rearsby, Leicester LE7 4YH

1 3 5 7 9 10 8 6 4 2

First published in the United Kingdom in 2012
by Choc Lit Limited

A CIP catalogue record for this book is available
from the British Library

ISBN 978 1 47120 596 5

Typeset by Palimpsest Book Production Limited,
Falkirk, Stirlingshire
Printed and bound in Great Britain
by MPG Books Ltd, Bodmin, Cornwall

MIX
Paper from
responsible sources
FSC® C018575

To Joyce and Raymond Fenton with love
Thank you for the wonderful Stocketts memories!

and

To Roger de la Stockette
May you find what you're looking for and RIP one
day

PROLOGUE

In the huge inglenook of the ancient manor house, the remains of the log fire collapsed with a hiss into a heap of smouldering ashes. A coil of smoke floated up the chimney, disintegrating slowly.

Nothing else moved in the room. The shadows that waited there gave no sign of their presence, apart from an occasional sigh that could have been mistaken for the draught blowing in under the badly fitting window frames.

Even so, the air crackled with restless energy and expectation. An electric charge suddenly galvanised the dust motes into a frenzied whirl, sending them spiralling towards the ceiling before they plunged downwards again in a never-ending dance.

The time had come to try again.

The time had come for the silent touch of shadows.

CHAPTER 1

Ashleigh Manor, Kent – Present Day

The driveway appeared quite unexpectedly after a sharp bend in the winding lane, taking Melissa by surprise. There were no signposts to advertise its presence and she almost missed the turning. Something made her slow down though and look to her right as they came around the corner. And there it was.

'Ashleigh,' she whispered to herself as she stared at the house through a pair of wrought-iron gates. Confusion filled her mind when she realised she recognised this place, and yet she was sure she had never been here before.

The old manor house nestled in a hollow, as if it had burrowed into the ground for comfort. Picture perfect, it was built of timber and orange-red bricks, with tiny leaded windows and tall chimney stacks. The colour gave an impression of warmth, reinforced by the sunlight reflected off the myriad of windowpanes. A shiver snaked up Melissa's spine. The view was eerily familiar.

'Is this where the old lady lives?' Her twelve-year-old daughter Jolie sighed and removed the ear plugs of her iPod, then directed a look of suffering at her mother which Melissa ignored.

'Yes, I think so,' she replied, but really there was no doubt about it. She knew this was the right place and didn't need to check the written directions. The sensation of *déjà vu* was so strong it made her frown. Perplexed, she continued to stare through the gate.

'Do we have to stay long?'

It was Melissa's turn to sigh. 'I told you we're invited for the whole weekend. Weren't you listening? I've never met great-aunt Dorothy before, so it would be nice if we could at least make a good first impression. Come on, please stop sulking now. You'll survive. Who knows, you might even enjoy it.'

Jolie made a face and muttered, 'Fat chance,' then turned up her music once more, oblivious to the beautiful countryside surrounding them. Melissa shook her head and climbed out of the car to open the gates. She had to admit to some apprehension herself, as her great-aunt's invitation to come and stay for a weekend had been totally unexpected. Dorothy's phone call a few days earlier was the first communication anyone in the family had had with her for over fifty years. Apparently Dorothy had fallen out with her sister Ruth, Melissa's grandmother, and no one had heard from her since.

So why the sudden change of heart? And how had Dorothy found her after all this time? A recent electoral roll perhaps, or had she hired a sleuth?

The crisp air made Melissa pull the edges of her unbuttoned jacket together, but she soon forgot the cold as she breathed in the earthy smells of the countryside. It was like stepping into a greenhouse where you instinctively fill your lungs to capacity from the oxygen-rich air, and Melissa couldn't seem to get enough of it. Although nature was only just waking from its winter slumber, there was plenty of greenery around, which made a welcome change from London. Melissa stood for a moment simply admiring the view.

They continued up the drive and parked next to a yew hedge, which surrounded a part of the lawn and flower beds immediately in front of the house, creating a cottage garden within the main grounds. The hedge had been trimmed to velvety perfection and grew thick and deep. A profusion of snowdrops peeped out from underneath the bushes, looking as if they were wondering whether it was safe to come out yet.

Before Melissa had even switched off the engine, a woman emerged from the front door and came down the path towards a gate set in the hedge. 'Welcome, my dears,' she called out. An excited little white terrier with a patch of black over one eye trotted behind her. When he caught sight of them he started jumping up and down, barking furiously.

Melissa assumed the woman must be her great-aunt since no one else came out. They shook hands in a rather formal way, which made Melissa feel as though she ought to curtsey or something. Dorothy was all smiles, however, so she gathered it was just old-fashioned manners.

'Hello, lovely to meet you,' Melissa said.

'And you, I'm so glad you could come.' Dorothy turned to wag a finger at the terrier. 'Now stop that, Russ, you're too noisy,' she ordered, but he wouldn't settle down until he had been made a fuss of by his guests. 'I'm sorry, he has no manners. He's just so happy to have visitors. I think he's hoping your daughter will play with him later.'

'I'd love to, can we go now?' The sulky expression had miraculously vanished the instant Jolie had caught sight of Russ. She bent down to scratch him behind the ears. 'I love dogs,' she added and giggled when the terrier tried to lick her chin.

Dorothy's eyes crinkled with amusement. 'Why don't you come and see the house first, then you two can go off and explore for a while before lunch?'

'Oh, all right then.' Jolie reverted to her previous near-teenage pout and ignored the warning look Melissa shot her.

Dorothy chattered on about the weather and this obviously wasn't the right time to ask awkward questions, so Melissa just nodded politely from time to time. Dorothy seemed amiable enough, although there was definitely a hint of steel in her

6

gaze as if she was used to ruling the roost. Well, she would have had to be pretty tough in order to stand up to Grandma Ruth, Melissa thought. She remembered all too well the terror that old lady had inspired in anyone who displeased her.

While Dorothy held forth, Melissa studied her surreptitiously to see if there was any family resemblance, but couldn't see any. Her great-aunt was tiny, with thick white hair and clear blue eyes, the complete opposite of Melissa's late grandmother. Dressed in navy blue trousers and a cashmere sweater, with a matching silk scarf knotted loosely around her neck, Dorothy looked casual but chic. She certainly didn't look her age, which Melissa guessed to be around seventy.

As they walked up the path to the porch, the sense of *déjà vu* returned and grew even stronger than when she'd first arrived. Melissa stopped to contemplate the house close up, searching for an answer to this phenomenon, but could find no logical explanation in the weathered brick walls.

'Are you coming, my dear?' Dorothy had turned to wait for her.

'Yes, of course. I was just, umm . . . admiring the façade.' Confused by her strange reaction, Melissa forced herself to ignore it and move on. Before their arrival, she had been excited about the prospect of visiting a house that had apparently belonged to her ancestors for generations, and she was determined nothing should ruin her enjoyment of this weekend.

Before she had time to think about it more, they were whisked into the house through a solid oak front door, which squeaked in protest as it slammed shut behind them. Suppressing the irrational feeling of recognition, Melissa tried instead to gaze with interest at her surroundings. They had entered a low, dark hallway lit by two dim wall lights. A strong smell of floor-polish hung in the air, reminding Melissa of her grandmother's house. In fact, polish seemed to have been rubbed into every surface; whether wood or metal, they all gleamed in the soft light. An old-fashioned bronze mirror distorted their images into comical shapes and Melissa saw Jolie peering into it from different angles to see what effect it would have on her features.

'This is lovely!' Melissa stopped and looked around at the smooth, plaster-covered walls, which had been painted white to contrast with the dark oak beams and planks around them. They looked ancient and solid and the sheer beauty of the workmanship was amazing.

'In here, dear.' Dorothy and Jolie disappeared further down the hall and her great-aunt's voice floated back to her, muffled by the thick walls. Melissa tried to follow the others, but was suddenly overcome by emotion at the thought of all the generations of ancestors who had walked here before her. She felt as if she was being enveloped into a collective embrace by them all and had to swallow hard. Taking a deep breath, she composed herself and made her way to the sitting room, where Jolie waited impatiently.

'Mum, look, isn't this huge?' She was obviously impressed enough to have forgotten to sulk and her honey-brown eyes opened wide as she took in the generous proportions of the room. Her winter jacket had been flung onto the floor and Melissa bent to pick it up, her reaction automatic.

'It used to be the great hall when the house was first built some time in the fifteenth century,' Dorothy told her. 'If you think it's huge now, you should have seen it back then – open all the way up to the ceiling. If you go up into the attic you can still see the soot from the cooking fire on the roof beams, left over from before they constructed this fireplace.' Dorothy pointed to an enormous inglenook, which took up more than half a wall.

Melissa closed her eyes and was shocked at the detailed picture that formed in her mind. She could see the big hall clearly, including the massive ceiling rafters, the benches along the walls and even the haze of smoke from the central hearth drifting upwards to a hole in the ceiling. At either end she glimpsed doorways leading to storage rooms and steps up to small private sleeping chambers above. The sounds of feet scraping on the floor and the barking of dogs assailed her.

A voice came out of nowhere, calling for ale, but the man spoke with an unfamiliar dialect which made Melissa wonder where he might come from. There were candles burning in sconces set at intervals along the walls, and their distinctive smell caused Melissa to wrinkle her nose. They cast their flickering light over floorboards that weren't very clean, and in one corner a couple of dogs were fighting over a bone.

When Melissa inhaled sharply, the stench of unwashed humans and cooking clogged her nose and throat. It made her gag in disgust and she blinked, shaking her head to clear the images away. She looked around the room for the source of the voice, but there was no one there now except Dorothy and Jolie. They were still talking and didn't look as though they'd heard or seen anything unusual. Completely disorientated, Melissa stumbled after the others when they moved on.

'The whole of the first floor was created later to make space for more bedrooms,' Dorothy was saying, 'and an extension added in the seventeenth century made the house L-shaped.' The old lady was obviously very proud of her home and Melissa dutifully admired everything that was pointed out to her. She had no trouble making the right noises; it really was beautiful and just the sort of house she would have liked for herself. She'd been fascinated by history for as long as she could remember, so to her, living in a building this old would be paradise.

To her relief, Jolie was becoming more animated by the minute and showed great interest in what Dorothy told them.

'So this house is six hundred years old?' Jolie said. '*Six hundred* is, like, *ancient*.'

10

Dorothy chuckled at her expression. 'Yes, you'll get used to the idea. Isn't it nice to know that it was built to last? Just think how many storms it must have weathered. I always feel so safe here.'

Jolie nodded, but Melissa shivered involuntarily as she thought of all that must have happened during the past six centuries. Births, deaths, marriages, the house had seen them all. Laughter, sadness, love, *grief* . . . As the others moved on again, a gut-wrenching sadness overwhelmed her without warning and made her gasp out loud. She wanted to curl up on the floor and howl with some dimly remembered pain. When she followed this instinct and doubled over, clutching at her clenched stomach muscles, the emotion disappeared as quickly as it had come. Melissa straightened up and took in a shuddering breath.

What on earth is the matter with me?

She felt suddenly cold and glanced over her shoulder, but there was nothing. She shook her head at her own stupidity and hurried to catch up with the others before any more strange things happened.

'I'm so pleased you could come. I've been meaning to contact you ever since I found out that both your mother and grandmother had passed away,' Dorothy said. 'But my beloved husband, Charles, also died last year and it's taken me a while to come to terms with that.'

They were having a chat by the fire in the sitting room and Melissa felt herself relax into the deep armchair. Entering the room for a second time, she'd been relieved not to experience any more strange sights or sounds. She put the unusual images down to an overactive imagination. It was a very old house after all.

'Of course,' she said now. 'Grief isn't easy to cope with. When I lost mum I found it so hard to accept. She was the only one I had left, apart from Jolie, of course.'

'Yes, and what a terrible shame, dying so young. Cancer is a dreadful disease.'

Melissa nodded. It wasn't something she wanted to dwell on. She still couldn't quite grasp that her mother was really gone. 'I have to admit your call came as quite a surprise. Grandma hardly ever spoke of you and I didn't expect to hear from you.'

Melissa hadn't even known of Dorothy's existence until she began to trace her family tree and started asking questions, but she thought it best not to mention that. When pressed as to the reason for this estrangement, her mother had told her Dorothy wanted no contact with their part of the family and then muttered something about 'letting sleeping dogs lie'. This was intriguing and Melissa hoped she would finally get some answers.

'Oh, it was all so silly.' Dorothy shrugged. 'Ruth and I had an argument and we were both very stubborn. The years went by and before we knew it, it was too late to patch things up. It was just one of those things, but it's all in the past now. It needn't concern us.'

Melissa felt sure there must have been more to it than that, but before she could ask Dorothy for details, the old lady changed the subject.

'So what is it you do exactly? I gather you're divorced, so presumably you work, at least part time?'

'Yes, that's right. I'm a professional genealogist. I prepare family trees for private clients and I also do freelance jobs for several law firms, helping them to find people mentioned in wills. Some of the work can be done from home, which makes it ideal for me.'

'Sounds fascinating.' Dorothy looked as though she meant it and Melissa was just about to tell her more when they were interrupted by the sound of the front door slamming. The noise made Melissa's stomach muscles clench with sudden anxiety. She was still trying to puzzle out this irrational reaction when, seconds later, Jolie burst into the sitting room, closely followed by a panting Russ. They were both oblivious to the trail of mud behind them as Jolie rushed to her mother's side and Russ trotted over to lie down on a little dog bed next to Dorothy, looking tired but happy. Melissa cringed and tried in vain to signal to her daughter, but Dorothy made no comment.

'Mum, you won't believe it. There's a swimming pool outside. A huge one!' Jolie turned to Dorothy. 'Can I go for a swim, please?'

'In February? Goodness, no, I'm afraid you'll have to wait until May at least,' Dorothy laughed. 'I can't afford to heat that monstrosity.'

'Oh.' Jolie looked disappointed, then brightened up again. 'So can we come back in May, Mum?'

'Perhaps you should just wait to be *invited* back?' Melissa replied pointedly, and shook her head at Jolie.

'Oh, yeah, right.' Jolie flung herself into a deep armchair near the fireplace and stared into the flames.

Melissa sighed inwardly, but at least Jolie seemed to have forgotten that she didn't want to spend the weekend in the country 'with a stuffy old aunt'. She'd gone off to explore the enormous garden of the manor house with her canine companion, eyes sparkling with excitement.

'Of course you're welcome any time, dear.' Dorothy stood up. 'Now I expect you're thirsty after all that exercise. I'll get you some squash, shall I? And some biscuits, perhaps? You young-sters are always hungry, I understand.'

'Er, do you have Coke?' Jolie looked mildly offended to be offered a drink she considered fit only for babies.

'I'm sure Jolie could find her way to the kitchen to fetch something for herself,' Melissa protested. Since her divorce from Jolie's dad the previous year, she'd been trying hard to make her daughter more self-reliant. 'And water is fine, thank you.'

'No, no, it's no bother. I shan't be a moment and I'll see what I can find.'

'Great, thanks.' Jolie nodded and, as soon as Dorothy had left, she whispered, 'Your aunt is really nice, Mum, I like her. And I like this house, too.'

'Great-aunt,' Melissa corrected automatically, 'and yes, I think I like her, too.' She felt it was early days yet and she didn't really know Dorothy well enough, but at least they had made a start. 'She might like you better if you take your shoes off next time you come in from the garden, though.' She glanced at the rapidly drying mud on the carpet.

'Oops.' Jolie grinned and Melissa couldn't help but smile back.

She shook her head at her daughter. 'You're impossible.'

'But you love me anyway,' Jolie shot back with a cheeky grin, her red curls bouncing. Her hair was of a particularly vivid shade of red, unlike Melissa's own which was more a warm auburn.

'Hmm,' Melissa said, but they both knew she found it hard to be stern and she loved Jolie to bits.

She took a deep breath and tried to relax again, soothed by the peaceful setting. It really was an amazing house, she had to agree, although a slight feeling of unease still lingered in her mind. 'It must be wonderful to live here,' she said, ignoring a little voice inside her which insisted that somehow she knew exactly what it was like. 'Aunt Dorothy is a lucky woman.'

As she prepared for bed that night in the guest room she was sharing with Jolie, Melissa thought about the odd sensations she'd been experiencing all day. Was she just imagining things, affected by the unusual surroundings? If not, what else could be causing them?

Dorothy had confirmed that neither Melissa, nor her parents, had ever visited Ashleigh, so she definitely couldn't have any real memories of the place. There must be another explanation. Had her grandmother told her tales of the house when she was a little girl, perhaps? But she couldn't recall Grandma ever doing anything except tell her not to put her sticky fingers on her furniture.

It was a mystery.

With a sigh, she crept into bed and listened to Jolie's soft breathing. She was glad now that her daughter had insisted they share, even though Dorothy had offered them a room each.

'I'd rather stay with you, Mum,' Jolie had whispered. 'Just this first time.' Melissa knew what she meant as waking up in strange surroundings was always daunting.

She closed her eyes and as she drifted off to sleep her mind filled once more with bewildering images. Images that teased at her brain, tantalising, beckoning her. Melissa concentrated hard. She wanted to remember more, much more, but someone was calling her . . .

CHAPTER 2

Ashleigh Manor, Kent – 1460

'You are to return by this afternoon or I'll fetch you myself, girl!'

Her father's bellow echoed through the hall as Sibell scurried to the door. She bit back a sharp retort while fumbling with the latch in her haste to escape his presence. 'Girl' he called her, even though she was a woman grown and a widow to boot. Not that it made a difference to him, she thought, she was still his chattel to dispose of as he wished. She gritted her teeth in frustration and a sigh of relief hissed out of her as she finally slammed the sturdy front door shut.

For the moment, at least, she was safe.

'Freedom!' The very word was an exclamation of joy. Although she only dared whisper it, Sibell savoured the feel of it on her tongue. She gulped in huge lungfuls of the clean, sweet country air, and revelled in the warmth spread over her face by the late February sun. Its feeble rays caressed the dusting of freckles across the bridge of her nose and probably highlighted the pallor of

17

her translucent skin. Forgetting herself, she laughed out loud with sheer pleasure, then clapped a hand over her mouth. She glanced back towards the house in fear and froze for an instant.

All remained quiet. No one had heard.

Sibell set off towards the lane at a brisk walk, but soon had to slow down. Three days with only meagre rations of food had sapped her energy and she was still sore from the beating she'd received before being locked in. Out of sight of the house she stopped to catch her breath for a moment before continuing. The track, which passed for a road in this part of the world, was unbelievably muddy. Sibell's wooden pattens made a slurping noise for each step she took, and became heavier by the minute as the thick substance stuck to the soles. Normally she would have ridden her docile mare, as befitted a lady, but this luxury had been denied her today since she was in deep disgrace.

She had to reach her destination. *It's my only hope.* This thought spurred her on and after a quick glance over her shoulder, she began to trudge along the lane.

'Your pardon, mistress, but could you direct us to the manor of Idenhurst, please?'

The question, although civil enough and asked in a reasonable tone of voice, made Sibell jump. Her euphoria at being outside the confines of her chamber evaporated in an instant as she became aware of two horsemen who had halted just beside her. They were staring down at her from the intimidating height of their steeds. How could she possibly have missed hearing the approach of two riders? These were dangerous times and she needed her wits about her. She scanned her surroundings surreptitiously, but there was no one within sight who could come to her aid.

'Forgive me, I didn't mean to startle you.' The deep voice was gentle and soothing, but as Sibell squinted up at the man, shielding her eyes from the light with one hand, her breath caught in her throat. A shard of fear stabbed her sharply. She swallowed hard. It seemed to her that she had exchanged one peril for another.

Seated on a giant war horse of shimmering grey was a huge warrior. Golden hair fell to his shoulders, where it brushed the top of his cerulean blue cloak. Strength and power radiated from every taut muscle and the determined set of his jaw indicated that he wasn't a man to be crossed. Sibell had no doubt he was dangerous; no doubt at all.

As he raised an eyebrow in amused enquiry, however, the feeling of terror subsided. She recalled that he was expecting an answer. His horse champed at the bit and pawed the ground with a massive front hoof, as if he too was tiring of the wait.

'I-Idenhurst?' she stammered, embarrassed by her lack of courtesy. 'I am going there myself and it's but another few miles along this track.'

'My thanks.' The man smiled, showing even white teeth, and adjusted his seat in the saddle.

Sibell blinked. He had the most incredible smile and she couldn't help but stare, though she knew she shouldn't.

He continued, 'Since we are travelling the same way, perhaps you'd care to ride with me and save your skirts from the mire? It's the least I can do for such a beautiful lady.'

Sibell's eyes widened and she felt the heat of a blush spread across her cheeks. He had paid her a compliment. But . . . ride with him? Only an arrogant stranger would think to ask a lady such a thing.

'No, I thank you, sir. I am enjoying my walk. Truly, it's not far.' Although her voice sounded far from convincing to her own ears, she resolutely ignored the chafing of her dress against the sore welts across her back. Likewise, she did her best to ignore the sea of mud in which she was standing. The offer of a ride was most tempting, but she couldn't possibly accept.

She managed an awkward curtsey intended as a dismissal, but when she straightened up, the riders hadn't moved an inch. The golden-haired one was staring at her with a thoughtful look in his eyes. Perhaps he wasn't used to having his invitations refused, Sibell thought. Most ladies would likely have jumped at the chance to ride with him, but not her. *I dare not.* She flushed again and looked pointedly at the ground, waiting for their departure.

'Oh, I see what the problem is,' she heard him

say smoothly. 'I haven't introduced myself and of course no respectable lady can ride with a stranger.' Against her better judgement she looked up as, half-standing up in the saddle, he bowed to her. 'I'm Sir Roger of Langford and this is my squire, Hugone.' He indicated the second rider, a gangly youth with straight, dark hair whom Sibell had almost forgotten. The squire had faded into insignificance next to his master, but she now saw he was goggling at her with his mouth open. He blushed at the introduction and bowed low over the neck of his horse.

She inclined her head in his direction before dropping another curtsey to his master. 'And I am Sibell of Ashleigh, but . . .'

'I won't listen to any refusals, mistress.' The knight held up his hand to stop her from arguing. 'My conscience will not allow me to leave a lady by the roadside, alone and unprotected. These are dangerous times,' he added, unconsciously echoing her earlier thoughts. His tone was haughty now, that of a man used to having his orders obeyed, she guessed.

But conscience? Sibell doubted very much he possessed such a thing and the only person she needed protection from was him. She was about to say so when she noticed a distinct twinkle in his eyes. Could he be laughing at her? She tossed her head and drew herself up to deliver a scathing retort, but he forestalled her once more.

'As you see, you are suitably chaperoned by

Hugone, who wouldn't dream of allowing a lady to come to any harm.' The young squire cast a look of confusion at his master, who ignored him and continued. 'So let us be off, for I have urgent business with Sir Gilbert Presseille at Idenhurst.' Sibell's protest was cut short by another devastating smile and she found to her consternation that her mind had stopped functioning. The intended reprimand died on her lips.

Sir Roger had thrown down the gauntlet of a challenge. He stretched out his hand peremptorily, daring her with mischievous eyes to refuse once more.

Rebellion suddenly stirred within Sibell and a treacherous voice in her mind asked, 'Why shouldn't I ride with him?' Hadn't she vowed to fight her father with any means at her disposal these last few days? She must have paced her bedchamber a hundred times at least, cursing him and his edicts. Well, here was her chance to defy him.

Her mind made up, she put her small hand in Sir Roger's large one without further hesitation. She felt the strength of his fingers as he pulled her up behind him. She was lifted effortlessly, as if she weighed nothing at all, and found herself sitting on the huge rump of his war horse. He nudged the destrier and the animal set off at a slow walk.

'His name is Snowflake.' Sir Roger patted the horse with affection as they ambled along the lane.

'His white mane and tail and gleaming coat made it the only choice of name for him, so what could I do? I had to bow to the inevitable.' The knight laughed, a rich, glorious sound that sent vibrations of pleasure shooting through Sibell. 'It's not really a name to inspire awe in my enemies though, you must agree, but I try to keep it a secret. You'll not tell, mistress?'

He glanced over his shoulder at her, his blue eyes twinkling. At such close quarters she noticed that his otherwise regular features were marred by a long scar running from the tip of the left eyebrow down towards his firm jaw line. An old wound, neatly healed, the puckered welt wasn't ugly or frightening. Sibell wasn't in any way repelled by it. In fact, strangely enough, she found it attractive, although she had no idea why that should be so.

She shook her head, unable to speak. He was trying to put her at ease, but she was too aware of him as a man to relax in his company. Of necessity she had to hold on to his lean waist in order to keep her seat, but she tried to keep her touch as light as possible. Even so, there was a strange tingling in her fingers every time she felt him move with the horse. She could have sworn she heard a smile in his voice when he said, 'Hold on tight, Mistress Sibell. We wouldn't want you falling off.' Could he read her mind?

The morning was cold, despite the best efforts of the sun, and the warmth from Sir Roger's steed was very welcome indeed. Sibell wasn't convinced that riding with him was good for her peace of mind, but she had to admit it was definitely preferable to plodding along muddy tracks on foot. *As long as no one sees me.* Her father wouldn't approve of her so much as talking to this man, let alone riding with him. Sibell shivered with remembered pain and concentrated on her surroundings.

A pox on her father, she thought defiantly.

A searing pain in her back woke Melissa abruptly in the middle of the night, dragging her out of a dream, which faded away even though she struggled to hold on to it. With a sigh, she turned over and tried to go to sleep again, but her back was very sore and she couldn't get comfortable. She wondered what was wrong with it and grimaced as she tried to stretch.

Slowly, she became aware of a pungent smell in the room – horse or farmyard if she wasn't mistaken. It would be impossible to imagine such a strong odour, so it had to be real. *Perhaps there's a farm nearby? That might explain it.* It was a far cry from the noxious exhaust fumes outside her London flat, and strangely enough she found it less repellent. For some reason, it made her feel at home.

Still hurting, she sat up and felt her back to determine the cause of the pain, but it was subsiding rapidly now. Within seconds it had disappeared completely. Puzzled, she fumbled for the light to have a proper look, then remembered she was sharing the room with Jolie. She would have to look in the morning. Irritated, she lay down again.

The timbers of the old house creaked and she heard the wind whistling down the chimney in the tiny fireplace. The sounds didn't disturb her. On the contrary, they gave her a feeling of security. She burrowed deep under the cover once more. If she closed her eyes, perhaps she could imagine how it must have been to live here hundreds of years ago, when there was no electricity or central heating. Only open fireplaces, horses and bold knights roaming the countryside. Bold knights . . .?

'Isn't this much better than walking?' Sir Roger asked cheerfully after they had been riding for a while. 'We'll be at Idenhurst in no time.'

Sibell didn't know how to reply. It seemed to her he was going incredibly slowly and she wanted the journey over with in case they were seen. On the other hand, she enjoyed his banter and it made a nice change to be treated as though she was of consequence for once. Lately, she'd been ignored so often it felt as if she didn't exist.

She heard the sound of horse's hooves in the distance and turned swiftly to scan the surrounding area.

'You don't fear robbers, do you, mistress?' He kept glancing over his shoulder at her.

'What? Oh, no.' Sibell sighed. *Robbers – if only it was that simple.*

A tress of hair had escaped her headdress and impatiently she tried to push it back underneath the linen, then froze as she heard Sir Roger's sharp intake of breath. She saw him stare, mesmerised, at the red colour of her hair. Embarrassed, she turned away. He was probably as appalled by its fiery hue as she was, she thought, but he recovered quickly and looked away.

'I can assure you I'm well able to defend you against all but an army of men.' He patted the lethal-looking sword dangling at his waist and Sibell glanced at the weapon. She didn't think it an idle boast. Most men would likely think twice before challenging someone like him. With another inward sigh, she decided to tell him the truth. No doubt he'd hear all about her anyway if he stayed in these parts.

'No, it's not outlaws I fear, Sir Roger, but my father,' she admitted.

'Ah.' Sir Roger nodded slowly, comprehension dawning in his eyes. 'Is there perhaps another route we could take where the chances of meeting anyone would lessen?'

'Why, yes.' She was grateful for his quick understanding and gave him directions and they soon turned off the track into a small forest instead. 'It's only slightly further this way. You don't mind?'

'Not at all, it's a fine morning for a ride after

all.' He grinned at her. 'And with such lovely company, how could I complain?'

Sibell felt her cheeks turn rosy yet again. It had been a long time since anyone had teased her in this manner and she wasn't used to the attentions of men such as he. The horse's gait was soothing, however, and eventually she relaxed in his company and even managed to smile back as Sir Roger continued with his banter.

'There, I knew it,' he exclaimed, casting a triumphant look over his shoulder. 'You do indeed have dimples. A face as perfect as yours had to have them, it was a foregone conclusion.'

'What nonsense.' A giggle escaped her before she could stop it. 'I can see you're practised in the art of flirtation, sir, but I shall ignore you. No doubt you speak that way to every female you encounter.'

He pretended to look mortally offended and she had to laugh at his expression. 'You wound me to the quick, mistress,' he protested. 'I swear, everyone else will seem sadly wilted after your vibrant beauty.'

Sibell just shook her head. She couldn't possibly take him seriously, but she enjoyed his compliments all the same. They were a far cry from the comments she usually received at home where nothing she did ever seemed to please anyone.

As they came out of the forest and approached Idenhurst in the distance, however, Sir Roger's expression hardened. The jovial man seemed to disappear in an instant, to be replaced by the frightening stranger she had first met. 'Tell me,' he said, 'what do you know of Sir Gilbert? What manner of man is he?'

'Sir Gilbert? Why he's the best of men,' she replied without hesitation. 'One to be reckoned with, but honest and honourable at all times.'

'Truly?' Sir Roger didn't look convinced.

'Yes. He was my father-in-law, you know. That is, until my husband died last year . . .' Sibell felt the sorrow wash over her once more as she recalled the circumstances that had triggered her present predicament. As always, she tried to suppress the memories. 'I met with nothing but kindness at Idenhurst.'

'He must have died very young, your husband?'

'Yes, Roland was barely twenty. He died in the recent fighting.'

'Is that so?'

Sir Roger looked as though he was about to add something to this comment, but he must have thought better of it since he turned away and said no more. Sibell saw him concentrate on his surroundings as they came closer to their destination. He looked around with keen eyes, obviously noting every detail with interest. To Sibell, Idenhurst had been a much-loved home, but she now tried to look at it from a stranger's point of view.

It was a large, moated manor house built of creamy yellow stone with red-tiled roofs. To reach

28

it, they had to pass over a bridge and under a small tower into a cobbled courtyard, which was teeming with people going about their daily business. Directly opposite the entrance tower was the enormous hall, which had clearly been designed to impress visitors with its proportions and grandeur. It had more than the usual number of windows for a building of this size, indicating that Sir Gilbert was a man of means as well as power. A wealth of other buildings surrounded the courtyard quadrangle, effectively enclosing it. Outside were gardens and an orchard, as well as a series of large fishponds.

Idenhurst was not intended as a fortress. Nonetheless, there were a number of fighting men lounging about in the morning sun, polishing their weapons and sharpening swords and daggers. A group of young squires were practising swordplay in one corner under the watchful eye of a seasoned warrior. Several huge destriers were being curried to glossy perfection by the stable grooms.

'Very nice,' Sibell heard Sir Roger mutter sarcastically and it suddenly occurred to her to wonder what his purpose in coming here was. She fervently hoped he wasn't an enemy of Sir Gilbert's. That would mean he'd be sent packing instantly and she realised she didn't want that.

She wanted him to stay.

CHAPTER 3

'**N**o!' Melissa came to in the hazy half-light of dawn, shaking with a mixture of anger, frustration, attraction and fear. Her heart hammered frantically at the bars of her ribcage. On the one hand she desperately wanted to stay with the handsome warrior instead of returning to grim reality, but on the other lurked the fear of being hurt by a man again. She cursed under her breath. *Can't I be left in peace, even in my dreams?*

'Hormones,' she muttered. 'That's all it is, nothing more.' Her body was obviously confused and lonely.

'Mum? What's the matter?' Jolie mumbled sleepily.

'Nothing, sweetheart, everything's fine.' Melissa had forgotten for a moment that they were sharing a room, but Jolie was soon asleep again.

Melissa tried to calm her breathing, while wondering why she had dreamed of a medieval knight of all things. It had never happened before, but then she'd had lots of strange dreams since the split from Steve. Her sleep was disturbed most nights and it had been ages since she'd felt truly rested. With all the worries about money and their future, it was no wonder. She sighed. Perhaps she should go to the doctor and ask for sleeping pills? She had, after all, been through a lot lately. Somehow it seemed like giving in though.

How about counselling? *What for? An inability to accept that my husband has left me?* That would be too embarrassing for words.

'No.' Melissa punched the pillow for emphasis. She'd never admit her weakness to anyone. And she *would* get over Steve. Somehow.

Taking another deep calming breath, she tried to go back to sleep. The minute she closed her eyes, wisps of the dream began to tease her brain with tantalising glimpses of the knight. She frowned into the darkness. What was it about him that had attracted her so? Surely mere good looks couldn't create such yearning for a man? Or could they?

Annoyed with herself for even thinking about it, she closed her eyes tightly and tried again to go to sleep. Using a trick someone had taught her of deliberately trying to see only the colour black on the inside of her eyelids, she managed to concentrate for a few moments. Then the pictures of the knight began to hover around the perimeter of her vision, teasing, waiting to pounce.

Melissa wanted to curse out loud with frustration, but that would wake Jolie again, so instead she turned over to glare at the wall.

Why did this particular dream seem so real? She

could still feel the texture of the man's woollen cloak and remember the rhythm of the horse's gait. Still smell the animal and the leather of its harness, hear the jingling of it and the clanking of his spurs as he urged the horse into a trot. She wrinkled her nose. Come to think of it, there was a distinctly equine smell in the room.

Impossible. It had to be the farmyard odour she had detected earlier. She snorted quietly. Her imagination was truly working overtime. *I really must get out more.*

The handsome warrior on his huge destrier was *not* real. Of course he wasn't. It was only in her dream that he came to take her on a ride to a night of bliss, leaving her sated and languorous the way Steve used to do before he . . . She ground her teeth and redirected her thoughts with an effort. Such perfect men existed only in fairy tales. These days there was no guarantee of a 'happy ever after' even if you did happen to find your dream man.

I should know.

As a naive nineteen-year old, she thought she had found hers. She'd been carried away all right, a whirlwind romance that resulted in marriage and a child, just as in the books she loved to read. But it seemed today's knights were allowed to tire of their wives and simply walk out, asking for a divorce, and leaving behind them a gaping hole of emptiness.

'I need space. I need to find myself,' Steve had

said the day he left so abruptly. 'For Christ's sake, we were too young, they shouldn't have let us get married at that age. We hadn't really lived, you know.'

Melissa was stunned. She'd thought they would do their 'living' together; had foolishly imagined their love would sustain them through whatever came their way. Obviously, the love had been one-sided. So why couldn't she let it go? *Why do I still want him?* And it had all been a lie anyway, because he had left her for another woman, not to 'find himself'. He was just too cowardly to admit it at first.

She drove her fist into the pillow once more. *Bastard. I hate you*, she thought, but she knew it wasn't true. If he walked through her door this minute apologising, she'd take him back, no questions asked. It was pathetic, she told herself, but it made not the slightest difference.

She pulled the covers up over her ears. She didn't want to think about men, they were nothing but trouble. Except for the one in her dream, of course . . .

No, I don't want you either. You're probably just the same.

There was no escaping him, however. A while later when she yawned and turned over, he was still waiting for her and just as before, she found it impossible to resist him. Snuggling down, she gave up the fight, relaxed and smiled in her sleep.

★ ★ ★

'Mum, time to wake up or you'll miss breakfast. Can't you smell it? Auntie Dorothy has been cooking for ages.'

Jolie burst into the guest room without preamble and Melissa stared at her in sleepy confusion. Bright sunshine was pouring in through the leaded windows, and the canopy of forest leaves in her dream faded away, leaving only floral curtains and smooth plaster walls. She tried to focus on her daughter.

'What? Breakfast? Oh, right.' She sat up too quickly and had to sink back down as her head spun like a fairground ride.

'Yes, hurry up, it's almost ready.'

'Okay, okay, I'm coming.'

Satisfied with that answer, Jolie rushed off again, leaving Melissa to make another attempt at sitting up. She took her time, admiring her surroundings while she waited for her brain to catch up. The room was small and cosy – almost too cosy with the two beds in there, but that was the only flaw. A wealth of exposed ceiling beams, none of which were straight, made it quaint. In one corner was a tiny fireplace with a stone surround and all the furniture was of heavy oak, highly polished and smelling slightly of beeswax. The overall effect was charming and Melissa couldn't help but smile. It was certainly a far cry from their London flat, which was, to put it mildly, rather shabby.

No point thinking about it now. She wanted to enjoy her stay at Ashleigh and was determined not to allow any depressing thoughts to ruin things. She stood up and went to get dressed.

The large, rustic kitchen at the back of the house could have been copied straight from the pages of a glossy interior magazine. Stripped pine cupboards and granite work surfaces complemented the leaded windows perfectly. Worn flag-stone flooring, a pine dresser and an Aga completed the picture. Bunches of herbs and dried flowers, tied together with colourful ribbons, hung from little hooks in the exposed roof beams, their scent mingling with the aroma of cooking.

A collection of copper pots gleamed in the morning sun, giving the room an aura of days gone by. This was reinforced by old-fashioned blue-and-white crockery, displayed in neat rows on the dresser. A large pine table, worn smooth with age, stood in the middle of the room looking as though it had been there for hundreds of years. Jolie was sitting at one end, already tucking into bacon and eggs, looking very much at home.

'Good morning. You're just in time,' Dorothy said and handed Melissa a heaped plate, while preparing one for herself. 'Do start, so it doesn't get cold.'

'Thank you, but you didn't have to go to all this trouble just for us.'

'It's no bother, I love cooking, always have. I've missed having someone to cook for. Somehow it's not the same when you're on your own.'

Melissa knew that feeling all too well. Although she still had Jolie to cater for, she missed the look of appreciation on Steve's face every evening as he sat down to his meal. He'd been very easy to please in that department, eating anything and everything with enjoyment. She shook herself mentally, refusing to dwell on the past. Instead she concentrated on the conversation between Dorothy and Jolie.

'So you liked my garden?' Dorothy was asking.

'Oh, yes, I would love to have all that space to run around in. And a dog.' Jolie's face took on a wistful look which Melissa tried to ignore. 'Mum won't let me have one.'

'You know we're not allowed to, so it's not up to me. The landlord hates pets.' They had already had this discussion at least a dozen times and Melissa didn't want to be drawn into an argument in front of Dorothy. She decided to change the subject and looked around the kitchen. 'This is so different from what we're used to. We're in a horrible rented flat, but I'm in the process of trying to find a better one. Our lease is running out soon.'

'Why don't you move to the country?' Dorothy asked.

'To be honest, I hadn't thought about moving out, we've always lived in London.' Melissa nibbled on her second piece of toast, which seemed to taste so much better here than it did at home.

'Do you need to be in town for your work? You

did say a lot of it was done from home, didn't you?'

'Well, yes, but I also travel around to various record offices.'

'And you have to live in central London for that?'

'No, I suppose I could reach them almost as quickly from outside London as from Putney. It might make the journeys slightly longer, but not significantly so,' Melissa conceded.

'What about you, Jolie? Would you be willing to change schools and make new friends?'

'Sure, I'd love to go to a new school. I hate the one in Putney.'

'You do?' Melissa looked at her daughter in surprise. 'You never told me that.' Jolie shrugged, but didn't answer. The school she attended at the moment had started off as a temporary measure until they were settled somewhere. Unfortunately nothing had come of Melissa's attempts to obtain a mortgage and Jolie had ended up staying put for the last two years.

After the divorce, Melissa and Steve had decided to sell their old flat and split the money. However, since they hadn't paid off much of the mortgage, there wasn't enough left over for a down payment on a new one. No matter how much she scrimped and saved, Melissa hadn't been able to scrape together enough to satisfy the bank or building societies she'd approached. It was incredibly frustrating.

'Well, then, it seems to me I have the perfect

solution,' Dorothy announced. 'Why don't you move in with me?'

Melissa and Jolie stared at the old lady in stunned silence, before exclaiming inelegantly in unison, 'What?'

'Are you serious?' Melissa's hands were suddenly shaking and she had to put her teacup down before the contents spilled out onto her lap.

'Yes, of course I'm perfectly serious. I have to admit it is why I invited you down here. Well, that and because I wanted to get to know you, of course.' Dorothy smiled, but wouldn't quite meet Melissa's eyes.

'But surely you wouldn't want us cluttering up your home? And we've only just met.' There was something going on here that Melissa didn't understand. She was also rather embarrassed by this kind offer. Although she'd told Dorothy about her difficulties following her recent divorce, she didn't want to be seen as a poor relation needing assistance. She was doing just fine by herself. Well, more or less. *If only Dad hadn't gambled away all his and Mum's savings on the wretched horses, leaving Mum with a house mortgaged to the hilt, then I might have had at least a small inheritance now . . .* But there was no use crying over spilt milk.

'Nonsense,' Dorothy was saying. 'It's not much fun living here all alone. It's been very quiet since dear Charles died. I would welcome the noise and someone to talk to occasionally. And there is plenty of space; this house is really too big for just one person. If you want to bring your own furniture, I'm sure we could come to some arrangement. There's a lot of old stuff here that could be got rid of.'

'No, I really don't think . . .'

'Oh please, Mum, it would be brilliant and I could see Russ every day,' Jolie pleaded, her face taking on an expression Melissa knew only too well. 'We could even buy a puppy, couldn't we, Aunt Dorothy?'

'Why not? I'm sure Russ would like a friend. Seriously, you would be doing me a favour, Melissa,' Dorothy added. 'I would feel much safer knowing there was someone I could call on for help if I needed it. I'm not getting any younger, I'm seventy-two you know. Unfortunately, Charles and I were never blessed with children.'

Melissa hadn't thought of that aspect. Of course Dorothy must be lonely and in need of assistance with the big house. Despite having a cleaning lady once a week, it was probably too much work for her.

'You don't have any other relatives? On your husband's side, I mean.' Melissa knew perfectly well there was no one left in her own family.

'No, there is no one. Charles was an only child.'

'But, no, really we couldn't impose on you, Dorothy. It wouldn't be right.'

'Oh, Mu-um . . .' Melissa cut short Jolie's protest with a stern look. She would prefer them to discuss the matter in private later on. They hardly knew

Dorothy. The idea of moving in with someone who was almost a complete stranger seemed like madness. And yet, she couldn't deny it was tempting.

'When exactly does your lease expire?' Dorothy asked.

'At the end of this month.' Melissa was uncomfortably aware that time was running out. It was only the second of February, but that still left only four weeks, as it was such a short month.

'And have you seen any flats you like?'

'No, that's the problem. There are very few available in our area at the moment. At least of the kind I'd consider suitable and at a reasonable price.'

'Well then?'

Melissa hesitated, then shook her head. 'If you don't mind, I'd like to think about this before rushing into anything.'

'Of course, I'm sure it is all a bit sudden, but please do consider it. Honestly, I'd love to have you both.'

The old lady tactfully dropped the subject, but Melissa couldn't stop thinking about it. *I'm coming back.* The thought popped into her head involuntarily, and she wondered where it had come from. This was all happening too fast. She was sure there must be a thousand reasons why she should object. A part of her was deliriously happy at the possibility of living here and urged her to accept, whereas another part of her insisted on caution.

She didn't understand why this should be so. It was as if the house attracted her and repelled her at the same time. She was like a fly lured by an irresistible sparkling spider's web. It shimmered and beckoned, but if she came any closer, would she be unable to turn back?

CHAPTER 4

'There you are at last, my dear. I was beginning to think you weren't coming.'

Lady Maude Presseille came bustling towards Sibell and her escort, wearing a rose-pink houppelande and matching cloak. She tugged the edges of the latter together against the cold. Several strands of strawberry blonde hair were refusing to be confined by her simple headdress, but the lady ignored them. In her pale blue eyes was a look of relief and Sibell found herself clasped to Maude's soft bosom in a lavender-scented embrace. She tried not to flinch as Maude's hand inadvertently touched the sore part of her back, but drew in a hissing breath and gritted her teeth. When she glanced at Sir Roger, she saw him frown as if he'd noticed, but he made no comment.

'Lady Maude. It's so good to see you again.' Sibell had to bite her lip to prevent herself from bursting into tears. Maude had been a friend of Sibell's mother and when the latter died, Maude had insisted Sibell must come and live at Idenhurst. Saddled with a ten-year-old girl he didn't really want, her father had agreed readily enough. He'd been even more pleased when at the age of sixteen Sibell married Maude's only son, Roland. During the years she spent in the Presseille household the two women had become very close. Sibell wished for at least the hundredth time that she could have stayed at Idenhurst forever, but now Roland was dead she was once again her father's pawn.

Maude de Presseille was not noted for her beauty, but her intelligent gaze missed nothing. Sibell saw that the lady's eyes immediately went to the tall knight who had escorted her. Maude stepped around Sibell to greet Sir Roger, craning her neck to obtain a better view of him.

'I am Lady Presseille. Welcome to Idenhurst, sir.'

'Sir Roger of Langford at your service, my lady.' He executed a perfect bow to Lady Maude.

She frowned slightly and studied him, her head to one side. 'Have we met before?'

He gave her his lazy smile, which made Sibell's insides flutter even though it wasn't directed at her. 'I hardly think so, my lady. I would have remembered you, of that I am certain.' The implied compliment flustered Maude and she cleared her throat.

'Well, umm, just so. Thank you for escorting my daughter-in-law. It was most kind of you.' Turning towards Sibell she chided gently, 'I cannot think why you didn't at least bring a groom, my dear. Traipsing around all alone! Why, the very thought of it makes me tremble.'

Sibell knew why Maude looked so worried.

There had been rumours of outlaws roaming the forests close by, some reputedly vicious. Anyone alone and on foot would be an easy target. Sibell murmured something about the grooms all being unavailable that morning, then turned to Sir Roger and added her thanks to those of Maude for his assistance. Sir Roger smiled politely.

'You're welcome, Mistress Sibell. Any time I can be of assistance, just let me know.' He looked her in the eyes as he spoke, and Sibell had the feeling he wasn't just talking about mundane tasks such as escorting her. His gaze told her he'd defend her against anyone, should she wish it. She almost gave way to the threatening tears at the thought that there was someone who could help her. *If only I had the right to call upon his assistance.* She was in sore need of a champion.

'Come into the hall, you must have some refreshment after your journey.' Lady Maude ushered her guests towards the main entrance of the manor house. 'I assume you are here to see my husband, Sir Roger?'

'Indeed, my lady, if he can spare the time.'

They entered the great hall, a room of splendid proportions designed to impress, yet not overly ostentatious. Maude led the way towards the dais at one end and asked a serving maid to bring wine.

'Please be seated, Sir Roger, while I send someone to fetch my husband. He shouldn't be too long.'

Maude issued orders to another servant to this effect, then made small talk until heavy steps

44

heralded the arrival of Sir Gilbert. Sibell looked up as her former father-in-law came striding towards them, tall and loose-limbed, with corn-coloured hair cut just below his ears and covered by a slightly floppy hat which he removed just before he reached the dais.

'Sibell, my dear, how lovely to see you. I trust you are well?'

'Very well, thank you, Sir Gilbert.'

'Good, good. And here is another visitor. Welcome to Idenhurst.' He greeted his unexpected guest politely, as good manners dictated. 'Sir Roger, was it? I'm told you wish to speak to me?' Sir Gilbert frowned slightly as he studied his guest closely, but the young knight appeared to take this perusal in his stride. Indeed, Sibell didn't think Sir Gilbert would glean anything from his study. The man was dressed without extravagance. His blue cloak and matching tunic were of good-quality cloth, but apart from an embroidered edge to the tunic, there was no decoration, nothing to show whether he was wealthy or not. Even his sword, although undoubtedly of good craftsmanship, was curiously unadorned, with a plain handle. She wondered if this was done on purpose.

'Yes, Sir Gilbert. Thank you for taking the time to see me.' Sir Roger's deep voice washed over Sibell and kept her rooted to the spot, but a nudge from Maude recalled her to the present.

'We had better be off then. Come, my dear.' Maude towed Sibell towards a door in the far corner.

Risking a further peek, she saw the two men sit down in the huge carved oak chairs on the dais while a servant poured them wine. They began to speak as soon as they had a cup each and Sibell strained to catch their words. She desperately wanted to know why Sir Roger had come, but Maude pulled the door shut behind them.

'Stop eavesdropping,' she admonished with a smile. 'Gilbert will tell me everything in good time and you know I'll pass on any interesting gossip to you.'

Despite being consumed with curiosity, Sibell had to be content with that.

'. . . to have and to hold, till death do us part, according to God's holy law, and this is my solemn vow.'

The words reverberated around the old stone church, but as soon as Steve had repeated them after the vicar, Melissa knew they were a lie. A promise he would never keep. She could hear the deceit in his voice, as clearly as if he had spelled it out for her, and she imagined it was almost possible to taste his fear of commitment. It surrounded him like an aura and she'd been a fool to think she could change him.

There would be no happy-ever-after for her.

With panic churning in her gut, she turned to stare at the man she was marrying, the man she loved, hoping he would deny her premonition of doom. But predictably he couldn't look her in the eye. He just shook his head, taking away the last trace of hope.

'I'm sorry, I can't,' he mouthed, giving her one quick,

guilty glance, before fading slowly into a shadowy world where she couldn't reach him. Huge sobs welled up inside her as she stretched out both hands, trying to pull him back.

'No, you're mine, I won't let you go,' she cried, but it was no use. He had disappeared from view completely.

A collective gasp of horror went up from the congregation, but in the next instant it changed into a buzz of excitement as another man stepped forward to take Steve's place.

'I do,' he said solemnly, as if answering the vicar's earlier question, and held out a gauntlet-clad hand in invitation.

Melissa's breath caught in her throat as she realised who he was – her medieval knight, complete with deadly sword, spurs and a long cloak of finest, deep-blue wool. She stared up at him, confused, afraid and exhilarated at the same time. She felt instinctively his was a voice she could trust. And, although she had no idea how she knew, she was sure he would never lie. His blue gaze penetrated hers with not a shadow of guile in it.

She hesitated only a moment before placing her hand in his. As soon as she did so, however, warning bells began to ring all around her, penetrating every nook and cranny of the little church until the sound became too painful to endure. Filled with panic, she snatched her hand away, lifted up her skirts and ran full tilt towards the door . . .

Melissa sat up in bed, her heart beating so hard she thought it would surely burst, her nightdress drenched in perspiration and her mind in turmoil. The last misty images of the dream hovered on the periphery of her vision. She blinked, trying to focus on the here and now in order to banish the strange scene in the little church. The leathery smell of the knight's outstretched gauntlet lingered in her nostrils and she could still hear the clanging of a bell. It was unbearable and she was just about to put her hands up over her ears when she realised the noise had nothing to do with weddings.

She was back in London and someone was ringing her doorbell.

Hurrying out of bed, she stuck her feet into a pair of worn slippers and snatched up her dressing gown. Yawning hugely, she rushed down the hall and peered through the spy hole, sighing when she saw who was outside.

'Oh, hell,' she muttered and drew in a steadying breath before opening the door.

'It's about bloody time, I haven't got all day, you know. You deaf or something?'

'Excuse me?' Melissa stifled another yawn and tried to focus on her apparently angry landlord, Mr Donne. He glared at her, two red spots highlighting his pasty cheeks, but she pretended not to notice. He had dragged her out of a well-deserved Saturday morning lie-in, and she wasn't in the mood for his histrionics.

'I've been standing here for ages. A man has better things to do,' he grumbled.

'Yes, quite.' Like sleep, she wanted to add, but

didn't. She was so tired it was an effort just to keep her eyes open. It had been a long, hard week and she desperately needed a rest. Thoughts of Ashleigh and her great-aunt's kind offer had kept her awake most nights, as had a backlog of genea-logical charts and ongoing research projects which had forced her to stay up long past her usual bedtime. The last thing she wanted was a conver-sation with Mr Donne. 'What did you want to talk to me about?'

'For starters, you can tell that brat of yours to turn the TV down. It's so loud a person can't hear themselves think downstairs. I've told you before, I won't stand for it.'

'It can't be as bad as all that, I can barely hear it from here.' Melissa tried not to show the irrita-tion rising rapidly inside her. Jolie did have a tendency to turn the sound up too much, but today it was at a perfectly reasonable level for most people.

'Then you need your hearing tested, Ms Grantham.'

'Very well,' she said curtly, 'I'll ask Jolie to turn it down. Perhaps you could do something for me in return? The heating doesn't seem to be working and as I believe it was supposed to be included in the rent, I'd be grateful if you could fix it as soon as possible.' She shivered, despite wearing the thick bathrobe and slippers. The little flat was perpetually damp and cold, no matter what the weather was like outside.

The landlord puffed out his chest in indignation, his beetle brows almost meeting in the middle as he fixed her with a malevolent look. 'There's nothing wrong with the heating, Ms Grantham, it's working perfectly downstairs. If you've broken any radiators, it's up to you to have them seen to.'

'But . . .'

'And if you don't like it here, you're welcome to leave at any time. In fact, that's what I came to say. I want you gone by next week because my son needs a place to kip for a while. You're nothing but trouble anyhow. You and that noisy kid of yours.'

'What? You can't do that. The contract said we have rented this flat until the end of this month. If you wanted to change it you'd have to give one month's notice in writing.'

'Well maybe I did write to you. Perhaps the letter got lost?' He smirked, looking pleased with himself for coming up with that little lie. 'I'll give you a copy.'

Melissa narrowed her eyes at him, anger finally getting the better of her. 'Now you listen to me, Mr Donne. I'll be very happy to leave this disgusting hovel, but I'm not going for another three weeks and if you try anything, I'll get on to my solicitor.' She slammed the door in his face, restraining the urge to shove the self-important little man down the stairs.

'The nerve of the man!' Righteous indignation sustained her as far as the kitchen, then despair

50

hit her with full force. 'Shit, shit, shit . . .' She banged a fist into the nearest cupboard door, but regretted it the instant pain streaked up her arm. She sank onto one of the two rickety bar stools which served as kitchen chairs and slumped over the counter, her head cradled on top of her arms. *What am I going to do?*

This was the third flat she'd rented in two years and something always seemed to go wrong. It was difficult to find properties within walking distance of Jolie's school. She didn't have much hope of finding another, especially at such short notice. In fact, it would be downright impossible. If they were staying in London, they needed to be close enough so that Jolie could walk back on her own on the days Melissa worked away from home.

But were they staying in London? Melissa still couldn't make up her mind.

Heaving a sigh, she stared out of the grimy window, which overlooked a railway track and the back of a windowless building. Filthy bricks, covered with graffiti, stretched as far as the eye could see; a thoroughly depressing sight and one she definitely wouldn't miss. She thought she must be mad to hesitate for even a fraction of a second, but she still felt there was something strange about her great-aunt's sudden offer. Not to mention her timely appearance in Melissa's life. It was simply too good to be true.

A train rumbled by, causing the house to shake as if in an earthquake, but she barely noticed any longer. Instead she wondered idly how the graffiti-artists managed to get up so high to do their paintings. Surely it wasn't possible to bring a ladder onto a busy railway and paint away without anyone noticing?

Trying her best to put all thoughts of her problems firmly out of her mind for the moment, she thought that now she was awake, she might as well stay up and get on with some work. She'd had a breakthrough on one of the family trees yesterday and needed to write up her notes. First things first, though. She went to ask Jolie what she'd like for breakfast.

'Shh, I'll miss the end of the programme,' was the reply.

Melissa opened her mouth to tell Jolie off for being so rude, then decided it wasn't worth the effort. She didn't want to start the weekend on bad terms and lately Jolie had become very difficult and moody, even more so since the visit to Ashleigh. Melissa supposed it was the onset of puberty, but it was definitely another thing she could do without right now. 'Fine, get your own breakfast then,' was all she said.

She headed back towards the kitchen and wished that she could start the day all over again. She barely made it as far as the hall before the doorbell rang once more, however. As she reached for the handle, she realised she'd forgotten to tell Jolie to turn the sound down. This made her even more cross and she yanked the door open.

'Yes, I was just about to tell her,' she started to say in a belligerent voice, only to stop mid-sentence. 'Oh, it's you.'

Steve was the last person she'd expected to see and the impact was therefore doubly devastating. Although her brain had accepted the fact that he'd left her for someone else, her body had not. It was always a struggle not to show him that a part of her still wanted him back. Normally, when she knew a meeting was inevitable, she had time to steel herself beforehand and retreat behind a carefully constructed shell of indifference. Not so this morning. His rugged good looks had the sort of effect they'd always had on her and she fought hard to regain her composure. Clenching her fist inside the pocket of her bathrobe, she felt the nails digging into the palm of her hand. She concentrated on the pain it caused rather than the wave of longing that swept through her.

'Nice to see you, too.' Steve looked almost as irritated as she herself had been only a moment before. 'Is she ready?'

'Who?'

'Jolie, of course. Who d'you think?'

'Ready?'

'What's the matter with you? Had a heavy night last night or something? I said I was coming to pick her up at ten and you said that was fine.'

'Oh, for your mother's birthday lunch.' Melissa's brain, which had temporarily stopped working, crunched into gear. She frowned. 'But you said Sunday. Surely, her birthday is tomorrow?'

'Yes, yes, but I said we were having lunch today, Saturday, because I've got something else on tomorrow. Don't tell me she isn't ready? We're going to be late as it is.' He groaned and ran a hand through the silky dark hair Melissa remembered so well. It brought back memories she didn't want to dwell on and she shivered with the effort to keep them suppressed.

'I'm sorry, I must have misunderstood. Just give me ten minutes and she'll be ready, okay?'

'Ten minutes, not a second more.' Without so much as a 'goodbye', he stomped off down the stairs and slammed the door to the street, making Melissa wince. She expected Mr Donne to come charging out to complain yet again, and shut her own door hurriedly.

'Jolie, come on, quickly, you've got to get dressed,' she shouted, springing into action.

They managed it, but only just. Melissa thanked her lucky stars she had at least bought and wrapped her former mother-in-law's present, a silk scarf in the exact shade of green that was Beatrice's favourite colour. She shoved the parcel into Jolie's hands, gave her a quick hug and waved her off. 'Behave yourself now, you know what your gran is like.'

She wasn't really worried, however. Beatrice was strict, but Melissa also knew that Steve's mother had a soft spot for Jolie and the two of them had always enjoyed each other's company. Once you got to know her, Beatrice wasn't half as scary as she seemed on first acquaintance and Melissa still had a good relationship with her, despite the divorce.

She stood for a moment by the window, watching as the car sped away down the street with an angry roar. Apart from Jolie and her father, it also contained Daisy, the woman who had lured Steve away, and a toddler who was apparently Jolie's half-sister. The thought of that child, conceived while Melissa and Steve were still married, was like a knife-edge of pain slicing through her and Melissa quickly pulled away from the window.

She stood in the silent flat, battling the feelings of resentment, depression and heartache that always followed a meeting with Steve.

'. . . to have and to hold, till death do us part . . .'

The words from her dream echoed through her mind once more, but she shook her head to free herself from its cloying tentacles. Steve had spoken those vows once, but he hadn't meant them in real life, any more than in the dream. Or if he had, he'd quickly forgotten.

No, there was no happy-ever-after for Melissa.

CHAPTER 5

Although servants scurried around putting up trestle tables for the main meal of the day, Roger was happy to see they were out of earshot. What he was about to discuss with the lord of Idenhurst was no one's business but his own. He preferred to be without an audience.

They chatted about the weather and the state of the roads at first while they sipped their wine. At the same time, Roger surveyed the hall with curiosity. It was impressive, with a series of windows facing the courtyard and a huge oriel window in the middle of the opposite wall. On either side of this were two enormous fireplaces with carved stone surrounds. They looked newly built and must have replaced the customary open fire in the middle of the room. They struggled to heat the vast chamber, belching puffs of smoke into it from time to time, which made the air heavy. Fresh rushes were being strewn on the floor, and Roger guessed that Lady Presseille ran her household in a well-ordered and cleanly fashion. There were no dogs looking for scraps, so he assumed they'd been banned.

When the ladies had disappeared, a little of Sir Gilbert's bonhomie had gone with them. 'So, you wished to speak to me,' he said now, raising his eyebrows.

'Yes. It's with regard to a matter that concerns my late mother, Lady Emma of Langford,' Roger began, unconsciously lowering his voice a little. He thought he saw a flicker of surprise in the older man's eyes, but it was quickly masked and he couldn't be certain.

Sir Gilbert said only, 'Oh, yes?'

Roger tried to see through the polite façade. He needed to judge what manner of man Sir Gilbert might be. His lordship had, at first glance, looked affable enough. Usually skilled at weighing up his opponents, in Sir Gilbert he perceived hidden depths. Judging him proved more difficult than he had anticipated. Roger already knew about the death of Roland Presseille, Sir Gilbert's only son, because he'd actually been present when it occurred, but he wasn't about to mention that. Although obviously tired and drawn by grief, the older man appeared calm and collected, with an innate courtesy not always present in a person of his high standing. Roger decided he was probably fair and honest, as Sibell had said.

'I'm a bastard,' he continued matter-of-factly, 'and have never felt the lack of a father. However, I have to admit to a certain curiosity as to who my sire might be. My mother assured me that my father was nobly born, but she always refused to tell me his name. On her deathbed, however, she relented and told me to seek you out.'

The older man's eyes narrowed a fraction, but he held his tongue.

Roger went on, 'She claimed my father was a member of the Presseille family, and said that if you were as honest as she remembered, you would help me to find him.' He held out his hand and removed a ring from the smallest finger. 'She said this might help nudge someone's memory.'

'I see.' Sir Gilbert's expression remained calm, but to Roger it seemed almost too carefully neutral. His lordship took the ring and gave it a cursory look before handing it back quickly, as if it burned him, then frowned.

'And have you come to claim recompense of some kind then, or were you simply hoping he would buy your silence?' Sir Gilbert sounded unaccountably defensive and a muscle twitched in his jaw.

Roger resented the implied insult. He gritted his teeth to keep his anger contained. 'I want nothing from my father except perhaps recognition of my existence,' he growled. 'Is that so much to ask? I've made my own way in life. I have acquired some wealth in the service of noble lords, and will one day inherit my uncle's manor as he has no children of his own. I'm happy with my lot. But I would very much like to know who fathered me, and why he didn't marry my mother as he'd promised. Surely, that's understandable, my lord?'

Sir Gilbert looked into Roger's eyes, blue clashing with blue. 'Didn't your mother give you a reason why she never married your father?' he countered.

Roger hesitated. 'No, and I can't understand it. She was of noble birth, and extremely beautiful. I see no reason why she should have been rejected.' He sighed. 'She said only that circumstances prevented it. I assume she meant the man was already married. He must have duped her.'

'I see. How old did you say you are?'

'Three-and-twenty.'

'And did your mother never marry anyone else?'

'No. She insisted she couldn't love anyone except my father, and so she would have none other for a husband. Besides which, everyone knew she was a "fallen woman".' Roger's jaw tightened at the thought of how some people had treated his mother on account of this when to all intents and purposes she'd been lured into someone's bed under false pretences and left with the consequences. He added, 'I was proof of that. We lived with my uncle, and he brought me up until I was sent away to board at the age of ten.'

Sir Gilbert was silent for a long time. Finally he said, 'I'm sorry, Sir Roger, I don't think I can help you. Although you have something of the look of a Presseille, you could be the by-blow of any one of my four brothers, who are all dead. It was a long time ago. Can you not be happy with what you have achieved for yourself? These things are often best forgotten and after all, you've survived for twenty-three years without a father. You don't need him now.'

Sir Roger swallowed hard. He knew Sir Gilbert was holding something back, but wouldn't force him to speak against his will. His pride forbade it. 'Very well, so be it. I thank you for your time and apologise for intruding upon you. I shall, as you say, have to be content with what I have.' He stood up and bowed curtly, before turning to leave.

'Wait! Won't you stay as our guest for a few days? It's the least I can do when you have come so far especially to see me.'

Roger hesitated. Perhaps there were others here who would know more, if only he could make them talk to him. That thought settled the matter. 'Thank you. I'd like that.'

'Excellent. I look forward to seeing you later then.' Sir Gilbert seemed relieved, although why, Roger wasn't sure.

It didn't matter though. He was here now and he'd make the most of his time at Idenhurst. He bowed again, and left the hall without a backward glance.

Jake Precy woke in a panic, hopelessly tangled up in his duvet. With a muttered oath he twisted and turned until he'd managed to extricate himself, then flung the clinging material away. He stilled. The silence in Ashleigh Cottage was oppressive, unbroken apart from the hooting of an owl. And the bedroom was hot and airless even though it was only February.

'Christ Almighty!'

He put up a hand and dragged his fingers through his tangled hair. Images crowded into his mind, flashing by with lightning speed, then all of a sudden they joined into a coherent sequence and he remembered his dream clearly.

He'd been on a huge horse, riding for what seemed like forever, saddle sore and bone weary. Then he'd met a woman and she had joined him, sitting behind him with her soft hands at his waist. A shadowy figure, he couldn't remember her features, but he knew by his body's reaction that he'd found her beautiful. Desirable. Her very nearness had made him forget his aches and pains, and her scent lingered in his nostrils, tantalising him with overtones of lavender.

'Damn it all . . .'

Jake gritted his teeth and tried to steer his thoughts in another direction, but his body wouldn't let him. He sighed. For the first time in forever, he'd felt lust, but only for an imaginary woman. Why couldn't he feel that way for someone real? Why couldn't he move on?

His wife, Karen, was dead and he needed to put the past behind him once and for all.

The dreams didn't seem to be connected to her, though. In fact, he'd had them on and off since they had moved into Ashleigh Cottage, although never quite as vivid as the one tonight. And where before he'd always been alone on the horse, riding without destination or purpose, now his mind had dreamt up a female companion. This disturbed him more than anything else.

'What the hell does it all mean?' He shook his head. 'Maybe I need a shrink.' But he didn't really want to discuss it with anyone. *It's my problem and I'll sort it.*

He took a deep breath and tried to forget the dream. Instead, he allowed his mind to return to the subject of Karen. He'd wanted *her* once with the single-mindedness only those newly in love experience. He'd craved her touch, yearned to make love to her. But in the end, she had killed his feelings stone dead and he hadn't wanted a relationship with anyone ever again in case they hurt him the same way.

'*I would never do that . . .*' The soft lilt of the dream woman's voice washed over him, as clear as if she'd been real. Jake blinked and shook his head. He was imagining it. He couldn't erase her from his memory though, and remembered once more the feel of the woman's soft curves against his back, the way her husky voice had sent shivers down his spine. Another jolt of desire shot through him.

'No, this is crazy.' He cursed under his breath. He'd sworn never to involve himself with a woman again, relationships were too painful. When he closed his eyes, Karen's face returned to taunt him. She had been beautiful too, but her beauty had only been skin-deep.

'You're so boring, Jake! I don't know why I had to go and marry a country vet. Honestly, all you ever do is work. No excitement, just work, work, work.' The sneering tone and hard eyes were etched into his memory.

Karen had never been a good mother either, and had refused point blank to have any more children. Jake strongly suspected their daughter had been a mistake on Karen's part, but he could never regret having her. She was his life now.

Karen's remarks during their last evening together had destroyed any love Jake had ever felt for her, and he'd wished her good riddance. Perhaps that was why she had driven off at such speed, without paying attention properly. Maybe it was why she had lost control of the car and spun into a tree? He'd never know now and there was no point thinking about it.

Jake straightened his duvet and lay down with one arm flung across his eyes. Almost immediately, the faint scent of lavender returned to tease his senses and his body reacted as if the dream woman was right there in bed with him. He swallowed hard. It was definitely time to move on. Time to forget. *They can't all be like Karen. I'll just have to be more careful in my choice of partner*, he thought.

He was so tired of being alone.

'Come, sit by me and tell me all that's been happening in my absence.' Maude had just returned from a pilgrimage to Canterbury Cathedral to pray for her dead son's soul. Sibell wished she could have gone with her, but there had been no point in even asking. Her father would never have given his permission. Maude patted a cushion on the comfortable window seat next to her, and Sibell obliged willingly. 'Spare me nothing, I beg you, there's no need to pretend with me,' Maude added.

They were ensconced in Idenhurst's beautiful solar, warmed from within by a goblet each of mulled wine, and heated on the outside by two sturdy braziers. Sunshine poured in through the unusually large glass window, which gave plenty of light for sewing or reading. The room was further made comfortable by a multitude of brightly coloured cushions and tapestries. Most of these had been made by the ladies of the household, and the latest work in progress was spread out on a large table nearby. It was a room to relax in, and Sibell allowed herself to do so for the first time in months.

'I'm afraid things are not going well.' After glancing around to make sure there was no one to overhear their conversation, she proceeded to pour her troubles into Maude's sympathetic ears. 'Since I last saw you, my father has kept me closely guarded. Indeed, for the past three days I've been locked in my chamber with hardly any food.' Sibell swallowed hard. 'That was after he beat me.' She looked up at the older woman, tears of despair hovering on her lashes. 'He-he means to m-marry me to Sir Fulke of Thornby. The man is old enough to be my grandfather, and known to have abused at least three wives into an early grave.'

Sibell shuddered in distaste before exclaiming, 'I simply couldn't bear it. I'd rather die.'

Maude patted her arm. 'It is as I thought, he will sell you off to the highest bidder in order to increase his own status.' She tut-tutted. 'Sir Fulke is indeed a bad choice, but I suppose your father was swayed by the man's connections and wealth. I've heard that he is very powerful.' She shook her head. 'Life is most unfair, especially for us women. To an uncaring father, a girl child is but a chattel to be sold into marriage or made use of in any way he sees fit.' Maude sighed. 'I had hoped he would make a better choice for you.'

'I almost agreed to the marriage,' Sibell confessed. 'Being confined in such a tiny space for so long was simply unbearable. I felt as if I couldn't breathe, and I was afraid he would keep me there until he had my agreement.' She swallowed a sob and bit her lip. 'He refuses to listen to me. He says that my views are not important, that I will become used to Sir Fulke. And once I have given him an heir he won't touch me anyway because I'm so tall and freckle-faced. But I don't want him to touch me at all. Ever!'

'No, I can most certainly understand that, my dear.' Maude gave Sibell another reassuring pat. 'Don't worry, we'll try to think of something. You know I'll help you in any way I can.'

'You will? Oh, thank you! I'm so glad we had this opportunity to talk. Now that I know I'm not alone, I won't let Father win. I will find a way to defy him.' She would do whatever was necessary. 'Thank the good Lord your summons came today. Nothing else would have induced Father to release me until he had my agreement.'

'I'm so sorry, my dear, I had no idea things were that bad. We should have insisted on you staying here after . . . when we heard the news about Roland. Gilbert and I both thought you'd be happier with your own family, rather than in a place which reminded you of your marriage, but I see now we were wrong.'

'I'm sure you did what you thought was best.' Sibell didn't want to admit that she'd longed for Sir Gilbert to insist she stay at Idenhurst until a new husband was found for her. At least then her father would have had more trouble browbeating her into submission, even if he did have the right to wed her to anyone he chose.

'Well, it's not too late. Why don't I invite you now?'

'No, please don't! Father will know I've spoken to you on the matter and then he'll find a way to punish me. He's forbidden me from mentioning it to anyone.'

'Hmm.' Lady Maude stared out of the window, deep in thought. 'Do you know, I believe your best course would be to go along with it for now, just to appease him,' she mused. 'While he's busy with contracts and such like, we can think of a better solution.'

'You truly think so?'

Maude nodded. 'Of course.'

'I don't know . . . If only I'd had a child, then I would have had to stay here, surely?' Her inability to conceive had been a great worry to Sibell during her marriage, but they had only been married a few months when Roland took it into his head to go off and fight. Maude had assured her these things often took time, but since Roland never returned, Sibell hadn't found out whether she was right.

'Perhaps. Knowing your father, I'm not so sure.' Maude squeezed Sibell's hands in sympathy, then abruptly changed the subject. 'Now tell me, wherever did you meet that handsome young man you arrived with? It's very strange, but I'm sure I have seen him before.' She shook her head. 'At any rate, he seemed rather smitten with you.'

'No, no, it was all friendly banter. He meant nothing by it.' Sibell felt her cheeks heat up in a fiery blush, and began to stammer more denials, then stopped as she saw the teasing smile on Maude's lips. 'Now, Maude, you know a man like that would never be interested in a red-headed beanpole like me,' she said sternly. 'You'll have to think of something better.'

Maude's eyes twinkled. 'We'll just see about that.'

CHAPTER 6

'Pleeeeease, Mum! I hate it here and I don't want to keep moving all the time. The flat we looked at yesterday smelled *gross*.'

Melissa sighed and dug her knuckles into the side of her throbbing head in an effort to ease the pain. 'Jolie, are you sure you're not just saying that because you want a dog? You'll get tired of taking it for walks in no time, you know, and then where will you be? At a new school that might not be any better than the one you're in already.'

'Yes, it will. Anything would be better than this one. The kids here are a bunch of wankers.'

'Jolie!'

Jolie's expression turned mulish. 'Well, they are.'

'Maybe so.' Melissa didn't have the energy to argue about her daughter's use of inappropriate words just then. 'But why had you never told me before we went to Ashleigh that you hate your school?'

'I don't know.' Jolie shoved her hands into her pockets and refused to look at her mother.

'Come on, there must be a reason.' Melissa lifted Jolie's chin gently so she could see her expression.

'Tell me. Has someone been bullying you and saying it would get worse if you told on them?'

Jolie shook her head.

'What then?'

'Well, I do get bullied sometimes, but it doesn't matter 'cos I don't like the other kids anyway. I hate the teacher, though, she's always picking on me. Nothing I do is ever right.'

Melissa could well believe it. Mrs Olsen was not a very sympathetic woman and Melissa had often wondered what had made such a person want to be a teacher. She nodded slowly. 'I know what you mean. Perhaps we could get you moved to the other class, would that help?'

'No. I don't want to stay here. I want to move to Ashleigh.'

'Jolie, let's talk about this sensibly. You're not a baby any more so you should be able to understand my arguments, too. Now, do you really think we would cope, living with an old lady? She's probably set in her ways and although she said she wants people around her, I don't think she realises what it would mean. Loud music, noise, having to adapt to change . . .'

'It was her idea.'

'I know, but maybe she hasn't thought it through. And what if we do move in, but find that we hate living in the country? Dorothy might be terribly sad and even more lonely if we changed our minds and moved out again.'

'Mum, you said yourself that sometimes people

have to try new things, even if they don't turn out the way you think.'

'I said that?'

'Yes, when we were talking about Daddy. He wanted to try something new, so why can't we? If we don't, how will we ever know whether we like it or not? We already know we hate it here, so . . .'

'I don't hate it, it's just not ideal.'

'Yes, you do. You're always going on about the landlord and stuff and you're always miserable. And now we can't find a new flat, so you're flapping about that. Maybe in the country you'd be happy.'

Melissa bit her lip. She hadn't realised how much her unhappiness had affected Jolie or how perceptive her daughter could be.

The truth was that her inexplicable reactions to the house had unsettled her more than she cared to admit. And because she was at such a low ebb, she was apprehensive about leaving London and all that was familiar. She had never been one to take chances, but the temptation to just pack up and leave was great. Ashleigh Manor occupied her thoughts constantly and it was almost as if the house was calling to her, urging her to return. And yet at the same time, something about it set off warning bells in her mind . . .

Could a house be in your blood? In your DNA? *No, that's ridiculous.*

She thought for a moment, then forced herself

to come to a decision. 'All right, I'll tell you what
– how about a compromise?'

'What kind?'

'I think you're right, we should try living in the
country for a while. What if we agree to stay with
Dorothy for a few weeks while we look around for
a place of our own in the same area?' Melissa
suggested. 'That way, we could be near her so
she's not lonely, but without intruding on her
space. Renting a little cottage or something should
be much cheaper in Kent and if there's a garden,
you can have your puppy. How does that sound?'
Even as she made the suggestion, Melissa was
worrying that it wouldn't work out, but she felt
she was desperate enough to at least try.

'Okay, I guess.' Jolie didn't sound totally
convinced. 'You promise I can have a dog?'

Melissa smiled and pulled her daughter close for
a hug. 'Yes, sweetie, as soon as we know we want
to stay there for good. I promise.'

Sibell smiled to herself as she made her way
towards the stables at Idenhurst. Maude was right,
of course – the simple act of agreeing to the
marriage contract would probably free her from
incarceration. At least to the extent that she would
be allowed to visit her former mother-in-law and
thus be able to make further plans. *I'll thwart
Father's schemes yet, see if I don't . . .*

It was dark inside the stables and she stood still
for a few moments while her nose adjusted to the

smell of horse. When she could breathe easily again, Sibell put out a hand to feel her way along the wall. Maude had insisted that she borrow a mount for her journey home and she was just about to call out for the grooms when she heard the sound of low voices. She hurried towards them, then stopped when she realised the people talking weren't grooms. There was something furtive about the conversation. On silent feet, she crept closer, crouching down to remain hidden from view.

'You have need of my services, my lord?' The whisper was barely loud enough to be heard.

'Indeed I do.'

Sibell peered over the top of the dividing wall and saw Sir Gilbert standing next to a burly, thick-set man she vaguely recognised from her time at Idenhurst. Sir Gilbert motioned the man closer and Sibell tried to blend into the dark shadows around her.

'Walter, I need your help. It's a delicate matter and, as usual, I trust you to keep it to yourself.'

'Naturally, my lord. What would you have me do?'

'Did you happen to notice the young knight who arrived here this morning? Tall, fair and with a squire in tow.'

The servant permitted himself a lop-sided grin. 'If you'll pardon my saying so, he's a mite hard to miss, that one. If he stays, he'll cause a riot among the womenfolk, he will.'

'Aye, so I thought.' Sir Gilbert stroked his chin. 'It should make your task easier. He says his name is Sir Roger and claims to be from a place called Langford.' His tongue stumbled over the name and he paused for a moment, only continuing after he had cleared his throat. 'I believe it's situated north of London, not far from Letchworth, near Hatfield. I want you to go there and find out more about him. As much as you can. And fast.'

'Very well, my lord. I'll set out immediately.'

'Excellent.' Sir Gilbert untied a leather pouch from his belt and handed it to Walter. 'This may help to loosen tongues. And Walter, take a good, strong horse. I'll try to keep Sir Roger here until your return. I want him where I can keep an eye on him.'

If Walter was surprised at his task, he hid it well and, to Sibell's annoyance, neither did he ask his master why he had developed this sudden interest in the young knight. With a bow he turned to leave.

'Walter?'

The servant stopped and looked over his shoulder and Sibell held her breath, hoping for an answer after all. 'Yes, my lord?'

'Thank you, and God speed.'

Sibell let out the air she'd been holding in, suppressing the feeling of disappointment. She tried to tell herself it was none of her business, but Sir Gilbert's words refused to leave her mind. Why was he so interested in Sir Roger?

Did he mean him harm? *And why should it matter to me?*

She waited until the men had left, then quickly made her way out of the stables. So quickly, in fact, that she collided with something very solid in the doorway. Shaken, she looked up, expecting to be taken to task for eavesdropping. She blinked.

'Oh, it's you, Sir Roger. I thought you were . . .' She bit her lip to stop the words from tumbling out, then sank into a curtsey to cover her confusion.

'Mistress Sibell. This is a pleasant surprise.' He took her hand and quickly pulled her up. 'No need for that.' He smiled. 'We're old friends, are we not?'

'I . . . I . . . if you say so.' She drew in a deep breath and wished that she could speak two words with the man without blushing. He must think her a complete nodcock. 'I thought you long gone from here,' she said, then wished she hadn't. She didn't want him to realise she had been thinking of him at all.

'Indeed, I should have been on my way, but Sir Gilbert invited me to stay a few days.' He grinned. 'Do you wish me far away then?'

'No, er, no, of course not. I mean . . . it doesn't matter to me. You must come and go as you please.' She stopped to take in another huge gulp of air. It was no good. She'd had no practice in the art of flirtation, whereas he had obviously done nothing else all his life. She sighed. 'I must go and

74

find a groom. Lady Maude is lending me a horse. I bid you good day, sir.'

'I hope to see you soon again, mistress.' He bowed, but before he did she saw the twinkle in his eyes. For some reason that made her cross. Wasn't the man ever serious? Or was he hiding something behind this carefree façade? If only he hadn't been so charming. If only she knew why Sir Gilbert was worried by his presence.

Thoroughly out of sorts, she went in search of a groom.

Melissa's surly landlord seemed to have given up on trying to evict her immediately, so she felt it was almost a shame she wouldn't be staying until the end of the month as she'd said she would, just to spite him. Still, she didn't trust him and it was a relief to know she wouldn't have to deal with him for much longer.

'I shall expect you to return my deposit in full since we haven't damaged anything,' she told him. She couldn't ask for the rent back, as that was paid monthly, but he owed her the deposit at least.

'The sooner you're gone, the better, and I'll be making a deduction for the heating,' he muttered, true to form, but she fixed him with a fierce glare that seemed to startle him.

'Don't you dare! The contract clearly says that the heating is your responsibility and my lawyer informs me I can sue you for not keeping the flat warm enough.' This was an outright lie, as she hadn't consulted anyone, but she figured Mr Donne didn't need to know that. He blustered for a bit, but finally agreed to give her a cheque for the full amount. Melissa was very proud of herself for securing this small victory.

She also knew she had to inform Steve of her plans, vague though they were, so the following week she steeled herself to call him. His secretary took it upon herself to disturb him in a meeting, despite Melissa's protests that the matter wasn't urgent. Consequently, by the time he came to the phone he was already in a bad mood. Melissa's heart sank.

'Yes, what is it? Has something happened to Jolie?' he barked.

'No, not at all. I'm just calling to tell you that we'll be moving soon.'

'Couldn't you just have sent me a letter with the new address as usual? Or are you going to Outer Mongolia?'

Stung by his sarcastic tone, Melissa replied with some asperity. 'No, to Kent, actually. I'm sorry to have disturbed you. I just felt it would be courteous to inform you, but if you're not inter-ested . . .'

'Kent? What the bloody hell do you want to move down there for? What about Jolie's schooling?'

'We're going to find a better school for her there; she hates the one she's at now. The other children have been bullying her and the teacher is a nightmare. And another reason we're moving to Kent is to be near my great-aunt Dorothy. She's getting on a bit and needs some support.'

'Great-aunt who? I thought you didn't have any aunts, great or otherwise. Look, this is going to make things very inconvenient for me. It's bad enough having to come all the way from Islington down to Putney to see Jolie, but to Kent? It's fucking miles away, not to mention having to use the M25 each time. It's always choc-a-bloc with traffic.'

'I'm sorry you feel that way, but I really can't afford to stay in Putney any longer. And if Jolie is unhappy, I have to do something about it. We're going to live with my great-aunt at first so I can economise for a while.'

'You can't be that hard up with all the money I pay you each month.'

'All the money? It barely covers Jolie's food and clothing, never mind anything else!' Melissa could feel the discussion heading in the direction of a major row, something she didn't need right now. She decided to end it before things got out of hand. 'I've got to go, Steve. I'll send you the address and phone number. If you find it difficult to get down there, I can always bring Jolie up on the train to Victoria and you can pick her up from there. Bye.'

She was shaking by the time she put down the receiver, but she was pleased. For once she hadn't allowed him to provoke her into a full-blown fight.

She only prayed she wasn't making a huge mistake in leaving London. Somehow, this had to work.

Dorothy was more enthusiastic when told of their plans. 'Excellent,' she said, 'but if after a while you find that you like it here at Ashleigh, then please feel free to stay. Really, I'd love it. Now have you thought about schools? Shall I call the ones around here to see if any of them could offer Jolie a place, then you can go and have a look as soon as possible?'

'Thank you, that would be great.'

After that everything happened with lightning speed. They moved in with Dorothy while Melissa started to make enquiries about a cottage, and Dorothy was as good as her word and found a school for Jolie within cycling distance of Ashleigh Manor. Although Melissa was worried at first, she soon realised her daughter could manage very well on her own. Unlike in London, there were no busy roads to cross and not much traffic.

'I'll be fine, Mum,' Jolie assured her. 'I'm not a baby, you said so yourself. This won't be any worse than walking home from school in Putney by myself.'

Fortunately, their move coincided with the winter half-term break and Jolie was able to start school soon afterwards. She returned in high spirits after her first day, barely pausing to lean her bike against the gatepost.

'Mum, I've made a friend already,' she announced,

running to give her mother a hug. 'She's called Amy and she lives in a cottage just up the road. Can I go over there this afternoon? She has her own horse and she's going to teach me how to ride. Please?'

'That's wonderful. Of course you can go.' Melissa felt some of the tension of the past few weeks drain out of her.

Arriving at Ashleigh, she had experienced the strange apprehension again and had there been anywhere else for her to go, she might have turned and run at that point. Since there wasn't, she had no choice but to stay, even though she was almost sure she shouldn't have come. Jolie's happiness now made her feel a lot better and she decided to stop worrying. 'What about the other children, were they nice?'

Jolie shrugged. 'Oh, they were okay, but I didn't really talk to them much. Some of the boys called me "carrot-head" and "newbie", but I ignored them and then they stopped. Amy says they sometimes call her "four-eyes".'

Melissa shook her head. Perhaps it was as well to let Jolie fend for herself. It was probably not the last time she'd be teased about her hair colour. If she could take such comments in her stride, so much the better.

A warm feeling of contentment spread through her body as she followed Jolie into the house. She told herself everything was going to be fine.

★　★　★

Jolie's new friend came over after school the next day. She was tiny and blonde, with enormous cornflower blue eyes behind her glasses, and Melissa immediately warmed to her.

'I live with my dad,' Amy told them while they were having tea in the kitchen. 'Mummy died in a car accident two years ago.'

'Oh, yes, I remember.' Dorothy nodded. 'I read about it in the local paper. So sad for you. I expect you miss her a lot.'

'I don't miss her at all,' Amy stated and helped herself to another chocolate biscuit. The others stared at her in surprise. 'She was never home anyway,' she explained, shrugging her slight shoulders as if that took care of the matter. 'She was always busy. Now we have Mrs Johnson. She does the cooking and cleaning.'

Melissa would have liked to ask more questions, but didn't want to pry. She suspected Amy had had to grow up a little too fast after her mother's sudden death, but she sensed the girl was still very vulnerable, despite her bravado.

'Tell us about your horse,' she invited instead. 'Is it a big one or just a pony?' This subject was seized upon with great enthusiasm by the two girls and half-an-hour later Melissa had begun to regret having asked. Horses had never been her passion. Apart from the one belonging to her night-time warrior, of course. She smiled to herself and let her thoughts wander. The dreams had returned several times since their move, but her memories of them were always frustratingly vague. The only thing that stood out clearly was his face – she knew each and every part of it in intimate detail now. Had she been an artist, she would have been able to draw his likeness without any problems. She sighed and gazed into space, propping her chin up with one hand.

'Mum. *Mummy!*'

'Sorry?' Melissa came reluctantly out of her daydream and it took her a moment to focus on her daughter.

'I said, we're going over to Amy's house now so I can have my second riding lesson,' Jolie said, speaking slowly as if she was talking to an idiot. Melissa realised she must have been far away and hurried to make amends.

'Of course, dear, but you will wear a riding helmet, won't you?'

'Yes, Mum. Amy has a spare one.' Jolie rolled her eyes in exasperation. 'Don't worry, I won't fall off.'

'I wouldn't be too sure about that.'

'I'll take care of her,' Amy assured her. 'She'll be fine.' The confidence she saw on the little girl's face made Melissa smile.

After the girls had left, Melissa wandered towards the sitting room with the intention of reading the paper. As she walked along the corridor she experienced a prickling sensation between the shoulder blades, as if someone was watching her. Turning around swiftly, she thought she caught a glimpse of a shadow disappearing quickly into the wall. A shadow in the shape of a human.

She shivered and went slowly over to the spot where it had vanished. It was just an ordinary wall. Smooth plaster painted white. Nothing else.

'What are you doing, Melissa?' Dorothy appeared behind her and Melissa jumped as if she'd been jolted by an electric charge. She put a hand over her heart to stop its frantic beating.

'Dorothy, you scared the life out of me.'

'Sorry, dear. You were so engrossed I suppose you didn't hear me coming. What are you looking at?'

'Er, this wall.' Melissa cleared her throat and tried to come up with a plausible excuse while studying the wall for something that might be of interest. At the top, she found what she was looking for. 'I was just wondering why the wood was shaped like that.' She pointed to a piece of cross-timbering in the shape of a semi-circle. 'All the others are straight.'

'Perhaps there used to be a door here before they added on the back part of the house,' Dorothy replied, stepping closer to have a look. 'Yes, this section is about the right shape for a door, wouldn't you say?'

Melissa had a sudden vision of a sturdy door, rounded at the top, and set with iron studs in an attempt at crude decoration. She closed her eyes and heard the squeak of its hinges as it opened and shut slowly. The sound grated on her nerves and she had to clench her teeth together firmly to stop from groaning.

'Yes, I'm sure you're right,' she murmured faintly. 'Well, never mind architecture, I think I'll go and read the paper now.' And she escaped into the sitting room, clutching the newspaper in front of her like a shield. She didn't know what she needed protection from, but there was definitely something strange going on in this house.

With a frown she tried to concentrate on the day's news, but she still felt as if someone was watching her. The room was quiet, almost eerily so, but nothing untoward stirred. There was a slight draught from the windows moving the curtains, and in a pale beam of sunlight the dust motes danced merrily as always, but there was no sign of the shadow from the corridor. Melissa scanned the room twice, just to make sure, then returned her attention to the newspaper.

The log fire suddenly collapsed, making Melissa's heart jump almost as far as her throat. She put up a hand to still its beating and drew in a deep breath.

'For heaven's sake,' she grumbled to herself. 'It's an old house, it makes noises. Get used to it!'

She felt foolish, but she couldn't help it. Something was making her edgy and no amount of reasoning with herself could shake the feeling that she was being observed, perhaps even appraised. Was the house judging her to see if she deserved to live here? Would she pass muster?

Shaking her head to rid herself of such stupid thoughts, she gave up her attempt at reading and left the room.

As she ran upstairs, however, she couldn't help but wonder if she'd been accepted.

CHAPTER 7

John of Ashleigh was not a patient man.

Sibell tiptoed along the corridor outside the main hall of her father's house, hoping to avoid a meeting with him before the evening meal. He'd been in such a foul mood that morning and she had no doubt it would have worsened during the day while he waited anxiously for her return. She knew he was in awe of Sir Gilbert Presseille, the most powerful man in the district. She was also sure he'd be terrified in case she should manage to persuade her former father-in-law to help her thwart his plans for the marriage to Sir Fulke.

'Don't you dare breathe a word of it to anyone, do you hear, or it will be the worse for you,' he'd threatened before she left, as she'd told Lady Maude.

'Hah!' she thought now. 'As if that would have swayed me if I had seriously thought Sir Gilbert could help.' Even if Sir Gilbert disapproved of the match, he had no authority to forbid it. He could voice his concerns, of course, but Sibell doubted her father would take any notice because once he was related to Sir Fulke by marriage, he would

85

have a much more powerful ally and protector. Besides, there was no reason why Sir Gilbert would want to disrupt his relationship with either man just for Sibell's sake. In the greater scheme of things, Sibell's well-being and happiness would not be worth him fighting for.

What her father failed to reckon with, however, was help from a woman, but Sibell realised that if anyone could find a way out for her, it was Lady Maude. Stealth and cunning were needed and Lady Maude had both in abundance, but John of Ashleigh would never believe that.

'Well, just you wait and see,' Sibell whispered mutinously. She was certain her faith in Lady Maude was not misplaced.

She peeked into the hall and drew back hastily as she caught sight of her father, pacing the floor with his hands behind his back. He was muttering under his breath and when her heartbeat had slowed a little, she was able to hear him clearly.

'Damn the girl! I shouldn't have let her go, but how could I have done otherwise?'

Sibell watched him through the crack between the door and the wall as he continued his pacing. Clearly impatient, his face was turning scarlet with anger now and she shrank back. She wanted to escape, but there was nowhere to run to.

'I cannot afford to offend Presseille and his wife,' he was mumbling. 'Not yet. It's too soon.'

Sibell shivered behind the door, the fear spreading through her once more. Her father was cursed with a temper he couldn't seem to keep in check these days. She had an awful feeling it would lead him to do something truly dreadful. The mere sight of her was enough to set him off sometimes, although she did her best not to goad him in any way.

'Where the hell is the little shrew?' she heard him say and knew that she couldn't delay the inevitable. Squaring her shoulders, she silently retraced her steps to the front door. She opened it as quietly as she could, then shut it with force before walking down the hall to face her father's wrath.

Melissa stretched lazily in her new bedroom at Ashleigh with a small smile on her face, pleased that her knight had visited her again last night. She had stopped worrying about it. After all, what harm could it do? It was just a fantasy and a lot easier than a real-life relationship. The fact that the dream was becoming more vivid only added spice to it, and as she snuggled up under the duvet she caught the faint odour of horse and leather again. And man.

She closed her eyes and saw his face clearly, then tried to remember more. What had the rest of him looked like? She wasn't sure. There was only a blurred image of someone big, solid and golden. Never mind, she would see him again, she was certain. A warm feeling of contentment spread through her body.

Getting up at last, she dressed quickly before padding over to the window to gaze at the breathtaking view. An enormous smooth lawn, bordered by a perfectly clipped hedge, was followed by an endless vista of rolling fields, all ploughed and ready for the spring sowing. In the distance to one side, she could see an old orchard, yet again of huge proportions. She leaned on the window sill and counted at least thirty trees. Their branches were bare now, but soon they'd be filled with blossom. Melissa wondered idly what on earth Dorothy did with all the fruit they must yield every autumn.

The main building was flanked by a stable block to the right and a huge barn with an oast house on the left. A small pond, surrounded by weeping willows and bushes, was set between the barn and the gates. At present, all the trees had stark, leafless branches. The only flashes of colour were the dark green leaves of ivy, interspersed with the occasional glint of yellow from a late-flowering winter jasmine. Later during the spring, these would be superseded by the profusion of climbing plants that grew all over the walls of the house – roses, wisteria, honeysuckle and more. No doubt those provided a riot of colours and scents.

Melissa flung open the casement and breathed deeply of the fresh country air, closing her eyes to savour the moment. It was a relief to finally have a home again, without having to worry about the rent or renewing the lease. Now they had the time to look around for a house of their own without being under pressure. Dorothy had been so good to them and wouldn't hear of accepting any payment. To think that only a few weeks ago they hadn't even met her.

'You're doing me a favour, my dear,' Dorothy had protested when Melissa wanted to pay rent and no arguments could sway her. So Melissa backed down, but insisted on paying for all the food and half the bills instead. She didn't want to lose her new-found independence. It made her feel better to know she was contributing in some way, apart from being here for Dorothy if she needed help.

'*Sweeting*.'

The unexpected word startled Melissa and she turned around to scan the room. There was no one there.

'Oh, God, I'm hearing things again.' She put a hand to her brow and bent her head, shaking it slowly.

'*Sweeting*,' the voice whispered again and at the same time Melissa felt something caress her cheek. She gasped and put a hand up to her face, her eyes searching the room once more.

It must have been the wind. A small laugh of relief escaped her as she realised her mind was playing tricks on her. Of course it had to be the wind. She closed the window with a bang and walked on slightly shaky legs over to the bed, where she sank down and drew a deep breath to calm her erratic heartbeat.

'*My love . . .*' This time the voice was stronger, and Melissa almost choked on her hastily indrawn breath.

'No, this isn't happening.' She shook her head again. 'Whoever you are, go away.'

She heard laughter, deep and rumbling, echo round the walls and then felt another soft caress on her cheek. For a moment she remained motionless on the bed, petrified into immobility. Then the urge to flee overcame everything else and she found she could move her limbs once more. She jumped up and headed for the door, her legs moving faster than she had ever thought them capable of. In her haste, she stubbed her toe on a loose floorboard. 'Ow, ow, ow! Damn!' she swore, trying to ignore the flash of pain shooting through her foot as she rushed out onto the landing.

She ran down the stairs as if pursued by demons. The strange laughter was still ringing in her ears when she slammed the front door shut.

Roger couldn't stop thinking about Sibell of Ashleigh. The hunted look in her eyes and her obvious distress when she mentioned her father had intrigued him and he wanted to learn more about her circumstances. He didn't want to draw attention to his interest in the young widow, however, so he set Hugone the task of finding out more about her. The last thing he wanted was to make matters worse for her.

'Now then, Hugone, have you been listening to gossip as I instructed?' They were exercising their horses on the forest tracks around Idenhurst and there was no one within earshot.

Hugone grinned and nodded. 'Yes, sir. There's plenty of tattle about Mistress Sibell so it weren't too hard to learn a few things.'

'Go on then, don't keep me in suspense.' Roger smiled back to show that he was half-joking. He liked the boy and they had an easy relationship, more like brothers than master and servant. Hugone was hard-working and earnest and not averse to keeping his eyes and ears open on Roger's behalf.

'Right, well, to start with, her father, John of Ashleigh, isn't well liked hereabouts. Thinks highly of himself, but in fact, he's only of yeoman stock. He has ideas above his station and claims to have Norman ancestors, despite the fact he has no proof of such a connection.'

Roger nodded. 'It's not unusual. Mostly these things can't be proved one way or another.'

'Oh, but they can in this case, sir. It's common knowledge John of Ashleigh's father was but a humble English foot soldier in the recent war with the French. Ruthless, he was, and he got his hands on a small fortune in ransoms and booty. With it, he bought up land around Ashleigh and increased his holdings tenfold. John, the son, was sent to a noble household to be trained in the arts of fighting and manners.' Hugone smirked. 'It seems although he learned much about fighting, no trace of the manners remain.'

Roger laughed. 'I see. And who had the misfortune to marry such a man?' He was curious about Sibell's mother.

'He's had two wives, sir. The first one died birthing their fifth son in as many years, but 'parently her husband didn't mourn her much. By all accounts he was much more upset when the oldest boy, named John after his sire, was killed in an accident a few years back. Anyway, he remarried quickly to a woman of gentle birth, but small fortune, p'rhaps hoping this would secure him entry into higher levels of society. He treated his new wife well simply because she was a friend of the Lady Maude, but the second wife died as well and the daughter was boarded out at the age of ten. When the girl turned sixteen and was offered a marriage with Sir Gilbert's only son, John's joy knew no bounds, so I'm told.'

'Hmm, I can see why,' Roger commented wryly.

Hugone's eyes danced with mischief. 'Ah, but alas, his joy was short-lived. The marriage lasted only a year, during which time Mistress Sibell failed to produce an heir to the Presseille holdings. The young man took it into his head to run off and fight for the Yorkists against the King and he was killed, as we know.'

Roger nodded to acknowledge this fact, but didn't want to think about the way Roland had died. It could so easily have happened to him as well. Hugone threw him an uncertain look, then continued. 'John's wrath at hearing this piece of news was amazing to behold.'

'John's wrath? Don't you mean Sir Gilbert's?'

'No, sir. I don't doubt Sir Gilbert grieved for

92

his son, but John of Ashleigh's reaction was the complete opposite when he was told of it. Bellowed in rage, he did, ranted about what a stupid, young fool master Roland had been. Sir Gilbert wasn't best pleased to hear his late heir described in such a manner, I can tell you.'

'The saints preserve us,' Roger muttered. 'So I take it tact isn't the man's strong point?'

'You could say that again, sir,' Hugone agreed. 'That wasn't all though. He then turned on his daughter in front of some of the servants. "And you! What have you to show for a whole year of marriage?" he shouted at her. "Not a thing, that's what! God's bones, but you're no damned use at all!" Those were his very words. A shame Sir Gilbert wasn't there to hear him. He'd gone off to see about his son's burial by then, or so I was told.'

Roger shook his head. 'What a fool.'

'Yes, sir, indeed. Took Mistress Sibell home that very day, and she weren't even allowed to pack her belongings. Last thing they heard John of Ashleigh shouting was apparently, "I'll find a use for you, see if I don't, and this time don't you dare fail me!"'

'The man sounds like a complete oaf.' Roger suppressed a shudder at the thought of what Mistress Sibell must have suffered at the hands of such a man. No wonder she'd had that anxious look about her. He sighed and returned his attention to his squire. 'You've done well, thank you for your efforts, Hugone. Please keep your ears open for more.'

'There you are, Melissa, I've been looking for you everywhere.'

Melissa was still sitting on a bench by the pond an hour later, despite the cold nip in the air, and turned to see Dorothy coming towards her. She knew she should be indoors doing some work, but had been unable to force her legs in the direction of the house. They still shook whenever she thought about what had happened.

'Sorry,' she mumbled.

'What are you doing out here?' Dorothy sat down beside her and peered at her, an anxious expression in her eyes. 'Is something wrong?'

Melissa sighed and decided not to beat around the bush. 'Do you think my bedroom might be haunted? Does Ashleigh Manor have a resident ghost?'

Dorothy's eyebrows lifted ever so slightly. 'Haunted? What makes you think that?'

'I thought I heard a voice this morning. In fact, I'm pretty sure I did. And there have been other instances, things I can't explain.'

Dorothy shrugged. 'It's possible. It is, after all, a very old house. I've never noticed anything odd, but then they say only certain people are sensitive to paranormal phenomena. Perhaps you're one of them?'

'I'd rather not be.' Melissa shuddered. She'd

been hoping Dorothy would give her some completely rational explanation for her experiences. She didn't want to believe in ghosts and definitely didn't want to share a house with them.

'Even if there is something, shall we say unusual, I've never heard of anyone being harmed in this house. It's certainly never bothered me and I've lived here all my life.'

'So it's not a poltergeist then. Well that's something to be thankful for, at least,' Melissa said sarcastically.

'Do you want to change to another room, dear? I understand that ghostly phenomena are often connected with certain places.'

Melissa thought about it, then rejected the idea. 'No, I . . . I guess I have to get used to it if I am one of those people who are sensitive to such things. Besides, I really love that room, it's perfect. I feel at home there.'

Dorothy looked out over the pond and smiled. 'Do you know, I would love it if someone could prove ghosts exist. I'd find it comforting to know that our souls can live on. It gives one hope, don't you think? Perhaps dear Charles is watching over us as we speak. And your mother.'

'I suppose so.' Seeing Dorothy so calm and matter-of-fact about this subject made Melissa feel silly for having over-reacted. She had always prided herself on being a practical woman, surely she could cope with a ghost playing pranks on her occasionally? As long as that was all it was.

But when she followed Dorothy inside and felt that strange apprehension seize her as soon as she neared the house, she wasn't so sure.

The rustling of paper woke Jake and he realised he must have fallen asleep on the living-room sofa while reading the newspaper. He'd been doing extra shifts at work lately and this wasn't the first time he'd nodded off early during his infrequent evenings off.

He sighed and closed his eyes again. *Not much point moving really, I may as well stay where I am.* He wriggled to try and get more comfortable, but instead he began to feel cramped and hemmed in. The sensation grew until he was sure all the air in his lungs was being squeezed out. He had to fight for every breath and, if he hadn't known better, he would have said something or someone was jostling him. In fact, not just one or two people, but a whole crowd were now pushing and shoving him, keeping his arms pinned to his sides.

'What the hell . . .?' he muttered.

Frowning, he tried to open his eyes, but his eyelids refused to co-operate. They stayed stubbornly shut and suddenly, on their insides, images appeared out of nowhere. It was like watching a DVD without access to a pause button, and what Jake saw was so horrible his heart began to hammer loudly.

He was indeed in the middle of a huge throng of people, and they were all hurling abuse at some unfortunate men on a make-shift scaffold. A young man was at the front, his hands tied behind him, and Jake gasped when he saw the man's features. They bore an eerie resemblance to his own – the same slightly sharp nose and blue eyes, with straight hair falling across his brow, although this man's was more of a reddish hue than Jake's own golden blond. *A mere youth, not really a grown man!* Jake felt empathy tear through him at the sight of a youngster in such grim circumstances.

There was no time to register any more details, however, as someone in a black cape stepped forward and blocked the view. The official-looking man read out a decree, most of which Jake didn't catch. It was impossible to hear much with the crowd baying for blood and pushing at him from all sides. The only words he heard clearly were '. . . *Roland . . . traitor to the crown . . . executed by beheading . . .*' *Roland?* The name wasn't one he recognised, and yet it was as if he watched these events through the eyes of someone who did, because he felt no surprise. His mouth formed a silent scream of 'no' at the cruel sentence being read out, but he still couldn't open his eyes and he was forced to watch what happened next.

The strawberry-blond young man was lead towards a crude block, a squarish piece of wood with slightly uneven sides. Someone shoved him between the shoulder blades and he was made to kneel and put his head on the rough surface. Jake saw him fight his gaolers one last time to raise his terrified gaze to heaven, muttering something. He guessed it was a prayer, because there seemed no chance of halting the proceedings.

With one final, anguished look at the crowd, the young man closed his eyes and placed his head on the wooden block. He seemed calm now, but Jake could see that despite this bravado, the youth couldn't keep the rest of his body from shaking. He was quite simply petrified. *And who wouldn't be?*

Although he wanted to intervene and stop this from happening, Jake knew there was no hope of doing so, and he couldn't move in any case. He swallowed hard and resigned himself to the inevitable, the way the youth had already done. A huge man with his head covered by a dark hood stepped forward and lifted an axe with a wide blade into the air. The crowd quieted and held its collective breath. The only sound to be heard now was a muted chanting from a priest who was standing at the back of the scaffold.

The sharp blade flashed in the sunlight and came down with a sickening thud. Jake flinched, as if it had severed his own head from his shoulders, and he had to fight hard not to throw up at the sight before him. He knew the young man had been lucky in that the executioner had succeeded in his task with just one blow, but all he felt was nausea and a bone-chilling bleakness.

Invisible fingers plucked at his sleeve and a voice hissed, 'Master, we must leave. We can't stay here, it's madness. They could take you next!' He was aware of being pulled out of the crowd by someone with dark, straight hair, and followed blindly. Somehow he knew he'd been fortunate to escape the fate that had befallen the youth. It could have been him up there on the scaffold.

Slowly the images faded away and Jake was able to blink open his eyes. The modern living room came into focus all around him and he pushed himself upright, no longer feeling restrained. He couldn't forget what he'd just seen though. Why was he dreaming of things like that? Was it a dream or some memory encoded in the cottage walls? He'd heard about such theories, but never believed them until now.

Or was it possible to relive the experience of some long-dead ancestor? Something embedded deeply in his DNA? *But in that case, why was I seeing it through someone else's eyes?* There was no doubt in Jake's mind that the youth on the scaffold was somehow related to him, yet Jake hadn't been seeing things from his point of view. He swallowed hard and got off the sofa, too restless to stay still.

None of this makes sense!

Either way, he never wanted to see such horrors again.

CHAPTER 8

'So the high-and-mighty Sir Gilbert isn't coming to your aid, eh?'

Sibell's father smirked at her across the table and chewed noisily on a piece of coarse bread, before taking a large swig of ale and then burping repeatedly. He seemed in a particularly good mood for once and Sibell bit back a sharp retort. Instead she sent him a wide-eyed look, as if she had no idea what he was talking about, although she knew full well why he was gloating.

For several days after her visit to Idenhurst, he and her brothers had kept a close watch over her. It was as if they expected someone from the manor to come riding to her rescue, even though she'd taken Maude's advice and pretended to agree to the marriage. Now that a week had passed, her father obviously felt able to relax, sure in the knowledge that she had failed to secure assistance.

'Of course, he knows as well as I do that he has nothing to say in the matter. Still, he could have made a nuisance of himself if he'd so chosen,' he continued. 'Seems you misjudged him. He's a sensible man, won't meddle where he's not wanted. And you are nothing to him any more.' He chuckled.

'I didn't speak to Sir Gilbert, only Lady Maude,' Sibell answered quietly. 'It was she who sent for me after all. And I followed your instructions.' She crossed her fingers under the table since this wasn't strictly true.

Her father's expression darkened at the mention of Lady Maude. 'Meddlesome old crone. I don't doubt she'd go pleading your cause with her husband if she felt so inclined. Just as well you said nothing, or else . . .' He left the threat hanging in the air between them and Sibell suppressed a shiver. She didn't think he would ever do any harm to Lady Maude if he found out she'd been meddling, but one never knew with her father. He was so unpredictable and his temper was definitely spiralling out of control. She shuddered again. *No, he must never find out.*

Thankfully, his improved mood meant that he also relaxed his vigilance. Sibell was at last able to go about her normal duties, both indoors and out, without a watchdog on her trail. After finishing her many tasks that morning, she took the opportunity to escape out of the back door while no one was looking, and headed for a small forested area nearby.

It was a beautiful day, unseasonably warm and with hardly a breeze stirring the branches of the trees. Spring had always been Sibell's favourite time of year and she noted with pleasure all the signs of its coming. There were trees with fat leaf buds ready to burst, fruit blossom, birds serenading each other and flowers peeking up through the thick layer of dead leaves on the ground. All these lifted her spirits and she decided to simply enjoy the moment, leaving her worries behind. It was impossible to stay dejected on such a day.

Although she knew it was dangerous to venture too far into the forest alone, she thought she'd be safe as long as she stayed within hearing distance of the house. Surely any outlaws would be targeting travellers on the roads, rather than ordinary local people going about their business, she thought. Besides, she was wearing an old cloak borrowed from one of the kitchen maids. Everyone knew servants had nothing worth stealing so she hoped she'd be mistaken for one and left in peace.

Underneath the beech trees she found primroses peeking out here and there, and a veritable carpet of wood anemones brightening up the forest floor as far as the eye could see. Sibell stopped to admire this lovely sight. Although she'd seen it many times before, she knew she would never tire of it. She leaned her back against the nearest tree and closed her eyes, savouring the moment. There was a promise in the air, a hint of wonderful things to come, that made her heart beat faster in expectation.

'So, the little bird has flown the nest at last,' a deep voice said behind her.

Sibell whirled round so fast her cloak caught on a nearby branch. She wrenched it free with trembling hands and stared at Sir Roger of Langford, who had materialised behind her like a wraith out of the ground. 'I . . . I . . .'

'Forgive me, I didn't mean to startle you again.' He laughed. 'It seems to be my misfortune to scare the wits out of you whenever we meet. I promise, that is not my intention.'

'Where did you come from? I didn't hear your approach.' Sibell strove to calm herself and pulled the cloak together in front of her. Yet again he'd caught her unawares.

'You must have been truly engrossed then. I made no secret of my presence.'

Sibell wasn't convinced. Anyone walking in the forest was bound to step on at least the occasional twig, but she'd heard nothing. 'You are on foot today?' she remarked suspiciously, wondering what could have brought him so near her home in stealth. Was he spying on her father?

'Indeed. It is too beautiful a day to ride. I prefer to observe nature at close quarters and what better way than going for a walk? Isn't that what you're doing yourself?'

'I, er . . . I merely came to look for herbs.'

'Ah, but of course.' The look he gave her told her clearly that he knew she was prevaricating and Sibell thought it best to change the subject.

'Didn't Sir Gilbert warn you there are outlaws hereabouts?'

103

Sir Roger laughed again. 'I thought we established last time we met that neither of us feared them. As you can see, I have brought my trusted sword just in case.' He gave the weapon an affectionate pat, then grew serious. 'However, a woman alone shouldn't venture too far from home. It would be foolhardy, I think.'

'I haven't. I'm still close to the manor,' she defended herself, although she could see now that had he been an outlaw, she would have had trouble escaping him. It occurred to her to wonder whether he was actually one of those desperate men himself. Was that why he was sneaking around in such a furtive manner? Was he on his way to a meeting with other outlaws, supporters of the Duke of York perhaps? She frowned. If he was, he was taking a huge risk, wandering about in broad daylight.

'You're not enjoying this fine day?' he asked, seeing her expression. 'Perhaps you don't care for flowers?'

'Of course I do, only . . .' She couldn't tell him he had spoiled her enjoyment of them. It would sound too churlish. 'You frightened me, is all.'

'Well, perhaps you'd allow me to make amends? Come for a walk with me and we can appreciate the beauty of spring together.' He held out his arm for her and looked at her expectantly.

'But I barely know you.'

'Nonsense. I'm a guest of the Presseille family. Surely you don't think I would jeopardise their goodwill by mistreating one of their neighbours

104

and a former daughter-in-law of Lady Maude's at that?' He smiled at her to indicate how ridiculous he thought her suspicions. 'I only wish to walk and talk with you.'

Sibell felt foolish for doubting him. He certainly didn't look like a brigand, nor act like one. Perhaps he was the opposite – someone sent to root out and apprehend the Duke's supporters? With a sigh she gave up thinking about it and remembered her decision to enjoy the here and now. 'Very well,' she said and placed a few fingers on his forearm. 'I see no harm in walking a little way. There is a brook not far from here which is in full flow at this time of year; a lovely sight.'

'Then let us find it.'

The smile he gave her banished all her doubts for the moment. But they soon returned.

This is all wrong! Sibell knew that to spend time with a virtual stranger, and a male one at that, went against everything she had been taught. To do so in the seclusion of the forest was even worse. And yet, she couldn't deny she was enjoying every moment.

Sir Roger's enthusiasm for everything around them was infectious, as was his laughter, which rang out frequently. Here was obviously a man who lived life to the full, who never looked back with regrets, but only forward. Unlike the men in her family, who seemed to be forever brooding over something and always wishing for what they didn't have.

'Why so sad?' he enquired, pulling her out of her reverie.

'I'm not sad, merely thinking.'

'You're still worried about your father? Is he likely to have followed you?'

'Oh, no. He's busy this morning. It was nothing, really.'

He had stopped to face her and was regarding her with a serious look for once. 'I wouldn't want to put you in a difficult position. You must tell me if you wish me to leave.'

'No! I mean, don't leave on my account. I'm enjoying your company.' The confession escaped her before she could stop it and she felt her cheeks heat up in embarrassment.

'And I yours.'

The look that accompanied this statement sent her heart into a frenzy, but she told herself sternly that it was just his way. He was merely indulging in a light flirtation to pass the time.

He means nothing by it and I'd do well to remember that.

Roger was enjoying himself hugely, a fact which surprised him somewhat. Although he hadn't sought out Mistress Sibell on purpose this morning, he realised now he'd unconsciously walked this way in the hope of seeing her. He was quite sure it was the last thing he ought to have done. So why had he?

The answer seemed to be that he couldn't help himself. He simply had to see her again.

It was strange, for he wouldn't normally have given her a second glance. He'd always liked small, merry, buxom armfuls, the kind of women who knew the rules of the game and gave as good as they got. Easy-going and worldly wise, never demanding any serious effort on his behalf. Sibell most definitely didn't fit that description. If anything, she was the complete opposite.

She was tall and reached at least up to his chin. Although the full-length cloak she wore prevented him from assessing her figure properly, he judged her to be of slim build. But he remembered from their ride that she had curves; he'd felt them as she leant against him. Her face was almost gaunt, though, and an air of sadness hung over her like an invisible veil. She also appeared to be extremely innocent, despite having been married. His flirtatious glances and comments were mostly met with either a shy smile or a look of bafflement. It was as if no one had ever teased her before.

He couldn't understand it.

Something about her fascinated him, however. He'd gathered from further gossip overheard at Idenhurst that she'd been well-loved as the daughter-in-law of Sir Gilbert and was a favourite with Lady Maude. With such patronage, her father ought to have been concerned for her welfare. *So why was she walking alone through the countryside? For that matter, why had she been walking at all?* Even Lady Maude had questioned her lack of a mount.

As he slanted her another brief glance, the wide grey eyes, thickly fringed with dark lashes, regarded him solemnly, almost apprehensively. There was none of the coquetry he usually met with, and Sibell seemed sublimely unaware of her own charms, such as they were. He had to acknowledge she wasn't a beauty in the true sense of the word, but he would allow that she was passing pretty. The silvery eyes were set in a piquant face together with a small, straight nose, which was slightly tilted at the tip. The bridge of her nose was covered in freckles, which some men might have found offensive. Roger thought them charming. He knew she had dimples either side of her generous mouth and he suddenly had an irresistible urge to kiss her.

He shook himself mentally. *This is madness and I should go.*

There was something infinitely appealing about her, though. Her aura of fragility stirred his inherent chivalry to uncharted heights and made him want to protect her against the entire world. And when she tilted her head to one side and sent him a look full of trust and dawning hope, he knew he was lost. He couldn't leave her.

Perhaps not ever.

On his return to Idenhurst, he forgot about Sibell for a while, however, when Hugone sought him out and drew him to one side.

'Sir, I have some news. A servant of Sir

Gilbert's by the name of Walter came riding into the yard earlier, looking as though he'd been on a long journey. I decided to follow him and shortly after his arrival he met with his master in the stables.'

'And why the secrecy?' Roger's interest was piqued. He suspected his host was a supporter of the Duke of York, but if so, he'd kept quiet about it. Officially, he was loyal to the King.

'Well, they spoke about you.' Hugone looked slightly uncomfortable and Roger frowned at him.

'Me? What did they say?'

'It sounded to me as though the man Walter had been sent off to find out more about you, check your background, as it were.'

Roger nodded. 'Didn't trust my story, eh? Can't really blame him, I suppose. And what was the verdict?'

'I heard Walter say that everything you'd told Sir Gilbert appeared to be true and he'd had no bad reports of you, only good.' Hugone bit his lip. 'Although . . .'

'Spit it out. What else did he say?'

'He'd been told of your possible involvement with the Duke, sir. Nothing definite, but there were rumours, apparently.'

'Hmm, no one can prove anything, but we'd do best to be on our guard. Not that I think Sir Gilbert will hold it against me, quite the opposite, but until we can talk of such things freely . . .' He fixed Hugone with a stern gaze, but knew it wasn't really necessary. The youth was completely trustworthy.

'Not a word, sir.'

'Excellent. Thank you for your vigilance, and remind me to pay you extra this month.'

CHAPTER 9

'A snowstorm in March? Now I've seen everything.' Dorothy threw up her hands in disgust and let the heavy velvet curtain fall back into place.

Melissa, the room's only other occupant, sneezed violently in reply and burrowed further into the huge winged armchair next to the fireplace.

'Can I get you anything, dear?' Dorothy asked.

'No.' Melissa blew her nose and added, 'I mean, no thank you. Sorry to be so grumpy, but I don't feel too good.' Her head was aching like the very devil and she thought her sinuses might be in imminent danger of exploding.

'Hmph. You're a worse patient than my Charlie and that's saying something.'

Melissa couldn't disagree with that statement since she'd never met the late lamented Mr Cummings, so she merely sniffed and reiterated her apology.

Dorothy headed for the door. 'Some hot soup is what you need. If anyone wants me I'll be in the kitchen.'

'Uh-hmm. Thanks.'

The oak-beamed sitting room at Ashleigh Manor

was a warm haven, cocooning Melissa from the violent snowstorm raging outside. The log fire in the enormous inglenook kept the room at just the right temperature, and had the added advantage of making the dark oak furniture gleam warmly in the reflection of its bright light. Large Persian rugs in shades of russet and red added insulation and a welcome splash of colour.

Melissa sighed. 'I hate being ill,' she muttered, and leaned back to let the softness of the chair envelop her. Dorothy was right, she was a very bad patient. Russ, who was lying in front of the fire, raised his head and gave her a sympathetic look.

The old timbers of the house creaked from time to time and the occasional gust of wind whistled down the chimney, but nothing else moved. Melissa could hear humming and the distant clatter of cooking utensils from the kitchen, but the noise seemed far away. A sense of unreality stole over her, and she was lulled into sleep.

Without warning, Russ suddenly shot up and growled furiously in the direction of the wall opposite Melissa's chair. His hackles were up and he performed a series of little angry jumps while keeping his eyes firmly glued to the wall.

Melissa blinked. 'What's the matter with you?' She rubbed at sleep-heavy eyes and stared after him as, claws scrabbling on the slippery floorboards, he bolted for the door into the hall. She turned back to see what could have made the little dog act in such a strange manner and froze.

There was a face on the wall and it was staring at her.

The hair on the back of her neck stood on end and a vice began to close around her throat. She couldn't breathe, and although she wanted to scream, she found it impossible. She tried, but only a pitiful whimper emerged. Squeezing her eyes shut, she regained the use of her lungs, although only for small, painful gasps of air.

'Oh, my God,' she whispered. Was she really so ill she was conjuring up faces on the wall? *But wait, Russ must have seen it, too.*

She raised her eyelids just a fraction. The face was still there, and this time he smiled at her. She drew in another rasping breath and opened her eyes fully. Sheer terror kept her rooted to her seat and her eyes riveted to the strange image.

It was a he, no doubt about it. He had an incredibly masculine face, although it was framed by long, blond hair. It slowly came into focus, as if an invisible lens was adjusting the picture and Melissa found herself gazing into a pair of ice-blue eyes that seemed strangely familiar. She noticed a long scar down the left-hand cheek, which made him look slightly piratical and that was when she made the connection. *He's the man in my dreams!*

She wondered fleetingly if she'd gone to sleep and was dreaming now, but somehow she knew that wasn't the case. The vivid eyes blinked and she exhaled slowly to calm herself.

'No, this can't be happening,' she breathed, but his smile widened as if to prove her wrong.

Little by little, she felt the terror ebb out of her and curiosity took over. How was this possible? Another brief attempt at closing her eyes to make him go away didn't result in any change. The man's face remained and his lips moved as if he was talking to her, although she couldn't hear anything.

Melissa began to wonder if someone was playing a trick on her. She looked around for a possible source for the image on the wall, but couldn't find anything obvious. There was no one else in the room, and no logical place in which a tape recorder or film camera could have been hidden. The smooth plaster wall would be an ideal place to project an image onto, but in that case, there should have been a beam of light emanating from somewhere. There wasn't.

'Impossible,' she muttered and returned her stare to the man's face.

All of a sudden her body began to tingle and her head felt as if someone was stuffing it full of cotton wool. A strange groping sensation spread inside her, little tentacles searching, questing. Melissa shook her head and blinked several times. *What is happening to me?*

Unaccountably, the fear she'd felt before was dispersing and it was replaced by something else. A burgeoning warmth, the niggling sensation that she knew this man, liked him even. She tried to shake her head once more, but this time it didn't obey her. In fact, none of her limbs moved at her command, but appeared to be guided by some other force, a force that wasn't of her making.

She had no choice but to stare at the man. His smile suddenly made her go weak at the knees, despite sitting down, and as if in a trance she felt her body lean forward to catch his words. There was an urgency compelling her to listen, and she became frustrated when at first she couldn't make out what he was saying. Slowly, however, his voice grew louder and began to echo inside her head until she could hear him clearly.

'Sweeting. Help me, please!' His voice was a caress, flowing over her softly, causing her breathing to become laboured.

Feelings of love for the man exploded inside her, taking her by surprise. She couldn't understand why she should feel anything for him at all, but the warm love flowed through her as if she had no control over her emotions whatsoever.

At the same time little tendrils of fear crept up her spine, but she realised that it wasn't fear *of* him, but *for* him. She didn't want to lose him. The urge to cry was overwhelming and she desperately wanted to tell him of her love, but the words stuck in her throat. In agony, she clenched her fists and his voice receded. The pain helped her regain control over her limbs momentarily, but then the voice rang out once more inside her head.

'Please, my sweet . . .' The force within her returned with a vengeance, slamming into her gut.

A yearning for him went through her, stronger than anything she'd ever experienced before. She drew in a ragged breath. She wanted this man, more than anything.

When his features began to fade, Melissa panicked and found she could move once more. 'No, wait! Why are you saying that?' she cried, erupting from her chair and stumbling towards the opposite wall. 'Don't go yet. Please, tell me who you are.'

She heard a chuckle, a rich vibrant sound that made her body sing with the remembrance of pleasure, and then came a faint reply. *'Roger, sweeting. Help me . . .'* The face faded away completely as Melissa reached out to touch the wall. Her fingers encountered only cold, hard plaster and an unbelievable sadness welled up inside her.

She was shaking so badly she could hear the charms on her bracelet jangling and she stood for a long time leaning her forehead against the wall. The alien force inside her seeped away slowly, leaving her with huge tears rolling down her cheeks unheeded. It wasn't until Dorothy came bustling into the room some time later that she came out of her stupour.

'Ah, you're up and about. Are you feeling any better? The soup will be ready in . . .' Dorothy stopped short as she noticed Melissa's distraught expression. 'Why, what's the matter?'

'A ghost, Dorothy,' Melissa whispered. 'I saw the ghost.'

There was a slight hesitation before Dorothy replied. 'You saw it?'

'Him, it was a he. Definitely.'

'Really? You know, you don't look at all well, my dear. Let me fetch you a cup of tea. Some aspirin, perhaps?'

Melissa frowned. Dorothy didn't seem to be taking this at all seriously and she wanted to shake the old lady to make her understand. 'I'm not making this up. I'm not that ill,' she insisted.

'No, no, of course not, but do sit down or you're going to get worse. Let me fetch you a hot drink and you'll feel much better.'

'Dorothy, I . . .' But her aunt had already left the room and Melissa was left to grind her teeth in frustration. 'I am *not* going crazy,' she whispered to no one in particular.

But deep inside she was beginning to wonder.

The bout of flu lasted for nearly a week, and Melissa was sure it was the worst one she'd ever suffered. It left her feeling low and listless and she thanked her lucky stars that Dorothy was around to help. The old lady took care of all the cooking and washing, and even helped Jolie with her homework.

'It's really kind of you,' Melissa said. 'Although I'm sure Jolie can manage on her own.'

'It's no bother and I've noticed she gets it done faster with a bit of encouragement.'

Melissa could see Dorothy enjoyed being needed,

so she didn't protest too much, only thanked her again. Indeed, after the first few weeks at Ashleigh, she'd more or less given up even thinking about renting a place for herself and Jolie. Dorothy had made them so welcome and seemed supremely happy to have them living with her. It seemed pointless and churlish to move out just for the sake of wanting to be independent. The phrase 'cutting your nose off to spite your face' came to mind and Melissa was pragmatic enough to accept that they were fine as they were.

The only drawback was the fact that she continued to be plagued by unsettling dreams and vague feelings of disquiet. Even though the ghostly face hadn't hurt her in any way, the experience had frightened her badly and it wasn't something she wanted to go through again. She took to glancing over her shoulder whenever she had to walk anywhere in the house alone and jumped at the slightest sound. Although she berated herself and tried to reason away this nervous reaction, she couldn't help it.

'This is ridiculous,' she muttered on more than one occasion. Had anyone asked her previously whether she even believed in ghosts, she would have laughed, but now . . . How could she doubt her own eyes?

Far more unsettling than merely seeing the ghostly face was the fact that her body was gripped by a yearning for the man that was almost painful. She was sure he was the same man as the one in her dreams; there could be no mistaking him. The dreams of him became a nightly occurrence, evermore sensuous. Every time she woke up, it was to find her body in a state of turmoil and longing, such as she had never known before.

Was it possible to imagine something to the extent that it turned into a hallucination? she wondered. Melissa didn't know, but whenever she closed her eyes she could still hear the caressing voice and she found it utterly frightening that she didn't want it to go away. She wanted to listen to this Roger forever.

Melissa prided herself on being an intelligent, rational woman, but she began to wonder if the difficult times she'd suffered recently had affected her more than she had thought. Could the dreams and the face on the wall simply be a figment of her imagination, a reaction perhaps to the trauma of divorce? Since Steve had walked out on her, she hadn't had the slightest desire to meet other men, let alone sleep with one. Instead, she concentrated on her work and Jolie. Steve was still the only man she wanted, or so she'd thought. It therefore seemed plausible that her mind should come up with a dream substitute, a perfect man who would never betray her, would never leave or disappoint her.

No matter how much she mulled this over, she couldn't come to any other conclusions and it weighed heavily on her mind. As the days went by, however, and no more spectres appeared, she began to calm down and the turmoil lessened somewhat. Always practical, she determined to wait and see whether it happened again.

'Melissa, telephone for you.'

Dorothy's voice summoned Melissa out of yet another reverie concerning the ghost and she shook herself mentally. She really must stop thinking about it, it wasn't healthy.

'Coming.' She rushed down the stairs and arrived by the phone slightly breathless. 'Hello?'

'Melissa, it's me, Steve.'

'Oh, hi.' She hadn't heard his voice for weeks now and her heart performed a little extra tattoo, although she refused to allow herself to think he was calling because he'd realised his mistake at last. That would have been tempting fate. She was also determined not to let him know she was pining for him, so she made her voice slightly sarcastic. 'To what do I owe this pleasure?'

'I'm just calling to let you know I won't be paying maintenance much longer.'

'You what?' Melissa's voice rose to a squeak, all her good intentions to stay calm when speaking to him forgotten. 'What do you mean? You can't just stop paying when you feel like it. Jolie is your daughter, too.'

'I know that, but now you're living the high life in a grand mansion, I'm sure you don't need my paltry contribution. I checked it out the other day; it's quite the little palace, isn't it? It's all right for some.'

'Grand mansion? Palace? Are you mad? This isn't my house and we're only staying here until we find a cottage of our own. A very small cottage. I told you!' Melissa decided Steve didn't need to know that she'd stopped looking for one. It was beside the point. Frustration made her voice rise to a much higher pitch than she'd intended, but he didn't take any notice.

'Yeah, yeah, and pigs might fly,' he sneered. 'You think I was born yesterday? I know as well as you do that you don't have any other relatives, so that house will probably go to you as soon as the old lady snuffs it. It's just a question of time. I saw her pottering round the garden, looked pretty frail to me.'

'Don't you dare talk about Dorothy like that! She's only seventy-two and in excellent health.'

'Whatever. The fact is, I can't afford to pay any longer. Me and Daisy are having another baby soon and Daze wants us to get married. Although not until after she's recovered from the birth and all that.'

Melissa leaned her back against the wall and slid downwards until her backside connected with the floor. She felt as if someone had just punched her guts into smithereens and a sudden tightening in her throat prevented her from breathing.

'Melissa? Are you there?' Steve sounded impatient. 'I haven't got all day.'

'Yes.' The word came out as a whisper, but it was all she was capable of. Her mind was grappling with the concept of Steve having another child with his current girlfriend and wanting to marry the woman. All that after he'd told Melissa he hated being tied down and didn't want any more children. How much more tied down could he get? One love-child he could have walked away from, especially since he'd confessed he wasn't even sure it was his, but two? She swallowed past the heavy lump in her throat.

'I just wanted to tell you so you don't make a big fuss. You don't have a leg to stand on,' Steve said.

Righteous anger filled Melissa to the exclusion of all else and her powers of speech returned. 'No, you listen to me, you scumbag. I don't have a single penny more than I did before I moved into this house and I can prove it. Jolie is your daughter and, unless you want her to grow up deprived of every-thing a child her age should have, you'd better keep paying. I don't care how many other kids you have, that's your problem. Jolie is still half yours and you owe her! You'll be hearing from my solicitor.'

She slammed the phone down, then burst into tears. They were mostly tears of anger and frus-tration. She had finally allowed herself to feel financially secure, since she wasn't paying the exorbitant London rents any longer, but now it seemed she was back to square one. Hiring an expensive solicitor was the last thing she wanted, and because she and Steve only had an informal agreement regarding the maintenance payment it could also turn into a lengthy business if the matter had to go to court.

And how could she ever prove whether Steve could genuinely afford to pay the amount he was sending her at the moment? He was a self-employed IT consultant. She knew for a fact he didn't declare even half of his earnings, so anyone investigating his affairs might come to the conclusion that he earned very little. It was infuriating.

Mixed in with her anger was a feeling of utter despair. The money was important, but even worse to her mind was the fact that Steve was marrying someone else, having children with someone else. He really wasn't coming back. Ever.

It was time to face the truth, but how could she when it hurt so badly?

Melissa definitely couldn't afford to be ill now so, despite the lingering effects of the flu, she went back to work in between heated discussions with a local solicitor recommended by Dorothy.

'I agree your ex-husband is in the wrong,' he told her, 'but you will have to fight every step of the way and it will cost more money, I'm afraid.'

Money she didn't have. This only made her more determined, however, and she fought off the tiredness, ignored her sore nose and went off to do as much research as she could.

It was a relief when Saturday came and she was able to take some time off to go shopping in the nearest town to Ashleigh. The little High Street was crowded and Melissa was jostled several times as she made her way up the steep hill, but she didn't mind. She worked her way down her shopping list and was almost sorry when she reached the last item, bread.

In the window of the bakery, there was a beautiful three-tiered wedding cake, decorated with a profusion of pink roses and white swirls of icing. Melissa paused to have a look at it before entering the shop. It was vaguely similar to the one she and Steve had shared at their wedding, all those years ago, and it brought back memories. She'd been so young and naive and actually believed she was marrying the perfect man. *What a fool I was!*

Perhaps she and Steve hadn't been right for each other, only she'd been too immature to realise it at the time? No, they had both been in love, she was sure of it. The doubts came later. And the harsh words. She shook her head impatiently. She mustn't let herself brood over it. The past was over and done with and, judging by his recent behaviour, he really wasn't worth pining over. With a sigh, she turned towards the entrance of the bakery.

The bell above the door jingled and a man stepped out of the shop, holding the door politely for her to enter. Melissa looked up with a smile to thank him for his courtesy, and stopped dead, the smile fading from her lips.

'Oh, my God!' she gasped. Suddenly her head felt very light and there was a buzzing noise in her ears. She couldn't breathe properly; a vice

124

closed around her chest, squeezing hard. As if in a dream, she felt her hands go limp and heard the dull thud when the various carrier bags hit the pavement. In slow-motion, she followed them downwards and heard herself cry out. The startled man began to disappear rapidly from her vision as a pinprick of darkness grew ever larger. She was only vaguely aware of him swearing softly. In the next instant everything turned black.

'Bloody hell!'

Jake dropped the bag of doughnuts he'd just bought as he caught the woman's crumpling body at the last minute. He didn't have a chance to do anything about her shopping bags and could only hope they didn't contain anything fragile.

She wasn't all that heavy so he was able to lift her without much effort and carry her into the shop. The little bell jangled furiously as he kicked the door open wider with one foot. There were exclamations of surprise and murmurings of sympathy from other customers as they moved hurriedly to make way for him and his burden. Three chairs were arranged against a wall, presumably for the use of elderly customers, and he lay the unconscious woman down across them.

'Dear me, what happened, young man?' he heard someone say. He turned to find some kind soul had retrieved his doughnuts and the woman's carrier bags from the pavement outside and was depositing them next to the chairs.

'Thanks,' he murmured somewhat distractedly, his attention focused on the woman. There was something about her that disturbed him, but he couldn't quite put his finger on what it could be.

'It's been a long time since I saw a young girl swoon at the sight of a handsome man.' The comment, together with a stifled cackle of laughter, came from somewhere behind him and he turned in irritation to glare at the person who had uttered it. There were several elderly ladies watching with avid curiosity, and he couldn't say for sure which one of them had spoken so he gave them all a stern look before turning back to the prone woman. *Of all the stupid things to say*, he thought, but stifled the urge to comment out loud.

The woman stirred and her eyelids fluttered. As he chafed her hands in an attempt to revive her and waited for her to come out of her faint, he heard the voice behind him add in a loud, theatrical whisper, 'But he's handsome enough to make even an old lady like me swoon.' Gritting his teeth, he resolutely ignored it.

The woman was trying to open her eyes and finally succeeded.

'Ah, good, you're waking up,' Jake said, while she blinked in confusion. 'How are you feeling?'

As she looked up into his face, he saw her frown. All of a sudden, her gaze widened and she swallowed hard. At first she didn't answer him, but then she whispered, 'Roger?'

'I'm sorry?' It was Jake's turn to frown.

'No, it can't be.' She stared at him. 'You . . . you look different, somehow. Oh, it's your hair, you've had it cut. Shame, I liked those long golden tresses, but that short, layered style quite suits you.' She smiled at him, showing two perfect dimples, and Jake drew in a sharp breath. The smile transformed her face from merely pretty to breathtakingly beautiful and he felt as if he'd been floored by a heavyweight champion. But what had she meant by 'long golden tresses'? She was quite clearly barking mad. *A real shame.*

'I think you must be confusing me with someone else,' he informed her gently. 'My name is Jake Precy. I'm the local vet, and I don't think we've met before, or have we?'

He said the last part of the sentence as if it was a question, because he *had* felt a small stirring of recognition himself. Surely he would have remembered meeting this woman, though? With her long, wavy, auburn hair, cool silvery eyes and incredible smile she was definitely unforgettable. And although she had felt light as a feather when he carried her into the shop, her tall figure was nicely rounded in all the right places. A shaft of desire suddenly snaked through him, taking him by surprise, and he gave himself a mental shake. What was the matter with him? He hadn't reacted to a woman in ages, not since . . . well, since that damned ridiculous dream. But perhaps that was the trouble.

'Do you have a pet?' he added, hoping against hope this would solve the mystery.

'No, I . . .' She was still staring at him, looking totally bewildered now. 'Oh, dear. I'm sorry, you must think I'm crazy, but you look so much like . . . like someone I know,' she finished lamely.

'My long-lost twin, perhaps?' He tried to smile reassuringly, but the words echoed round his brain in a very disturbing way.

He saw her shiver and thought he heard her murmur, 'Goodness, but he's even more attractive in real life. *No!* What am I thinking . . .?'

He had no idea, but he knew he needed to put some distance between them. Fast. 'Are you all right now?' he asked. 'I must get back to work.'

'Yes, yes of course. Th-thank you for your help. I really don't know what came over me, it's never happened to me before.' She sat up, obviously still fighting the dizziness, and tried to compose herself. Several of the onlookers were still peeking at the little tableau from time to time, and Jake could see that she disliked being the centre of attention. Her cheeks flamed and she took a few deep breaths, as if in an effort to cool them. 'Thank you again. It was very kind of you to help me,' she said more firmly, leaning over slowly to pick up her shopping.

Jake bent down at the same time to retrieve his own mangled bag, and as he did so, his hand brushed against hers. Her eyes widened in surprise and she drew in a sharp breath, as did he. A strange sensation had shot through his fingers, and he knew she'd felt it, too. He tried not to give any sign of

128

having been affected by the contact, however, merely straightened up and gave her a polite nod.

'You're welcome. It's not every day I have women fainting at the sight of me,' he joked. He smiled again, and cast a challenging look towards the old biddies by the counter, daring the one who had spoken earlier to repeat her comments. No one moved.

With a quick, 'Goodbye,' and a wave of his hand, he left.

One block away, however, he had to stop and lean against a wall as a wave of dizziness washed over him. The soft susurration of the woman's voice echoed round his brain and he shook his head to clear it. He felt bewitched, as if someone had cast a spell on him, but such things didn't happen in real life.

'I need to get out more,' he muttered. He'd had his wish at last. A woman had affected him, and if she could do it, so could others. He just had to leave his comfort zone a bit more often.

Perhaps he should try going on some dates? He could start by offering to take the lovely red-head to dinner to make sure she'd recovered from her faint.

But damn, I didn't even ask her name!

CHAPTER 10

Melissa drew in another deep breath and tried to compose herself. Seeing Roger's *doppelgänger* like that had shaken her badly, but she told herself it was just a fluke. Or maybe she had remembered wrongly and it was just the fact the vet had blond hair and blue eyes. He had certainly been attractive. She reflected wryly that he probably did have ladies swooning over him, but perhaps not quite so literally. She smiled to herself.

When he disappeared, however, she suddenly felt bereft, as if something very precious had been taken away from her.

I guess I really am going crazy, she thought, and struggled to her feet. *Or maybe I need to rest more.* Yes, that was probably it. The flu had made her over-tired.

But as she made her way home, she couldn't stop thinking about the man she'd just met. His features were etched into her brain alongside those of Roger and a little voice kept telling her the vet had been right. *They could have been twins.*

★　★　★

The delicious aroma of homemade vegetable soup permeated the kitchen when Melissa came marching in upon her return from the shopping expedition, but she didn't notice. Instead, she dumped her bags on the kitchen table with a thump, and vented her barely suppressed frustration on her great-aunt.

'Dorothy, there's something weird going on around here. Now, I know we haven't known each other for very long, but as your only relative, I think I'm entitled to the truth. I have a feeling there are things you're not telling me and it's driving me nuts.'

The old lady swivelled round to look at her great-niece in surprise. 'The truth about what?'

'This house. Us. The strange things that keep happening. I don't know, but . . . You can't have lived here all your life and not have noticed anything? Please, I would really appreciate some answers now.'

Dorothy turned back to the cheese board she was preparing and began to unwrap a piece of Stilton slowly, as if stalling for time. 'What makes you think there's something strange going on, dear?'

'I told you, I hear things in my bedroom and I saw a ghostly face in the living room. I also have weird dreams all the time, well, one particular dream actually.' Melissa held up a hand to forestall any protests as Dorothy turned round again. 'And don't say I was hallucinating about that face, because I wasn't. I saw him quite clearly and I assure you I was wide awake and I only had a cold, no fever, nothing. Besides, Russ also saw him. He growled and his hackles were up.'

'Oh, yes?' Dorothy raised an eyebrow in enquiry.

'Yes, and not only that, but I've just seen him in the High Street, too.'

'What?' This time Dorothy looked puzzled. 'Surely not?'

'Not the ghost, but a man who looked exactly like him. In fact, I was so shocked by the likeness that I fainted at the sight of him in the baker's shop,' Melissa admitted, her cheeks turning hot just thinking about it.

Dorothy burst out laughing and Melissa felt some of the aggression drain out of her. Her great-aunt's laughter was infectious and she thought to herself that perhaps she was taking this a bit too seriously. There had to be a logical explanation for these strange occurrences and maybe she was over-reacting.

'That must have amused the clientele no end, dear,' Dorothy said. 'You'll be the talk of the town. No doubt I'll hear all about it when I play bridge next week.' She grew serious again. 'Are you sure it was the same man? Did he say who he was?'

'I swear, he was the spitting image of the plaguey ghost, although he said his name was Jake, not Roger. Jake Precy.'

Dorothy's eyes widened. 'How on earth do you know the ghost's name?'

'He told me. It's Roger. He said he wants me to help him, but I don't know with what. I thought perhaps you could tell me.' Melissa sat down at the table and scowled. As she looked out of the window, her mind filled with images of the two men again. So alike and yet, not quite. The vet's face had lacked the long scar, for one thing.

'Er, what exactly did he look like, this ghost?' Dorothy put the cheese board on the table and took a baguette out of the warming oven of the Aga. She cut it into two-inch pieces with great precision and put them in a bread basket.

'He was tall and blond.' Melissa's face grew warm once more. 'And extremely handsome. Just like that damned Mr Precy.'

Dorothy bustled around setting the table. 'So Mr Precy looks like the ghost you saw? Are you sure?'

'Of course I'm sure! You don't think I normally go around fainting at the sight of a good-looking man, do you? I know I'm single again, but I'm not that desperate. It was most embarrassing, I can tell you.'

Dorothy chuckled. 'Yes, I can imagine. What did Mr Precy think of it all?'

'Oh, he was very kind and gentlemanly. He put me on some chairs to recover and tried to joke about the whole thing. But I could see he was uncomfortable, especially when I called him Roger.' Melissa sent Dorothy a pleading look. 'Please, if you can shed any light on this at all, I'd be really grateful. I'm starting to think I'm going mad.'

Dorothy sighed. 'Well, the truth is that others have seen the ghost, too. I just didn't want to upset you any more the day you asked, so I thought it better not to tell you. I was afraid you would leave before you had a chance to settle in and I so wanted you to stay. It would be so lonely here without you.'

'I see. So the house is definitely haunted?'

'Yes, but not everyone notices. I've never seen anything myself and I've lived here all my life.'

'How strange. You haven't noticed anything at all?'

'No, although as I said, I'd love to. I can't believe your ghost talked to you, that is most unfair. After all the years I've been here. That's gratitude for you.'

'Hah, I'd much rather he didn't, thank you very much. You're welcome to him.' Melissa tossed her hair out of her eyes. 'Actually, I was going to ask you if there are any old papers or anything about the house that you could show me. I want to research its history, see if anyone called Roger lived here. I have to get to the bottom of this, see if there are any facts or documents to back this up.' She had thought of nothing else all the way home from town. She wasn't a genealogist for nothing and this was a challenge she simply couldn't refuse.

Dorothy shook her head. 'No, I've never seen

any papers. But you're not going mad, dear. I told you, you're not the only one to have seen ghosts at Ashleigh.' She hesitated, as if she didn't quite know where to begin, then pulled out a chair and sat down opposite Melissa. She took a deep breath and plaited her fingers together on the table in front of her.

'You're right. Perhaps it's time for the truth.'

Sibell stifled a sigh and tried to ignore the discomfort of sitting ramrod straight next to her father during the evening meal. He had a proper chair with an ornately carved back and armrests, while she had to make do with a bench. She wished herself a hundred miles away. Or at least as far as Idenhurst. She wondered idly if Sir Roger was still there and, if so, what he would be doing at this hour. Was he, like her, sitting at table or had he retired for the night? Her face grew warm at the direction her thoughts were taking.

'I must stop thinking about him,' she chided herself, but she'd found it almost impossible during the last few days. Images of him came unbidden into her mind far too frequently for comfort and she wanted nothing so much as to escape to her chamber to daydream.

Normally she would have done so as soon as she had finished eating, but tonight she had to remain, since her father had guests. Some distant cousins whom he wished to impress with his worldly goods and standing. Hence the interminable meal. Sibell restrained the urge to rip off her headdress, which was making her head ache like the very devil. Out of sheer boredom, she began to pay attention to a conversation across the table. It was all about politics, a subject that wasn't normally of any interest to her, but it helped pass the time.

'There are rumours that the Earl of March is assembling a fighting force and plans to return to England soon to meet up with his father, the Duke of York, who is coming back from Ireland.' The speaker, a sparse man in his late forties named Robert, was her father's cousin on his mother's side. He had a nose as sharp as a razor blade and riddled with red veins, and he was telling his tale with relish. Sibell could see his eyes glowing with excitement.

'Oh, aye?' Another cousin, Ambrose by name, who was slightly older with a huge paunch, was clearly not impressed. He continued with his meal unperturbed. The excellent fare provided at Ashleigh appeared to interest him far more than the intrigues of his superiors.

Sibell had heard talk about the Duke's return for months now. No one seemed to know for certain whether there was any truth in this or merely wishful thinking on the part of his supporters.

'Yes, and the Queen isn't best pleased, apparently. She must have thought the threat from York was over after the King's victories last year, but there are many who think she wields too much power. They'd support York, should he return.'

It was rumoured that Margaret of Anjou, Queen of England, was an ambitious and unforgiving woman who had no intention of relinquishing her position. Apparently, she dominated her husband and the court completely, causing controversy among the lords who felt they could no longer give the King their whole loyalty. Sibell knew the Queen had given birth to a son seven years previously. This excluded York from the succession, but it would appear it wasn't enough to stop an ambitious man such as he. Could he really take the throne, though? It didn't seem very likely, but it was true there was a lot of opposition to a system of government dominated by the Queen.

Whatever Ambrose's private views on women in politics, his only reply to the sharp-nosed Robert's gossip was a grunt. The latter man continued undaunted, pleased to have an audience in John and his sons, at least.

'Yes, indeed. Lord March is said to be ready to rally to his father's cause.' The scepticism on the face of his listeners was obviously not to the man's liking. He drew himself up to his full height and tried to look important, despite the shabbiness of his clothing, which proclaimed his lowly status.

'And who will support him?' A third cousin was equally unimpressed.

'Why, he has the Earls of Warwick and Salisbury with him in exile and at least two Neville lords as well, it's said. There are many who are ready to join them when they land on these shores.' Robert was growing agitated now, his cheeks turning as red as his nose.

'I take it you're one of them?' The paunchy Ambrose had obviously tired of such treasonous gossip, which could easily be overheard and the words misconstrued.

'M-me?' Red-faced, Robert began to splutter indignantly as he belatedly realised his peril. 'I was only repeating what I've heard, cousin.' He sniffed. 'It's nothing to me what the Earl of March chooses to do. I am a loyal subject of his majesty the King.' Ambrose raised one eyebrow in disbelief and the gossipmonger obviously deemed it wise to retreat. Muttering something about needing the privy, he headed for the door.

Sibell saw her father watch the man scurry away, a pensive look on his face. She could tell he was digesting the overheard information to see whether it could be used to his advantage. He'd never been averse to finding ways of bettering his position, as she well knew. But he was canny enough not to rush into anything without being absolutely sure it would be to his benefit. Would the situation have any bearing on her own plight, she wondered? Perhaps if she prayed hard enough, Sir Fulke would join the fray and get himself killed in battle before the wedding. *Oh, if only . . .*

The woman on the horse was a red-head too!
This random thought popped into Jake's brain without warning later that day, causing him to

bump into the examination table as he led an elderly woman into the veterinary surgery. The strange dream he'd had came rushing back to him again. Taking a deep breath, he turned to the lady and asked politely what he could do for her, putting everything else out of his mind for the moment.

She didn't answer immediately, but placed a shoe box on the table and opened the lid. Inside, nestled on top of a pink tea towel, was a tiny hedgehog.

'I found him in the middle of my lawn this morning, Mr Precy. He wasn't moving and I thought the little mite was just cold, so I brought him indoors. He wouldn't touch a drop of milk, though, just lies there looking sorry for himself. You'd better have a look at him.'

With infinite care Jake felt for broken bones before lifting the little creature out of the box. He put it on the table and listened to its breathing. He had a shrewd idea what ailed the hedgehog, but examined him thoroughly before making a diagnosis.

'You did right to bring him, Mrs Wycliff. I think the little fellow has pneumonia. Can you hear his laboured breathing?' In the silence of the surgery, the wheezing noise coming from the tiny animal's throat could be clearly heard.

'Oh, yes, poor little thing!' The old lady tilted her head to one side to look at it.

'Not to worry, I'll keep him here for a while and put him on antibiotics. That should do the trick.

139

When he's feeling better I'll give you a call and you can keep him in your greenhouse for the rest of the winter, if you don't mind. That way he should survive.'

'Thank you, Mr Precy, that's very kind.'

'Not at all. You'll probably have to feed him, though. I don't think he's strong enough to hibernate this year. Just some dog food and milk once a day. Can you do that?'

'Of course. I'll see to it, don't you worry.'

He walked her to the door. 'Goodbye then, Mrs Wycliff. Thank you for coming.'

'Goodbye. I'll look forward to hearing from you.'

As he gently lifted the hedgehog to give him an injection of antibiotics, Jake's mind returned to the subject of the woman in his dreams. It was that other woman's fault, the one who'd fainted into his arms outside the baker's shop earlier on, he was sure. Meeting her had triggered something inside him, although for the life of him he didn't know what it could be.

Yes, he'd been attracted to her. He'd have had to be made of stone not to, in all honesty, but that wasn't all. No, something about her had struck a chord deep inside him. But why?

'You're cracking up, Jake,' he muttered to himself.

She was just a woman, and he'd been without one for too long. Holding her so close, his body had reacted predictably. End of story.

On auto-pilot, he settled the hedgehog into a cage and made sure there was fresh water and food within easy reach. He filled out a sheet of care instructions for his assistant and hung it on the cage door, while his brain returned to the subject of the red-headed female. Well, not red exactly, he corrected himself. A deep, rich auburn, like a fresh chestnut, just out of its shell. The kind of colour that would look wonderful in candle light . . .

Jake shook his head. *What the hell is the matter with me?*

The little hedgehog continued his wheezing and regarded him sadly out of huge brown eyes. Jake stared back. 'Yeah, little fellow,' he whispered, 'life is strange, eh?' But some things were stranger than others.

Perhaps it was time he found out more about Ashleigh Cottage. He was beginning to believe it might be haunted. *Or at the very least, a witch had lived there and she'd cast a spell on him . . .* He smiled at the thought. *Ridiculous!*

Another sneeze from the hedgehog made him snap out of this idiotic thinking. Still, it wouldn't do any harm to ask someone about the cottage's history, would it?

CHAPTER 11

'There's a story which has been passed down through our family,' Dorothy began. 'Long ago a daughter of the house fell in love with someone unsuitable. Her name was Sybil, I believe, and she was supposedly the daughter or grand-daughter of the man who had Ashleigh built, so this must have been some time in the fifteenth century.'

Melissa felt as if a warning bell sounded inside her head; the name seemed very familiar. She had to force herself to concentrate on Dorothy's next words.

'Unfortunately,' her aunt continued, 'Sybil's father had already decided that she was to marry someone else, so she wasn't allowed to marry her beloved. I don't know his name, but perhaps he was the Roger you mentioned? The lady was, of course, deeply unhappy with this and refused the man her father had chosen for her. She was crazed with grief and it's said that she turned to a witch for help in exacting revenge. The witch cast a spell on the family so that all Sybil's brothers died before their father, and Ashleigh manor came to her on her father's death as she was the only child left.'

Dorothy paused for a moment, then went on, 'I think the young man had been her lover because she bore a child, a daughter. The house has been passed from mother to daughter ever since. And it has been reputed to be haunted for centuries.' Dorothy looked at Melissa with an apologetic shrug. 'It's probably all rubbish, but it made a great tale to tell the children round the fire in the evenings.'

'Hmm. I've learned to take most family stories with a pinch of salt. I hear an awful lot of them from my clients. This one does sound a bit more credible though – apart from the bit about the witch, that's just silly – and it could be the explanation. But why didn't Sybil marry her lover after the rest of her family died? She could have done whatever she wanted then. And why is he haunting this place and not her? Surely it should be the other way around?'

Dorothy shrugged once more. 'I don't know. Perhaps he was already dead? There is no mention of his name in the story and those were uncertain times. There is more though.'

'What?'

'This ghost that you have seen appears to all the red-haired women of this house. So you see, you're not the first one he has haunted. Please, do try not to become too affected by it all.'

'Oh. I wondered why he picked me. You've lived

here for so much longer than I have, I thought surely he should have shown himself to you too.'

Her great-aunt looked sad. 'No, I was blonde.' She paused. 'But my sister saw him.'

Melissa gasped. 'You mean Grandma Ruth?'

'Yes.' Dorothy grew silent and Melissa waited for her to explain, but her aunt hesitated. Finally she sighed again. 'I see that I shall have to tell you everything. I was going to wait until you'd been here a bit longer, but I suppose you might as well know now.'

'Know what?' Melissa was about to expire with curiosity. She was finally going to learn the reason for the estrangement between the sisters and now Dorothy was stalling. She couldn't bear it. 'Go on, please,' she urged impatiently.

'Very well. As I said, Ashleigh Manor has been in our family for centuries and it has always been passed down from mother to daughter and never, as far as I know, to a son. Now your grandmother, my sister Ruth, was the eldest and as such the house should have been hers, but my mother decided to give it to me instead. There was nothing to prevent her doing that.'

'The house isn't entailed in any way, then?'

'No.' Dorothy shook her head. 'There's nothing written down. The tradition has been carried on anyway, a sort of pact between mothers and daughters, if you will.' She paused to take a deep breath. Melissa was spellbound and waited silently for her to continue. 'Unfortunately Ruth and I were

144

forever quarrelling and when our mother left this house to me, well, that was the end really. My sister never spoke to me again.'

'But why would your mother exclude her like that? Didn't Grandma Ruth get anything?' Melissa was puzzled.

'A little bit of money, but most of it is tied up in the house and a lot is needed for the upkeep.'

'How very odd. As far as I can remember, Grandma was extremely staid. I can't imagine that she'd ever done anything of which a parent could disapprove that strongly.'

'That she was. I'm not sure what happened, dear, there was some argument. I tried to have the will revoked, but Mother had made absolutely certain it was all legal. And I couldn't sell the house either and give Ruth half the money. The will stipulated that if the house was ever sold in my lifetime the proceeds would go to charity. In other words, I'm only the custodian until it passes to the next generation. Since Ruth and your mother are no longer with us, and I have no daughters, this house will therefore be yours one day.'

'Mine?'

'Yes, dear.'

'Oh, no!' *So Steve was right after all.* That was annoying, although Melissa didn't see how it affected her economic situation in the short term. 'But . . . but are you sure you can't leave it to anyone else? You have only known me for a few weeks.' Melissa was genuinely confused.

'No, I could never do that. Ashleigh Manor belongs to our family and I intend it to stay that way. If you don't want it, I will make a will in favour of Jolie.'

Melissa stared at her aunt. 'I'm stunned, Dorothy. I don't know what to say. I mean, this is totally unexpected. I didn't even know the house existed until a couple of months ago.' She frowned and recalled the reason why the subject had come up in the first place. 'But what does all this have to do with Grandma seeing the ghost?'

'Ah, yes, I was coming to that. You see, I have a feeling the quarrel between my mother and her had something to do with Ruth's obsession with this ghost, but I'm not sure. I was much younger and not allowed to participate in any family discussions.'

'That's a shame. You're sure she saw the same ghost?'

'Oh, yes. You do know she had reddish hair, just like you? That must have been why she saw him. She told me about him once and she looked completely besotted. I heard her scream to mother that she never wanted to marry because she had found her one true love already.'

Melissa shivered involuntarily. *Besotted.* That was exactly how she had felt at the sight of Roger. Weak at the knees, butterflies in her stomach, erratic heartbeat. Completely and utterly in love. Another tremor, but of fear this time, passed down her spine.

'And yet, she did marry eventually and produced my mother, so she must have forgotten. Maybe the infatuation wears off?'

'Yes, I believe it does, with time and distance. But by then, we were already estranged so I can't know for sure.'

'Perhaps the ghost gives up, when he realises he's not going to get the help he's asking for. Assuming that's what he does with everyone and not just me.'

'Well, yes, and if he's still here, then no one has succeeded in helping him, I guess,' Dorothy added.

Melissa nodded slowly while thinking this over. 'Is there anything else you can tell me? I really want to get to the bottom of this.'

Dorothy smiled. 'No, nothing else, dear. I think that's quite enough for one day, don't you?'

'Oh, absolutely.' Melissa hesitated, then decided she had to enlist Dorothy's support. 'Umm, could I ask you a favour, please?'

'Of course, anything.'

'I'd be very grateful if you don't tell anyone that I'm going to inherit this house. You know, because of Steve.'

'Don't worry, I won't breathe a word. No one is allowed to see my will until I'm gone so he can't prove a thing. I'll lie like a trooper if anyone asks me. Don't you worry. He won't be able to wriggle out of paying maintenance for Jolie as is right and proper.' Dorothy had a steely glint in her eye and Melissa smiled at her having mixed up her metaphors, but she was grateful for the support.

'Thanks, I really appreciate it.' It was wonderful to feel that she wasn't alone any more. There was someone on her side. She stood up, full of determination now. 'Do you know if the local library is open this afternoon?'

'Why, yes, I believe it is.'

'Good. I might as well start my search there. Or at the very least, they can point me in the right direction.'

'A strange occurrence, wasn't it? Snow in March? I didn't look to see you for weeks, my dear, judging by the state of the roads.' Maude enveloped Sibell in a scented embrace and the latter relaxed, as always.

'Indeed, most unusual. All those lovely spring flowers completely covered. I do hope they survived. But how do you all fare?' Sibell hadn't been able to stand the stifling atmosphere at Ashleigh a moment longer, and had taken her mare onto the muddy road to Idenhurst, despite dire warnings from the groom.

'Very well, thank you.' Maude's eyes took on a mischievous glint. 'And your handsome young man was forced to remain as well. He told me he daren't risk an injury to his precious destrier.'

Sibell felt herself blush. Maude obviously hadn't given up her match-making, even though it was doomed to failure. 'Maude, he is not "my" young man. I told you . . .'

'. . . that he'd never look twice at a red-headed beanpole, yes, yes, I know.' Maude wagged a finger at her. 'But that's not what you look like. Why, your hair is a gorgeous shade of chestnut and there is nothing wrong with your figure at all. Some men like tall women and those freckles are simply charming. So, no more such talk, if you please.'

Sibell shook her head, but said nothing more on that subject as they simply wouldn't agree. 'Well, it must have been irksome for Sir Roger to remain so long,' she commented.

'On the contrary, he's kept himself very busy.'

'Really? Doing what?'

'Training his squire in fighting and swordplay. I've watched them occasionally and he drives the boy hard, but not unfairly, while practising diligently himself. Even some of Gilbert's men are taking note and have offered to let him train with them. I believe he's teaching them new skills this very moment and I wouldn't be surprised if—'

The door burst open and Maude was interrupted in mid-sentence. One of the newer maidservants almost tumbled head first through the door in her haste, a stricken expression on her face. 'Oh, my lady, come quickly! There's a fight going on and it looks likely to be serious. You must stop them!'

'Who?' Maude demanded, standing up and craning her neck to try and see out of the window. 'Who's fighting?'

'Why, it's Sir Roger and two of the Ashleigh brothers, my lady. Only, it's so unfair, them being two against one.'

Sibell and Maude looked at each other, then headed for the stairs and out into the courtyard at a half-run. They immediately spotted the throng of people who formed a ragged circle round the combatants, and hurried to join their ranks.

'What is happening here?' Maude demanded of the nearest man, elbowing him to gain his attention.

'That young knight has offered to teach the Ashleigh brothers a lesson,' the man replied with a smirk.

Sibell felt her insides go cold. She knew Simon and Edmund caused a lot of mischief and weren't well liked, but she didn't want to see them badly hurt. Nor Sir Roger, of course.

'I'll put a stop to this,' Maude said and tried to push forward, but the man, who happened to be Sir Gilbert's steward and therefore a man of some authority, held her back.

'No, my lady, don't. I think it best to leave them to it. Look over there, your husband isn't doing anything to intervene.' Sir Gilbert was indeed to be glimpsed on the opposite side of the circle and this stopped Maude.

'What on earth started this then?' she asked, clearly irritated.

'One of them called him a "whoreson". Couldn't stand for that, now could he?'

'Hmph, men,' Maude muttered, but she and Sibell were soon as caught up in watching the spectacle before them as everyone else.

'Dear Lord, don't let him be hurt,' Sibell prayed, before realising she ought to be asking God to help her brothers, not Sir Roger. They were family, after all. But she couldn't deny to herself that he was more important to her and if anything happened to him, she would be devastated.

As for her brothers, they deserved no prayers from her if they'd started this.

Roger didn't often get angry, but the Ashleigh brothers had been trying to rile him for days and he'd finally had enough. It was one thing if not everyone welcomed his advice on swordplay; outright insults altogether another.

'I don't know who he thinks he is, coming in here and lording it over the rest of us like a cock on a dung-heap,' stocky, red-haired Simon had been heard to complain loudly to his brother that morning after practice.

'Yes, a whoreson, that's what he is!' Edmund, equally stocky, but with a blond tint to his red thatch of hair, spat on the ground for emphasis and grinned maliciously.

It wasn't unusual to be born on the wrong side of the blanket, and no one had ever held it against him before, but to infer that his mother was a whore was more than Roger could stomach. He couldn't possibly let anyone slight her like that, especially two such cocky youths whose own mother didn't seem to have instilled any manners into them. His jaw had tightened and he had decided to deal with them once and for all.

'Perhaps you'd care to teach me a lesson?' he'd suggested, 'after you introduce yourselves, as the gentlemen you undoubtedly are.' He knew their names already, of course, but they'd never spoken to him directly.

The two young men glared at him, hearing the sarcasm and underlying menace in his voice, then smiled at each other. They were clearly spoiling for a fight and confident of victory.

'With pleasure,' the red-haired one sneered. 'I am Simon of Ashleigh and this is my brother Edmund. At your service.' He gave an exaggerated bow, copied by his brother, who was snickering under his breath.

Even though he knew it was the truth, Roger still found it hard to believe these two were related to Mistress Sibell. No siblings could have been more unalike, in temperament at least. No wonder she looked so despondent. With half-brothers like these uncouth creatures, her life must be hell. And if the father was the same . . . he shuddered to think what the poor girl was going through. He hadn't missed the fact that she'd flinched when her back was touched. If it had been a mere accident, she would have mentioned it to Lady Maude, but her silence told him the truth. Besides, her fear during their ride had been almost tangible, and some of the anger at her treatment returned when he saw the swaggering looks of the two men in front of him. He determined to pay them back for her suffering.

'Unsheath your swords,' he snarled, pulling his own gleaming weapon out of its plain scabbard.

CHAPTER 12

The lady at the library who staffed the desk in the corner marked 'Local Studies' looked a bit dubious when Melissa asked her about Ashleigh, but pointed to a shelf of musty tomes. 'There might be something over there. I know one of them is an old history of the parish and there are a couple of books that mention prominent local families.'

'Thanks, I'll have a browse, then.'

Melissa settled down at a desk with a pile of books and soon learned a lot about the village and its past. But, although the manor house itself was mentioned several times, she could only find one reference to one of the owners – a Dionise of Ashleigh who had married in the sixteenth century. Melissa sighed.

'That's too late, then.'

She turned her attention to the books that dealt with the history of the area in more general terms. She had always found it useful to link important events with the lives of the people she researched, as it was good to see how they fit into the wider context. Obviously things like the Civil War and other periods of unrest would influence their lives and Melissa knew the choices they made at such times could have devastating effects on their futures.

The period when Ashleigh was built wasn't one she'd studied lately, so she decided to mug up on that first to remind herself of the basics. She soon found plenty of interesting information. Skimming through the sections on the fifteenth century, she jotted down that King Henry VI ruled for a large part of the century, from 1422 to 1461, although Richard, Duke of York, was several times appointed Protector when the feeble-minded King temporarily went mad. York secretly coveted the throne and it seemed he had the common people on his side, especially in London and Kent. 'Aha!' Melissa muttered. 'I remember now.'

In one book, she found a couple of intriguing sentences.

> The Duke of York raised a rebel army and fought against the King's forces, but was routed in October of 1459. He fled to Ireland, while his son the Earl of March went to Calais with other allies, and there followed severe persecution of Yorkist supporters. As the Duke was especially popular in Kent, the numbers of men in hiding were larger there than anywhere else. Many of them turned vicious out of sheer desperation . . . .

Could Sybil's lover have been one of the outlaws? Melissa wondered. Was that why she wasn't allowed to marry him? If her father had been for the King, then of course a Yorkist supporter would have been out of the question as husband material.

'Well, it's a start,' she told herself as she gathered up her belongings. There didn't seem to be anything else of interest here, so she decided to go to the nearest record office as soon as she had the time.

On her way out, she stopped by the helpful lady's desk once more as a thought struck her. 'Excuse me, but do you know if there is a local historian in the town? Someone who specialises in this area?'

'Yes, indeed. One moment and I'll find his number for you.'

Armed with the address and phone number of this individual, Melissa went home feeling as if she had made some progress at least.

The fight between Roger and the Ashleigh brothers quickly became the centre of attention of all the menfolk of Idenhurst, as well as a good number of the women. To begin with there was encouragement for both sides, but as the bout continued, the crowd became vociferous in Roger's favour. The Ashleigh brothers had been training with Sir Gilbert's men for over a year, but hadn't made themselves very popular. There were plenty of people who would welcome someone who could teach them a lesson. As Roger fought first one, then the other of the pair, there were cheers when he rebuffed them at every turn.

Finally, in pure rage, the two attacked him at once, causing mutterings of outrage among the older members of the household. However, Roger had been defending himself since boyhood, and didn't lose his head. A sharp slash across his forearm halted him momentarily, and the sight of blood drew gasps from some of the women present, but he didn't let it distract him. Instead it spurred him on to a flurry of thrusts with his flashing blade and very soon the Ashleigh brothers were soundly beaten. As first Edmund, then Simon was disarmed, their swords knocked clean out of their hands, the yard erupted in clapping and cheering.

'Bravo, Sir Roger. That was as fine a display as I have ever seen, I think.' The deep voice of Sir Gilbert rang out above the din as he made his way through the crowd.

Roger looked up and saw admiration plainly written on the man's face. This turned to a grimace of disgust as he briefly turned to the Ashleigh brothers and ordered them to go and get cleaned up. Roger knew they weren't badly hurt, but mostly winded, with a few superficial cuts and bruises. So it proved when, without a word, Simon pulled Edmund to his feet before dusting himself off. The two of them stalked away, pushing their way through the crowd. Despite having bested them today, Roger was sure this wasn't the last he'd hear from them.

'Might I have a word with you in private, please?' Sir Gilbert continued.

Roger nodded, feeling slightly dazed, and followed his host into the hall.

'Please, have a seat. You there, some wine if you please,' Sir Gilbert added to a passing servant before sitting down himself. He came straight to the point. 'Sir Roger, I've been watching you for a few days and it seems to me you are exceptionally good at what you do. I therefore have a proposition for you. Would you care to stay for a while and train my men? My sergeant was taken ill before Christmas, and since then there has been a lack of discipline among them. Perhaps you can rectify that? I will, of course, pay you whatever you deem suitable.'

'Well, I don't know.' Roger hesitated, battling with a handkerchief to try to staunch the flow of blood on his arm. 'Actually, I'm half-expected at the castle of Lord Lydbury come May. He offered me employment, should I want it.'

'I will pay you double whatever he said he'd pay you. I really am in need of your services, and I don't doubt he can do without you for a while. He and I are friends, so if I write to him and explain the situation, I'm sure he won't mind.'

Roger's eyebrows rose a fraction. 'Double? Very well, I can't turn down so generous an offer.' He smiled and held out his hand. 'You have a bargain, Sir Gilbert.' They shook hands on it.

'Oh, and one more thing. Please keep an eye on

those two hotheads from Ashleigh. They have two older brothers and are apt to go raising hell at every opportunity. They've been sadly indulged by their father, I fear.'

They grinned at each other in mutual understanding before Sir Gilbert beckoned to his daughter, who was passing by on her way to the kitchens.

'Katherine, come and make yourself useful girl. See to Sir Roger's wounds, will you?'

'Of course, Father, it will be my pleasure. If you'll come with me to the stillroom, sir?' Tall and gangly, the girl nevertheless held herself with an assurance unusual in one so young. Roger had been told she was fourteen, and he admired her poise. She turned on her heel, sending a blonde braid as thick as his wrist flying out behind her, and with a smile he followed her out of the hall.

Outside in the courtyard, they ran into Lady Maude and Mistress Sibell. When told where they were heading, Maude said, 'I'd better check that she does it properly. We'll come with you.'

'Mother,' Katherine protested. 'I'm perfectly capable of dealing with a wound. You've taught me yourself.'

'Yes, but you're always in such a hurry. I want to watch, that's all.'

Roger didn't mind having an audience, especially not one which contained Mistress Sibell. He made the most of it, engaging young Katherine in teasing banter, but glancing at the older girl every now and then. Katherine answered him in kind, not at all self-conscious or shy. Soon the pair of them were talking and joking as if they'd known each other for years.

'Are you sure you know what you're doing?' he teased when he'd made her laugh so much she dropped a bandage. 'No man will want such a clumsy wife, although I suppose your beautiful hair might make up for any deficiencies.' He flicked her braid with his free hand and grinned at her. 'I swear, it's like a sunbeam trapped on earth. Did some goddess descend to bestow this gift on you or was there magic involved?'

Katherine shook her head at him and retorted, 'For shame, Sir Roger, I've never heard such rubbish. Sunbeam, indeed. Why, your own hair is the same colour. That goddess must have been awfully busy, in that case.'

They both laughed, but Roger heard Lady Maude draw in a hissing breath, as if she'd been shocked. When he looked up at her, he caught a strange expression on her face, which was quickly masked. To ease the sudden tension, Roger turned his charm on the older woman instead. He hoped she wasn't offended, he'd meant no harm. 'No need to worry, my lady. Joking aside, I have seldom been tended with more care,' he assured her.

'Naturally, Sir Roger,' she replied with a slightly forced smile. 'Katherine has been well taught. I'm pleased she has been of assistance to you.'

'Oh, indeed she has. She'll make some lucky man an excellent wife.'

'That she will,' Lady Maude agreed, with an edge of steel to her voice as if to say, 'but not you, young man; most definitely not you.'

Although it made him angry that she didn't find him good enough for her daughter, Roger was nevertheless in complete agreement with her since he wasn't interested in marrying the girl. To clearly demonstrate this he added, 'A shame that I'm promised elsewhere, indeed a great shame.'

He saw Maude relax slightly, but she remained in the stillroom until he took his leave, thanking Katherine for her services. He winked surreptitiously at Sibell before he left, but there was no answering smile on her face. Instead, she looked as if she'd just received a blow and he cursed his tongue for running away with him.

This was not the time to tell her the true meaning of his words, however. He'd only just realised it himself.

Melissa was determined to find out more about Ashleigh Manor and its history, but with solicitor's fees to pay, her job had to come first. For the next week she was so busy she didn't have any time to herself. Even thoughts of the ghostly face faded into the background, until on the Friday evening when she sank into the soft armchair in the sitting room once more. She glanced nervously towards the opposite wall, and was relieved to find it blank.

Shaking her head, she began to sort through her notes, trying to concentrate on making sense of a family tree she was putting together for a new client by the name of Tylson. Jolie was upstairs doing homework, but Dorothy sat next to Melissa watching television and she felt reassured by her aunt's presence.

The little table in front of her proved woefully inadequate, and soon she had spread her papers all over the carpet as well. She had a list of entries from various church registers relating to the Tylsons, several copies of wills and a few marriage certificates obtained from the Registrar General, as well as details of census records for the family at different times. Her job now was to put this information into some semblance of order which wasn't unlike doing a giant jigsaw puzzle. Melissa began with the most recent information and worked her way backwards, stopping every now and then to check she hadn't missed anything. It required deep concentration.

Eventually Dorothy stood up and said, 'I think I'll go to bed now, if you don't mind, dear? It's getting late. I'll check on Jolie, shall I?'

'Mm-hmm, please. Goodnight,' Melissa replied rather absently. She wasn't really paying attention. She frequently lost herself in her work. Pedigrees of all kinds were a constant source of fascination, and once she had begun she became completely absorbed in the enjoyment of creating a family tree.

The next time she glanced at her watch it was five to midnight. 'Good grief, how did it get so late already?' She yawned and bent to gather up her papers. *Organised chaos.* She chuckled to herself. Although it usually worked this way, she really must devise a better system for her notes, she thought.

Halfway through her task she caught a slight movement out of the corner of her eye. With a frown she straightened up and glanced towards the inglenook. A little shriek escaped her and all the papers slithered to the floor with a whoosh.

'Roger!' She gripped the armchair for support and sank into it, shock making her heart settle halfway to her throat, thudding painfully.

This time he was standing by the fireplace, leaning on it nonchalantly with one arm draped over the mantelpiece. She could see all of him, not just his face. His long hair shimmered in the light from the dying fire and his blue eyes were sparkling. He smiled at her.

He was so close, only a few feet away, and the impact on her senses was devastating. As she detected his distinctive scent and recognised it from her dreams, she could hear the blood roaring in her ears. His smile widened, and her insides turned slowly to jelly. What was it about this man that made her feel like this? Inebriated, like the heady fizz of champagne thrumming through her veins. Or like a schoolgirl infatuated with a pop star, wanting to scream at the mere sight of him.

No, not man, she corrected herself. *Ghost! I can see the television through him, for goodness' sake.*

He looked so real, though. His tall, muscular body was dressed in some kind of dark tunic and his legs were encased in tight-fitting hose, which showed off powerful thighs. He was wearing short leather boots and at his waist hung a gleaming, lethal sword. The man was confidence personified, and she almost expected him to sling her over his shoulder and carry her off to bed. She wouldn't have lifted a finger to resist him.

The realisation hit her with sickening clarity that she was sitting there grinning like a love-sick adolescent at a ghost, but she couldn't help it. She had absolutely no control over her emotions concerning this man, and she simply stared at him, waiting. For what, she didn't know.

'Sweeting, you must help me, please.' His voice broke the spell. As before, it seemed to come from far away at first, but when he repeated the words she heard them clearly. The terrible sensation of loss assailed her again, and she felt the tears begin to roll down her cheeks.

'How?' she managed to whisper. 'How, Roger?'

He said nothing for a moment, but his gaze grew pensive. *'The ring will help you. Search, sweeting . . .'*

The apparition faded slowly, but Melissa stayed motionless in the chair for a long while afterwards. Indeed, her limbs felt as if they were made of the heaviest granite, and the unbearable sadness filled her mind to overflowing. A shuddering sigh went through her and she tried to gather her wits.

Am I going crazy? Her fingernails dug into the palms of her hands as she clenched them in frustration. No, as far as she could make out she was entirely sane. The first time she had been ill, and could possibly have been hallucinating, but tonight she was healthy and completely awake. Therefore she could only conclude that ghosts really did exist. She just couldn't doubt her own eyes.

There had to be a logical explanation for his presence in this house, however. Who was Roger? Was he indeed Sybil's long-lost lover, the father of her child? Was he a Yorkist outlaw? And how was he connected to Ashleigh? Melissa was entirely convinced now that somehow, somewhere he had existed. Tossing her long hair over her shoulder impatiently, she stood up, raising her chin in determination.

'Well I'm damned well going to find out,' she vowed. She would start on Monday, and never mind Mr Tylson's family tree. He could wait.

CHAPTER 13

'Sir Gilbert. Good of you to see me.'

John of Ashleigh strode down the hall towards the dais, where his host awaited him, stony-faced. Sibell trailed a few steps behind. Her father had allowed her to accompany him to Idenhurst, but she'd been told to keep quiet and stay out of the way. 'And we're not staying long,' her father had added.

Her father attempted an ingratiating smile, obviously trying his best to be jovial, but his attempts fell flat. His discomfort in the other man's presence was making him squirm visibly and Sibell bit her lip. Although Sir Gilbert was normally a cordial host, there was an underlying coldness in his manner this day which appeared to be penetrating even John's thick skin. Sibell wished herself anywhere but here.

'Please, be seated,' Sir Gilbert said, but Sibell noticed that they were not offered any refreshment. He turned to Sibell. 'Why don't you run up to the solar, my dear? I'm certain Maude would appreciate your company.'

Sibell glanced to her father for permission and

he nodded reluctantly. He looked as if he had chewed on something sour, but his face soon became wreathed in smiles once more when Sir Gilbert called for wine at last. Sibell made her escape.

The solar was empty and Sibell sent a serving maid to look for Maude. While she waited, she became absorbed in a beautifully bound book called *Troilus & Creseyd* by Geoffrey Chaucer, which was lying on the table. It was the story of a perfect, gentle knight and Sibell seized on it with alacrity, although she treated it with great care, since she knew it was very valuable. She loved Chaucer's stories, and anything that offered escape from reality, if only for a while, was a welcome distraction. Reading was one of her favourite pastimes, and one she'd learned here at Idenhurst. Unfortunately, she seldom had the opportunity to indulge in it, since her father considered books a waste of money.

'Mistress Sibell, we meet again.'

Sibell looked up, eyes widening. 'Sir Roger!' She leapt up from the bench. He had managed to startle her yet again. The man moved as gracefully as a fox and just as quietly. Sibell felt herself blush furiously as she recalled that his was the face she had pictured while reading about the perfect Troilus. Perhaps her thoughts had conjured him out of thin air. She frowned slightly and wondered what he was doing there. 'Should . . . should you be up here?' That sounded rude, so she attempted a feeble joke. 'This room is normally full of women and only the bravest of men walk into this lion's den.'

'You don't think me courageous enough? Once again you wound me, mistress.' The broad grin on his face belied his words, even as he dramatically put a hand over his heart. 'To be honest, I wouldn't have ventured here if the Lady Maude hadn't told me to come and keep you company,' he admitted. 'She's been detained for longer than she thought and didn't want you to become bored.'

Sibell's mouth fell open in astonishment. 'Keep me company?' she managed faintly. Had her former mother-in-law lost her mind? There was no one in sight to chaperone her, and although she was officially a widow, at eighteen she was still considered in need of protection. She surveyed the room surreptitiously, but they were indeed completely alone. As Sir Roger moved closer, she backed away slightly, ready to flee if the need should arise. Quite what she feared, she wasn't sure, but she knew it would be wrong to let him stay.

Roger seemed to sense that his presence was unnerving her and he walked over to study the view outside the window for a while. This gave her time to become used to his nearness, but when he returned his gaze to her, she still felt her heart increase its rhythm.

'What brings you here this fine day?' he enquired politely.

'My father had business with Sir Gilbert. Something about a bridge between their properties which has been damaged by the recent weather.'

'I see. Well, come and tell me how you have been faring,' he urged, settling himself at her feet on a large cushion. She cast him a wary look – he was still far too close for comfort – but he patted the bench she stood by and she reluctantly sank down on it.

'I . . . I am well, thank you.' She swallowed hard and picked up the book she had been reading to hold as a shield in front of herself.

He leaned forward and caught her gaze. 'Truly?'

'Well, yes, why shouldn't I be?'

'No more beatings then?'

She gasped and dropped the precious volume, then turned her head away. 'No,' she whispered.

He retrieved the book and put it gently on a nearby table. 'I just wanted to make certain. During our ride together, I couldn't help but notice that you were in pain.'

Sibell raised her chin a notch. 'That was due to a misunderstanding between my father and myself. He has arranged a marriage for me, which I was reluctant to consider at first.' Her lips tightened. 'I know it's my duty to obey him, but when he told me he expected me to marry Sir Fulke, I own I was a bit taken aback.'

'Not Sir Fulke of Thornby?' At her nod, his brows came together in a heavy scowl. 'Why, that's barbaric. The man must be, what? Three score?'

'Perhaps not quite as old as that . . .'

'Almost then. I don't wonder at it you were unwilling.'

'It's a brilliant match according to my father.' Sibell's voice wasn't entirely steady and had lost its defiance. She blinked away unshed tears.

'No, it's impossible. Can't Sir Gilbert help you? I mean, he was your father-in-law until recently. And surely you've told the Lady Maude you are being coerced?'

'Yes, of course I have and she's doing her best, but we are no longer related, so there is little either of them can do, at least officially.' Sibell paused and looked around, making sure they were truly alone. 'Can you keep a secret?' she whispered. She didn't know why she trusted him, but for some unknown reason she did.

'Upon my honour, your secrets are safe with me.'

'Lady Maude is trying to think of a way to rescue me. If all else fails, she will take me to stay for a while with her sister who lives in the north. Without informing father, of course,' she murmured into his ear, then realised just how close he was. Her breathing quickened.

He opened his mouth to reply, but stopped and gazed at her instead. An arrested expression entered his eyes, then he sighed and shook his head as if capitulating. Sibell felt as though she was drowning in a sea of emotion and didn't understand what was happening. Roger brought

170

up a hand to caress her cheek, a slight frown still creasing his brow.

'I think perhaps there may be another way,' he told her softly.

His hand was warm and a bit rough and his touch sent a shiver down her spine. There was a faint smell of horse and leather on his skin, but also some exotic spice and a clean scent that was all his own. Sibell breathed it in, storing it in her memory. She didn't draw away from him and when he rose to his knees before her, she knew he was going to kiss her. Mesmerised, she watched Roger's mouth descend towards her own. For some reason, his nearness had ceased to alarm her. Instead, she revelled in it and closed her eyes in expectation of his touch.

His kiss was soft and feather-light, a mere brushing of lips against lips, but his mouth returned to caress hers again and again, until neither could stand it any longer and sought to increase the contact. He stayed on his knees in front of her, his head on a level with hers. With a groan he wrapped his arms around her and pulled her tightly into his embrace. The kiss deepened and Sibell felt as if she was spinning in a maelstrom of sensations. Only his strong arms were holding her upright. She leaned into him and returned the kiss measure for measure. Never had she experienced anything like it.

'Sibell, you are so beautiful,' he murmured against her cheek, as they paused to draw breath.

Sibell didn't believe his words. She knew she wasn't a beauty and never would be, but it didn't matter just now. She was also fully aware that she should not allow this to continue, but his soft breath stirred her senses even more. When he returned his mouth to hers and sought entrance with a questing tongue, she opened for him willingly. He tasted wonderful.

The spell was broken by the sound of a door closing on the floor below, and heavy footsteps on the stairs outside the solar. Reluctantly they drew apart, still staring at each other in wonder, until with a shuddering sigh Sibell began to straighten her head covering.

'I'll come and see you at Ashleigh,' Roger whispered, just before Maude entered the room carrying refreshments. When Sibell raised anxious eyes to his, he added, 'I'll be careful, never fear.'

The journey to Maidstone took the best part of an hour in the morning traffic, but once there Melissa quickly found her way to the Kent History and Library Centre. She knew the records for mid- and southern Kent were held there – including those for the area around Ashleigh Manor – following a recent move into this new purpose-built facility.

As she entered the building and made her way to the records department, she reflected on her good fortune in having a job she enjoyed so much. And now that Jolie had settled happily into her new school and had Dorothy to come home to in the afternoon, she felt better about leaving her in order to do the necessary research.

In the reception area Melissa signed in at the desk and confirmed her booking of a seat and microfilm reader. She deposited her jacket and bag in a locker and, armed with a pencil and notepad, she headed for the search room.

As always, it was a hive of quiet activity even this early in the day, with scores of eager family historians beavering away over their microfiche or film readers. They were mostly elderly people who pursued their elusive ancestors as a hobby, but Melissa noticed there were a handful of professional researchers present as well. Some of them were known to her and she nodded to a few.

Behind the information desk, Melissa saw the archivist, who was a good friend of hers. She and Jenny had been at university together and the two had become very close, sharing as they did a love of all things past. She waited while Jenny attempted to explain the index system of the 1851 Census to a lady in her early seventies. It proved to be a monumental task, as the woman had a faulty hearing aid and everything had to be repeated at least twice. Melissa saw Jenny heave a sigh of relief when the woman finally took herself off. When she turned to her next customer with a friendly smile firmly plastered to her face, she found Melissa grinning at her.

'Melissa, I didn't see you there. How are you?'

She hurried round the counter to embrace her friend.

'Fine thanks, and very happy not to have to deal with that kind of aggravation every day.' She glanced towards the old lady and they both giggled.

'Now, now, it's part of my job and I enjoy it most of the time. It's wonderful to be able to help people. But what brings you here? Another Kent family to research?'

'No, as a matter of fact, I'm here for myself today and I was hoping you could help me out.' Melissa told Jenny about the move to Ashleigh and that she was curious to find out more about the history of the house and its occupants. 'My great-aunt thinks it was built sometime in the late fourteenth or early fifteenth century. Could you have a look for any old documents which might mention Ashleigh, please?'

'Of course. It sounds like fun. I'll go and see what I can find right away. You make a start on the parish registers and wills. The indexes are out here on the shelves and you know where to find the relevant microfilms, right? I'll take a look in the archives room.'

'Thanks, Jenny, I appreciate it.'

Melissa was soon seated by a microfilm reader. Most of the parish registers for the villages in the area surrounding Ashleigh began around 1590, but although she found Ashleigh mentioned, there was no one called either Sybil or Roger. She put

174

together a list of people connected with the house before moving on to the wills index.

This time she was in luck. One of the earliest wills listed was for a Sibell of Ashleigh and with mounting excitement she ordered the document from the stores. Could this be the Sybil that Dorothy had talked about? The name was similar enough. The minutes crawled by before one of the assistants finally brought it to the table where she was seated, together with a pair of white gloves.

'This is incredibly old, so if you wouldn't mind wearing these, please? Jenny tells me you know to handle this kind of document with care.'

'Yes, of course, thank you.' Melissa knew that for it to have survived this long was a minor miracle. She could hardly contain a whoop of delight as she carefully picked up the will and began to read.

The sounds of the search room faded into the background and in her mind Melissa was transported back to another age. The modern table in front of her disappeared and she saw instead a sturdy oak trestle with a candle on either side of the parchment and a small, black-clad man scratching away at it with his quill. Next to her was an unfinished baby's smock of embroidered linen and an inkstand, and she could hear the crackling of a log fire. The heat seared her on one side while a cold draft caressed her body from the opposite direction. Instinctively she tried to adjust a nonexistent shawl.

Strange memories came flooding into her brain then. Memories of dictating to the scribe while being heavily pregnant, of being filled with a mixture of hope, anger and despair as he quickly translated her words into Latin. A lassitude crept over her, a tiredness which was bone-deep, born out of almost unbearable sadness.

When at last the images faded, she put the will on the table in front of her and repressed a sob. The urge to burst into tears was almost over-whelming and she didn't know why. *What is happening to me?* With a great effort she pulled herself together and began to write down an English translation of the Latin wording with shaking fingers.

IN THE NAME OF GOD AMEN, I Sibell of Ashleigh in the parish of Idenhurst in the County of Kent, being of sound and perfect mind and memory, God be praised, therefore do make and ordain this my Last Will and Testament in writing in manner and form following, That is to say, first I recommend my soul into the hands of Almighty God and my body I commit to the earth, and as for my worldly estate wherewith it hath pleased God to bestow upon me, I give and dispose thereof as follows, viz

I give unto James Norice, Mary Pettit and Aline Goodhew, my faithful servants, the sum of one pound each, and to my dear friend Ingirith

Waite the sum of five pounds. All the rest and residue of my personal estate, goods and chattels whatsoever I give and bequeath unto my unborn child with love, and it is my wish that said child be named Roger should it prove to be male or Meriel should it prove to be female.

If said child is female, it is my wish that her guardians ensure the house and lands of Ashleigh remain her personal possessions even after marriage so that she may bequeath it to her first-born daughter, that the estate may pass down the distaff line for all eternity.

I do make and ordain Sir Gilbert Presseille of Idenhurst full and sole Executor of this my Last Will and Testament, and in witness thereof I have hereunto set my hand and seal this fourteenth day of January in the thirty ninth year of the reign of our Sovereign Henry the sixth King of England. Anno Domini One Thousand Four Hundred and Sixty One.

Signed   Sibell atte Ashleigh

Roger. Melissa stared at her own handwriting, mesmerised by that one word. So the Sybil of Dorothy's story had, in fact, been Sibell of Ashleigh. And if she wanted her child named Roger then it had to be because that name had special significance for her. There was no mention of a husband, thus it followed that the child she was expecting was going to be illegitimate.

'Progress at last,' she whispered.

As Roger left the solar, he turned for one last look at Sibell. He knew she hadn't believed him, but she really was beautiful and he'd been right about her figure. Although tall and lithe, she certainly had curves. Her gently rounded bosom strained against the russet-coloured fabric of her plain woollen gown, which seemed a little too small for her. And the gloriously coloured tendrils of hair, still escaping from her headdress despite her best efforts, together with her wide silver eyes, tempted him beyond belief. He wanted to free the flaming tresses and run his hands through them, feel their silkiness against his fingers, bury his face in them . . .

Roger took a deep breath and blew her a kiss behind Lady Maude's back, a mixture of happiness and excitement bubbling up inside him. Sibell's cheeks turned pink and she looked away. He found her shyness endearing. She was like a frightened fawn, but he'd make her come out of her shell. He'd protect her. She was his now, although why he'd allowed himself to succumb so readily he wasn't sure.

He'd been determined to think it over first, consider all his options. When he had gazed into her crystal clear eyes, however, Roger had known he was already lost. He was inexorably drawn to her and was helpless to prevent it. He would have laughed at the irony of it, if it hadn't been such a serious matter. He, who had for years evaded the lures of women of all ages, had finally been caught by a woman who'd done nothing to snare him. A woman who had no idea of the feelings of chivalry she had awoken within him. Somehow, within the space of only a few meetings, she had penetrated his guard.

There was only one course open to him now and to his utter amazement, he was looking forward to it.

CHAPTER 14

'We're having guests for tea today, dear, so would you mind helping me make some sandwiches, please?' Dorothy came into the kitchen looking fresh and relaxed. It was Sunday and Melissa, never at her best in the morning, looked up from her breakfast with what she knew must be a grumpy expression. She wondered where the old lady got all that energy from so early in the day.

'We are? Who's coming?' she enquired absently, while trying to focus her tired eyes on the Sunday paper lying next to her plate. She felt as if she had been wrung out in a mangle, absolutely exhausted physically and mentally, and it was all Roger's fault.

Last night she had dreamt that he was fighting with two red-haired youths on her behalf. She had cheered him on, hating his opponents with a vehemence foreign to her nature, and feared for Roger when he was hurt. There had been blood, lots of it, but she didn't think it was all his. She was sure he had beaten them in the end, despite a two-pronged attack that nearly made her heart stop.

The entire dream had been so vivid, she woke up with the stench of sweat and blood in her nostrils. She had just succeeded in convincing herself she was being silly, when Jolie marched into the room and immediately wrinkled her nose.

'Eeeuuw! It stinks in here, Mum. What have you been doing? A work out?'

Struck dumb, Melissa was unable to answer, and a sensation of panic washed over her. If Jolie could smell it as well, at least she wasn't imagining things, but that was scant consolation. She gave herself a mental shake. *This won't do. I'm becoming completely fixated by that ghost!* And Dorothy had warned her against that.

'Just Amy and her father.' Dorothy's casual answer to her question brought her back to the present.

'Sorry?'

'I have invited Amy and her father,' Dorothy repeated patiently. 'Amy said the poor man was always alone on weekends, probably pining for his dead wife. It's the least we can do for a neighbour, don't you think? And with Jolie spending so much time over there, I'm sure we owe them.'

'Yes, I suppose so.' Melissa was only half-listening, lost in her own thoughts again. Her dreams were becoming a real problem and they were a nightly occurrence now. On the one hand she found herself looking forward to going to bed because she wanted to be with Roger, but the rational part of her knew this wasn't normal. She wondered if the dreams meant anything. *Perhaps he's trying to tell me something more via my subconscious?* If only she could recall what had been said.

She shook her head. 'For heaven's sake,' she muttered and shook out the paper in frustration. 'This has got to stop.' With as much determination as she could muster, she concentrated on the day's news.

'Could someone get that please? I can't leave the oven just now,' Dorothy hollered from the kitchen when the doorbell rang later that day. The wonderful aroma of freshly baked scones wafted towards Melissa as she came down the stairs, vaguely annoyed about having to change into nicer clothes on a Sunday. Wearing skirts made her feel like she was working. She much preferred a pair of soft, comfortable jeans at the weekend and had planned on a relaxing afternoon, perhaps taking a long walk through the fields. As yet there hadn't been an opportunity to explore the countryside around the manor and she also needed time alone to think.

'All right, I will,' she called back, walking towards the front door, adding *sotto voce*, 'I just hope they don't stay too long.' She fumbled irritably with the door latch, which had a tendency to stick. She had a faint suspicion Dorothy might be match-making. *A divorcée and a lonely widower with daughters the same age, what could be more suitable?* Well, she'd catch cold at that. Melissa wasn't interested in men at the moment, not even Steve, after his latest announcement. Although a part of her still loved him obviously – feelings didn't evaporate that quickly – he also irritated the hell out of her. Living here at Ashleigh, she was beginning to see him from a new perspective and it made her wonder why she hadn't noticed his domineering tendencies much before. *Perhaps I would have come to resent that with time?*

'Sweeting . . .' The voice inside her head goaded her beyond endurance.

'No, go away, Roger!' she muttered. 'You're annoying me, too.' She opened the door with more force than was necessary, making the hinges squeak loudly in protest and the guests outside jump.

The fake welcoming smile died on her lips as Amy pushed past her with a quick, 'Hello, Ms Grantham,' and she was left staring at the girl's father.

'Mr Precy!'

The stunned expression on his face told her he hadn't been aware of her identity either, which was a relief. *At least he's not in on Dorothy's plans, then.* He recovered first and stretched out his hand. She took it reluctantly, afraid his touch might affect her the way it had at their previous meeting. It did, and the electric jolt reverberated all the way up her arm this time. As before, he appeared not to notice.

'Jake, please, we're neighbours. And you're Ms Grantham, I take it? I forgot to ask your name last time we met. It's a pleasure to see you again.'

'Er, Melissa.'

He shook her hand and added with a smile, 'You're not about to faint again, are you? Only, I wouldn't mind a bit more notice this time so that I can catch you properly.'

Melissa managed a stiff smile in return and thought 'Ha, ha, very funny.' Aloud she said, 'No, I'm not going to faint. I'm really sorry about that, it has never happened to me before.'

He handed her a bouquet of yellow flowers and greenery, beautifully wrapped in cellophane with a large matching bow at the bottom. 'For the hostess, or should that be hostesses?'

'Thank you. Do come in and make yourself comfortable in the sitting room.' Melissa pointed him in the right direction, before making her escape to the kitchen to put his offering in water.

'Dorothy,' she hissed accusingly, 'you knew, didn't you?'

Dorothy smiled blandly. 'Knew what, dear? That Mr Precy was Amy's father? Of course. They're our neighbours and he's also Russ's vet. Besides, Amy did say her name the first time she came. I thought you heard her.'

'Why, you . . . you know I didn't. Don't you think maybe you should have warned me? Or were you hoping I'd swoon into the man's arms again?'

'Well, the thought did cross my mind, but . . .' Dorothy stopped when she caught sight of the expression on her great-niece's face. 'Now, now, Melissa. It was just a harmless joke. Of course I knew you'd do no such thing. And he really is lonely, Amy said so. Just you go back in there and be nice to him. I'll bring the tea in a minute.'

'Can't you do it? I'll prepare the tea.'

Dorothy shook her head and grinned, making shooing motions with her hands. 'Away with you.'

There was nothing for it and, with a mutinous glare, Melissa returned to the sitting room with the flowers crammed into a vase.

'Interesting arrangement,' Jake muttered in amusement when Melissa entered, but she ignored his comment and pointedly made small talk about the weather until Dorothy and the two girls appeared with the tea tray.

During the ensuing conversation Melissa had the opportunity to study Jake further and she came to the conclusion that she'd been right. He was the spitting image of Roger. Jake's hair was cut short at the back and sides with a long fringe at the front which had a tendency to flop over his eyes, but apart from that they could have been twins. The resemblance was uncanny, in fact. To her great annoyance she felt herself flush every time Jake looked at her as she remembered the feelings Roger had awoken in her. If this was really what Roger had looked like, she could very well understand why Sibell had succumbed to him, if indeed he was her mysterious lover.

Melissa clamped down on her thoughts with determination. This wasn't Roger and she wasn't Sibell. Even if the ghost could make her go weak at the knees through some unearthly magic, there was no reason why this modern-day replica should affect her the same way. She wouldn't fall under a man's spell as easily as her ancestor had obviously done. She'd had enough of men for a while, especially charming rogues.

Jake looked around with interest. 'This is a wonderful house, isn't it? I can't believe how big it is compared to ours.' He smiled. 'I gather Ashleigh Cottage used to be where your servants lived.'

'Yes, we had a cook, a maid and some grooms when I was young,' Dorothy said. 'I believe your house was divided between them.'

'That sounds right. We knocked through quite a few walls when we bought it, as did the previous owner who must have bought it from you.'

'They have lots of stables here too, Daddy, while we've only got the one,' Amy interjected. 'If we lived in a house like this we could have at least a dozen horses.'

Jake laughed and held up his hands in mock horror. 'Oh, no we couldn't. One is quite enough in our family. He's eating us out of house and home as it is. Besides, you wouldn't have time for your schoolwork if you had to look after any more animals.'

'Oh, but Daddy . . .'

'Anyway, I think our house is quite big enough for the two of us.'

'Well, I want a horse, too.' It was Jolie's turn to enter the conversation. 'Mum, Auntie Dorothy says that I can use any one of the old stables if I want to.'

'Does she really?' Melissa made sure her dry tone indicated clearly what she thought of the fact that this matter had been discussed without her. 'How about you learn how to ride one first? You've only been having lessons for a couple of weeks.'

'Oh, but I'm getting really good at it, Amy says so. Don't you?'

'Yes, she is and . . .'

'We'll discuss it in a few months, okay? I'll have to earn enough money to buy you a horse first, *if* we are buying one at all. Besides, I thought it was a dog you wanted. Have you forgotten that already?'

'No, of course not, but Mum . . .'

'End of discussion, Jolie.' The two girls knew when they were beaten and retreated to Jolie's room to play loud music. Melissa wondered inconsequentially whether the ghost could hear things like that. If he could, he was probably going deaf at that very moment.

To Melissa's further irritation, Dorothy disappeared with some flimsy excuse or other, leaving her alone with Jake once more. She squirmed in her chair, trying to think of a safe topic of conversation and cursed Dorothy under her breath. She had no doubt whatsoever that her great-aunt would stay in the kitchen for quite a long time.

'So what do you do, Melissa?' Jake enquired politely.

'I'm a genealogist,' she replied and told him a bit about her work.

'That must be fascinating. I've always wanted to research my family tree, but I've never got around to it. Too much to do at work.' He shrugged. 'And then there's Amy, of course.'

'Well, if you're feeling rich I could do it for you. That's my job,' she joked, and then regretted her words instantly since they made him smile at her in bone-melting fashion that reminded her strongly of Roger.

'But of course! That would be wonderful. How much do you charge?'

'That depends . . .' Melissa quoted a figure that should have made the man blanch, but he didn't bat an eyelid. *Damn it all*, she thought. *I don't want to research his family tree.* It would mean seeing him again and, although she had to admit she found him attractive, she didn't feel ready to even think of forming a new relationship. *Especially not with Roger's long-lost twin.*

'When can you start?' The eagerness in his voice made her feel ashamed for deceiving him.

Melissa felt trapped, but she had been hoist with her own petard and couldn't see a way out. Stifling a sigh, she replied, 'I'll try and fit it in as soon as I can, but I do have a lot on at the moment. It would help me if you could give me as many details as you have of your parents and grandparents and so on. Any old papers you can lay your hands on will also be useful. Birth certificates, marriage lines, wills, anything like that.'

'I'll see what I can do,' he promised. 'I'll have a

look when I get home, there's a box of old stuff in a cupboard.' Melissa resigned herself to her fate. She would just have to steel herself against his – or was it Roger's? – charm.

At last, Dorothy returned to the sitting room and interrupted their *tête-à-tête*. Melissa heaved a silent sigh of relief.

'Have you been doing the spring cleaning?' she asked mildly, but she should have known that sarcasm would have no effect on her great-aunt.

'I'm sorry, but at my age everything takes so long.' Dorothy made a great show of levering herself into a chair, as if every bone ached. Melissa raised an eyebrow in disbelief. From what she'd seen so far, Dorothy could do the dishes at least three times faster than she herself could and there was nothing wrong with her at all. She conceded defeat. Soon her ordeal would be over.

Her relief was destined to be short-lived, however, as the older woman somehow managed to persuade them to go for a walk around the fields.

'Didn't you say you were going this afternoon, dear? I'm sure Jake would love to show you the area. He's lived here so much longer than you, after all.' Dorothy's expression of innocence didn't fool Melissa for an instant and she gritted her teeth in frustration. When Jake protested half-heartedly that he hadn't brought his boots, Dorothy conjured up an old pair that had belonged to her late husband. Melissa only had time to change quickly into a pair of old jeans and a sweater before being shooed out of the door. The pair set off down the lane in strained silence, with Russ running ahead of them, nose to the ground and tail wagging. Well, at least he's happy, Melissa thought rather grumpily.

'I'm sorry about my great-aunt.' She turned to Jake as soon as they were out of earshot of the house. 'I'm afraid she's a bit bossy.'

'Don't worry, I like her. And she's not the first in this town to try her hand at match-making.' Jake grinned. 'All the ladies seem to feel that because I'm a widower with a young daughter I must need a wife. I have learned to ignore it.'

Melissa felt her cheeks heat up and turned away. She should have realised that he would see through her aunt, too. Dorothy had been rather obvious, after all.

'Perhaps we could be friends, though?' he suggested. 'Since our daughters seem to be practically glued together at the moment, we might as well grin and bear it. I promise not to hit on you, as Amy would say, if you promise not to hit on me.'

Melissa had to laugh at that absurd statement and the conversation became decidedly more friendly. They found they had a lot in common and once the barriers were down, they enjoyed each other's company. As they continued their walk, Melissa began to relax at last.

★ ★ ★

They crossed a stile into the open fields, while the little dog found his own way through a hedge. When Melissa jumped over first, Jake discovered he quite liked the view. Her old jeans clung to her behind in a way that made him feel decidedly hot under the collar. He swallowed hard and determined to be the first one over the next stile. *This won't do,* he told himself. He'd offered her friendship, and friendship he would give her until they were both ready for something else. He took a firm grip on his wayward thoughts and led the way along a well-trodden bridle path.

It was the beginning of April and the countryside was definitely waking from its long slumber. The footpaths meandered along the perimeters of fields which had been ploughed and were ready for spring sowing. A few groups of daffodils still remained in the shadier locations, and some primroses were to be found hiding under the occasional hedge. Both types of flowers provided a welcome splash of colour. The smell of wet sods and burgeoning greenery combined to tease their nostrils.

'Mmm, I can't get enough of this earthy scent,' Melissa said, closing her eyes and drawing in deep breaths. 'And the air is so pure, too.' She laughed. 'I never knew I'm a country girl at heart.'

'Yes, spring is wonderful here,' Jake agreed.

'It's so unbelievably green,' she enthused. 'Fresh and minty, it's beautiful.' She shook her head, sending her hair flying out behind her. Jake couldn't help but admire the red highlights brought out by the sunshine and the way her eyes sparkled with enjoyment of the day. He wondered if she, herself, realised how beautiful she was. She didn't seem vain though, so he thought not.

'I can't believe I lived in London for so long,' Melissa continued. 'Now that I'm used to this, I don't think I could ever go back,' she added. 'I do hope Jolie doesn't change her mind.'

'I know what you mean. My wife and I lived in Fulham for a while when we were first married, and I absolutely hated it. I had a temporary job there for six months and was so relieved when I was offered work here, instead. Unfortunately, Karen didn't feel the same.'

'She didn't like it here?'

'Well, she enjoyed having the cottage decorated and all that, but once it was finished she found country life boring. She was a bit of a social butterfly and, as you've probably noticed, there isn't much going on around here.'

Melissa laughed. 'Actually, I haven't had time to notice things like that yet, but I'm more of a stay-at-home kind of person anyway. A good book and some chocolate is my idea of fun, although the occasional party can be great, too.'

'My feelings precisely.'

They smiled at each other.

Their walk eventually brought them to a small river. 'This is the river Idun,' Jake said. 'Come, I want to show you something really pretty.'

'Ok, but we'd better keep an eye on Russ so he doesn't fall in. Here, boy, heel.' Russ was very obedient and trotted just behind her, still looking excited to be outdoors.

Jake led them along the riverbank for quite a long way until they came to a bend. Just behind a clump of trees an old bridge came into sight and Melissa drew in a sharp breath.

'Oh Jake, it's lovely! It must be ancient.'

'Yes, I'm not sure how old exactly, but I do know it's a listed monument. I often come here when I want to be alone. It's a lovely spot, don't you think?'

Pointed in the middle, like the gable end of a house, the little bridge was charming. A rounded brick arch underneath let the torrent of spring water through, and the rest was constructed of stones of different shapes and sizes. One end jutted out into the river more than the other, making it appear slightly lopsided. Some of the lichen-covered stones were coming loose where the mortar was missing. In the middle of the bridge a rusty old gate hung precariously, separating the property of Ashleigh manor from that of its neighbour.

Melissa went to have a closer look, but as she came nearer her limbs suddenly became numb with fear and refused to move. She vaguely heard Russ growling at something, then alarm bells went off inside her head, causing her heart to beat faster in a rhythm of pure, abject terror. She began to shake and put her hands out for support. The only thing they encountered was the solid form of Jake, who looked at her in surprised concern.

'What's wrong? Are you feeling faint again?' He took her arm and led her over to an old tree-trunk nearby. Her knees buckled and she sank down gratefully.

'I'm okay,' she lied. 'Sorry, but I've been ill recently, bad bout of flu. I think perhaps the walk was a bit too much for me.' She didn't want to tell him of the fear, since she knew it was completely irrational.

'Put your head down and breathe deeply,' Jake instructed, and Melissa did as she was told. His hand on her back, unconsciously stroking her with soothing movements, helped to ease the rigidity of her muscles. At last the panic subsided and she started to breathe normally again.

Melissa looked around. 'Where's Russ?'

'Over there.' Jake pointed along the path. 'I think he's ready to go home. Maybe it's his dinner time?'

They stayed for a short while longer, before heading back to the manor house and, walking next to Jake, Melissa felt safe. Safe from what, she didn't know. She only knew that she'd never go near the bridge again if she could help it.

CHAPTER 15

'*Psst*. Sibell, over here.'

The softly hissed words made Sibell jump and look around in a panic. There was no one in sight, but the sound had come from the walled kitchen garden. She made sure no one was watching, then with a few hesitant steps, she went through the gate.

A pair of huge arms enveloped her swiftly and held her in an almost vice-like grip, but she wasn't frightened. She knew instinctively who her captor was and she didn't resist but smiled and looked into eyes as blue as the forget-me-nots in the nearby flower beds. A tremor of pleasure coursed through her.

'Roger.' She glanced around furtively once more. 'You are taking a great risk. If my father or brothers should see you, they'd beat you to a pulp.'

'Do you think so?' His smile was infectious, but she tried to stay serious.

'Well, they'd try anyway.'

'Shhh . . .' He put a finger to her soft lips. 'Don't worry. Hugone tells me they all rode out a while ago. It's unlikely they'll return for some time.' He grinned and pulled her closer. 'And Hugone is keeping watch.' He lowered his mouth to capture hers in a searing kiss.

She tried to protest. 'You shouldn't . . . we can't . . . I mean, it isn't right.'

He took her face between his hands and looked into her eyes. 'Yes, it is. I love you, Sibell, so nothing could be more right than this. Now do you trust me?' She nodded. 'Then just love me back and all will be well.'

Without further thought she twined her arms around his neck. 'I do,' she whispered. 'Oh, I do.'

It was a long time before she emerged from his embrace.

As he rode back to Idenhurst some time later, Roger had to admit he wasn't as confident as he'd pretended to be. For one thing, he wasn't getting anywhere with his quest to find out who his father might have been. And for another, he knew Sibell's father would never tolerate a match between them, even if she hadn't already been spoken for.

There has to be a way.

'Hugone, do you think I've run mad?' he asked.

'What? No!' The young squire looked startled to be asked such a direct question, but when he saw Roger smile at his response, he added with a cheeky grin, 'You're just in love, sir. They say that's a madness in itself, don't they?'

Roger sighed. 'Yes, it surely is.' He shook his head. 'Never thought it would happen to me. In fact, I was determined not to allow it, but God decided otherwise.' He had a vague feeling he might be blaspheming here, since what he felt for Sibell was more earthly than godly. But since his intentions were honourable, he felt sure the Lord would understand.

'Happens to everyone, so I'm told,' Hugone commented. 'And she's a lovely lady, to be certain.' He blushed as only an adolescent could, a fiery red that spread to the tips of his ears.

Roger laughed. 'Well, I'm glad I'm not the only who thinks so.'

'Oh, no. I've heard lots of other men commenting as she passes at Idenhurst, sir.'

'Have you now?' Roger didn't like the small demon of jealousy that rose up at hearing this. He'd never been jealous of anything or anyone in his life before. He forced himself to relax. Sibell was his and no one could change that.

All he had to do was make it legal somehow.

Jake was as good as his word and came over two days after their walk to hand Melissa some old papers he'd found in the attic. She was shocked at how pleased she was to see him again and did her best to suppress a wide smile of welcome. This was business, nothing else, and the fact that he looked like her dream lover was neither here nor there, she told herself firmly.

'I've jotted down as many details of my family as I could recall, like you said.' He handed her a

197

separate sheet of paper. 'I called my mother and my aunt and they filled in a few gaps for me. It's amazing the things some people remember.'

'Yes, old people are a great source of information, although you can't always trust them. They often try to hide the skeletons in the cupboard while embellishing the family's origins. You wouldn't believe how many people claim to be related to royalty, one way or another. Then they get annoyed with me when I can't prove it. Thanks anyway, this will help me get started.' Melissa glanced at the information he had written down. 'Oh, so your family came from this area?'

'Yes, I have many happy memories of visiting my grandparents here when I was a child. I think that was part of the reason I jumped at the chance to work in this town.'

Melissa put the papers on the hall table, then made the mistake of looking up into Jake's eyes. Her breath caught in her throat and the strange feelings of *déjà vu* returned. She stared at him, unable to move so much as a finger, and he appeared equally captivated. A door opened somewhere at the back of the house, but she hardly noticed. They remained motionless. Nothing existed except this man, this moment. She desperately wanted him to kiss her and her eyelids half-closed in anticipation.

'Hello, Jake, nice to see you again.' Dorothy's cheery voice broke the spell. Melissa came out of her trance and hurriedly looked away. Fortunately

Dorothy continued on her way and didn't stop for a chat. Melissa studied the stone-flagged floor, incapable of speech.

Jake cleared his throat. 'I, er . . . I was just about to tell you how nice you look today.'

Her eyes flew to his to see whether he was joking as she wasn't wearing anything special, but he seemed perfectly serious. Her stomach did a little somersault. 'Why, thank you. It's very kind of you to say so.'

'Not at all. I always tell the truth. Vets aren't allowed to lie, it's against the rules.' He winked at her. 'Right, I'd better be going then. Let me know how you get on. Bye.'

Melissa was left staring after him in confusion. Did he really find her attractive? Was she attractive? After Steve's departure she had seriously begun to doubt it, but having coped on her own for over a year her self-confidence was slowly returning. Anyway, didn't they say that beauty was 'in the eye of the beholder'? Well, that brought her back to her first question – whether Jake found her attractive. With a muttered oath she cut off this train of thought and stomped off down the corridor, grabbing the papers from the table as she went. She wasn't supposed to care what he thought. She didn't want a man in her life.

'Except me.'

The whisper caught her off-guard and she swore again. 'Go away,' she hissed. 'This is probably all your fault. Well, I'm not Sibell and Jake isn't you. So leave us alone.' The stupid ghost was affecting her thinking and she had to stop him. But how?

Melissa loved her job and when she set out for Maidstone yet again the following day it was with a familiar feeling of excitement. Every genealogical quest was a puzzle to be solved and the exhilaration she experienced whenever she was successful was headier than any wine. It never failed to thrill her. This time it was more personal, which added spice to the search.

The road to becoming a genealogist had been long and hard for her, but it had been her goal ever since she'd understood the meaning of the word. History was her favourite subject at school. While her friends read magazines and romantic novels, she had her nose stuck in what they called 'stuffy' books about the past. It wasn't until she discovered historical romances that she showed any interest in light reading at all.

She was in her second year of studying history at university when she met Steve and Jolie was conceived. Despite her growing bulge, Melissa finished the summer term that year, and as soon as she had recovered from the birth she resumed her studies by correspondence via the Open University. With a small baby to look after, distance learning was her only chance to continue. Her perseverance paid off and she completed her degree despite Steve's grumblings.

'You're wasting your time. Why are you studying history anyway? If you want to do something useful, then take a secretarial course or something so you can earn some money and help with the rent.' Melissa ignored him most of the time, although she did attend an evening course in typing and computer studies. Steve was pleased, thinking she'd finally seen sense. He never realised that both these subjects were invaluable to a genealogist.

He'd finished his IT studies and landed a fairly good job with a reputable firm in the City. However, his salary, although adequate for their needs, wasn't large enough to cover a nanny's wages. And as there was no one else who could take care of Jolie, Melissa stayed at home. Steve later decided to work freelance as a consultant and there was even less money. To pass the time she took another Open University course in genealogy, followed by several more in specialised subjects such as Latin and medieval manuscripts. When Jolie started school, Melissa began to do the odd job from time to time and built up some contacts in the business. It was a slow process, but ultimately rewarding.

Her growing workload proved to be a lifeline through the difficult time of her divorce. Losing herself in old records and family trees kept her sane and she knew that without genealogy she would have been lost.

'Back again so soon?' Jenny greeted her cheerfully as soon as she walked through the door of the search room.

'Yep, I'm nowhere near finished. And now I have another client from the same area, so I'm afraid you'll be seeing quite a lot of me.'

'Tell me what you're after and I'll help you make a start. It's awfully quiet in here today and I much prefer a quest to dull old cataloguing work.'

Melissa spent hours at the Kent History Centre and, with Jenny's assistance, found a wealth of information, both about Ashleigh Manor and about Jake's family tree. To her surprise she had hardly any trouble at all in tracing his line back to the beginning of the baptismal records of the local church at the end of the sixteenth century.

'God, what a boring lot,' she commented. 'These Precy's don't seem to have moved around much at all. No spirit of adventure whatsoever.'

'Guess they loved it here then,' Jenny said with a smile. 'Like your vet.'

'He's not *my* vet in the least.' Melissa frowned at her friend. 'But you're right, Jake really did return to his roots when he relocated from London. His ancestors have lived in the area for generations.'

Some had owned or rented properties, which made the task of tracing them much easier. Melissa always found leases and other property transactions very informative, as they often mentioned several members of a family and were witnessed by others.

'Looks like they couldn't make up their mind how to spell their name though,' Melissa commented. The spelling of the name Precy varied a lot through the ages. There was *Pressy*, *Preecy* and *Presay* and quite a few others besides, which made Melissa smile. Some of the curates keeping the records had recorded the name phonetically and some had probably misheard their informant. Others were simply incapable of spelling correctly. She noticed one poor chap in particular who even spelled the word "burials" with two r's and two l's.

It wasn't until she got back to the beginning of the seventeenth century, however, that the spelling *Presseille* appeared, startling Melissa no end when she recalled where she had last seen it.

'Good God,' she mumbled. 'I should have seen that one coming.'

'What's that?' Jenny came bustling over, having caught sight of Melissa's expression.

'Look here. This must mean the man who was executor of Sibell's will could be related to Jake. Intriguing, don't you think?'

Jenny considered the matter. 'Yes, I suppose he could be, but you'll have a hard time proving it. From 1460 to 1600 is quite a gap.'

'I wonder why she appointed this Gilbert Presseille her executor?' Melissa chewed her bottom lip, lost in thought. Could he have something to do with Roger?

'Don't read too much into it. I'm sure it was just a formality. You said the lady supposedly had no other relatives, and this man may have been an important neighbour or kinsman, so who else would she have asked?'

'Yes, I guess you're right.' Swallowing her

disappointment, Melissa was nevertheless extremely pleased with the information regarding Jake's family. 'Could we try to trace this Sir Gilbert, though? Let me see, I'm pretty sure the will mentioned where he was from.' She riffled through her notes and found what she was looking for. 'Yes, here it is – Sir Gilbert Presseille of Idenhurst. Any idea where that is?'

'Nope, but I'll check the computer database of all the really old manuscripts we have here. Some of them go back as far as the eighth century, isn't that amazing? There may be some references to that place among the documents that aren't on public display. Come on, in here.' Jenny led the way into the back room where normally only archivists were allowed.

They found that Idenhurst had been a large property and it was mentioned in quite a few documents. Painstakingly they sifted through the material, discarding most of it as it was of a later date. It wasn't until late in the afternoon they finally had a real breakthrough when Jenny unearthed an old manor court roll from Idenhurst.

'Oh, brilliant, Jenny, just what we need.'

'Yes, this should be interesting, as long as it's not too damaged.'

Manor court rolls were records of the proceedings of manorial courts, which provided justice at a local level in medieval times. For a genealogist, they could be an absolute goldmine so Melissa was thrilled they'd found one. Among other things, they might give information about such issues as ownership and occupation of land, inheritance and enforcement of law and order. Held at regular intervals, usually with the lord of the manor in charge, these rolls were full of richly detailed accounts of the life of the local people.

'I do hope they had a diligent clerk at Idenhurst, who didn't miss anything out,' Jenny muttered.

A manorial clerk was employed to write down everything the court decided, usually in a cursive court hand that was hard to decipher. Melissa and Jenny had both been trained to read this, however, so it wasn't an obstacle. Neither was the fact that the records were written in abbreviated Latin, using many archaic terms. It was something they were used to.

'Okay, careful now.'

Melissa didn't need to be told. The old parchment roll was exceedingly fragile and she knew they had to take great care when unrolling it. Both of them wore soft gloves, so as not to harm the document further, but Melissa still held her breath a lot of the time, certain that it was going to crumble in her hands.

Thankfully most of it was legible and they worked on deciphering it together, delighted with all the details it contained. When they reached the late fifteenth century, Melissa couldn't contain a gasp of delight.

They had hit the jackpot.

CHAPTER 16

As always, Sibell attended Sunday mass with her father and brothers. The little church was full to overflowing and the lack of air made breathing difficult. Sibell brought her rose-scented handkerchief up to her nose surreptitiously, trying not to gag at the rank smell of too many people crammed into too small a space without ventilation.

There was a scuffle at the back of the church where the poorer members of the community had to stand throughout the service. For obvious reasons, a place near the wall was coveted and more often than not there were those who gained their places by the judicious use of sharp elbows. There was a continuous hum of noise as people coughed or sneezed and children were hushed by their elders. Babies wailed, regardless of the efforts made to quieten them. Sibell felt for the mothers as the priest turned a baleful eye in their direction.

The tiny stained-glass windows didn't throw much light onto the congregation. Father Jacob had lit numerous tallow candles, which only added to the fug already created by wet clothes drying slowly in the warmth. Sibell glanced at the stone carvings that were the church's only decorations and tried not to think about Roger. Unfortunately, she had thought of nothing else during the last week.

Since their first meeting in the walled garden he had come as often as he could without giving rise to suspicion. The garden had become their refuge and they found time to talk as well as share the magical kisses that made her dizzy with desire. He told her of his life as a knight and she confided her fears and tribulations, gaining strength and confidence from their conversations. He gave her hope for the future and when he was near she wasn't afraid of anything.

She still found it hard to believe he could possibly love her, rather than all the beautiful ladies he had met on his travels, but he assured her it was so.

'You are different, sweeting,' he told her. 'You don't make sheep's eyes at me and there is no artifice in your manner. You are everything I have ever wanted.' His every caress made her feel special and whenever he wasn't near she craved his touch.

Sibell sighed quietly. The images which came before her eyes every time she closed them refused to be repressed. Even in this holy place she couldn't keep them at bay. The feel of his lips on hers, his hands caressing her and words of love whispered softly, lingered in her memory. A frisson meandered up her backbone, leaving a tingling sensation in its wake. She shifted uncomfortably on the rock-like wood of the bench. If ever there was a penance for having inappropriate thoughts in church, then sitting like this was definitely it.

Roger was standing on the left hand side of the church, not far from where Lady Maude and Sir Gilbert were seated, and Sibell knew he was as aware of her presence as she was of his. She dared not look. As she risked a peek at her father, who was on her right, a shard of fear pierced her. *If he should ever find out* . . . No, she wouldn't think of such things. They would be careful.

The priest had chosen to preach of the Temptation of Jesus in the Wilderness from the gospel of Saint Matthew. Sibell almost broke into hysterical laughter at the aptness of his choice. *Temptation.* The word had taken on a whole new meaning for her lately. With great effort she controlled herself.

'Practise in the light of Christ's message,' the priest urged them in a voice which promised retribution to all who didn't follow his orders. 'Overcome temptation. Battle it with all your might!' Sibell felt the guilt stain her cheeks and she bowed her head. Even the Lord's Prayer reproached her. 'Lead us not into temptation, oh Lord . . .'

But how could she possibly resist when she didn't want to?

'I reckon it was just pure luck. You'd never beat us a second time, knight. Fancy trying again?'

Roger was one of the last people to come out of church and the Ashleigh brothers must have been lying in wait for him. Three of them emerged from the shadows of the porch now and blocked his way. He drew in a calming breath, determined not to rise to their bait. There were still people about and they couldn't do him any actual harm here.

'Nothing to say for yourself today?' The red-headed one sneered. Roger could never remember which brother was which, but he did know the biggest one, an ugly brute who hardly ever spoke, was Henry, the heir.

'We can train together again any time you wish, gentlemen,' he replied evenly. 'But not, I think, on a Sunday.'

'You're just afraid we'll beat you,' the blonder brother said and spat on the ground. 'And with Henry to back us up, we will. Won't be no training bout, neither.'

'Yes, don't go wandering around after dark.' The red-head chuckled, as if he found his threat hilarious. 'Wouldn't want you to be caught unawares, now would we?'

'Simon, what are you about? Father is calling for us.'

Roger looked to his left, where a fourth brother came towards them. This one never spoke much either, but Roger had gathered it wasn't because of a lack of wits, as was the case with Henry. He watched with interest as the other three scowled at their brother, but still sauntered away. They sent Roger menacing glares over their shoulders, which didn't scare him.

'Ignore them, Sir Roger, they're young and foolish, or in the case of Henry, just foolish.' To Roger's surprise, the fourth brother had stayed behind and was staring after his siblings with narrowed eyes. 'But have a care. I wouldn't put it past them to try something underhand.'

With that comment, he too left, and Roger watched him go. The warning had been unnecessary, but he was pleased to find that Sibell had at least one relative with some brains and manners. A shame there weren't more of them.

'I can't believe this, Jenny, we've got confirmation of a connection to Jake's line.' Melissa grinned at her friend, who was equally delighted.

'Yes, incredible piece of luck. I can't see any mention of that Gilbert fellow, though.'

'Well, we've only gone back to 1495, perhaps he was dead by then. Let's see, does it go any further?'

This was when their luck ran out, however. To their immense frustration, they discovered the innermost part of the roll appeared to be stuck together. Jenny tried to gently prise it open, but it wouldn't budge.

'Damn,' she muttered. 'I don't dare force it.' She shook her head. 'It's no good, I'm going to have to ask the conservation guys to take a look at it and see if there's any way of opening it without ruining the writing. Aargh, this is so annoying! Just when it was getting interesting, too.'

Melissa giggled. 'Any normal person would think

us insane, getting so excited about an old document.'

'Yes, but they have no idea how addictive this is. Better than any drug, if you ask me. Leave it with me and I'll see what we can do. I'll give you a call, all right?'

The minute she was outside the Record Office, Melissa called Jake on her mobile phone to report on her progress.

'Jake? Hi, it's Melissa Grantham. Do you have a minute? Good, listen, I have great news. I'm getting on really well with your family tree and I found a manor court roll today which is all about your ancestors. We can trace them back to the fifteenth century now. It's an incredible piece of luck.'

'You found a what?' Jake said, sounding baffled.

'Sorry, let me explain. Normally, it's almost impossible to go back further than the beginning of the seventeenth century when putting together a family tree. That's when baptisms began to be recorded in most churches, so before that it's very hit and miss. Unless you're of noble birth or your family has owned land for much longer, that is. What we found today was a record of a manorial court, which was held at some place called Idenhurst, apparently a large manor somewhere near Ashleigh. And it was owned by your ancestors.'

'Really? That's fascinating. So I should really be a lord, then?' Melissa could hear the smile in Jake's voice.

'No, no. If there ever was a title, it passed along a different line to yours. You are descended from the lords of the manor, but I'm afraid you're still plain mister. The manor itself seems to have been inherited by a daughter and her husband. But listen, the manorial roll mentions lots of names in the daily transactions recorded and that means I can go a lot further back. It's very unusual and exciting.'

'I see. Well, I'm very grateful for your hard work. Can we get together one evening so you can show me what you've found so far?'

Melissa shivered. Just hearing his voice was enough to make her feel strange again. She wasn't at all sure she should meet him alone anywhere. Fiddling with her car keys, she hesitated, then told herself sternly not to be so stupid. She was meeting him in a professional capacity after all, nothing more.

'Sure,' she managed finally. 'Give me a few days to put the information together into a proper family tree, then I'll show you.'

She'd intended to start as soon as she got home, but just as she walked through the door, she was distracted by a phone call from the local historian, Colin Parsons. She had tried to call him weeks ago, when she was given his number by the lady at the local library, but he'd apparently been away until now, and she'd almost forgotten all about him.

'Oh, thank you for ringing back, Mr Parsons.

Yes, I have some questions about the history of this area and I was wondering if you would have time to meet me? It might take a while to discuss everything, so I would rather not do it over the phone.'

'Sure, I'm always happy to help. I live at number two Vicarage Close, not far from the old church. Why don't you come round, say, tomorrow evening?'

'Perfect. Would seven o'clock be okay?'

'Absolutely.'

CHAPTER 17

Colin Parsons was shorter than Melissa and fairly rotund, with intelligent, smiling eyes behind thick-rimmed glasses. She guessed his age to be somewhere around fifty, but couldn't tell for certain. Although he had greying hair with a bald patch, his face was almost entirely free of wrinkles, almost boyish in fact. He was dressed haphazardly, as if he'd pulled out the first thing he could find in his wardrobe without bothering to check whether it matched anything else he was wearing. Melissa found this rather endearing. She noticed that one of his socks was brown and the other blue, but he seemed sublimely unaware of his appearance.

'Come in, come in.' She was ushered into a large, but extremely cluttered, sitting room, where Colin cleared some papers off a worn leather chair so she could sit down. He then picked up several other items from the coffee table – a newspaper, a calculator and several pens – and looked around for somewhere to dump them. Since every available surface was already occupied, however, he became slightly flustered and finally pushed everything under the sofa while muttering under his breath. Melissa watched him in amusement.

'Sorry, I haven't had time to do any cleaning lately,' he said. 'As I said, I've been away. Now would you like a cup of tea?'

'Yes, please, if it's not too much trouble?' Melissa noticed the lack of a woman's touch and wondered if he was a widower or a bachelor. Probably the latter, she concluded. The house didn't look as if a woman had ever had any say in its decor or furnishing. It was very much a man's domain – dark colours, no flowery patterns and no knick-knacks. Books and papers were everywhere, overflowing the bookcases that lined one wall and lying in untidy piles on the floor.

Soon after he had gone off to the kitchen, a small, sleek tabby cat sauntered into the room and came up to assess the newcomer. Melissa gathered she must have passed the inspection, since the cat proceeded to rub herself against Melissa's legs. 'Come on, then.' She patted her knees in invitation, but the little feline turned her back on Melissa and wandered round inspecting her territory instead.

Colin returned surprisingly quickly, balancing a tray containing two mugs of tea and a packet of Rich Tea biscuits. He shrugged apologetically. 'I'm afraid I live alone, so this is as good as it . . . oh, hell!'

Melissa gasped as he tripped over the cat and almost dumped the contents of the tray onto her lap. With a dexterity she hadn't thought him capable of he managed to right himself and somehow the mugs of tea survived intact. Only the packet of biscuits went flying, and she caught it in mid-air and placed it on the table.

'Damned cat, always in the way,' he muttered. 'I see you've met Duchess.' The cat meowed loudly and gave her master an affronted glare. 'Yes, yes, I know it's not your fault that I can't see beyond the end of my nose, but you should know better than to walk in front of my feet by now. Honestly, you are a stupid animal.' He shook his head. 'But I love you dearly, you know that.'

'Duchess has been keeping me company. And I love Rich Tea biscuits, Mr Parsons. I didn't expect to be entertained with a formal tea, I just need some information. Preferably lots of it.' Melissa smiled at him to show there was no need for him to be flustered.

'Right, well I hope I can help you, but please, call me Colin. "Mr Parsons" makes me feel ancient.'

'All right then, if you'll call me Melissa.'

They chatted about the local town and the surrounding villages in general while they sipped their tea and Melissa found that his enthusiasm for history was equalled by his knowledge of the subject. In the space of ten minutes she learned more than she had during the whole of the previous month, things that none of the weighty tomes in the library had mentioned. Colin had delved deeper and had managed to unearth additional information in various private archives around the area. He was delighted to discover a fellow devotee.

'It's so nice to speak to someone who understands what I'm talking about.' He beamed at her and pushed his glasses onto the top of his head before picking up his mug.

'Likewise.'

'So tell me, what was it you wanted help with in particular?'

'Well, I'm researching the history of Ashleigh Manor, which has apparently been in my family for generations. My great-aunt owns it now and she's told me some old stories about it that made me want to find out more. I'm also interested in another property called Idenhurst, which is supposed to have been somewhere in the neighbourhood, but I can't find it on any maps of the area.' She showed him the documents she had come across at the Record Office. 'The earliest map of the village I have found so far is dated 1694 and although Ashleigh is on there, it doesn't show Idenhurst.'

'Yes, I've seen this one before. Hmm, the name Idenhurst rings a bell, but I'll have to look into it.' Colin expressed great interest in the information she had gathered. He was able to add a few things about Ashleigh's more recent history, but Melissa was impatient to learn more of earlier times.

'One of the stories my great-aunt told me was

about one of the owners, a woman by the name of Sibell, who apparently had a lover called Roger. I would very much like to find out more about them. As far as I can make out she must have been born around 1430-1440, or thereabouts. I have a copy of her will, which is dated 1461, although I don't know if that was when she died or if it was merely a precaution. She seems to have been pregnant at the time and I think she subsequently gave birth to a daughter called Meriel.'

'Ah, yes, Mistress Sibell. I know her well.' Colin nodded enthusiastically.

'Sorry?'

To Melissa's amazement, Colin set his mug down with a thump and stood up. 'Come, I'll introduce you to her immediately.'

Her eyes widened. 'Introduce me?' For a wild moment, she wondered if the entire village was seeing ghosts, or indeed going mad, but then rational thought returned and she told herself she must have misunderstood.

'Yes, I'll take you to meet her now. Let me just fetch a torch.' He scurried off and returned to his startled guest a few minutes later carrying a huge flashlight and a bunch of very large keys. 'These are the keys to the church. I act as warden from time to time. Come on, follow me, it won't take long.' He ushered her into the hall and Melissa was caught up in his excitement, pulling on her sweater as they went. As they reached the front door, however, he stopped short and began to feel in his pockets, as if he was searching for something. 'Hold on a minute,' he muttered and rushed back into the sitting room. When he came back he was frowning.

'What's the matter, have you lost something?' Melissa asked.

'Yes, can't find my glasses. I'm sure I had them a minute ago.'

Melissa stared at him, speechless, and then burst out laughing.

His frown deepened. 'This is no laughing matter. Without my glasses I'm almost blind.'

'I'm s-sorry.' Melissa tried to compose herself. 'It-it's just that . . . they're on your head.' She managed to turn another fit of laughter into a cough, so as not to offend him, but he grinned at her broadly, his relief at finding the glasses palpable.

'Of course, I should've known. Sorry, I do that a lot.'

His house was only a few doors away from the village church and within a short space of time he was turning the largest key in the old lock of the door. It swung open with an unearthly squeak from the old hinges and they entered the dim interior. Colin switched on the ceiling lights, but they were old and gloomy and cast insufficient light, making the torch a welcome addition. Their footsteps echoed eerily on the stone floor and Melissa shuddered and stayed close to her guide.

He shone the light in a wide arc, giving her a glimpse of a low, vaulted ceiling, tiny stained-glass windows and carved pillars, before proceeding down the aisle. Shortly before the altar he came to a halt and turned left, then right again. He headed for a dark corner where there was a small opening into a private chapel protected by an ancient wrought-iron gate.

'Now which key is it again?' Colin muttered, rattling the bunch until he came to a small, twisted one with an ornate top. It took a lot of force and several tries before he managed to push the gate open. It screeched loudly and Melissa gritted her teeth against the sound.

'Over here,' Colin said, and directed the beam of light onto the floor to her left, where a large brass plaque glittered dully. 'Hardly anyone comes in here except me. Now, say hello to your ancestor, Mistress Sibell of Ashleigh.'

Melissa knelt down and stared at the image of a young woman. 'So this is where you're buried,' she whispered. A deep sadness welled up inside her, followed immediately by a hollow sensation of loneliness. Sibell was unhappy; Melissa could feel it with every fibre of her being. The sound of anguished crying suddenly bounced round the small, enclosed area and she winced.

'Did you hear that, Colin?'

'What?'

'That noise. Sort of like wailing.'

'Oh, you mean the wind outside. Yes, it's really picking up, isn't it? Always seems to whistle round the church, it's so draughty in here.'

Melissa dropped the subject. It was obvious that Colin hadn't heard anything out of the ordinary. Instead she bent to study Sibell's grave. The plaque was beautifully executed, obviously the work of a true craftsman, and Melissa marvelled at the detail. Sibell's dainty hands were clasped together over her chest in pious prayer. Her gown had been depicted falling in graceful folds to her feet, which peeped out from underneath the hem. Long tresses of wavy hair cascaded down to the narrow waist.

Finally, her eyes came to rest on Sibell's features and she frowned. 'Can you shine the light on her face please, Colin?'

'Sure.'

Melissa reached out and traced the portrait of Sibell with reverent fingers – a small, straight nose with a slight tilt at the end, high cheekbones, finely sculpted brow, a generous mouth and a chin with a small indentation in the middle and . . . With a gasp, Melissa put up a finger to the dimple in her own chin.

'I say, she looks an awful lot like you, don't you think?' Colin cleared his throat when he caught sight of Melissa's expression. 'Well, in this light anyway, but that's not to say . . .' He stopped again and coughed.

There was no denying it, however. Looking at Sibell was like staring into a dull mirror, one that needed polishing badly, but which still showed your features clearly. Melissa stood up and took a step backwards. She tried to gather her thoughts, to stop herself from panicking. Averting her gaze from the brass itself, she concentrated on the surrounding area instead.

Carved into the stone floor around the edge of the grave was a Latin inscription, and Melissa began to read aloud. *'Hic iacet Sibella . . .'*

'Here rests Sibell, much mourned by those who loved her,' Colin put the words into English. 'Yes, I've read it many times, but it says nothing about her being a wife. It's puzzled me that, I must admit. I thought perhaps her husband didn't like her.'

'I don't think she was married.' The sadness returned in full force, almost knocking Melissa off her feet. When she closed her eyes to the dull ache which had begun to throb inside her head, she heard chanting and the sounds of grief. Her eyes flew immediately to Colin's, but he didn't appear to have noticed anything this time, either.

She looked at the end of the inscription, where a date had been added. 'MCDLXI,' she murmured. 'So you did die in 1461, how sad.'

Colin put a hand on her arm. 'Come, there's something else I want to show you.' Impatient once more, he pulled her up and dragged her over towards the other side of the church, slamming the little gate shut behind them. The torch illuminated a carved inscription on the wall. 'Have a look at this,' he commanded.

'Meriel, beloved wife of Guy de Manton,' Melissa read. 'Oh, Colin, do you think . . . .?'

'Yes, exactly. This must be her daughter. You said

her name was Meriel, not precisely a common name, and the dates fit. I haven't come across anyone else called that so far. But she's over here, next to the Presseille graves and not with her mother. Why should that be? Was that Roger bloke a member of that family?'

'Presseille? How odd, I've just been researching that name for a, umm, client. It seems to be cropping up all over the place. A Gilbert Presseille was executor of Sibell's will, too. Hmm, Roger Presseille.' She tried the name out and as it echoed round the walls of the little church, a sudden tremor shot through her. 'Yeees, it's possible. Perhaps he was already married when he and Sibell were lovers. Then when his wife died he could have acknowledged Meriel as his?'

'Yup. That would explain it, especially if Sibell was already dead by then as well.'

'Hmmm, I don't know, Colin. Something isn't quite right, I can sense it.' But there seemed to be no other logical explanation. Melissa sighed. 'I shall have to look further. I didn't come across any Roger Presseille's at all, but that's not to say he didn't exist. There is so little material left from those days.' She smiled at Colin. 'Thank you so much for showing me, anyway. I really appreciate your help. I hadn't got round to visiting the church yet, and even if I had I'm sure I would have missed Sibell's tomb, hidden away as it is.'

'Anytime,' he mumbled, 'anytime.'

CHAPTER 18

The great hall at Idenhurst was at least three times the size of the one at Ashleigh and Sibell watched her father looking around in envy. She followed his gaze towards the great oriel window Sir Gilbert had recently had installed to brighten the room. It was a beautiful piece of architecture and must have cost a great deal. She knew it galled her father that he couldn't aspire to anything so grand, although he was hoping her marriage to Sir Fulke would change things.

'With his connections, I'm sure he'll be able to help me rise to a more prominent position in society,' he had been heard to boast to his sons. 'Then we'll see about buying a larger manor house and more land.' The fact that his daughter had to be sacrificed for the sake of his ambitions seemed not to matter.

Sibell saw his eyes wander upwards towards the cavernous ceiling, where the great roof timbers were decorated with corbels carved in the shape of serpents' heads. An involuntary shudder passed through him, as if he found them intimidating rather than decorative. Sibell had to admit the snakes looked ready to strike at any time.

They had been invited to a feast in honour of the powerful Lord Blaine, an acquaintance of Sir Gilbert's, and the entire Ashleigh family was present.

'I wish we could have refused to attend,' her father grumbled to his eldest son Henry, who was seated on the other side of him, 'but Blaine is on good terms with Sir Fulke of Thornby. He'll want to look Sibell over on behalf of his friend.' He glanced at his daughter and, by the expression of distaste that crossed his features, she gathered he found her wanting, as usual.

'Well, I hope he doesn't look too closely then,' she heard Henry mutter. The guffaw that followed this thoughtless remark did nothing to improve her father's temper. He cuffed the boy, wiping the smirk off his face in an instant.

'Shut your mouth, fool,' he hissed. 'You had better pray the man likes what he sees, or else there'll be no wedding. You know full well the advantages of the match and should we fail there's no one else half so powerful who'll have her. By the saints, that a man should be so plagued with a lackwit for a son, and my heir to boot now . . .' He continued to curse under his breath for some time and Sibell looked round to make sure no one was listening.

Henry was the largest and strongest of her brothers, with fists the size of small hams, but the good Lord did appear to have forgotten to give the boy a brain. He had ever been slow to grasp things, frustrating his impatient sire who often said he had no idea how Henry would ever manage Ashleigh. His only hope was that his other sons would help when the time came.

Simon leaned across Sibell and whispered to his father, 'I heard a rumour that Thornby is occupied with the young wife of an elderly knight. She's apparently not averse to lifting her skirts for anyone who asks. Perhaps he'll change his mind about Sibell?'

'He had better not,' came the growled reply, together with a glare which boded ill for Sir Fulke should he renege on his word. Simon quickly leaned back.

Although the marriage negotiations were progressing, Sir Fulke hadn't yet bestirred himself to visit them, preferring to rely on trusted messengers. Sibell was very grateful, since it gave her more time to think of a solution. No doubt Sir Fulke had been told she wasn't a beauty, tall and lanky as she was and with these accursed freckles of hers. Nevertheless, Sir Fulke had agreed to the match in principle, perhaps swayed by the considerable dowry her father had used as bait, and that thought was disheartening.

'If the contract isn't signed by Midsummer, I suppose I'll have to ride over to Thornby and speed things up.' Her father cast another sour glance towards her, then narrowed his eyes. 'I don't doubt you're playing some deep game, but don't think you can best me, girl. You'll be married before summer's end, even if I have to beat you black and blue.' He took a deep swallow of the excellent burgundy wine, which was flowing freely. 'It's your duty to do as your father wishes, damn you. I shouldn't have to force you.'

Sibell lowered her gaze and kept silent.

Musicians, jugglers and even two dwarves had been hired to entertain the guests, but Sibell found no enjoyment in their antics. The dwarves and jugglers irritated her, and the scraping of fiddles and banging of drums was making her head ache. Her father seemed to agree with her.

'Damned cacophony,' he muttered into his goblet, then turned his attention to the highly spiced food on his trencher.

Sibell stirred restlessly. Someone was looking at her, she could feel it, but as always she had to be cautious. Turning to the finger bowl on her left, she carefully rinsed her hands and under the pretence of looking for the drying-cloth she peeked across to an adjoining trestle. Her eyes met those of Roger and she stilled, unable to drag her gaze away.

He was leaning back against the wall behind him, ostensibly deep in conversation with a pretty lady seated next to him, but his expression of barely suppressed boredom told her the woman meant nothing. It was Sibell he wanted, and a delicious tingle went down her spine at the promise she read in his eyes. As a juggler walked past, momentarily shielding him from view, Sibell drew a shaky breath. The warmth spreading through her veins was threatening to spill over into her cheeks. She had to control her thoughts or she'd give herself away.

She shot a watchful glance at her father, but he was busy devouring his meal. He ate with a single-mindedness that never failed to astonish her, but she was grateful for it now. With her father occupied, Sibell risked another look at Roger. He was speaking to the woman and pointed to something behind her. As she looked away he quickly mouthed, 'Later,' at Sibell, before returning his attention to his table companion.

Sibell checked to make sure none of the members of her family had noticed the exchange, but her father was still lost in his fare and her four brothers were too deep in their cups to see anything. She heaved a sigh of relief and shivered in anticipation. How soon was 'later'?

The following day was Open Day at Jolie's new school, so Melissa was forced to take a break from her research.

'Would you like to come with us?' she asked Dorothy, who always took an interest in everything Jolie did, but the old lady shook her head.

'Thank you, but not this time. Russ has been a bit under the weather this morning, so I think I'd better stay with him. Probably just a temporary side-effect of the annual booster shot he had yesterday, but still, I don't want to leave him.'

'No, of course you must keep an eye on him, poor little chap.' Melissa bent to pat the little terrier, who lay with his head on his paws, his expressive brown eyes mournful. 'Hope he feels better soon.' He was a sweet, intelligent dog, and she and Jolie had both come to love him very much.

Melissa could have done with Dorothy's support, however, and left the house feeling nervous, checking and re-checking her make-up and clothing. She had informed Steve about the event – via his secretary, since she didn't want to talk to him directly – and now she couldn't decide whether she wanted him to come or not. It would, of course, be good for Jolie's sake if he put in an appearance, but as for herself she'd much rather not see him. She wasn't sure she could handle it.

As they left the car in the school car park, she was still fretting. 'Do I look all right?'

Jolie looked her over critically, then grinned. 'Of course you do. You look great, Mum. I like the grey of your jacket, it goes with your eyes, and that black skirt is very pretty and swirly.'

Melissa smiled and gave Jolie a hug. 'Thank you. So you won't be ashamed of me, then?'

'Don't be silly.'

Growing serious, Melissa raised the matter of Steve. 'You know your dad is very busy, so don't be too disappointed if he doesn't show up.'

'I know. He never came to the Open Days at Putney, so he probably won't today, either.' Jolie sounded resigned, and Melissa wanted to strangle Steve, although to be fair it wasn't always easy for parents to get time off for school events. 'Come and see everything I've done, Mum.' Jolie led the way up the stairs and Melissa followed her to the classroom.

The children's work had been spread out on top of their desks and it took a while to look at it all. Melissa sifted through one workbook after another and was seriously impressed. She was just about to tell Jolie, when the teacher, Miss Kavanagh, came up behind them and said, 'She's doing really well, isn't she, Ms Grantham. You must be very proud of her.'

'Oh, yes, of course I am, and I'm so glad she's happy here.' Melissa glanced at her daughter, whose cheeks were slightly pink with embarrassment at the praise. Jolie really did seem to be thriving and was working very hard. 'I'm very grateful to you and the rest of the staff for being so supportive and helpful.'

'Not at all, Jolie is a joy to teach. Never any bother.'

Melissa hardly dared to believe Miss Kavanagh's words, they were so far from what she had been used to hearing from Jolie's teacher in Putney. She looked at her daughter and smiled, enveloping her in a quick hug. 'Well done, sweetie.'

'Mum! Not here.' Jolie struggled to disentangle herself.

Melissa laughed and let her go. 'Sorry, I forgot. Hugging in public is un-cool, right?'

'What's this I'm hearing? My little girl doing well? I don't believe it.'

They both looked up to find Steve standing next to the desk, larger than life and as handsome as ever. Melissa's stomach lurched, and she inhaled sharply, waiting for the usual despair to flood through her. Nothing happened. To her surprise, there was no wave of longing, only mild irritation caused by the anger still simmering inside her. She was hugely relieved, but also slightly confused. He nodded curtly at her, bent to give Jolie a quick kiss on the cheek, then asked her to show him her work.

Melissa stood beside them in silence, mulling over her lack of reaction to Steve, while Jolie went through everything once more with him. Jolie soon led the way on a tour of the school, stopping in various places such as the science lab, where there were demonstrations of experiments going on. Later, in the art room, they bumped into Jake and Amy.

'Hello there, everything all right?' Jake ruffled Jolie's red curls, prompting a squeal of outrage from Amy.

'Dad, don't do that, she's not a baby.'

'Sorry, just couldn't resist.'

He laughed and the sound made Melissa feel all funny inside. She had an insane urge to throw herself around his neck and never let go. This was such a contrast to how her body had responded to Steve's arrival, it almost made her gasp out loud. Instead, she took a deep breath to control her wayward emotions and introduced them to each other. The two men shook hands, both with a slightly wary look about them, like two fighters squaring off, weighing up their opponents.

They chatted about the school for a while and Steve grudgingly admitted that it seemed to have done wonders for his daughter.

'It's the atmosphere, I think,' Jake said. 'And they're just wonderfully supportive of each child as an individual here.'

Melissa wasn't really listening and only made noises of agreement now and again. She was still disconcerted by her different reactions to the two men. It seemed to her everything had turned upside down and the only way she could account for it was to blame it on Roger. Had he messed with her brain? Infiltrated her thought processes and changed her way of thinking? No, she refused to believe it. *He's a ghost, he doesn't exist!*

The logical explanation, however, was that she had at last fallen out of love with Steve, alienated by his attitude. And perhaps slightly *in* love with Jake. *But I barely know the man and I'm not even sure I want a relationship right now.* Did it matter? People could fall in love at first sight and she had been attracted to him from the start, she couldn't deny that. Besides, was there ever a right time for these things? It just happened. *No, this is Roger's doing, it's all his fault.* She put a hand up to her temple, trying to massage it surreptitiously. She wanted to go home and think things through in peace and quiet, but there was no chance of that yet.

Just then, their conversation was interrupted by someone practically shrieking Jake's name across the room. Two women with almost identical sleek and high-lighted hairstyles sashayed over and began to monopolise him. One leaned forward to kiss his cheeks in an exaggerated show of affection, while the other put a proprietorial hand on his arm. Their behaviour made Melissa want to grit her teeth.

'Jake, darling, how are you? You never turned up for Anne's party last week, we were so worried about you. Was it work again?' The taller of the two fixed Jake with a look of concern that was as fake as her spray-tan.

'Er, yes, too much to do as always.' Jake nodded, a slight frown appearing, as if he didn't like being questioned like that.

'Poor man, you work too hard. All work and no play, it just won't do, you know, we've told you before.' The other woman playfully smacked his arm as if he'd been a naughty schoolboy. 'Come on, let's go and have a cup of tea. They must have started serving it by now. The girls can make their own way down to the dining room.'

The two chattering women started to lead Jake away, but he dug in his heels and protested. 'Hold on a minute. I was just talking to Mr Jones and Ms Grantham. Perhaps they'd like to join us?'

The women turned enquiring glances on Steve and Melissa and for once she was glad when Steve answered for both of them. 'Thanks, but we're not quite done here yet. Maybe we'll catch up with you later.'

'Of course. Come and join us when you've finished looking at your daughter's little efforts.'

The woman's words made Melissa see red, since they seemed to imply that Jolie's artwork was nothing to write home about. 'Patronising bitch,' she murmured without thinking after their retreating backs, then looked up as Steve chuckled.

'Too right. Come on, princess,' he ushered Jolie towards the display, 'show us your "little" efforts. I bet they're a hundred percent better than anything that woman's kid can produce.'

His words helped to smooth things over and made Jolie laugh. Melissa was grateful to him. Jolie's self-confidence was still fragile and the stupid woman could have done more damage than she had intended if it hadn't been for Steve.

She watched Jake leave the room and a sensation of acute loss overwhelmed her. It was like a pain twisting her insides and she wanted to bend double to contain it. With an effort she stayed upright, cursing under her breath. *This is crazy.*

'Mum, come and see! And look what Amy's

done. She's incredibly talented and she wants to be an artist when she grows up.'

'Hmm? Oh, yes, very nice.'

Melissa dutifully admired Amy's paintings, which really were extraordinarily good, but her mind was still on Jake. She breathed a sigh of relief when they finally made their way to the dining room for the promised tea. Soon she would be able to leave, then she could escape back to her ordered world of family trees where she felt safe.

'Really, Sir Roger, you seem to have led a most interesting life. It sounds so romantic, being a knight.' The Lady Isobel sighed, laying a dainty hand on his muscular forearm as she spoke. He had to force himself not to snatch his arm away; the gesture felt too familiar after such a short acquaintance.

'Do you think so, my lady?' Roger privately thought that only a silly, empty-headed female could perceive any romance in the life of an itinerant knight. The reality was for the most part tedious and a lot of hard work, although there were moments of excitement from time to time.

'Oh, yes! Only think of all the wonderful places you must have visited, the sights you have seen. We poor ladies seldom travel much.' She fluttered her eyelashes at him, but her limpid blue eyes failed to impress him in the slightest.

Roger realised that before arriving at Idenhurst, Lady Isobel was precisely the type of woman he would have admired. Small and exquisitely beautiful, well-rounded and with a ripple of corn-coloured, elaborately coiffed hair peeping out from under her headdress, she was similar to any number of women he had dallied with in the past. Her rather blatant overtures would have pleased him, rather than repulsed him as they did now, and he would have gladly taken what she was offering. Now, however, he yearned only for one woman. A tall, red-haired female with grey eyes and dimples. He wanted no other.

'Later,' he had promised her, and he suppressed a sigh as he resigned himself to spending more time with Lady Isobel first. She was an important guest, and it wouldn't be wise to offend anyone if he wished to stay on in this household. For the moment, he most certainly did.

And he wasn't leaving without Sibell.

Jake stifled a sigh and followed Anne Dowling and Celia Montgomery to the dining room. They'd been friends with Karen and, since her death, they had been trying to persuade him to socialise, claiming it wasn't good for him to sit at home and brood. Although he knew they were right about that, spending time with them wasn't the answer, he was convinced of that. He couldn't stand either of them.

'Now Jake darling, you are coming to Caroline's party this weekend, aren't you?'

'Party?' he echoed, vaguely remembering a fancy

embossed invite which he'd tossed onto the table without really reading.

'Really, Jake, it's the social event of the season around here. Even you must know that.' Celia laughed and Jake wondered why her low, seductive voice and lovely features didn't have any effect on him. He was sure she was the sort of woman most men would fancy, but she did nothing for him.

'Umm, I'm not sure if I'm free,' he hedged. 'Lots of people off on their holidays still, you know, so we're run off our feet.'

Anne tut-tutted, as if he were a naughty child. 'No, that simply won't do. Tell the others you've got to have a night off. We insist, don't we, Celia?'

'Absolutely.'

Jake felt hunted, trapped by two predators with no way out. But perhaps they were right? What harm could it do to go to a cocktail party, after all? They normally didn't last very long and if he remembered correctly, Caroline whatever-her-name-was entertained on a lavish scale. The canapés would be to die for.

'All right, I'll see what I can do,' he said, caving in. 'Remind me again about the details?'

Anne and Celia were only too happy to fill him in and made him enter the date and time in his diary.

'Now don't you dare stay at home, or we'll come and drag you out of your lair,' Celia purred and slapped him playfully on the arm again, just as Melissa and her ex-husband and daughter entered the dining room. Jake mumbled some reply to Celia, but his entire attention was focused on Melissa, whose brief glance at his two companions was decidedly unfriendly.

For some reason that pleased him, as did the fact that she kept her distance from Steve and carefully positioned Jolie between them when they sat down. The green-eyed monster which had stirred when he was introduced to Steve subsided and a warm glow spread inside him.

There was hope.

CHAPTER 19

A sob escaped Sibell as she undressed in her little chamber at home, folding her best gown carefully and putting it in the chest at the foot of her bed. Roger hadn't kept his promise and she was back at Ashleigh without having exchanged so much as one word with him.

In all fairness, Sibell didn't know how he could have managed it. Her father hadn't let her out of his sight all evening, even going so far as to send one of her brothers to stand guard over her when she went to the privy.

'Rotten swine,' she murmured. They were all in it together. Her brothers knew there would be rewards for them if they helped to marry her off safely to Sir Fulke. 'Curse the lot of them!' She kicked her shoes out of the way and they hit the wall with a satisfying thump.

Too angry to sleep, Sibell tossed and turned on the narrow bed for ages, listening to the loud snores emanating from the next room, where her brothers slept. All was quiet in the hall below, which housed everyone else except her father. He slept alone in the solar at the other end of the hall in a magnificent four-poster bed, big enough for at least four people. Tonight he'd had to be carried in, too drunk to walk. Sibell hoped his head would be extremely sore in the morning. If he asked her for a tisane to help him cure it, she vowed to make him some foul concoction that would make it worse instead.

At first she didn't hear the faint scratching noise, but when it grew louder she sat up in bed and peered into the darkness. It sounded as if it was coming from the window and she padded over on bare feet to have a look. She opened the casement and barely had time to draw in her breath before she heard a muted 'Shhh!' Her heart stopped beating until she realised who was outside.

Roger manoeuvred himself in through the window with some difficulty, only just managing to squeeze his large frame into the narrow opening.

'Roger, have you taken leave of your senses?' she breathed, terrified he might wake her brothers.

He smiled in the faint moonlight and took her into his arms. 'No, sweeting, but I made you a promise and I always keep my promises.' He kissed her to stop any further protests and all thoughts flew out of her head as she melted into his embrace.

Her joy knew no bounds. He had come after all and suddenly everything was right with the world. Her family was forgotten, as was her anger. Roger would somehow protect her and save her from Sir

Fulke and there would be nothing anyone could do about it. Her faith in him was absolute. She hugged him tightly and revelled in the feel of him, so solid, so strong.

His kisses were gentle at first, in the way she had come to expect from him, but soon they became more demanding. Sibell wasn't alarmed and followed his lead without hesitation. A delicious warmth spread through her, right down to her toes, and there was a fire building within her which couldn't be quenched by anyone other than him.

When a while later he lay down next to her on the bed, she made no objections, nor when his questing fingers undressed her. It seemed the most natural thing in the world to give herself to this man, who in a few short weeks had become so precious to her. His caresses awakened longings within her that she had never known existed. She wanted him, as she had never wanted her husband, with an intensity that was almost painful. Roland had been a fumbling boy, whereas Roger was a man. She soon found out the difference it could make as a whole new world was opened up to her. When he guided her to the final shattering explosion he took her cry of pleasure into his mouth. Even if her brothers had been wide awake, they would have heard nothing.

By morning he was gone and only the scent of him remained. Sibell inhaled it and smiled, restraining the urge to sing. Her whole body felt vibrant and alive as never before. She had no regrets.

The room Melissa had chosen as her bedroom wasn't large, but it had the advantage of a private bathroom, as well as the magnificent view. If anyone had asked her, she would have been unable to explain why she had chosen that particular room. She'd had a choice of at least two larger ones, but she hadn't hesitated for a second. She felt at home in this one.

The walls had been in need of redecoration, so she'd painted the plaster with a soft primrose yellow, and bought matching curtains, giving the room a warm and welcoming aura. In one corner was the smallest fireplace she had ever seen, with an exquisitely carved stone surround. She never needed to light a fire in it, so instead she'd put an arrangement of dried flowers in the little grate. They, too, matched the overall colour scheme, as did an old-fashioned quilt Melissa had inherited from her grandmother, which had always been a favourite of hers.

Waking up, the morning after the Open Day, she stretched and gazed around the room contentedly. Somewhere near the ceiling a fly buzzed lazily, and she watched him for a while as he continued his search for a way out.

Melissa rolled over onto her side and her right hand encountered warmth, as if the bed had been shared by someone. With a gasp she sat up and stared at the second pillow. There was an indentation.

Jolie. She must have sneaked in during the night, as she used to do when she was little, and then left before Melissa woke up. Relieved, Melissa drew in a deep breath and slumped back against the pillows with a grin. 'Cheeky little so-and-so . . .' but the smile faded as she recalled that Jolie had spent the night at Amy's house, a last-minute treat the girls had begged for as reward for all their hard work at school. A chill crept up her spine. *So who's been in my bed?*

She closed her eyes and snatches of a dream returned to torment her. Roger again, no doubt about it. He'd held her close, undressed her, caressed her bare skin and . . . The pictures which formed in her mind were too vivid for comfort and she gasped once more. She forced herself to breathe slowly in order to calm her erratic heart-beat, but in the next instant her nostrils detected the scent of him and she turned abruptly to sniff the pillow. Horse, leather and . . . man.

'Nooo!' She threw the pillow clean across the room where it hit the wardrobe with a thud. 'I'm going mad, totally mad.'

Casting the sheet aside she strode into the bathroom and turned on the taps of the shower full blast, as if the water could wash away her thoughts. She found that she was shaking and it took a long time before she calmed down enough to catch hold of the slippery soap. The softness of the lather on her heated skin was almost too much, however, and brought more fevered images into her mind. *His big hand, stroking her breast. The touch of his fingers, slightly rough, sending shockwaves through her body* . . . A sob of frustration escaped her.

The steam rose slowly up to the ceiling before sinking down towards the floor. The swirls floated about and Melissa could have sworn she saw the shape of a man coming closer. With trembling fingers she yanked open the glass door of the shower cubicle, but there was nothing outside except vapour dissolving gently. The cold air hit her skin and she shivered violently.

'Go away, Roger. Leave me alone, damn you!' With a muffled curse she banged the door shut and finished quickly. Once out of the shower she dried herself off with jerky movements, glancing round the room from time to time, but nothing stirred. He was gone. For the moment.

Why wouldn't he leave her alone?

A little moorhen was scuttling across the pond, hooting an anxious warning to her tiny chicks, who all came swimming obediently at her command. They propelled themselves towards safety as fast as their spindly legs could manage. In his haste to reach his mother, one tiny bird even walked on top of a lily pad, which was blocking his way. The long, thin legs on such a small, fuzzy body was both a comical and charming sight. Melissa watched as the whole family disappeared from view under an overhanging bush.

She drew in a deep breath and caught the scent of the enormous wisteria that was climbing up the gable end of the barn behind her. At the bottom the stems were as thick as her calves, and the lilac flowers and clinging tentacles covered almost the entire wall. Spring had arrived with a vengeance.

Absently throwing a piece of mouldy bread to the voracious carp that lurked in the mud at the bottom of the pond, she brooded on her predicament and wondered what to do about it. The fish eagerly sucked soggy bits of bread into their gaping mouths, making a curious smacking sound, but Melissa hardly noticed. She hurled another chunk of bread.

'Are you all right, dear? You look a bit tired.' Dorothy joined Melissa on the wooden bench.

'No, I'm not tired, Dorothy. It's just that I don't know what to do about Roger. He won't leave me alone.'

'You've seen him again?'

'Not exactly.' Melissa felt her cheeks turn warm, as an image of a man making love to her passed swiftly through her mind. She had seen entirely too much of him, in her opinion, but her traitorous body disagreed and responded to the picture by becoming heated, her heart increasing its rhythm. She gripped the bench hard and concentrated on the lovely view. 'I sense him all the time, as if he's trying to tell me something, and he haunts my dreams. I want to help him, but I don't know how. I don't even know his full name, so how can I find out what happened to him?'

'Have you considered hypnotherapy? Perhaps a hypnotist could make you remember more of your dreams. There might be a clue for you.'

Melissa felt herself blush again and shook her head. *God forbid I should talk to someone about sleeping with a ghost!* They would have her sent to an asylum for sure. 'No, I don't think that would help. There must be another way.'

'Come on, let's walk around the garden. It is really so pretty this time of year.'

They wandered aimlessly and Dorothy chatted about the garden, describing the various flowers and vegetables which were grown every year. 'Over there we have strawberries and raspberries – you'll have to try and keep the girls out of there or there'll never be any left to pick – and over here are the blackcurrant bushes. I usually make a lot of jam . . .'

While Dorothy continued with her commentary, Melissa tried once more to make sense of her dreams and Roger's plea for help. She felt sure there must be something she was meant to be doing, but she had no idea what it could be. Her brain seemed unable to come up with anything useful, other than to continue with her research about the house.

As they came to the back of the garden, Dorothy cleared her throat and brought Melissa back to the present. 'Melissa,' she began, 'you're getting too caught up in this ghost business. What I mean is, you're not the first person this has happened to. You remember I told you about my sister and that I overheard a shouting match between her and my mother?' Melissa nodded slowly. 'Yes, well, from what I can remember Mother said the handsome ghost haunts at least one woman of every generation in our family, but it will pass. As I told you, he seems to pick on the girls with reddish hair. Ruth's was almost the same colour as yours. Perhaps Sibell had red hair and he's looking for her? You mustn't let it disturb you, dear. I'm sure he'll give up soon.'

'That's easier said than done,' Melissa scoffed. 'What with Amy's father reminding me of Roger, and all those dreams, how can I forget it?'

'How can you be sure it's not Jake you're dreaming of? You two seemed to hit it off, or am I wrong? I think perhaps your imagination is working overtime and you have confused the two.'

'I wish I could believe you, Dorothy, but there's more to it than that. And although I do like Jake, I'm not sure whether it's just because of his likeness to Roger. The two are confused in my mind, almost as if they overlap somehow. Does that make sense? No, probably not.' An overwhelming weariness washed over her, and her shoulders slumped. 'I don't know about the others Roger has haunted, but this time I'm convinced he won't give up.'

'If you say so, dear.' Dorothy capitulated with a sigh.

Just past the greenhouse, where that year's tomato seedlings were almost ready to be planted out, Melissa stopped and looked around in confusion. 'Where has the walled garden gone?'

'I beg your pardon?'

'The walled kitchen garden. I thought it was over there. I could have sworn I saw it last time I was in this part of the garden.' Melissa pointed to her left, but then she noticed Dorothy staring at her and realised her mind had been playing tricks on her again. Her frustration boiled over and she shouted, 'Oh, for heaven's sake,' startling a couple of rabbits who hopped off into the bushes. She sank down onto the grass cradling her head in her hands.

Dorothy looked thoughtful. 'I see what you mean. Perhaps there is more to this than I thought. You're quite right, actually, there is part of a wall over there, behind those bushes, but I didn't know it was for a kitchen garden. It's very likely though.' She patted her great-niece's back awkwardly. 'I wish I could help you, but this is obviously something only you can sort out. Perhaps if you just wait, the answers will come to you. I think Roger will tell you all when he's good and ready.'

Melissa wanted to believe her, but couldn't rid herself of the despair. She hated the feeling of helplessness. She wanted to be in charge of her own destiny.

Most of all, she wanted to be free of Roger. Or did she?

'Are you sure I was invited as well?' Melissa asked for at least the tenth time as they climbed into Dorothy's tiny car and set off down the drive.

Dorothy sighed. 'Yes, dear. Caroline specifically asked me to bring you so everyone can meet you. You need to make some friends if you're staying in this neighbourhood, you know. And it will take your mind off things.' The words 'ghost' and 'Roger' hung unspoken between them.

Melissa knew Dorothy was right, but when her great-aunt had told her they were invited to a cocktail party at the grandest house for miles around, she'd felt daunted.

'It's just that I don't think these are my sort of people. You may be used to mixing in high circles, but I'm not. Rich people make me feel uncomfortable.'

'I'm rich. Well, comparatively . . .'

Melissa smiled. 'You're different.'

'Maybe there are some others just like me? You shouldn't tar them all with the same brush.'

'Yes, I guess you're right.' Still, Melissa would definitely have preferred to stay at home and put the finishing touches to Jake's family tree, as far as it went at the moment. She had put off calling him until she had it all ready, but she knew she couldn't stall for much longer.

'You're sure Jolie and Amy will be all right with

Savannah?' The grand-daughter of one of Dorothy's friends had agreed to keep an eye on the girls, who were having yet another sleepover, even though they'd initially insisted they were too old to be babysat.

'Of course, why wouldn't they be? Savannah's a lovely girl.'

Melissa stifled a sigh. She was being silly and she knew it.

Lights and noise spilled out of the large mansion as they parked on the driveway next to what seemed like hundreds of other cars. 'Good grief,' Melissa muttered. 'Have they invited the whole county?'

'Oh, Caroline's parties are always well attended. The canapés are out of this world. You'll see.'

They were greeted by their hostess, a stunning lady of indeterminate age, dressed in a glittering sheath and covered with chunky jewellery that had to weigh a ton. 'Dorothy, darling, how lovely to see you,' she gushed and Melissa cringed inwardly. 'And this is your lovely niece, is it? Welcome, my dear, I'm Caroline Brooke-Fearnley. So glad you could come. Do go through, I'm sure Dorothy will introduce you to everyone.'

Shedding their coats in the hall, Melissa tried to shrink behind Dorothy as they entered a room so big it could have been used as a sports hall. It had been decorated with flower arrangements and swags of greenery and there was a small orchestra at one end providing subtle background music.

They could have saved themselves the trouble though, since the noise level from the guests was deafening. Melissa could never understand how a group of people doing nothing but talking could possibly be so loud.

She looked around and wondered if this was what Cinderella had felt like. The only difference was that Melissa's fairy godmother had forgotten to provide her with the requisite sparkly outfit. Her black dress was plain and unadorned, its severity relieved only by a pretty diamond brooch that Dorothy had let her borrow. She was very thankful for that, at least, as every other woman present seemed to shimmer in one way or another. She felt like a peahen in a room full of peacocks, but she knew deep down this was what suited her best, so it didn't bother her much.

An hour later, her head was beginning to throb and her cheek muscles hurt from keeping up the polite rictus grin throughout boring conversations. Although everyone she'd talked to had been welcoming, so far she hadn't met anyone she'd really like to be friends with. All she wanted was to go home. And if one more person asked what she did for a living and where Mr Grantham was, she thought she would scream.

Where's Prince Charming when you need him? she wondered, taking a fortifying sip of her drink.

Just at that moment, the crowd shifted and she caught sight of Jake standing over by the wall.

She hadn't expected him to be there, although why not, she couldn't say. Her breath caught in her throat at the sight of him and she stood entranced, just staring in his direction. He looked different, perhaps because she'd never seen him in a formal suit and tie before, but unlike her, he seemed to blend in perfectly. He was talking to Caroline, who had one arm around his waist and was laughing up at him coquettishly. This made something ugly stir inside Melissa and she shook herself mentally and turned away.

'For heaven's sake, what is the matter with you?' she muttered. *Jake is not Prince Charming, any more than Steve was. And he's perfectly entitled to talk to any woman he likes.* Was Roger playing tricks on her again? she wondered. Could he influence her even in someone else's house? The thought gave her goose pimples.

She finished her drink and grabbed another glass of champagne from a passing waiter, then took a large gulp and headed for the door. Out in the vast hall, the air was cooler and Melissa breathed deeply. She was shaken by her reaction to Jake. There was no doubt she was very attracted to him, more so for every time they met it would seem, but why? Had she just struck lucky and happened to meet a man with whom she had exceptional chemistry, or was there something more sinister going on?

She rubbed a hand over her brow, trying to ease the tension. The simple truth was she didn't have any answers. Roger was clouding her mind, deluding her and . . .

'So this is where you're hiding yourself.'

Jake's voice, so like Roger's, made Melissa jump and she turned too quickly and spilled some of the champagne onto the floor. 'Oops . . . Hello, Jake. What brings you out here?'

He smiled and bent to whisper, 'Remember what you said about preferring a good book and some chocolate? I couldn't agree with you more right now.'

Disturbed by his nearness, Melissa found herself stammering. 'R-really? Well, I'm glad I'm not alone, then.'

He put his head to one side and studied her with an appreciative glint in his eyes. 'You look absolutely lovely tonight. You should wear dresses more often.'

Melissa felt colour flood her cheeks. 'Thank you, but I prefer jeans.'

He glanced again at her legs and murmured, 'Shame.' Pulling his eyes away, he cleared his throat. 'Well, now that I'm out here in the hall, I think I might just make my escape. Caroline won't notice with so many other people to talk to and I really should get back to the surgery. There are several patients needing attention, especially my favourite, a little hedgehog who had pneumonia. I want to check on them all.'

'Hedgehog with what? Surely not?'

'Oh, yes. They can get it too, quite badly. But

he's back to normal now after a course of antibiotics. I just like to keep an eye on him to make sure he stays well. You should come and see him sometime; he's a sweet little thing. Amy wants me to keep him, but of course that's impossible.'

'Impossible, yes . . .' *Oh, Lord, am I turning into a parrot now?*

'Right, well, I'll be off then. Please, don't tell on me.'

'No . . . no, I won't.'

Halfway to the door he turned. 'I nearly forgot. When can I come over to see that family tree you promised to show me? Would tomorrow be any good?'

'Umm, yes, sure. Tomorrow evening is fine.'

She leaned against the wall after he'd gone and closed her eyes. Something inside her was desperate to see Jake again and it scared the wits out of her.

If only she could be sure of the reason.

CHAPTER 20

'By all the saints, Sibell, what kept you so long?' Henry snarled as Sibell took her place next to him at the table. 'I swear you'll make Sir Fulke a useless wife if you can't even attend meals on time.'

Sibell muttered something about a kitchen disaster that had to be dealt with, but it was a lie and she hoped no one would question her more closely. She knew she was late, and had been for the past few mornings, but in truth she couldn't help it. Every day for the last week she had woken later than usual and as soon as she tried to get up her stomach rebelled and she'd been vilely sick. Fortunately, she had the little chamber to herself so no one else had found out about her affliction, but she had to tread warily. At first she'd thought it was something she had eaten, but when it happened again and again, she began to suspect another cause. And that was something she definitely had to hide.

'Henry's right, girl, tardiness won't be tolerated from the mistress of the household. Nor bad housekeeping – why is this bread stale?' Her father added his grumbling to that of his sons, and threw a half-chewed crust onto the table.

Sibell bit into her own bread, which wasn't stale at all, and guessed her father must be suffering from toothache. Anything harder than sops would hurt him to chew.

'Yes, it's grateful we'll be when we can hire ourselves a more efficient housekeeper,' Henry spat, giving her a sour look. 'I pity Sir Fulke, truly I do.'

Sibell kept silent and tried to stem the tide of nausea threatening to overcome her. She had learned early on that it was never any use retaliating or talking back since Henry would always exact his revenge somehow at a later date. No, far safer to keep one's mouth shut and endure his jibes.

It was with great relief that she escaped into the garden some time later to breathe in huge gulps of fresh air. She sank down under an old apple tree in the orchard and allowed her body to relax. To her relief, the nausea slowly ebbed away. Henry's parting shot was still echoing in her brain and she shook her head, unable to understand his unreasonable hatred of her. It had always been that way, for as long as she could remember, and one particular instance from her childhood came back to her as she closed her eyes.

'Who needs girls? Father says they're useless.' Henry's sneering voice had interrupted a nine-year-old Sibell as she was concentrating on her sampler. Tongue poking out slightly from one corner of her mouth, she'd been making a huge effort to set the tiniest stitches she could manage in order to please her mother, Elinor, who was unwell. She looked up with a frown.

'What do you know? You're just a nasty little boy,' she retorted and almost added, 'Mother says so,' but thought better of it.

Henry came to stand in front of her, closely followed by Edmund, who bent down to rip the piece of cloth out of her hands with a swift movement. Edmund and Simon always followed Henry's lead whenever their oldest brother, John, wasn't around.

'No! Give it back, you'll ruin it!' she shrieked, jumping up to try and grab her handiwork back. Edmund held it out of her reach and since he was so much taller, her puny efforts were no use. She felt tears prick her eyelids and tried to hold them back. She glared at her half-brothers. 'Why do you hate me so much? What have I ever done to you?'

'You don't belong here. We don't want you or your mother. She is forever scolding us, telling us to wash, mind our manners, not spit on the floor . . .'

'Well, you shouldn't behave like such oafs then, should you?' Sibell interjected.

'Hah! This is our father's house. We can do what we like and we don't need some weak-brained female telling us what to do. The sooner you're gone, the better.'

'Gone? We're not going anywhere.' Sibell frowned at him, baffled by his words.

'Well, maybe you're not, but your mother . . .' Henry shrugged and turned to leave the hall.

'My mother? Where is she going? What do you mean?' Surely her father couldn't send them away? But her half-brother didn't reply.

Edmund threw the by now crumpled sampler into her lap and gave her a smirk before following his brother out the door. Simon brought up the rear. Sibell stared after them with a sinking feeling in the pit of her stomach, wondering what they meant.

Godwin, the third oldest of her half-brothers, had watched the scene in silence from his perch on a bench near a window. He rose slowly now, and came over to pat her awkwardly on the head.

'Don't mind them, they're only making mischief. You are not leaving Ashleigh.'

She looked up at him with gratitude and a hesitant smile. Smaller than his brothers, and the only one with true blond hair rather than red, he had never treated her badly, but he seldom spoke to her or anyone else.

'I'm sorry I cannot defend you against them, but the others are all bigger than me . . .' He shrugged philosophically and walked away before she could reply. She knew he was always beaten into submission should he ever dare to question his brothers or his father, and there was nothing anyone could do about it. She didn't blame him for not coming to her aid.

When her mother died two days later she understood what Henry had meant, however. Everyone else had known that Elinor would not recover from her illness, but no one had thought to tell Sibell. Her life, which had been bearable as long as her mother was alive, became purgatory. For several months she endured abuse and neglect until her father unwittingly saved her by accepting Lady Maude's invitation for her to foster with the Presseille family. Sibell had thanked God for it ever since.

She sighed and stared at the blue summer sky now. Her life had once again become unbearable after her husband's death, but she was older now and she vowed to fight with every means at her disposal. She put a hand to her abdomen. As yet there was no sign there might be a life in there, but she was fairly certain she was with child. The thought thrilled and alarmed her at the same time and her heart increased its rhythm.

'Don't worry, little one,' she whispered, 'I'll make sure you don't have to grow up here with my father and half-brothers, no matter what it takes.'

Melissa dressed casually for her meeting with Jake, in black jeans and a charcoal-coloured sweater that hugged her figure, but she couldn't resist spraying on a whiff of exotic perfume.

'Idiot,' she murmured. 'He'll think you've made a special effort just for him.'

When he arrived with Amy in tow, however, she was inordinately pleased to see the appreciation in his eyes as they scanned her quickly. She hurried to put some distance between them, otherwise she knew she wouldn't be able to think, never mind speak coherently. Amy rushed off upstairs as usual and Jake followed Melissa into the dining room.

'Dorothy not in tonight?' he asked casually.

'No. Whist at the Partridges. She'll be back soon, I think.' Melissa tried not to show her nervousness at being alone with him in the room and took refuge in business. 'Right, here we are.' She had spread the family tree and other papers out on the dining table and launched into a lengthy explanation before he could ask any more questions. Jake listened without interrupting until she ran out of breath.

'So you mean my name should really be Presseille?' Jake grinned, pronouncing the word with a horrendous mock-French accent. 'That sounds awfully grand.'

A gurgle of laughter escaped her. 'Yes, but it would suit you, I think. Shame you don't own Idenhurst anymore. I wonder where it is, or was? I have looked on the map, but there doesn't seem to be a property of that name anywhere around here.'

'Perhaps it was renamed or fell into ruin?'

'Yes. The family might have moved to another

manor. Rich families usually had several and moved between them. I've been in contact with the local historian, but he didn't know either. He's going to try and find out so I'll let you know what he says.'

'So this Sir Gilbert fellow is the earliest Presseille you've found?' Jake pointed to the top of her chart.

'Yes, but I haven't connected you to him for certain yet. I know he was alive in 1461, but then there's a gap until 1495, which is as far back as we got with the manor court roll. There may be more, but we'll have to wait until the conservationists have had a look at it. The damn thing is stuck you see. Shame, I had hoped to find Roger.' Her hand flew to cover her mouth and she looked at him in consternation. Jake lifted an eyebrow questioningly.

'Roger? Who's Roger?'

'Oh, nobody. That is, er . . . someone connected with Ashleigh. I . . . I got confused and forgot which house we were talking about for a minute.' She turned away and fiddled with some of the papers on the table, trying to keep her cool.

Jake was nobody's fool, however, and now his curiosity must have been piqued. When Melissa looked up again she saw his eyes narrow. 'Hang on a minute, didn't you call me Roger that time when you fainted?'

Melissa ran a hand through her hair and sighed. 'Umm, yes.' She took a step away from him and hugged herself defensively. 'Look, I don't want to talk about it. If I tell you, you'll think I'm crazy and you won't let your daughter be friends with Jolie any more and then she'll be heartbroken, and how am I going to explain that to her and–' Her ramblings came to an abrupt halt as she glanced up and noticed him frowning at her.

'Melissa.' He took a firm grip on her shoulder with one hand and made her look him straight in the eyes. 'What's going on? I promise I won't think you're crazy, whatever you tell me.'

'That's what you say now,' she muttered, trying unsuccessfully to evade his hand.

He wouldn't let her go and as he looked into her eyes, she knew she had to tell him the truth. It was, after all, affecting him too, although he didn't know it yet. She sighed.

'Tell me, Melissa. Please?' he pleaded. 'This has something to do with me, I can feel it, so I think I have the right to know.'

'Okay, fine, but I'm sure you won't believe me. Let's go and sit down, this is going to take a while.' Her back straight, as if she were going into battle, she led the way into the sitting room. Jake took a seat opposite her in one of the huge wing chairs and waited patiently for her to begin.

Melissa silently cursed her big mouth. She had made up her mind to be businesslike during this meeting and had succeeded quite well for a while, but as she had explained to him about the various people on the chart and their relationships to one another, she had lost herself in the past. As always, she'd been caught up in the excitement of gene-alogy and Roger's name had just slipped out.

She fidgeted, trying to concentrate on the matter in hand, and decided that he deserved the whole truth. Hesitant at first, she told him about seeing the ghost. She described the uncanny resemblance between Roger and himself and recounted Dorothy's story about Sibell. She left nothing out, except the strange emotions Roger evoked in her, or the feelings he himself inspired. But Jake again came to his own conclusions.

'So you think that I'm Roger, returned from the dead, and you're Sibell reincarnated? Is that it?' He was frowning and she could tell the idea didn't appeal to him in the slightest. Obviously she'd been wrong and Roger was only working his magic on her. She wasn't sure whether that was a relief or not.

'No, not exactly, but . . .'

Jake shook his head and tried to make light of the matter. 'It sounds like that old horror movie *The Mummy* with Boris Karloff.'

'Don't be s-silly,' she stammered, realising how stupid it all seemed when discussed rationally. Nevertheless, she had seen a ghost and she couldn't doubt the evidence of her own eyes. 'I think perhaps he's influencing us somehow, bringing us together, but I don't believe in souls returning to possess people. Anyway, why would he ask me to help him, if his soul was already in you? It doesn't make sense.'

'No, it doesn't. Also, if they had simply come back as us there would be no need for a ghost, would there? Or there should be a ghost of Sibell too, but nobody has ever seen her, have they?'

'No, not that I know of. It's all so frustrating.' She bit her lip. 'I don't even know his surname, so I can't look for any record of him. That was another reason why I was hoping he was a member of your family. I was sure he must be, you look so alike.'

Jake shook his head and pushed back his floppy fringe with impatient fingers. 'This all seems a bit far-fetched.' He looked at Melissa. 'On the other hand, there *is* obviously something weird going on. Your strange reaction to me that first day proves you're telling the truth, at least as you see it. And as for me, well . . .'

'I'm glad you don't think I'm completely insane.' She gave a brittle little laugh. 'As long as Amy can still come over and hang out with Jolie, all is well.' With a resigned shrug she added, 'Could we just forget the whole thing? If he ever appears again, I'll ask for his full name, date of birth and every- thing else. Until then, let's leave it.'

'Good idea. Why don't we do something entirely normal, like go and see a movie? There must be something on at the local flea pit.'

Melissa knew she shouldn't go out with him, but suddenly she was past caring. Perhaps it would be better to get it out of her system. She had a feeling her attraction to Jake wouldn't go away by itself, no matter what she did.

'Sure, why not?' she heard herself reply and was rewarded by a blinding smile.

Letting out his breath slowly, as if he'd been unsure of her answer, Jake suggested they meet up in half-an-hour. He left soon after, taking his new family tree with him. Dorothy, when she returned from the whist playing, happily agreed to keep an eye on the two girls, who had already decided that Amy would spend the night at the manor.

'Have a lovely time, dear,' Dorothy trilled.

It sounded so normal, but Melissa knew her life was far from ordinary at the moment. Would it ever be again?

CHAPTER 21

The film at the local cinema was a comedy, but although she laughed in all the right places, Melissa could never afterwards remember which movie they'd seen. She was far too aware of the man sitting next to her, his thigh touching hers. Every time he moved, little sparks shot through her, making her heartbeat erratic and her stomach flutter. It was agony and ecstasy all at once. They shared popcorn and some chocolate and halfway through the film he took her hand, lacing his fingers with hers. She never wanted him to let go. She felt like a silly teenager on her first date.

As they poured out into the High Street together with the other cinema-goers, Jake kept hold of her hand. 'Do you want to share a Chinese take-away? I'm starving, and we can eat at my house since the kids are over at your place.'

Melissa just nodded, not trusting herself to speak. She was afraid of being alone with him, yet she felt safe at the same time. It was very confusing.

She followed him into his home after the short drive back. Ashleigh Cottage surprised her – although it looked small from the outside, its rooms were unexpectedly large and bright.

'Oh, this is lovely! How did you make it look so spacious?' she exclaimed, glancing round the living room with appreciation.

'We knocked down as many walls as we possibly could, without making the whole house come tumbling down, and then painted everything in light colours. Plus, we added an extension at the back. It was a compromise. Karen wanted a "cute cottage", but I can't stand small spaces, so this way we both got what we wanted. Sort of.'

Jake led the way into the kitchen and switched on the recessed lights. The walls were painted a warm shade of primrose and everything was spotlessly clean. Although the fittings were rustic and in keeping with their surroundings, Melissa could see that no expense had been spared in equipping the kitchen with all the latest gadgets, including a fridge with an automatic ice-making facility.

'This is nice too, and so tidy. You must be very domesticated, or is this Amy's doing?'

'Thank you. No, I'm afraid neither of us can take any credit for this. It's all due to Mrs Johnson, who keeps it sparkling clean.'

'Ah, yes, I remember Amy mentioning her. She's your housekeeper, right? She must be a real treasure.'

'That she is. We couldn't survive without her.' Jake set the food out on a counter and dragged two bar stools over. 'Would you like some wine? I think there's a bottle of white in the fridge.'

'Yes, please.' Perhaps it would calm her nerves, she thought. They appeared to be tauter than violin strings and about to snap any minute. When he handed her the glass, she sipped the drink gratefully and tried to slow her breathing as she waited for the alcohol to work its magic.

They ate in companionable silence and Melissa found she was ravenous, despite her inner tension. When they came to the dessert, however, she had reached her limit.

'No, thanks. I couldn't eat another bite. Honest.'

'Just try a small piece of this. It's heavenly.' Jake proffered a bit of sticky apple on expertly held chopsticks.

'Oh, all right. Just the one.' Melissa opened her mouth obediently, and Jake watched her with a strange look in his eyes as she took the morsel he was holding out to her.

Something happened in that moment and she felt as if she were under a spell. She chewed, swallowed and licked the sweetness off her lips. He gazed at her mouth the whole time and it appeared to have him spellbound. She knew without a doubt he was going to kiss her this time. Slowly he lowered his head towards her, giving her every opportunity to escape, but she remained motionless, just looking at him, waiting for the inevitable. She saw the icy blue depths of his eyes darken with desire and then he captured her mouth in a butterfly kiss. But it wasn't enough. Not nearly enough.

When she made no protest he deepened the kiss, and it was as if he had released a floodgate. Somehow they were no longer sitting on the bar stools, but standing up and her arms were round his neck. He held her as close as he possibly could without physically crushing her. It felt wonderful and she snuggled even closer. Jake groaned.

Melissa couldn't have stopped him if her life depended on it. His kisses were as intoxicating as the strongest drug and she loved the feel of him, hard against her softness. She ran her hands over his back, his arms, then through his hair. She couldn't get enough of touching him; she wanted more. She pulled him closer still, rubbing herself against him, and arched her back as his mouth explored her neck and below.

'Oh, God, Sibell, you're so beautiful!'

The words seemed to echo round the room and killed Melissa's passion faster than a bucket of ice over the head would have done. With a gasp, she abruptly let go of Jake and pushed hard against his chest.

'What did you say?'

He blinked at her in confusion, his eyes still hazy with desire. 'Nothing. I didn't say a word.' His arms were still around her and she pushed frantically to make him release her. 'What's the matter?'

'It was Roger. He's doing this to us.'

'Roger? What are you talking about?' He let her

269

go reluctantly and ran a hand through his hair, messing it up even further.

Melissa looked at him, biting her lip. 'The bloody ghost. He spoke to me, while we were kissing. He spoke to me as if I was Sibell and he was you. He-he said I was beautiful.' She turned away, shaking, and began to gather up plates and cutlery with unnecessary force.

'That's impossible. You shouldn't watch films like *The Exorcist*, you know. Besides, you *are* beautiful. The ghost has good taste.' Jake tried to make light of the matter, putting his hands around her waist from behind, but Melissa wasn't having it. She swivelled round to look him in the eyes, her own narrowed in anger.

'No. And that's not all. I also felt as if I knew how it would be to make love to you. *As if I'd done it before!* Now why should that be?'

Jake sighed and closed his eyes. 'I don't know, Melissa.'

'Can you honestly tell me you didn't feel the same?'

'I don't think so. I mean, of course I've fantasised about your body, but that was just my imagination. I have no idea what you really look like without your clothes on. Christ, I've been thinking of nothing but kissing you all week. That doesn't mean I knew exactly what it was going to be like.' He spread his hands in a helpless gesture. 'Come on, Melissa, this is crazy. It's just that you've been thinking too much about this ghost business. Your mind wasn't functioning normally. That's all there is to it.'

'No. I'm not buying it, Jake. Maybe he's not affecting you, but he's definitely put a spell on me.'

'So what you're saying is that if you weren't under a spell, you wouldn't look twice at me? Great. Thanks a lot.' Jake sounded hurt and Melissa felt torn, but at the same time she was so confused.

'No, of course not, but . . . Oh, I can't explain it.' Her voice was decidedly wobbly. She was shaking so badly she could hardly lift her glass of wine, but somehow she managed it and took a fortifying draught. She was scared. Terrified, in fact, and she didn't have a clue what to do about it. 'I knew I shouldn't have come here,' she muttered through clenched teeth.

Jake tried again and gathered her stiff body close. 'Melissa, darling, it will be all right. Let's just forget it. I didn't mean to rush you. We can take it slowly.'

She leaned against him briefly, wavering, then tore herself away. 'No, Jake, it won't work. Not until I've solved the mystery of what Roger wants. When I make love with someone I want to be sure I'm doing it for the right reason. I'm not having this. It scares the hell out of me.'

He walked her home in silence along the dark country lane. Not once did she look at him. She couldn't trust herself not to respond to him again.

She let him kiss her goodbye, but only on the cheek. It was as far as she dared to go.

'Well, Hubert, and what advice do you have for me today? I've made a right mess of things, haven't I?'

After a sleepless night Jake had gone to the surgery to check on his little hedgehog patient, among others, and to find something to occupy himself with. The silence in the cottage was oppressive and he couldn't stand it for another second.

Hubert made a small noise and looked at him out of eyes that were definitely as bright as they should be. The antibiotics had cured him and Jake noticed the little animal had eaten all the food left for him. He opened the cage door and fetched fresh water.

'I really don't know what happened last night. Do you think I'm possessed by a ghost? Could I have said something without noticing?' As if tired by the conversation, Hubert turned his back on Jake. 'No, it sounds too crazy, doesn't it?' Jake sighed deeply and ran tired fingers over the stubble on his chin, which he hadn't had the patience to remove before he left home. 'But I guess I should have mentioned those weird dreams I've been having, huh? They seem to be connected to the whole ghost business somehow. I don't really want to tell Melissa, though. If it's all in her imagination I don't want to make things worse. Heck, I don't even know if I imagined it all myself!'

He sighed again. 'But I can't just let her walk away either, Hubert. I've got to change her mind somehow.' It was Hubert's turn to sigh, or at least that's what his snuffling noise sounded like, and Jake smiled to himself. 'You're right, patience is probably the answer. I'll have to be patient like you, little guy. If she feels anything like I do, she won't let this silly ghost business come between us. Otherwise I'll just have to convince her, won't I?'

That settled, he went to check on his other patients.

CHAPTER 22

'Mum, come quickly!' Jolie burst into the sitting room a few days later and skidded to a halt inside the door.

'What? What's wrong?' Melissa had just sat down with a mug of tea and made herself comfortable. She scanned her daughter to check for cuts or bruises, but couldn't see anything. 'Are you hurt?'

'No, it's Russ. He's dying!'

Melissa took in Jolie's pale face and amber eyes wide with distress. 'Surely not?' She shot out of her chair. 'Has he had an accident?' She knew Jolie had a tendency to over-dramatise things, but this time she sounded serious.

'No, but he's in the kitchen and he's throwing up all over the place, and . . .'

'All right, all right. Calm down.' They headed for the kitchen at a run. 'He's probably just eaten too much, he can be such a little pig, you know. Perhaps he stole tonight's dinner? Dorothy left it on the counter.'

Upon entering the kitchen, however, she was filled with remorse at her words and had to admit Jolie had been right to be concerned this time.

The dinner was still intact while Russ was lying next to the Aga, shivering and looking extremely sorry for himself. He barely managed a small thump of his tail in greeting and let out the occasional whimper. As Melissa knelt in front of him, he looked at her out of sad, slightly glazed eyes, his nose resting on his front paws. All around him were the former contents of his stomach.

Jolie held her nose with two fingers. 'See, I told you.'

'Yes, well, he certainly doesn't look very well, poor thing, but I hardly think he's dying.' Melissa stroked the silky head and felt his nose, which was warm and dry to touch. 'Oh, dear, it's not cold and wet. I've heard that's not a good sign,' she muttered.

'We'll have to take him to the vet, won't we?' Jolie said. 'Auntie Dorothy isn't coming back for hours and we can't leave him like this.'

'No, we can't. You're right.' Melissa sighed. There was only one veterinary practice within easy reach and that was where Jake was a partner. She had successfully avoided him ever since their disastrous date, and she'd hoped she wouldn't have to meet him again until she had solved the mystery of Roger. Jake had called and asked to speak to her, but she'd told Dorothy to say she was busy.

Melissa caressed the little dog's head. There was no help for it, they had to go, and perhaps if she was lucky Jake's partner would be on duty. 'Stay with him while I ring and ask if we can bring Russ straight away.' Jolie nodded.

Fifteen minutes later they were ushered into the small surgery.

'Hello, Melissa, Jolie.' Jake smiled at them in welcome and Melissa tried to smile back while stifling a groan.

Just my luck. But she couldn't very well refuse to let Jake treat the dog. That would have seemed ridiculous.

He took Russ from her arms and lifted him onto the table. 'And what's the matter with you, little guy?' He examined the quivering dog carefully. 'He's been sick, did you say?' Melissa nodded.

'Yes, very.'

'Yep, nothing left inside him, definitely not,' Jolie agreed and made a face.

When Jake looked up at her, Melissa realised hiding herself away hadn't changed the fact that she still wanted him. And wanted him badly. Perhaps she had been a bit hasty and maybe he'd been right? How could a ghost possibly influence them? Then, with a shiver, she remembered the strange sensation that she had known exactly how it would feel to make love to Jake. Even if the voice inside her head could be ascribed to an overactive imagination, this eerie foreknowledge could not. No, Roger was up to his tricks, she had no doubt about it. She became aware Jake was saying something to her.

'I'm sorry, what was that?'

'I said, I think Russ has just eaten something he shouldn't have done in the garden or while out walking. Perhaps he took a lick at a dead rabbit or something. It's happened before. There's no need to worry, I'll just give him an injection and he should be okay soon. Don't feed him today and only give him chicken and rice tomorrow.'

'Well, that's a relief. He looked awful and I was afraid I would have to give Dorothy some bad news when she came home.'

Jake smiled. 'No, he's just feeling very sorry for himself.' He glanced behind him where Jolie was wandering around inspecting everything with curiosity. 'Why don't you go through that door,' he said to her, 'and say hello to Hubert. He's in the third cage from the left. In fact, you're lucky he's still here. He was going to leave a couple of weeks ago, but the old lady who brought him in had a fall and won't be out of hospital until next Saturday.'

'Hubert? Who's that?'

'Go and see for yourself.' Jolie didn't need to be told twice. As soon as she was out of earshot, Jake turned back to Melissa. 'I need to talk to you,' he whispered. 'Can't we have dinner or something? Please? I know you've been avoiding me and I understand your reasons, but I really want to see you.' Melissa felt herself weakening and he must have sensed it since he continued his persuasions. 'How am I going to convince you I'm right if you won't even talk to me? Come on, Melissa. What can it hurt to just eat together?'

Melissa wavered as he came to stand close to her. The look in his azure eyes almost made her give in, but she turned away and steeled herself.

'No, not yet. Please, you must give me more time, Jake, I . . .' She couldn't explain. Not even to herself. 'I need to work this out on my own.'

'Okay fine, but I won't give up, you know. I can't rationalise what happened, but I really think it has a logical explanation.'

'Maybe . . .'

'Oh, Mum, come and look! Hubert is a baby hedgehog and he's sooooo cute.' Jolie came hurtling back into the room and interrupted their private conversation. Melissa dutifully admired Hubert, but although she had to admit he was sweet, her heart wasn't in it. She returned to Ashleigh with Russ and her daughter, feeling torn, but determined. *Am I being silly?* She didn't think so.

Melissa had just finished the dishes and was coming out of the kitchen later that evening when she heard a scream from upstairs. She rushed over to the stairs, taking them two at a time, and collided with Jolie, who threw herself into her mother's arms and burst into tears.

'Sweetheart, what on earth is the matter?' Melissa looked at her daughter in dismay.

'Oh, Mum, I'm so glad you're all right,' Jolie sobbed.

278

Melissa raised her eyebrows and hugged her child close. 'But why shouldn't I be? I've only been washing dishes. Not a dangerous occupation, you know.'

'I . . . I thought Jake was going to k-kill you,' Jolie wailed. 'H-he had a huge sword and he went into your bedroom just now. At least I think it was him. Only, now he's g-gone . . .'

'What on earth are you talking about?' Melissa frowned. 'Come on, let's sit down on the stairs for a minute. Now tell me exactly what happened, from the beginning, please.'

'Well, I was doing my homework, listening to some music and then suddenly I felt someone touch my cheek. I thought it was you and kind of shook it off because I was in a hurry to finish my essay so I can go riding with Amy tomorrow. When it happened again, I got annoyed and turned around to tell you not to sneak up on me like that, but there was no one there.'

'I see.' A cold knot was forming in Melissa's stomach, and she waited anxiously for the rest of the story.

'So then I went over to the door and looked into the hallway. At the end, just turning right into the older part of the house, I thought I saw Amy's dad going towards your bedroom. It happened so quickly, like he was there one minute and gone the next, but I decided to run after him because I definitely saw a sword and that scared me.'

'A sword? You're sure about that?'

'Mm-hmm. It was sort of gleaming when he turned the corner. It . . . it looked very dangerous.' Jolie paused to take a deep breath and Melissa could feel her daughter's shoulders still shaking. 'I called out to him to wait, but he'd disappeared. The only room he could have gone into was your bedroom, so I panicked. I thought he'd gone mad!'

'So then what did you do?'

'I ran into your room, but there was no one there and the windows were all shut. It smelled funny in there, kind of like Amy's horse's stables and it was freezing cold. I thought I heard someone laughing. That's when I got really scared . . .'

Melissa gritted her teeth. 'You must have seen Roger.'

'Who's Roger? And why is he sneaking around the house with a sword? You can't let him do that, Mum.'

Melissa was silent for a long time, then said quietly, 'He's a ghost, dear, and I've seen him, too.'

'A ghost?' Jolie began to shake even more and Melissa gathered her close for another hug.

'Don't worry, sweetheart, I don't think he'll hurt you. It's not you he's looking for.' She patted Jolie's cheek soothingly. 'I think he's searching for his lost love, Sibell. I was hoping you wouldn't find out, but I think I'd better tell you the whole story.' She told Jolie everything she had found out so far.

'But, Mum, he touched me. He patted my cheek, just like you do sometimes. Only it felt cold.' Jolie shivered again and lifted her gaze to her mother's. 'What does it mean? What does he want?'

'I'm not sure, but I'm definitely going to find out.' Jolie seemed slightly reassured by the grim determination in Melissa's voice. 'As for why he came to see you, it was probably because he had a daughter, too. Perhaps he thought you were Meriel? At least, I hope that was the reason . . .' She decided not to tell Jolie that Roger apparently haunted a red-haired girl of every generation. Had he lost faith in Melissa and was now trying his luck with Jolie instead? That didn't bear thinking about. 'Anyway,' she continued brightly, 'you'd better finish your homework now. There's nothing to be frightened of, ghosts can't hurt you, but come and sit at the kitchen table and I'll keep you company.'

'Okay. And can I sleep in your room tonight, please? I don't want him sneaking up on me again.'

Melissa nodded, relieved Jolie had suggested it herself. She hadn't wanted to seem too panicky, but it would be good to have Jolie nearby during the night. 'Good idea.'

While Jolie went to fetch her homework, Melissa stayed on the stairs, deep in thought.

'Ghosts can't hurt you . . .' Brave words to soothe a child, but were they true? She wished she knew. The air around her was chilly and Melissa looked up, half-expecting to see Roger materialise in front of her, but the hall remained empty.

'I'm trying to help you, Roger, really I am, but

don't mess with my child. Do you hear me? Don't ever touch my daughter again!' She waited for a reply of some sort, a signal that he had understood, but nothing stirred except a slight draught that brushed her cheek.

'I'll take that as a yes,' she whispered. She found that she was shaking, too, and leaned her head on her knees with a deep sigh, adding, 'Damn you.'

The flames of the bonfire licked the dry branches carefully at first, but soon they devoured them with greed as they leapt higher and the wood began to disintegrate. Sibell watched from the shadows outside the circle of excited faces, wanting to see but not be seen.

The bonfire was lit every year on the eve of Beltane. Every cooking fire for miles around was extinguished and ritually rekindled the next day, celebrating the beginning of summer. The ceremony was an ancient one and no one knew for certain where it had originated. It was simply the tradition.

A grubby urchin had put the note into her hand in the general *mêlée* after church the day before, and she hadn't dared to read it until she was safe in her own chamber. 'By the fire tomorrow.' Only four words, but her heart had soared with joy.

She shivered slightly now and huddled closer into her dark cloak, making sure the hood shadowed her face and hid any wayward tresses of her shining, red hair. It hadn't been easy to escape from the house unseen, but with her skirts bunched around her waist she'd managed to climb to the ground via the tree Roger had used. Her father, who much preferred to drink himself into oblivion at home, had fallen asleep in the hall.

Three of Sibell's brothers, Henry, Simon and Edmund, were all part of the merry group around the fire. She shook her head in silent despair – really, someone should curb their excesses, she thought. Staggering around, singing bawdy ditties and grabbing anything in a skirt which came within grasp, they were highly conspicuous. Godwin stayed away from the others, but he was rowdy, nonetheless. Still, Sibell supposed she ought to be grateful to them this evening. They were of great help by diverting attention away from their sister.

She shivered. There were unpredictable forces at work this night and one had to beware of the supernatural. It was Beltane after all, a night of danger, when the powers of witches, fairies and the dead were strong. The priests forbade such beliefs, but they still lingered among superstitious country folk. Sibell prayed that whatever forces were present would be on her side tonight.

A large, warm hand appeared out of nowhere to envelop her smaller one and tug her gently into the shadows. She looked up, eyes shining in the moonlight, into the face of her beloved. He smiled, then pulled her further into the forest. There would be many couples in the bushes this night. If they wanted privacy, which they most definitely did, they had to find a spot as far away from the others as possible. Sibell followed him in silence, trusting him implicitly.

She would follow him anywhere.

CHAPTER 23

'**M**um! *Mummy!*' Melissa heard the impatient thump as Jolie threw her schoolbag down on the hall floor and ran upstairs, taking the steps two at a time.

'Up here, sweetie,' she called from the second floor, where she was sitting in a lovely, bright room she had recently converted into an office. Dorothy claimed the room had been empty for years and was happy for Melissa to redecorate it and install an internet connection. A dormer window showed far-reaching views of the surrounding countryside and the roof sloped on one side, giving the room a slightly lop-sided feeling, which added to its charm.

A large table, which Dorothy had unearthed in the attic, served as a desk and had been placed to face the window. Melissa found it a relief to be able to spread out all her charts and notes without having to move everything at mealtimes.

When Jolie arrived Melissa was on the floor on a faded old Chinese rug with a pile of notes spread out all around her. She looked up with a smile. 'Hi there. Had a good day?'

'Yes, fine thanks, but Mum, guess what? There's going to be a bonfire on Friday night and we all have to dress up as witches and warlocks and bring something to drink and a sausage to grill, or maybe marshmallows.' Jolie waved her hands around as she finally ran out of breath.

Melissa held up a hand, laughing. 'Whoa, hold on a minute. Calm down.'

'Yes, but can I go? Please?'

'I don't see why not, but what's this all in aid of?'

'Beltane, the most magical night of the year when all the supernatural things come out. Miss Kavanagh told us all about it today.'

'Supernatural?' Melissa felt a niggle of discomfort at hearing that word. She tried not to show it. 'Right, yes of course. I should have remembered. Okay, we'll find you some black clothes and I'll buy a witch's hat. Shouldn't be too difficult. Is Amy going?'

'Yes, yes, we're all going. And Mum, you can come, too. Grown-ups are invited, as long as you bring your own food.'

'All right, but do I have to wear a costume?' Melissa made a face. 'I hate dressing up.'

'Well, it would be more fun, you know. You have to enter into the spirit of it. The other kids' parents will probably dress up.'

Melissa sighed, resigned to her fate. 'Oh, very well then. I'll see what I can do.'

Over-excited children were running round madly, shrieking with laughter and totally out of control by the time Melissa and Jolie arrived at the bonfire. Parents stood in groups, chatting among themselves, oblivious of their offspring. Just about everyone in sight was dressed in black. There was an array of witches' hats of all descriptions and sizes and it was all Melissa could do to keep from giggling at the ludicrous sight.

'Good grief,' she muttered. 'This really is a witches' convention, isn't it? Which coven do you think I should join?'

Jolie scanned the crowd anxiously, ignoring her mother's comments. 'How am I supposed to find Amy when everyone looks the same?' she complained, craning her neck for a better view.

'Let's go over by the fire and I'm sure you'll find each other soon.' Melissa felt ridiculous in her outfit of long, black skirt, black sweater and a huge shawl with a trailing fringe. The plastic hat on her head was making her scalp itch and she longed to throw it into the flames, but of course she couldn't let Jolie down. The girl was fairly bubbling over with excitement and her happiness was infectious.

Everyone seemed to have congregated in groups round the fire to watch the leaping flames reaching up towards the night sky. It was a beautiful sight and Melissa found it mesmerising. As she stared into the molten centre, the sounds around her receded and she felt as if she were dreaming.

'My love, I have missed you so . . .' The voice made her jump and she looked around to see who would say such a thing to her, but there was no one there. *'Have you missed me?'* This time she knew the voice she had heard was only audible inside her head. And she recognised it. The deep, rich chuckle she remembered from before followed the words and made her shiver violently, but she realised it was a tremor of anticipation rather than dread. She loved that voice, every rich nuance of it, and wanted to hear more.

'Sweeting.' Out of the corner of her eye she caught a slight movement in a nearby grove of trees, and turned to look more closely.

'Roger,' she whispered.

He was standing in the shadows, a dark cloak tightly wrapped around him, but she could see his face clearly in the light from the fire. He smiled at her and beckoned for her to come nearer. Without thinking, she began to move slowly towards him, as if drawn by a magnet. Her gaze locked with his and she sucked in her breath as the full force of his love hit her. Her heart fluttered like a wild thing.

'Melissa, where are you going?' Jake's voice, so similar to the one echoing inside her brain, startled her, and she turned to look at him in confusion.

'Jake?' She blinked and swivelled round to look from him to Roger, unconsciously comparing the two. 'Jake, I . . . oh, no, wait!' She reached out a hand towards Roger, but he smiled sadly and faded into the shadows. In an instant he was gone and Melissa felt bereft.

'Who are you talking to?' Jake peered over her shoulder, and Melissa realised that of course he hadn't seen Roger. She tried to pull herself together.

'Oh, I thought I saw someone I knew, but I was mistaken.' She managed a slightly shaky smile and he smiled back, making her pulse rate increase again. She became aware that he had the same effect on her senses as Roger had and she suddenly understood how futile it was to fight against her feelings for this man. She swallowed hard.

Amy and Jolie had thrown themselves into each other's arms and chatted non-stop about their costumes and everyone else's. Without even asking, they linked arms and disappeared into the crowd. Melissa wasn't worried though, she knew Jolie wouldn't go far and she'd be safe here among her new friends.

'Nice outfit,' Jake commented, raising one eyebrow a fraction as he took in her clothes. Melissa stared back.

'Yes, well, you look very interesting yourself.' He was covered from head to toe in some sort of black cloak, which wasn't exactly the latest fashion. She looked him up and down critically, then burst out laughing as he opened the cloak with a dramatic flourish to reveal a crimson silk lining. At the same time he grinned widely to show a set of fluorescent-white Dracula teeth.

'Beware, or I will carry you off to my sepulchre,' he intoned in a deep, mock-scary voice, sending her into another fit of giggles.

'Don't you dare, or I'll cast a spell on you,' she threatened, disentangling a magic wand from under her shawl. She waved it at him in what she hoped was a menacing way and he retreated in pretended horror, before removing the teeth.

'Very well, I give up. You win, witch. I can't stand these things another second anyway, they were driving me mad.' He laughed, then leaned close to her ear and whispered, 'Besides, you have already bewitched me.'

As she tried to peer up at him in the darkness, Melissa knew it was mutual. Whether it was Roger's doing or not, Jake attracted her as no one else had ever done, and it was incredibly difficult to resist the magnetic pull between them. Staying away from him hadn't helped one iota. On the contrary, she wanted him more than ever. When he took a step closer she couldn't move, but stood rooted to the spot. They stared at each other.

'Mum, where are my sausages?'

'Yes, and mine?' The two girls were back and broke the spell temporarily. Melissa shivered and drew the shawl around her more tightly. She held out the bag she'd brought.

'Here, darling. Will you grill one for me too, please? I don't want to go that close to the fire. I might set this fringe on fire.'

'Okay, Mum.'

'You too, Amy, please. I'll keep Melissa company. But be careful, yes?' Jake was looking composed, but his voice sounded deeper than normal. Melissa was shocked to find that she had wanted to make love with him right here, in the midst of all these people. With an effort she reined in her out-of-control emotions.

'Melissa . . .'

'Not now, Jake. Later. We'll talk later.' Once more her eyes pleaded for time and he nodded in agreement. She knew he'd been remarkably patient during the past few weeks and had done what she'd asked. He had given her time, left her alone to come to terms with the ghost business. But enough was enough. Melissa was grateful and she sent him a look which she hoped spoke volumes.

'All right. Let's go and find a drink,' he said. She smiled at him in relief and rewarded him for his patience by not protesting as he twined his fingers with hers. It felt so right.

The fire had been reduced to a smouldering heap of ashes by the time the two girls had finally had enough of the proceedings. Tired, but happy, they were ready to go home, but not separately.

'Oh, please, can't Amy spend the night? We have so much to talk about.'

'What?' Melissa was still distracted by her feelings for Jake and hadn't been paying attention. Jolie repeated her request. 'But you've just spent the last three hours in each other's company. Surely you can wait until tomorrow? It's very late, you know.' It was a good try, but Jolie was nothing if not tenacious.

'It's Friday, Mum, and we don't have to get up early tomorrow or anything.'

Melissa hesitated and looked to Jake for assistance. The message she read in his eyes was no help at all, however, and only added to her indecision. In the end she gave in and led the two girls to her car. As they climbed in and busied themselves with the seatbelts, he pulled her out of earshot.

'Come to my house when they're asleep. Please, Melissa?' he whispered, and his voice fanned the flames already igniting inside her at his touch.

Melissa hesitated only for a fraction of a second before capitulating. Who was she kidding? She couldn't withstand him any more than she could her daughter. She was too weak. Or the feelings he evoked were too strong. She didn't really care which.

'All right.' She closed her eyes in surrender. 'But it might take a while.'

'I'll be waiting. All night if I have to.' With a quick goodbye to the girls, he was gone.

'I shouldn't be here, Jake.' Melissa was standing in the little vestibule of his cottage, with the smell of cold, fresh night air lingering around her. Jake swiftly pulled the shawl from her shoulders and kissed her on the cheek. Her brain was running around in circles of indecision.

'Stop worrying. Everything will be all right.' He took her hand and pulled her along behind him.

She closed her eyes and tried to let his voice soothe her. She was scared and nervous, but nothing could have kept her away from him this evening. Something or someone had compelled her to come. Perhaps Roger's powers were extra strong on this magical night. Or perhaps she was just in love with Jake. *I really hope that's what it is!*

In the living room the lights were dimmed and he had lit floating candles in a magnificent crystal bowl half-filled with water. The tiny flames flickered in the draught as they entered and the cut glass reflected prisms of light onto the walls. A bottle of wine and two glasses waited on a table and he led her to the sofa, pulling her down gently beside him. He took both her hands, rubbing her palms in a sensual rhythm with his thumbs, and looked her straight in the eyes.

'Melissa, I have tried to keep away from you these last weeks, because I could see you needed more time. I hate to push you, but I can't stand it any longer. I want to be with you, whatever the reason. I want you, more than I have ever wanted any other woman. Whether Roger is lurking somewhere and intends to share you with me, or wants to pretend that you're his lost love, I will still be the one making love with you, if you let me. No one else. Do you believe me?'

She nodded, unable to trust herself to speak. Emotion clogged her throat and tears were threatening, but she held them back.

'Then let's have a drink, relax and talk for a while, and I'll leave it up to you whether you want to take this any further tonight.'

Melissa accepted the glass of wine gratefully. If ever she'd needed something to bolster her courage, it was now. Because she knew with absolute certainty how this night would end and her wishes didn't come into it. Not that she didn't want to make love with Jake – she did, desperately – she just felt a lingering resentment that even if she'd wanted to hold back, Roger would somehow have persuaded her.

Well, this is my decision, Roger, so stay out of it! The fierce thought helped and she became calmer. *I am in charge, it's my life.*

When, later on, Jake took her in his arms, she didn't protest, but held him close in mute acceptance. Nothing existed except this feeling building between them and nothing could have stopped it from reaching its natural conclusion. She felt it was their destiny.

Their love-making was explosive, each one moving as if they knew exactly how to please the other. His fingers found her most sensitive spots at exactly the right time and she returned the favour, making him sigh with pleasure.

'You're the only woman who exists for me, the only woman I'll ever want,' he whispered, and Melissa believed him. She felt the same about him.

She'd never experienced anything like the sensations Jake created in her, and tried to concentrate her mind on the here and now. She didn't want to leave herself open to any of Roger's tricks, but it became increasingly difficult. She could sense him hovering on the fringes of her awareness, and she looked deep into Jake's eyes and whispered his name, over and over again to keep the ghost away. As they reached the final frenzy before the world exploded, the name Sibell echoed round the inside of Melissa's head with frightening clarity, but she kissed Jake fiercely, ignoring Roger. She wouldn't let anyone spoil this special moment, especially not someone who had been dead for six hundred years. She was making love with Jake and no one else.

As the aftershocks died down, however, the uncertainty returned and tears hovered on her lashes. For a long time she lay quietly in Jake's arms, but her mind was elsewhere. Jake noticed, of course.

'Was it difficult, love?' he asked gently.

'Yes. He was there, but I tried to ignore him.'

With a groan of frustration Jake pulled her closer, hugging her fiercely. 'I would do anything for you, Melissa, but I can't fight a ghost. It seems only you can do that, but I'll do whatever I can to help.'

'Thank you. At least it's nice to know that I'm not alone. I just wonder if Roger will ever give up?'

'Perhaps together we can make him?'

CHAPTER 24

The minty freshness of spring had given way to the darker greens of summer, and still the marriage contract had not been signed. With barely concealed frustration, John of Ashleigh set off to confront the lion in his den, taking two of his sons with him to Sir Fulke's manor. The other two, Simon and Godwin, remained to guard their sister and, unfortunately for her, took their duties seriously for once.

'I can't move an inch without tripping over one or other of them,' Sibell grumbled to Roger when at last she managed to give them the slip one afternoon. 'Father has promised them all some sort of reward if they help to marry me off safely. Even Godwin, who is usually kind to me, won't let me out of his sight. He knows it would be more than his life is worth.'

They were lying on a soft grassy mound by the river and she glared at the sky as if it was responsible for all her troubles. Roger nodded and chewed absently on a blade of grass.

'You are singularly unfortunate in your brothers,' he agreed.

'Half-brothers,' she interjected.

'They are like terriers with a rat, and just as pugnacious.' He sighed. 'I wish I could help you, sweeting, but my situation hasn't changed. I'd hoped Sir Gilbert would have relented by now, but he refuses to give me even a hint as to who my father might have been. No one else is willing to divulge anything to me.'

Roger had confided his reason for coming to Idenhurst in the first place to Sibell, since he didn't want there to be any secrets between them. He told her of his mother, the beautiful Lady Emma, who had kept the name of Roger's father a secret all his life. It was only on her deathbed that she'd hinted to him about a possible connection with the Presseille family. Roger had lost no time in trying to find out more, but without Sir Gilbert's help he had no chance.

'I feel sure he has the answer, but he stubbornly refuses to tell me.' Spitting out the grass now, Roger rolled onto his side to look at her and added vehemently, 'If only I had more to offer you than one paltry manor, and that not until my uncle dies, which could be many years from now. We could be married and I would take you away from here.' He caressed her cheek with loving fingers, touching the freckles reverently one by one, then pulled her close. 'I love every inch of you.'

'Roger, I don't care about your possessions or lack of them. Marry me anyway, please! Let's be gone from here before my father returns.' She beat her fists against his massive chest in sheer frustration. He captured her hands and kissed each finger in turn, but his face was serious.

'No, you know I can't leave Idenhurst until I have finished training Sir Gilbert's men. I gave my word.' He gathered her close again and dropped butterfly kisses onto her nose and cheeks. 'But if you're sure, then there is no reason we can't be married. In secret.'

Her eyes flew to his, wide with joy. 'Really? How would we do that?'

'It would be simple enough. We can both read and write, so we'll draw up our own contract of marriage and plight our troth in front of two witnesses. Even if the ceremony isn't blessed by a priest, it will be legal and binding. That's the law. We can have a church blessing at a later date. Is there anyone you can trust to vouch for you? Lady Maude perhaps?'

'No, I couldn't involve her. It wouldn't be fair. But . . .' She thought for a moment. 'I believe old Ingirith would help us. She has no liking for my father and was fiercely devoted to my mother because she was her personal maid. I know she can at least write her own name, I've seen her do it before.'

'Good. Then I'll draw up the document and bring Hugone. The lad is literate and loyal to me. When can you escape your gaolers next?'

Sibell hesitated, thinking furiously. 'Perhaps on Wednesday? I overheard them talking about a hunt they didn't want to miss. They'll probably lock me in, but Ingirith might contrive to let me out if I take her into my confidence.'

'Very well, Wednesday it is then. Meet me by the oak tree next to the river, the one with a hole in the trunk.'

'But, Roger?'

'Yes?'

'Are you sure you want to do this? You're not just feeling sorry for me because I am bound to marry Sir Fulke?' She still couldn't quite believe that a man like Roger could possibly want her enough to marry her. And without a dowry too, for she had no doubt her father would withhold her portion if she took this step.

He laughed and pulled her closer still. 'Don't you know by now that I love you more than life itself? I always will, I swear on my honour. For all eternity.'

Sibell breathed a sigh of relief. All would be well. She didn't need to be afraid of Sir Fulke any longer and her child would not be born a bastard. Soon she would tell Roger, when she was absolutely certain.

'Ouch!' Melissa stubbed her toe on the loose floorboard in her bedroom for at least the third time, and glared at the offending piece of wood. 'That's it, I'm going to nail you down if it's the last thing I do.' She set off in search of hammer and nails.

Hammer in hand, she knelt down on all fours to have a closer look. It seemed the whole board had come loose. She was gripped by a sudden urge to look underneath it and without thinking she lifted the wood to peer down into the cavity below. She couldn't see much, however, and gave a muffled shriek as a fat spider bustled out of his hiding place.

'Ugh, horrid thing! Out of my room this instant.' The spider scurried away, as anxious to put distance between them as she was. She shuddered.

Resolutely grabbing a torch which Dorothy had left for her by the bed – in case of power cuts, she'd explained – she had another look under the floor and noticed something sparkling in a corner. Melissa didn't like the thought of sticking her hand down into the hole, just in case any of the spider's friends or relatives were lurking there, so she found a pencil with which to poke around. To her surprise, she dislodged something glittery that rolled into the beam from the torch, and she picked it up to inspect it more closely. It was a ring.

Although it was dusty, it seemed to be made of pure gold and was quite solid. It was in the shape of a dragon biting its own tail and along the inside was an inscription of some sort, which she couldn't make out. The dragon's eyes were made of green gems, possibly emeralds, and Melissa thought she had never seen anything so lovely. She caressed the little head lovingly.

'Wow, you're a little beauty, aren't you?' She polished the grime off with the bottom of her T-shirt and held it up to admire its sheen in the sunlight.

She tried the heavy ring on various fingers and found that it only fit on the ring finger of her left hand. *A marriage ring.* The thought echoed around her head, and as she slipped the ring onto the finger again she shivered and sucked in her breath sharply.

Roger had said a ring would help her somehow. Was this it? But how could it possibly help her? She stared at the beautiful object, deep in thought for a while. She now had one answer, but also more questions.

Finally, she slipped the ring off and had another look at the inscription. Perhaps this was the clue, but she couldn't decipher the writing. She'd have to find someone who could.

Mr Smythson, the jewellery expert at Sotheby's in New Bond Street, kindly agreed to see Melissa at short notice when she called him and explained what she'd found. When she was ushered into his office, she discovered he was a tall, jovial man in his mid-fifties, with a shock of salt and pepper hair. He shook her hand enthusiastically.

'Have a seat, Ms Grantham, please.' He waved her into a chair opposite his desk. 'Now, let's have a look at your little find, shall we?' He sank into his own chair.

Melissa had thought it safer to wear the ring rather than carry it about in her handbag, and she now peeled the little dragon off her finger with great care. She handed it to Mr Smythson and he took it with an expression that reminded her of an eager schoolboy. Then he extracted a magnifying glass from his desk drawer.

'As I told you, I found this under the floorboards of my bedroom,' she said. 'I was wondering if you could tell me anything about it and, in particular, whether you can decipher the writing inside and also perhaps figure out how old it might be.'

He examined it closely from every angle, muttering to himself all the while, before looking up at her with a radiant smile.

'My dear Ms Grantham, this is a rare find. A rare find indeed.'

'It is?'

'Yes. This is a Viking ring, exquisitely crafted, as you can see. They were masters at creating jewellery of all kinds, but this is one of the finest examples I have ever seen, incredibly detailed. It's impossible to date it exactly, but I would guess ninth or tenth century. It may have been made here in England, or it may have come from Scandinavia. Their designs were similar and the dragon is, of course, a typical motif.'

'A Viking ring?' Melissa had to try really hard to keep the disappointment out of her voice. Then it couldn't have anything to do with Roger. Or

303

could it? She remembered the words she'd heard in her mind when she first put it on.

'Now as to the inscription, I'm afraid I can't tell you what it means. I am, unfortunately, not an expert on runes. But I think I know of someone who might be able to help us. Let me just copy the inscription down on a piece of paper and I'll let you know what I can find out.'

'Thank you, I'd really appreciate it.'

He studied the runic characters and copied them down carefully. 'Of course, I have no idea which ones come first,' he laughed, 'but it looks like there is a slightly larger gap between these two here,' he pointed, 'so I've started with the second one of those.'

'I'm very grateful for your help.'

'Not at all, it was a pleasure to see such a fine example of Viking craftsmanship. If you should ever wish to sell it, do come and see me again. You would be able to charge quite a large sum for such a rare piece of jewellery.'

'Thank you, but I don't think so. I want to keep it forever.' As she said the words, Melissa knew they were true. She could never sell the ring. It belonged in her family, she was sure of that.

As Mr Smythson ushered her out of his office, he said, 'I'll give you a call when I hear from my friend regarding the inscription.'

He was as good as his word and rang the next day. Melissa had been on her way out of the house and grabbed the phone in passing.

'Hello?' She was slightly out of breath.

'Ms Grantham? It's Michael Smythson here. My friend has come up trumps about the inscription I faxed him yesterday, so I thought I'd ring you straight away.'

'Oh, thank you. That was quick! And very nice of him. So what does it mean?' She found it hard to stand still, excitement and anticipation buzzing through her.

'Well, as to that, I'm afraid he can't say for sure. It seems to be a lot of runes chosen at random which don't really mean anything specific.' He paused and Melissa drew in a breath of disappointment, which she let out on a long sigh.

'What a shame. I had so hoped it would say something important. Never mind, I'll . . .'

'Hold on a minute, Ms Grantham, that wasn't quite all he said. Apparently runes weren't just used for writing with. I don't know if you've heard this – I hadn't – but they were also used for divination and fortune-telling. My friend thought that in this case these runes were put together in a particular way for some magical purpose. In other words, the inscription on your ring is either a spell or a curse.'

'Really?' Melissa was astonished and looked at the dragon on her finger. The tiny eyes twinkled up at her. 'I see. Well, thank you very much, Mr Smythson. You have been extremely helpful.'

'Not at all. Don't hesitate to call on me again if

you should find anything else of interest under that floor of yours.'

'Oh, I will.'

A magic spell or curse. Melissa stared at the ring. Was that the clue Roger had been talking about? But how could it be? There was no such thing as magic. *But then I didn't believe in ghosts until recently either . . .*

She sighed again in frustration. 'Oh, Roger, why can't you just give me a straight answer?' she grumbled. 'I'm no good at guessing games.' The hallway stayed eerily silent. Roger obviously wasn't going to reply.

'Okay, fine. Maybe it's time for some more concrete evidence then.' With renewed determination, Melissa dialled the number of the Kent History Centre and asked for Jenny.

'Melissa, hi, how are you? Sorry, I haven't got back to you before, but it's been really hectic round here. Everyone went down with some kind of flu.'

'No problem. I don't want to hassle you, I just wondered if there was any progress with that manor court roll yet? Have they managed to unravel it any further?'

'Not yet no, sorry. I checked with them yesterday, and as it's not really on their official work schedule, they haven't had time to look at it.' Jenny giggled and confided, 'But I think one of them has a crush on me and he's promised to do it soon. I sort of hinted that I might consider a date if he did . . .'

'You wicked woman, you.' Melissa joined in her friend's laughter, but inside the frustration was building up again. 'You will let me know as soon as you hear though, won't you?'

'Of course, I promise.'

Melissa hung up and looked round the hall, trying to find some inspiration. What next? What had she not investigated yet? 'Oh, yes, Idenhurst.'

It was time to call Colin again.

CHAPTER 25

'Here I take thee Roger to my husband, to have and to hold, until the end of my life and to this I plight thee my troth.'

The heavy ring slipped easily onto Sibell's finger and fit perfectly. Roger kissed her and old Ingirith wiped a tear from her eye. It was done. Happiness welled up inside Sibell and Roger's fingers tightened their grip around her own.

'Congratulations, Mistress Sibell.' Ingirith hugged her fiercely. She'd told Sibell how pleased she was that there was someone at last who could protect her from her brute of a father. 'And you sir, I wish you both well.'

'Thank you.' Roger clasped the older woman's hand. 'I shall be forever grateful for your support this day.'

'It was nothing, sir. I'm happy to help Mistress Elinor's daughter in any way I can. Such a kind, gentle lady she was.'

It remained only for them all to sign the marriage contract, wrap it in oilskin and hide it inside the trunk of the old oak tree. 'It will be safer there for now,' Roger said, 'that way it can't be found until we are ready to face the world as man and wife.' Sibell agreed and bent to sign her name.

As she finished with a flourish, however, she heard Roger swear under his breath. She looked up quickly, fear tearing through her gut. Had her brothers arrived after all to ruin everything? Surely, they were too late?

But it was neither Simon nor Godwin who emerged from the shadow of the trees, but Lady Maude and her daughter, Katherine. As they approached, the wedding party waited in tense silence, the only sound to be heard that of the swiftly flowing river and the birds singing in the branches of the oak tree. When at last they came to a halt before the wedded couple, Roger bowed and Sibell swept a curtsey, and to their immense relief Lady Maude smiled and then clasped them both to her bosom.

'So you're married?' she asked. Sibell nodded. 'Excellent. I thought something was afoot when Sir Roger came asking for parchment and quills. I said to myself, this one bears watching and so I set Katherine to spy on you. I hope you'll forgive me? I wouldn't have missed this for the world.'

Sibell felt light-headed and unable to do anything but laugh with joy. Roger was more practical. 'You mustn't breathe a word of this to anyone, my lady. Please? It's too soon.'

Lady Maude nodded. 'I know, but I can make sure there's no doubt as to the validity of the marriage. Hand me that parchment and we will sign it, too. Come, daughter, do your duty by your brother. He deserves no less.'

Roger drew in a sharp breath and blinked. 'What did you say?'

'Oh, it's there for anyone to see who has eyes in his head. My pig-headed husband might not want to acknowledge you yet, but I'll find a way to make him, see if I don't.'

'But . . . but how do you know he is the one? He said he had four brothers.'

'Pah! That has nothing to do with the matter. They would have been too young at the time of your conception; Gilbert is the eldest by far. And the moment I saw you with Katherine in the still-room, I knew why you had come.' She patted Roger's arm. 'Just give him time, he'll come round.'

'And you don't mind?'

'No, from your age I would guess you came along before I even met Gilbert. I never set eyes on him until our wedding day, you know. And I married him because I was told to; affection grew between us later. If he'd loved someone else first, that was his business, as long as he treated me well, which he did. So why should I mind? We lost one son, but if he will see sense, Gilbert can now regain another. If he is happy, I'm happy. Now enough of this, we'll speak more later. We must make haste.'

From a small leather pouch she extracted a quill and a container of ink, which she handed to her daughter. They took turns to sign their names at the bottom of the document, taking great care not to soil it. Finally, when the package was safely hidden away, the group dispersed, except for Ingirith, who held out a key to them.

'Here you are. I've prepared a little hideaway where you can spend the afternoon without fear of discovery. It's only my humble cottage, but at least it's indoors and clean.' She looked towards the sky where the clouds had turned a dull grey. 'And if I'm not mistaken, you'll be thankful to be somewhere dry.'

'Thank you, your kindness is much appreciated.' Sibell hugged the old lady. 'Will you go back to Ashleigh for now?'

'Yes, and if anyone asks for you, I'll tell them I sent you out to gather herbs. I have some in a hidden basket, should it be necessary to produce proof, and I can fetch you in a hurry if your brothers return betimes. Now go, enjoy your brief time together.'

They didn't hesitate and soon Sibell was alone with her husband at last. He still looked slightly dazed at Lady Maude's revelations, so she decided to change the subject.

'Where did you find this ring?' She slid it off her finger and twisted it to have a closer look. She inspected the perfectly formed shape of the little dragon biting his own tail. The tiny emerald eyes gleamed, shooting sparks of green fire at them. 'It is exquisite.'

'It was my mother's. She told me it has been in

311

our family for generations, perhaps since the Norsemen came to these shores.' He pointed at a runic inscription along the inside of the ring. 'See the writing? It's from their time. I don't know what it means, but Mother said each owner can make one wish and the dragon will make it come true.'

The ring was warm to the touch and she could almost feel it pulsating with a life of its own. It was truly magical. 'Then I had better think carefully before I make mine.' She looked at her new husband and felt love flowing through her. 'Besides, I have all I could wish for right here.'

When he gave her a lingering kiss, she decided the time had come to tell him her news. She was certain now.

'Come, let us not waste our precious time together. I have something to show you.'

'Oh, and what's that?' He smiled as she began to pull off her clothing. 'Ah, I see,' he murmured.

'No, I don't think you do.' It was her turn to smile as she stood before him, wearing nothing but her long, unbound hair. She took his hand and placed it gently on the swell of her stomach. 'Here, this is what I meant.'

His blue eyes opened wide, then darkened with emotion. 'You're telling me that . . .? Truly?' She nodded, awaiting his reaction anxiously, but his huge grin laid all her fears to rest. 'Oh, sweeting, that has made this day even more complete.' He pulled her close.

'So you're pleased?' She searched his gaze one more time.

'Beyond ecstatic, my lovely wife. Thank you for this wedding gift, it's better than anything I could have hoped for.'

'That nice Mr Parsons rang, dear,' Dorothy told Melissa when she returned from a research expedition a few days later.

'Oh, it's about time, I've been trying to get hold of him for days.'

Melissa was exhausted, however, and couldn't summon up much enthusiasm for Colin at that moment. She'd put aside the Presseilles and her search for Roger in order to concentrate on her other clients for a while. But it had been a long, hard day and she didn't have much information to show for it. That, she supposed, was part of the charm of genealogy. Sometimes you found nothing for ages, then suddenly, when you least expected it, you'd discover that elusive missing piece of the puzzle. The joy of such a discovery and the thrill of the search were addictive, at least if the growing number of amateur genealogists flocking to the record offices was anything to go by. When it was your day job though, it wasn't always as much fun.

'So what did he say?' she asked, putting her heavy briefcase down and collapsing onto a chair.

'He said he had some more information for you. Sounded terribly excited. I almost thought I could hear him jumping up and down.' Dorothy chuckled. 'He's a funny little man.'

'He may be funny, but he's been an absolute angel and refuses to let me pay him. Really, I don't know how to thank him enough.'

'Well, just invite him over for dinner. I'm sure he'd appreciate the company; he must get lonely living all by himself like that. I know I used to.'

'Hmm, good idea. I'll do that.'

As Colin came through the door the following evening, he juggled a stack of papers from one arm to the other in order to shake hands with Melissa, and almost lost his grip on the slippery bundle. She turned away to avoid looking at Dorothy, who disappeared off to the kitchen with a muffled chuckle.

'Colin, come in. Dinner will be ready soon. Would you like a drink while we wait?'

'Thanks, that would be great. A small whisky, maybe?'

He sank into the deep sofa in the sitting room. As he stretched out his hand for the glass, he forgot about the papers and they finally slid onto the floor. Melissa hid a smile and helped him to pick them up. He then spread them out on the coffee table and sorted them into the right order again.

'Look here, Melissa. I have some photocopies I think might interest you.' There was an air of contained excitement about him and Melissa thought he looked almost like a little boy about to unwrap his Christmas presents.

She perched next to him and picked up the first sheets of paper. They were photocopies of very old documents, or rather photocopies of microfilmed versions of them since, obviously, such ancient parchment couldn't be exposed to too much light. Melissa looked at court orders and decrees in the name of King Henry VI. The writing was faint with age, which was no wonder, she thought. Moving her lips silently as she read, Melissa gasped.

'Roland de Presseille . . . traitor to the crown . . . proven supporter of the attainted Duke of York . . . executed by beheading . . . Ludford Bridge, *Anno Domini 1459.*' She raised startled eyes to Colin's. He now wore the pleased look of the cat that got the cream.

'You see? That must be your man! You misunderstood the name and it was Roland, not Roger. Here's the reason why Sibell couldn't marry him – he was dead. Fits perfectly. Even the date is about right. Didn't you say her will was dated 1461?' He took a sip of his whisky, smiling smugly. 'The poor man got caught up in the Wars of the Roses and she was left as a pregnant mistress or fiancée.'

'*Noooo!*' The scream took her by surprise and she dropped the piece of paper to put her hands over her ears. Colin jumped and spilled some of his whisky. His smile faded as he saw the pained expression on her face.

'What's the matter? You don't agree?' He was so clearly disappointed not to have pleased her that Melissa came to a quick decision. She would have to come clean.

'Colin,' she began, 'I can't thank you enough for this. It's really helpful, but I'm afraid your theory is wrong. I can't prove it, but if you'll bear with me I'll try to explain.'

The story came pouring out of her, slightly jumbled, and Colin listened open-mouthed without interrupting her a single time. He stared at her and his eyes were enormous behind the thick lenses of his glasses, giving him the appearance of a startled frog.

However, when she stopped talking at last he exclaimed, 'How wonderful!' and beamed at her. 'Absolutely marvellous! Well, this changes everything.'

Melissa blinked at him. 'You mean . . . you believe me?'

'Of course. I've seen a ghost or two myself, but I've never been so lucky as to have a conversation with one.'

Melissa remained speechless for a moment, before smiling back at him. She had expected incredulity or even ridicule, but this unconditional acceptance was a complete surprise and very welcome.

'Why are you so sure Roland's not your man, though? Did he really say Roger? You've heard it only once?' Logical as always, Colin quickly returned to the problem at hand.

'He shouted at me.'

'Sorry?'

'Just now, when you gave me your theory about Roland, I heard a scream inside my head. That's why I was holding my ears. He said "no", emphatically. I don't know who Roland was, but he wasn't Sibell's lover.'

'Hmm, I guess it's back to the drawing board then.'

'Yes, I'm sorry to have disappointed you when you'd worked so hard on my behalf. And the information is useful anyway. You know even negative evidence is good to have. Besides, I'm not sure the dates do fit actually. If this Roland was beheaded in 1459 and Sibell didn't die until 1461, presumably in childbirth since she was expecting when she wrote her will, then that can't be right. She'd have had to be pregnant for two years.'

'Hmm, yes. Well, don't worry.' Colin patted her arm awkwardly. 'One way or another we'll solve this, I'm sure.'

Melissa wasn't sure she shared his optimism any longer, but thought it best to keep *schtum* for now.

'Tell me more about the Wars of the Roses.' Jake and Melissa were sharing another take-away in the kitchen at Ashleigh Cottage and she'd just told him someone who was a possible ancestor of his had been beheaded. It sounded like a harsh punishment for someone who had merely backed the wrong side in a conflict.

'Well, obviously it was a turbulent time in English history,' Melissa began. 'I've been mugging up on it myself to see if I could come up with any clues as to what to do next, and it's fascinating stuff.'

'Go on.'

'1459 was right at the end of the reign of King Henry VI. He was a ruler who wasn't much liked by his people, poor guy. A simple-minded man, controlled by courtiers and priests, his reign was dominated by feuds between the leading magnates. The most important of them was the King's former "heir presumptive" as he was called, Richard, Duke of York.'

'Yes, I remember all this from school history lessons.' Jake nodded. He'd quite enjoyed history, but had to drop it after O-levels in order to do more science-oriented subjects. 'And I know that even though the King had a son at last, York didn't want to give up his claim.'

'Exactly. It didn't help that when the pressures of state became too much for Henry, his feeble mind couldn't handle it. At least twice York was appointed Protector of the Realm, which must have fuelled his ambitions even more. And he was a great warrior, while Henry was just pious and gentle.'

'So the people were torn, like my ancestor, if that's what he was,' Jake said, 'trying to decide which one should rule them.'

'Yes, can't have been easy for them to choose.' Melissa looked pensive. 'The gentle Henry, a

318

totally ineffective king, and his young son after him, whose birthright it was, after all. Or the stronger Richard, whose veins contained an equal amount of royal blood. York's allies grew steadily in number and this Roland de Presseille must have been one of them.' She blinked hard. 'It's one thing to be killed in battle for a cause, but to be beheaded . . .' She shuddered.

But Jake had stopped listening and stared at her. 'Did you say Roland?'

Melissa nodded. 'Yes, why?'

'Jesus Christ.' Jake put down his knife and fork, his hands shaking.

'What's the matter? Are you ill?' Melissa glanced at his half-eaten dinner. 'I'm sorry, I didn't mean to put you off your food.'

'No, no, it wasn't you, it was . . .' He swallowed hard. 'Okay, this is really weird, but I think, no, I *know* I saw it happen.'

'Saw what?'

'The beheading.' Taking a deep breath, Jake explained. 'I didn't want to tell you before, but ever since I moved into this cottage I've had strange dreams occasionally. Like being a knight on a horse and riding through the forest and stuff, even though I don't know how to ride. One day, when I'd been dozing on the sofa, I had a really horrible nightmare. It was too vivid for comfort, let me tell you, and, well, I witnessed an execution. I'm sure they read out the name Roland beforehand, but I didn't hear the rest

319

of his name. Bloody hell! It can't be a coincidence.'

Melissa stared at him, her cheeks pale. 'Riding? So it's not just me then,' she finally said. 'I had dreams like that, too.'

Jake sighed. 'I guess that means we're in this together, although we kind of knew that already.' He gave a shaky laugh and pushed his plate away. 'Were you riding on your own?'

'No, with Roger.'

'So if I was him in the dreams, that means he was there when my ancestor met his death. Why else would I see it from a distance?'

Melissa gave a helpless shrug. 'God, this is all insane.'

'I know.' They were both silent for a while, then Jake said, 'I wonder why Roland didn't die in the fighting? There were battles, right?'

'Yes, York finally challenged the King openly, but the battle at Ludford Bridge ended in victory for the King, and the Duke was forced to flee to Ireland for a while. His poor followers seem to have been left behind and were persecuted. I bet Roland wished he'd died on a battlefield instead of a scaffold.'

Jake frowned. 'So what about Roger, then? Whose side do you think he was on?'

Melissa sighed. 'I've absolutely no idea. The bloody man just doesn't exist! I've had help from both Jenny and Colin to check through all the known sources for this period, but we've found nothing. I mean, yes, there were of course men named Roger, but we can't connect any of them to this particular area of Kent, and without a surname there's nothing more we can do. It's so frustrating.'

'Actually, I think I can at least tell you Roger was a Yorkist. The last thing I remember from that dream was someone telling me we should leave, that it was dangerous to be seen there. That must mean he was on the same side, don't you think?'

'I suppose so. Not that it helps much with finding him.'

Jake got up from his chair and went over to put his arms round Melissa. 'Don't give up yet. If this ghost really is as persistent as you say he is, he'll find a way to tell you more. Or me. We just have to be patient.'

She leaned her head on his shoulder and hugged him close. Jake felt her relax against him and nod slightly. 'Yes, you're probably right. Thanks.' She looked up at him suddenly with a smile that lit up her entire face and made him feel as though he'd just been punched in the gut. 'Sorry, I didn't mean to be such a bore. I'm sure you didn't ask me over here to give you a history lesson so let's try to forget it for now and concentrate on the present.'

He answered her with a kiss. 'Well, now that you mention it, I did have one or two ideas as to how we could spend our time together,' he murmured, trailing his hands down her back.

She shivered. 'Hmm, I bet you did. How about you give me a tour of the rest of the house? I don't think I've seen the bedrooms yet.'

Jake heard the laughter in her voice and grinned back. 'Exactly what I had in mind. Come on.'

As he took her hand to lead her up the stairs he forgot all about ghosts and ancestors. The only thing that mattered was Melissa.

He never wanted to let her go.

CHAPTER 26

'It is all decided at last, you'll be wed in September from here and then Sir Fulke will take you back to Thornby after a day of feasting.'

Her father rubbed his hands together in glee, which was understandable, since Sibell had overheard him say that negotiating the marriage contract had been a tiresome business. He must be pleased it was over with as he'd been forced to haggle for hours with the man over Sibell's dowry. Sir Fulke had apparently been merciless and her father had barely managed to hold onto his precarious temper. Presumably, only the thought of such an illustrious connection had made him keep a still tongue in his head, she thought sourly.

'Yes, Father.' Sibell looked out of the window and answered in a wooden monotone. He glared at her, then his gaze turned suspicious. He must have been expecting further histrionics or, at the very least, a quiet refusal to comply with his wishes. Instead, Sibell stood motionless and waited patiently for him to finish. Suddenly restless in the face of her unexpected acquiescence, he began to pace the room, slapping his leg with his riding crop as he went.

'Is that all you have to say on the matter? Dare I hope you have at last seen the error of your ways?' he asked, his voice dripping with sarcasm.

'Yes, Father.' She glanced at him briefly, before resuming her study of the scene outside the window.

He stopped his perambulations and grabbed her chin. 'Look at me when I'm speaking to you.' She did as she was told, but for once did nothing to hide the hatred she felt for him. His brows drew together and he fixed her with an angry stare. 'What are you up to now, hmm?'

'Nothing, Father.'

'Now see here, girl, if you're planning to make good your escape before September, you can think again. You'll be confined to this house from now on, and I will make sure you don't go anywhere unaccompanied. If necessary I will beat you senseless or break your legs. Is that understood?' he barked, emphasising his words with a slap of the riding crop for each syllable.

'Yes, Father.'

He made an angry noise. 'Well get yourself gone from my sight. And make yourself useful for a change.'

Sibell didn't say a word in her defence at this groundless accusation. She simply turned on her heel and strode out of the room with another, 'Yes, Father', which goaded him into picking up a pewter tankard and throwing it after her. It hit the door with a loud clang just after she shut it quietly behind her, but she ignored it.

'Damn the girl for defying me!' he bellowed.

Sibell smiled.

Up to her eyebrows in the Tylson family tree once again, and feeling very guilty for having neglected it lately in favour of her own search, Melissa was in her office when her mobile rang. She picked it up absently while she continued to go through a census record she was checking.

'Hello, Melissa Grantham.'

'Mellie, it's Steve.'

She dropped her pen in surprise and bent to retrieve it. The Tylsons were all forgotten in an instant. 'Steve! What a surprise to hear from you. I thought you only communicated via your solicitor these days.' Her unnaturally cheerful voice grated even on her own ears and she could picture him grinding his teeth. *Well good!* She ignored his deliberate use of a pet name he knew she hated and asked sweetly, 'What can I do for you?'

'I, er, well, it's been a while and I thought perhaps Jolie would like to come for a visit. I'm sorry but . . . things have been a bit tough.' He sounded embarrassed, and so he should, Melissa thought vehemently. It had been weeks since he'd seen his daughter. She was amazed he even remembered he had one.

Their divorce had granted her sole custody of

Jolie, but Steve was allowed to visit her any time. Melissa had made it clear she wanted her daughter to keep in close touch with her father, but for quite a few weeks now he hadn't bothered. Since he persisted with his claim that he wouldn't be paying child support any longer, Melissa had told herself she didn't care. But it wasn't fair on Jolie.

'I'll have to ask my solicitor. If you're not intending to pay for your child, then I don't know why you should want to see her.'

'Melissa, for Christ's sake, I told you I can't afford the payments. It's not that I don't want her. Come on, be reasonable, you know I love her. She is my daughter, too.'

'Precisely.'

'Look, all I'm asking for is a short visit. She, umm, she has a new sister she hasn't seen yet and I thought . . . oh, I don't know. Maybe it was a bad idea. Her last visit wasn't exactly a success.'

Melissa stared out of the window, her thoughts running round in circles. So Daisy had given birth already, another daughter for Steve. Why hadn't he told them? *He could at least have informed Jolie of the birth.* And presumably that meant he'd soon be getting married too, wasn't that what he'd said when he first rang about the payments? Melissa closed her eyes, expecting to feel hurt, but found that she couldn't summon up anything other than mild irritation. In fact, she couldn't care less any more what he did. She'd moved on.

But was he telling the truth about the money?

He certainly sounded frazzled enough, but she supposed that with two small children to cope with, he probably wasn't getting much sleep. Could his finances really be that bad? Still, it was the principle of the thing.

'I'll tell you what – if you write a letter to your solicitor saying that you'll agree to start paying for Jolie again as soon as you can afford to, you can see her. But I don't want any slippery excuses. The moment you're solvent, you pay. Is that clear?'

'All right, fine, but I still don't think it's fair. There you are with your big house and rich relatives . . .'

'For the last time, Steve, this is *not* my house and even if I were to inherit it one day, it won't make me better off financially. Quite the opposite. The damned thing practically eats money, the running costs are astronomical. Besides, Jolie and I have to survive on what I earn, which barely pays for food, clothing and petrol. Dorothy has sent a sworn statement to the lawyers to say she's not subsidising me in any way, so I'm sure you're fully aware that I am no better off now than I was before. The only difference is that Jolie is happy here and doing well at school.'

Steve sighed. 'Okay, okay, I'll send the damned letter. Now, when can she come?'

'I'll have to ask her. Did you have any particular date in mind? She breaks up from school on Thursday.'

'This weekend would be good. Could I pick her

up on Saturday morning and bring her back Sunday? Friday would be a bit difficult for Daisy . . .' His voice sounded strained and she wondered if he was having trouble with his partner as well. That thought didn't cheer her up the way it would have done only months ago, and she realised she was well and truly over Steve at last.

'I don't see why not.' Jolie may not want to go, but Melissa would make her. It was only right she should have some contact with her father, even if it was sporadic. 'See you Saturday, then.'

'Mu-uum! Do I really have to go?' Jolie wailed, a petulant expression on her face, her amber eyes dark and stormy.

'Come on. Why wouldn't you want to?' Melissa hugged her daughter close. 'You haven't seen your dad for ages. He's been rather busy with work and the new baby, but now he has more time,' she lied. Like a small child, she crossed her fingers behind her back in compensation. 'And be nice to your father's, umm . . . girlfriend.'

'But that's just it – I don't want to see his girl-friend or their brats. I hate them!'

'Jolie, of course you don't hate them. Those "brats" as you call them are your little sisters. I thought you liked babies? Last time you went, you said Tess was cute.'

'I do, but it's all their fault we're not a family any more.'

'No, Jolie. Listen to me. What happened between

your dad and me would have happened anyway, whether he'd met Daisy or not. You mustn't blame her, even though I admit I did too, at first. It takes two to tango, as they say – it was as much your dad's fault as hers in that case.' She sighed. 'And you know what? I realise now that your dad and I weren't really suited to each other, and . . .'

'Then why did you get married?' Jolie shouted, her hands fisted at her sides.

'Because we loved each other then, but people can fall out of love too, you know. If you fall in love with the wrong person, then eventually things will go wrong, with or without interference from others. And they did.'

'You said he walked out on us.'

'I was upset at the time and I still loved him then. Now I don't, I can see he was right to go.'

Jolie struggled with this in silence for a moment, then buried her face in her mother's shoulder. 'I still don't like it.' Her voice, muffled by Melissa's T-shirt, sounded small. Melissa stroked her back and held her close.

'I know, sweetheart, but sometimes things have to be difficult for a while before they can work out for the best.' She took her daughter's face between her hands. 'We're happy here, aren't we?' Jolie nodded. 'And your dad is happy with Daisy and the babies, so you see, everything's okay now.'

'You're not sad any longer? You cried so much for a while.'

'I'm fine now.' And Melissa realised with surprise

that she really was all right. It didn't hurt to think of Steve with someone else and all her anger had worked its way out of her system. She had learned so much during this past year and she was a person in her own right now, strong and independent. Her relationship with Jake was so different from the one she'd had with Steve. It had helped her to see that staying married to Steve would have been a disaster. Their teenage infatuation had been forced into something else by the birth of Jolie, but it couldn't possibly have lasted, she could see that now. What she'd felt back then was a mere shadow of the feelings she had for Jake. *And Roger*, the little voice inside her insisted. She ignored it.

'So what do you say, Jolie? Do you want to go? It's only for two days. You want to see your new baby sister, don't you?'

'I guess. And Tess was very sweet when I met her last time.' Jolie sighed. 'Oh, all right, I'll go. But if I don't like it, you'll come and get me?'

'Of course. Just call me. But, Jolie?'

'Yes?'

'Promise me you'll try and see things in a different way this time, okay? I think you're old enough to be mature about this. I'm sure Daisy must feel as awkward as you do when you're there. Situations like this are never easy for anyone.'

'All right, I'll do my best.'

Steve arrived shortly after nine, a heavy scowl marring his features as he surveyed the manor house.

'Nice little pad,' he commented.

'Yes, it's not bad, is it?' And if that wasn't the understatement of the year, Melissa didn't know what was. There was no need to add that if he hadn't been such an idiot he could have shared in her good fortune. She could see from his face he'd worked that one out for himself. 'Have a nice time.' She kissed Jolie goodbye and shooed her in the direction of the car. 'Try to behave yourself.' She winked at her daughter to show her she was joking.

'Yes, Mum.' Melissa hid a smile as Jolie sank into the front seat of Steve's BMW, one perk he could obviously still afford.

'So you couldn't cope with living on your own then?'

Melissa knew he was trying to hint that she couldn't cope without him, but now she finally could, his remark no longer had the power to annoy her. She smiled.

'Actually, I could. I was going to rent a cottage nearby, but Dorothy needed some company, so it seemed crazy not to accept her offer to stay here. This has worked out well for both of us. And I never have to worry about leaving Jolie all alone.'

'I see.' He looked surprised she hadn't risen to his bait. A year ago they would have been in the middle of a screaming match by now, but Melissa didn't feel the need to defend herself. It was a liberating discovery.

Steve looked at his ex-wife and opened his

mouth, as if he was about to say something else, then seemed to change his mind. She wondered if he had any regrets, but if he did he didn't show it. She knew he wasn't a sentimental man and wouldn't cry over spilt milk. He had made a new bed and would lie in it. He turned abruptly.

'See you tomorrow night, then.'

CHAPTER 27

'Maude, are you here? There's a matter I must broach with you and . . .'

Sir Gilbert put his head round the door to the solar and stopped in mid-sentence, his mouth open. 'By all the saints, what is the meaning of this?'

Sibell had pulled her head away from her husband's shoulder the moment Sir Gilbert began to speak, but Roger still held her hand. They were sitting as close to each other as two people possibly could in the window seat. It had been days since they'd seen each other, but at last her father had relented and allowed her a short visit to Idenhurst. Maude, kind as always, had arranged a private meeting.

'Well, we . . .' Sibell didn't quite know how to explain, but she was spared having to answer when Maude came bustling up the stairs, entering the room after her husband.

'Really, Gilbert, if you wish to speak to me you have but to send for me,' she said. 'Do come in and sit down and stop towering over everyone.' He obeyed, although reluctantly, a frown settling on his brow. 'Now, what did you wish to discuss, husband?' When he hesitated, Maude added, 'I have no secrets from these two, so please speak plainly.'

'Very well, I suppose that's just as well since it concerns this young man.' He nodded in Roger's direction and Sibell felt Roger stiffening slightly. She squeezed his hand and Sir Gilbert cleared his throat. 'When Sir Roger arrived, he spoke to me about a private matter and at the time I didn't feel able to help him. I have given it much thought, however, and believe it's my duty to try after all.' He looked at Maude, a shadow of fear in his eyes. 'But I am reluctant to do anything that would hurt you, my love.'

'I know you would never willingly hurt me, husband dearest.' Maude's voice was soft and soothing and this appeared to encourage him to go on. He took a deep breath.

'You know we were betrothed at a very young age and there was a time when, as a young man, I thought to rebel against my father's decision?'

'Uh-hmm. You did mention that once or twice.'

'Well, I hadn't even met you and didn't know how well we were suited. The year before we were to wed, there was a woman with whom I believed myself in love for a while. Her name was Emma.' He paused, waiting for her reaction, but when his wife didn't stir, he ploughed on doggedly. 'I foolishly promised to marry her and would have done so if my father hadn't reminded me of my prior obligation to you.'

'Emma of Langford,' Roger whispered, his eyes on Gilbert, who heard him and nodded.

'Yes. This young man is her son and I . . . well he may or may not be mine also.' Having come to the end of his confession, Gilbert hung his head, as if waiting for the verdict.

Maude rose from her seat and walked over to put her arms round her husband's neck. She leaned her forehead against the top of his head. 'I would say that you had an obligation to find out, my love, one way or the other. There must be some way of verifying it.'

He looked up, the relief in his eyes clear as he took note of her calmness and the fact that she had still called him 'my love'. He let out his breath in a ragged sigh and nodded.

Maude continued, 'Especially since Roger's future happiness depends on you.'

'Future happiness? Oh, you mean money. To be sure, but he is a man grown and has done well for himself already.' Roger nodded, still stiff beside Sibell, but holding her hand in a death grip.

'No, you dolt.' Exasperation tinged Maude's voice and she gave Gilbert a little push before crossing her arms over her ample bosom. 'Honestly, you men are so blind sometimes. Can't you see what's before your eyes?' She indicated the lovers in the window seat. 'Roger can't declare himself to John of Ashleigh without your support. How could he possibly compete with Sir Fulke of Thornby in his present situation? But if you were

335

to back his proposal, Sibell's father will not be able to deny him. To a man such as John it's the connection to a great family that counts, even if yours isn't quite as illustrious as Sir Fulke's.'

'But you said . . . I mean, we must first establish that Roger is really my son, surely?'

'You don't have much time and besides, there is no doubt in my mind, only yours.'

'How can you be so certain?' Gilbert looked thoroughly puzzled.

'Have you never seen Roger and Katherine laughing together?' Maude asked. When he shook his head, she continued, 'Well, I have. And you know how everyone comments on her likeness to you. It is a likeness Roger shares. It's there for anyone to see who cares to look. I couldn't be mistaken.' Gilbert stared at her in awe and took one of her small hands between his own. He kissed it gently.

'You truly are a remarkable woman, Maude. You don't wish to reproach me at all?'

'Only for not coming to me sooner. There is nothing else to regret. Except perhaps for this young man, who has had to grow up without a father.' Her gaze clouded over for an instant and Sibell knew she was thinking of Roland. Her own dear boy, so young and rash, who had never been given a chance to mature.

Sibell shivered as she remembered the dreadful secret Roger had shared with her regarding her former husband's true fate, and prayed Maude would never find out what had really happened to her son. *Please God, she continues to believe he died on the battlefield.* It was for the best.

Maude shook her head and returned to the matter at hand. 'Gilbert, you must do something. If you don't act soon, John will try to wed Sibell to Sir Fulke and you know my thoughts on that matter.' She shuddered in revulsion.

'Indeed. Very well, there is only one thing for it – we will leave for Langford the day after tomorrow. You spoke of having been raised by an uncle?' He looked at Roger who nodded. 'I remember the man, we were friends once, and if he confirms your story, I will take his word for it.'

'Gilbert, I take it Roger's mother is dead?' Maude suddenly sounded uncertain, which was very unlike her.

'Yes.' Gilbert looked deep into her eyes. 'And has been so to me since our marriage, my love. You have my word.' Maude smiled and Sibell let out the breath she didn't know she'd been holding. Perhaps all would be well now.

As the BMW pulled out of the driveway, another car, small and rather battered, drove up to the gate and stopped. Melissa shaded her eyes with one hand to see who it could be. The rotund figure that emerged from the driver's seat was very familiar and she smiled and called out, 'Colin!'

He waved excitedly, and she set off at a half-run down the drive to meet him.

'Hello, this is an unexpected surprise.'

'I found something else interesting at the British Library when I was up there yesterday.' He bent into the car and pulled out a large piece of paper. 'Look, it's a rough map of this area, dated 1523. And it shows Ashleigh and all the neighbouring properties, including Idenhurst. Now we can finally see where the Presseilles lived.'

She took the photocopy from him and studied it intently. 'Brilliant, Colin. Of course the local library would be too small to house such valuable documents; I should have thought of going up to London. Mind you, a copy of this ought to be kept at the Kent History Centre – I'll tell Jenny. This is great.'

Heads together, they peered at the map.

'Here is Ashleigh,' Colin pointed to the spot, 'and part of the Idenhurst lands are right next to it. There. I think that winding line is meant to be the river Idun and it looks like it's the dividing line between the properties. Let's go for a walk and see what we can find.'

'Okay. Let me just tell Dorothy. I'll be right back.'

They set off at a brisk walk along the same footpaths she had last trodden with Jake. Russ bounded ahead of them, very pleased to have been offered an extra outing. Eagerly, Melissa took off with long strides, but it was a very hot day and the sun was uncomfortably warm. She soon had to adjust her steps to those of Colin, who was finding it hard going, and they continued at a slower pace. As they drew nearer to the river, Melissa remembered the irrational fear she had experienced at the bridge, and glanced uneasily at the map.

'Is the old bridge the only way across the river?' She tried to make it sound like a casual inquiry.

'Uh-hmm, I think so, unless you want to make a long detour.' Colin appeared lost in his own thoughts and thankfully didn't notice the slight quiver in her voice. 'There it is.'

They had come upon it unexpectedly, just like the last time, and Melissa had to force herself to go on. *Don't be an idiot,* she admonished herself sternly. *There is nothing frightening here at all.* But her body wasn't listening to reason and her ribcage suddenly felt very tight. She breathed in rapid, shallow breaths. Russ, too, had stopped and seemed reluctant to go forward, although he wasn't growling this time.

'Come on, we'll have to climb the gate. It's rusted shut,' Colin said, and Melissa watched as he managed to scramble over the top. The rusty old hinges groaned in protest and she wondered if the tired metal would withstand another onslaught. There was no other way across, however, so she picked up the little dog and walked quickly forward. She handed Russ to Colin across the gate. Then she climbed over as quickly as possible and made it to the other side safely and without giving way to the threatening panic. Letting out her breath in a sigh of relief, she hurried after Colin and the dog along another path, slightly less worn, but distinguishable, nonetheless. The grass was higher on this side of the river and appeared to have been left to grow wild.

'I wonder who owns this now?' she said, but received no reply.

Wiping drops of perspiration from his brow with a large handkerchief, Colin stopped to have another look at the map and check their bearings. It was turning hotter by the minute. 'Lord, I haven't had this much exercise for years,' he panted. His face was a mottled red and he was trying to catch his breath. 'I wish I'd thought to bring a hat,' he muttered to himself, 'and had gone jogging every day for the last twenty years or so.' He traced their path on the map with his finger. 'Now then, we have to keep walking for quite a while, then I reckon the manor should be somewhere over there.' He pointed to their left.

'Okay, come on then.'

They finally stopped again what seemed like ages later, and Melissa looked around them. 'There's nothing here, Colin. Just grass.' Disappointment tinged her voice. She knew it was unlikely the manor house would have survived intact, but she'd thought perhaps a part of it would still have been standing. Lots of old houses remained, added onto by generations of owners. Here there was nothing at all.

'Well, we knew that, otherwise it would have been marked on later maps.' They wandered around a bit, wading through the high weeds, and looked for any signs of habitation.

'Ow!' With a string of expletives, Colin began to hop around on one foot, doing a funny little dance and Melissa had to turn around to hide her laughter. He looked like a rounder version of Charlie Chaplin.

When she had her face under control once more she took his arm solicitously. 'What happened?'

'Damned stone tripped me up.' He waved his hand in the direction of a huge, overgrown boulder and Melissa bent down to examine it. She pulled the vegetation to one side in order to inspect it more closely.

'I'm glad it did.'

'What?'

'I think you've probably just found what we were looking for.' She straightened up. 'That's not just any old boulder; it looks like a foundation stone.'

Colin stopped hopping about. 'It does? Oh, well in that case I suppose I'll have to forgive it.'

Further investigation of the area revealed the outline of a substantial building, but apart from a few low, crumbling walls, nothing else remained of Idenhurst.

'I wonder what happened to it?' They sat down to rest on a piece of the foundations and Melissa took some bottles of water out of a small rucksack she'd brought. She handed one to Colin and poured some from her bottle into a bowl for Russ, before quenching her own thirst. She closed her eyes against the glare of the sun, and tried to imagine what had occurred here.

'It must have fallen into disuse.' Colin stared out over the fields.

'Hmm. My guess would be that it was razed to the ground during the Civil War, otherwise such a fine house would have survived, surely? Slightly altered or added to through the ages, but not completely gone like this. I'm sure we could find out.'

'Civil War? But of course!' Colin hit his forehead with the flat of his palm. 'That's where I'd read the name. What an idiot, I should have remembered.'

'You saw it mentioned in a document about the war?'

'Yes, an old tome by some eminent local Victorian fellow that I read ages ago. I knew it rang a bell, but I couldn't for the life of me think where I'd seen it. I'll look it up again as soon as I get back and photocopy the page for you.'

'Thanks, Colin. What a shame though, not a single wall remaining. I would have liked to have seen it.'

For a long time they sat in the sunshine, lost in thoughts of the past, before heading back to Ashleigh.

'Melissa, will you marry me?' Comfortably ensconced in Jake's large bed, and half-asleep after their recent love-making, the question caught Melissa completely by surprise.

'What?'

'You heard me,' Jake growled. 'Damn it, Melissa, I don't want to sneak around like this. I want to show the world we're together.' She had begged him to keep their liaison a secret until she was sure of her feelings, and so far he had kept his word. 'I want to tell the girls about us, although from the strange looks I've been receiving recently I think they already suspect something's going on.' He lifted himself up on one elbow to look down on her. 'Melissa, I love you. Can't we at least become engaged?'

As she gazed into his blue eyes, Melissa knew he wouldn't lie to her. Not voluntarily. But how could she be sure he wasn't being prompted by Roger? It was true the ghost hadn't intruded on their love-making recently, but she could still sense his presence. Roger hadn't gone away and he was still haunting her dreams. He wouldn't leave until he had accomplished his goal. Whatever that was.

'Do you really love me, Jake? How can you be sure Roger isn't putting the words in your mouth?' The misery in her voice made him slam his fist into the headboard, and she could see him clench his jaw to stop from shouting his frustration out loud.

'For God's sake, woman! Of course I'm sure. What do I have to do to prove it?'

'Get rid of Roger,' she muttered, turning her back on him so he wouldn't see the tears rolling down her cheeks.

'Melissa . . .' Gently he turned her over and into his arms again. He wiped the salty droplets away with gentle fingers. 'Sweetheart. I can't get rid of him, but I'm sure in time he will leave of his own accord. Until then, there is nothing I, or you, can do. When he leaves, I swear I will still love you. Only you.' He stroked her back, murmuring soothing words as if she were a child, but the lump of misery remained inside her. She wished with all her heart that she could believe him, but at the moment it was impossible.

'I'm sorry, Jake, but I don't think it's fair of me to make any sort of commitment to you until I'm sure. I love you too, but at the same time I love Roger. When I see him or even just hear his voice . . . Well, I have the same feelings as I do when I'm with you. The two of you are confused in my mind and I'm having trouble keeping you apart. If you can't cope with that I'll understand. Perhaps if we stopped seeing each other for a while . . .?'

'No!' He startled them both with the vehemence in his voice. 'No,' he said more softly, 'I can't bear not to see you. I'll try to be patient for a bit longer.'

Melissa burrowed close to him, inhaling his scent, but all around them she could detect the odour of horse and leather. She wondered if Jake could smell it too, but she didn't dare ask.

CHAPTER 28

'You shouldn't have come, it's too dangerous.' Roger had once again taken the risk of climbing in through Sibell's window in order to say a lengthy farewell. He put a finger on her mouth and whispered, 'How could I have stayed away, my sweet? As it is, it will be far too long before I see your lovely face again.'

She needed no urging when his hands sought to free her from her garments, and it was nearly dawn before he reluctantly made his way back to Idenhurst.

'I'll return as soon as I can and then we will tell the whole world that we are man and wife,' he promised.

'Have a safe journey and may God go with you. And please, I beg you, be careful.'

Sibell watched from within the shelter of the forest as Sir Gilbert and half his men left later that July morning, intent on making their way north with all speed. They were an impressive sight, their weapons gleaming in the sun, the huge horses snorting their impatience to be off.

Her gaze sought out Roger, riding at the front

on his massive horse, Snowflake. His euphoria over the proposed journey had been almost tangible, his excitement infectious while he was with her, but now he was gone, her heart was heavy. She knew this was the only way and that he was confident of a positive outcome, but seeing the column of riders disappear in a cloud of dust, she felt utterly alone and defenceless.

There had been rumours that the Earl of March had landed at Sandwich just over a week earlier, together with his fellow earls, Warwick and Salisbury, and their men. Sibell was afraid Roger and the others might be caught up in any fighting which might ensue, although Gilbert had reassured his own wife he wouldn't do anything foolish.

'I'm not a hotheaded youth,' he told her with a smile. 'And this journey is necessary, you know that. I promise you we'll keep to smaller tracks and stay out of the way as much as possible.'

Sibell prayed he would keep that promise.

'Jake, how come you never talk about your wife?' They were having lunch in a lovely restaurant and Melissa didn't want him to spoil the day by talking about their future. She'd sensed that he was on the verge of saying something and grasped at this straw to distract him.

'Karen? Why do you ask?' Jake frowned slightly.

'I'm curious. You haven't been a widower all that long. Surely you must still be grieving?'

He sighed. 'Will you think me a dreadful person if I say no?'

Melissa looked up and saw pain in his eyes. She reached out across the table and put her hand over his. 'No, but I'd love to know the reason.'

'Very well, but it's a long story.'

'We have all day.'

He was quiet for a while, before beginning his tale. 'Well, Karen was very pretty – petite, blonde and vivacious – and when we met I was bowled over. I couldn't believe my luck when she agreed to go out with me, let alone marry me. We were happy at first. I think I told you that we lived in London, and Karen was a social butterfly, always doing something, always busy. When I was offered the partnership here in a small village practice, however, the endless arguments began.'

'She didn't want to move?'

'No. I persuaded her it was only for a short while, a step up on the career ladder, and that we could return to London eventually. But although she agreed to move, she didn't believe I would ever go back. Even so, she never made the smallest effort to adapt to living in the country, just went on endless trips up to London and her friends.' He sighed. 'Then after Amy was born, she suffered badly from post-natal depression, and things went from bad to worse.'

'Oh, dear.'

'Oh, dear, indeed. I tried to help her, honestly I did. I tried to be understanding and patient,

347

hiring nannies and babysitters so she could continue to go to town, but it didn't work. Giving her a taste of what she was missing only made her want to go back even more. She began to spend more and more time away from home, ignoring poor Amy. It nearly broke my heart.

'That final evening before her death Karen snapped completely. She was shouting at me, "I can't stand it any more, I tell you. I'm leaving, and don't try to stop me. I want a divorce immediately. You'll be hearing from my lawyers." There was no way of reasoning with her. I begged her to put up with the country for just a few more months. I couldn't just leave the practice without giving notice, with old Mr Montgomery, the senior partner, ill and no one else available, but I promised that as soon as things got back to normal, I would look for another job up in London.'

Jake stared into the flame of the candle on the table, his eyes blue pools of sadness. Melissa wanted to take him in her arms and comfort him, but he continued with the rest of his story. '"It's too late, Jake," Karen said. "Too late for us. Can't you see? You like it here. Either way, one of us will be unhappy." Clutching at straws, I asked what was to become of Amy if we divorced. I couldn't bear to think of losing her. "You can keep her here for the moment. She'll be fine with the nanny," Karen told me. I know she loved her daughter and she was probably only saying things like that to annoy me, but I was too upset to argue further.'

Melissa squeezed his hand tightly, feeling his pain as if it were her own. She knew exactly what he had been through, the turmoil and sense of incredulity that things could go so badly wrong. 'Then what happened?' she whispered.

'I knew deep down Karen was right. Our marriage was at an end, had been since the move, really. But then I made the biggest mistake of all – I let her leave before we had a chance to think more rationally. She was in a right state, as was I, and of course I should have stopped her from leaving the house, but I wasn't thinking clearly. She drove off at great speed without paying attention to her driving. Perhaps that was why she lost control of the car and spun into a tree.'

'Oh, Jake, you mustn't blame yourself. It was just as much Karen's fault, and surely the accident could have been caused by something else?'

'Maybe, the weather was pretty bad that night, but still . . .'

'No, stop it. It's not your fault and you can't change things, anyway. You've got to put it behind you.'

'I know it's time to move on. I'm so glad I met you, perhaps together we can face our demons. What do you say?'

Melissa sighed inwardly. She'd known he would ask eventually and she couldn't stall him forever.

'Yes, soon, Jake, soon. Please, just give me a bit more time.'

★　★　★

'So how was your visit?' Melissa stirred her tea before taking a cautious sip of the scalding brew and hoped her voice sounded casual. She was consumed with curiosity. It seemed her daughter had had a wonderful time. Jolie had come skipping in through the front door after waving goodbye to her father. Steve, on the other hand, had only nodded curtly before driving off at some speed.

'Great! Tess and Nell are really sweet, and they liked me a lot. Tess let me feed her, and Daisy says she hardly ever lets anyone other than her mummy do that. When I'm a bit older she'll let me babysit them, she said.'

'Really? And how's your father?'

'Oh, he's fine. Do you know, Tess cuddled me and wanted me to play with her. She's so small and cute.' A wistful look crept into her eyes. 'I wish I had brothers and sisters here. It was fun not to be the only child.'

'Well, now you know it wasn't so bad you can always go back soon. And here you have Amy. Isn't she like a sister?' Melissa resolutely ignored the little voice inside her head which reminded her that if she stopped being so stubborn, the two girls really would be sisters.

Jolie brightened. 'Yes, of course.' She was quiet for a while before adding out of the blue, 'She's actually really nice, you know.'

'Who, Amy?'

Jolie giggled. 'No, Mum, I mean Daisy. She's very pretty and all that and I could see why Daddy

350

likes her, but she's also a really nice person. I kind of felt sorry for her, she was a bit washed-out and looked really tired. She said the girls make her exhausted.'

'I can well believe it,' Melissa said with feeling. 'The little one's only a few weeks old, and the other one can't be much more than a year-and-a-half, right? I remember it was bad enough with one toddler, never mind a baby as well.'

'Yes.' Jolie was thoughtful. 'It's funny, Mum, but I didn't want to like Daisy, even after what you said. I still thought she ruined everything for us, but when I went there and talked to her a little everything seemed different. She said she felt bad about taking Daddy away from us and she was sorry, but she really loves him, even when he makes her mad.'

Melissa smiled. 'I guess that's okay then, because I don't blame her, either, not any more. And you want your dad to be happy, right?'

'Yes. Maybe he and Daisy and the girls could come and stay with us sometime?'

Melissa choked on a mouthful of tea. 'Really, Jolie, I don't think so. I'm supposed to hate her for stealing my husband.' Her protest sounded half-hearted, even to herself. It was strange, but the idea of having her ex-husband's partner for a visit didn't really sound as outrageous to her as it would have done a year ago. However, even though Daisy may not be the grasping, voracious man-eater Melissa had at first imagined, having her to stay might be taking things a bit too far.

Jolie grinned. 'But you don't, do you?'

'No, but that doesn't mean I want to be friends with her.'

'Why not? I'm sure you'd like her, you know.'

'Well, maybe, but I think it would be better if we didn't have them to stay quite yet. Perhaps in a year or so.'

In the days that followed she once again put her fee-paying work to one side and embarked on a frantic search for Roger or any mention of either Ashleigh, Idenhurst or the Presseille family. The thought of Jake's marriage proposal spurred her on and there was also a new sense of urgency within her, as if Roger had upped the pressure somehow. She enlisted the help of Colin, Jenny and a colleague who worked mainly in the counties north of London, but without much success.

They did find Sir Gilbert Presseille mentioned in an old document dealing with the battle of Northampton, which took place on the tenth of July 1460. The Earl of March, York's son, was victorious and the document mentioned some of the men to whom he owed gratitude for this feat. Sir Gilbert was one such.

'What was he doing all the way up there? Northampton is miles from here. Do you think he was a Yorkist all along?'

'It's possible. A lot of the people of Kent appear

to have been on the Duke's side, but it could have been a last-minute decision. Guess we'll never know.'

'Oh, this has to be the most infuriating case I've ever worked on,' Melissa grumbled. Unfortunately, it was also the most important one and she couldn't let it rest, even though it seemed the trail ended there.

'There has to be something else, there just has to be.'

A few days later she forgot all about Roger, however, as something even more momentous occurred, something which occupied her mind to the exclusion of all else.

'No, it can't be!' Melissa shook the little container as if that would make it change its mind. The line on the indicator remained stubbornly blue. Shocked, she sank down onto the closed toilet seat. It would seem Jolie would have her wish after all.

How could this have happened? They'd been so careful. *Except for that first time . . .* Melissa knew that was all it took. After all, this wasn't the first time she'd been in this situation. 'Damn, you'd think I would have learned my lesson then,' she muttered.

'Lord, I must be the most fertile woman on earth.' She glared at her reflection in the mirror. 'Melissa Grantham, you are a first-class idiot. Stupid, stupid, idiot.'

Jake would probably be delighted, and so would everyone else. Except her. Not that she didn't want more children, but this one hadn't been conceived under what she would call normal circumstances. What sort of child resulted from a union between a human and a ghost? A slightly hysterical laugh escaped her.

'Get a grip, woman,' she admonished the face in the mirror sternly. Ghosts could no more create children than they could come alive again. This was Jake's child, and no one else's. She lowered her face into her hands and tried to massage away the tension building steadily inside her temples.

'So what do I do now?' She thought she felt a caress at the nape of her neck and shrugged it away. If Roger was trying to pacify her now, he was too late. This was all his fault and she'd had enough.

If only she could solve the mystery. If only she could make Roger go away. But she had tried everything she could possibly think of . . . or had she?

'No, wait,' she exclaimed. She gritted her teeth in determination. There was one thing she hadn't tried yet.

CHAPTER 29

'Sibell, my love, you are a sight for sore eyes.'
'You're back!' Sibell was startled to find
Roger outside Ashleigh Manor's front door
in full daylight and alone, but since she was over-
joyed to see him again, she forgot everything
except the here and now. She flew into his arms
with a little shriek.

'Indeed I am and with excellent news. I've been
acknowledged by Sir Gilbert and have come to
formally ask for your hand in marriage.'

'Sir Gilbert is definitely your father? And he's
agreed to tell everyone?' At his nod, she laughed
and kissed him. Happiness bubbled up inside her
as he kissed her back with the pent-up passion of
many weeks and for a while they both forgot his
errand in their blissful reunion.

'What is the meaning of this?' The sneering voice
of Simon intruded on their idyll. He sauntered up
to the couple with his arms crossed over his chest
aggressively, closely followed by his younger
brother Edmund, who wasn't slow to add his
comments.

'Well, well, if it isn't the whoreson of Langford

making free with our sister. What do you think of that, brother?'

Roger froze and cursed under his breath. Sibell's heart disappeared into her throat and she swallowed convulsively. They shouldn't have been so careless, but in truth, the sight of Roger after such a long time had obliterated every other thought. When he was near she couldn't think rationally.

'I have come to ask for your sister's hand in marriage,' Roger informed the brothers stiffly, looking from one disbelieving face to the other. They quickly recovered from the shock and burst into loud guffaws of laughter.

'Marriage? To you? That's rich, upon my word.'

Sibell stamped her foot. 'Stop it, the pair of you! He's come to see Father, not you. Leave him alone.'

'Oooh, the little cat shows her claws.' Simon's childish jeer made her even more furious and she was on the verge of boxing his ear.

'Very well, this way, sir. I'm sure our father will be very interested in hearing what you have to say.' Edmund made their guest an elaborate bow and indicated the way into the hall. Roger managed a reassuring look at Sibell before marching past the brothers with his head held high. Into the lion's den.

Simon fixed Sibell with an angry glare. 'As for you, go away and leave this to us. It's men's business. I'm sure Father will call for you if you are needed.'

With a smirk he followed his brother and Sibell stood looking after him, seething with anger and nerves, but unsure what to do about it. Oh, if only she had been a man . . . Well, she'd be damned if she was going anywhere. She had a right to be present, too.

Exorcism was an ugly word. It conjured up images of angry demons, of people possessed by the devil and of evil practices. It made Melissa feel sick to the stomach, but she couldn't see any other way. There was simply no alternative. Once her decision had been made, she went in search of Dorothy immediately.

The old lady was doubtful at first. 'Are you absolutely sure about this? It sounds a bit drastic, you know.' It took all Melissa's powers of persuasion to make her great-aunt understand that this course of action was necessary.

'I just can't go on like this, Dorothy,' she told the older woman, 'and you have to admit I've tried everything else. It's driving me insane.'

'Yes, I suppose so, but . . .' Dorothy shook her head sadly. 'I just have this feeling it will do more harm than good, but on the other hand I hate to see you suffer. It's been so nice to have you and Jolie living here, I couldn't bear it if you left now.'

Melissa hugged the old lady and reassured her. 'Of course we won't leave. We love it here.' Ashleigh felt like home now and Melissa knew it always would. 'But I refuse to share the house with Roger. If he stays you'll soon be living with a raving lunatic. I mean it.'

'Well, if you say so.' Dorothy didn't protest any more, but Melissa knew she was still uneasy.

The Reverend Mr Brindle was a large, florid man, whose supreme self-confidence was evident in the way he carried himself. Here was clearly a vicar who believed himself chosen to lead the poor sinners of his congregation, Melissa thought scathingly. He obviously considered himself to be in a position to judge them as well. Quite why she disliked the man so much from the very beginning she couldn't say. She only knew she had to force herself to be civil when he looked down his long nose at her.

The Reverend Brindle had brought an assistant. Small and thin, and painfully new to his vocation, Mr Atwell didn't say a word beyond a polite greeting. His Adam's apple bobbed up and down nervously. He was clearly in awe of Mr Brindle, his gaze full of admiration whenever he looked at the older man.

'When performing the rite of exorcism it is vital that a second minister be present,' Mr Brindle informed them after the necessary introductions had been made. 'One has to be prepared to meet strong opposition, spiritual and psychic, and should one minister become incapacitated the other has to be ready to step in.'

Melissa almost laughed. She couldn't imagine

Mr Atwell stepping into the breach at a time of crisis. The poor man looked like he was wishing himself a hundred miles away. Anywhere but in this room. He was sweating profusely and kept rubbing his palms against his over-sized cassock.

She detained him by the door by placing a hand on his arm, and even that small gesture made him jump. 'Are you all right, Mr Atwell?' she whispered.

'I, er . . .' He cleared his throat. 'I'll be fine. It's just that I never thought . . . I mean we were taught about these things at college, of course, but I never imagined anyone actually . . . that's to say . . .'

Melissa took pity on him. 'You didn't think anyone did this sort of thing in real life, is that it?' He nodded, eyes wide with fright.

'Yes, yes that's precisely what I thought. And in my first week, too.' He hesitated and swallowed hard. 'I have to tell you,' his face went a shade paler and he leaned close to whisper confidingly, 'that I saw one once.'

'A ghost?'

'Yes, when I was a child. I've never been so scared in my life. It was an evil looking thing, floating about.' He shuddered. 'I would rather not repeat the experience.'

'I'm sorry, but I really am desperate, Mr Atwell. The ghost in this house has been plaguing me for months. If you were that scared just from one sighting, imagine how I feel having to live with one all the time.'

'Oh, of course. I hadn't considered that.' He made a visible effort to pull himself together. 'Well, I'm sure Mr Brindle will make every effort to help you and I'll try to assist as best I can.'

'Thank you, I really appreciate it.'

Their whispered conversation at an end, Melissa walked over to the Reverend Brindle. 'You have done this before then?' she asked. Her own body was shaking. This wasn't going to be any easier for her than for poor Mr Atwell.

'Several times, and I met with little resistance.'

Probably because there were no spirits there to resist you, but you might find it slightly more difficult in this house. Melissa kept her thought to herself and just nodded.

'Please, have a seat.' Dorothy indicated the sofa, and he sat down ponderously before rummaging in a large black bag. He brought out a Bible, a crucifix, some candles and a container of holy water. These items he placed with great care on a pristine white cloth, which he spread out on the coffee table in front of him. He proceeded to light the candles and they flickered, as if they too were uneasy. Mr Atwell perched nervously beside him, his eyes darting around the room.

Melissa's hands were clammy. A tension headache had been building steadily behind her eyes for the last hour, and she wished the whole process over and done with. *Thank goodness Jolie isn't here, at least.* Melissa hadn't told her about the exorcism and hoped it would all be over before her daughter came back from visiting Amy. She glanced at Dorothy, who was sitting quietly on the other side of the room looking resigned. The old lady's fingers were laced together in her lap as if in readiness for prayer. Melissa wondered if Dorothy had been right. Would they do more harm than good?

Exorcism. The word echoed inside her, and knifed the back of her head. The ache began to pound at her brain with the strength of a sledge-hammer. *Can't the stupid man hurry up?* She wanted to scream with frustration.

'You're sure this will work, Mr Brindle?' She plaited her fingers together in her lap to keep from biting her nails.

'My dear Ms Grantham, the Church exists to undo the devil's work and it certainly appears that you have some form of demonic presence in this house. We shall bring the power of God to bear on those poor souls who need deliverance from evil, and perform a spiritual cleansing of this dwelling. I think you will find it most helpful.'

Melissa still had serious doubts, but she kept silent as he prepared himself with a prayer.

'Nooo! Wait! Listen to me.'

The plea made Melissa jump and she received a look of irritation from Mr Brindle. She glanced at the other occupants of the room, but they didn't seem to have heard anything. *Roger, please, we must do this*, she answered the voice silently inside her head and tried to concentrate on the priest's words. *It's for your own good.*

The vicar stood up and began by blessing the house, sprinkling holy water into all four corners of the room. 'Peace be to this house and all who dwell in it,' he intoned. 'Let us pray together. Our Father, who art in heaven, hallowed be thy name . . .'

The familiar words of the Lord's Prayer flowed over Melissa and soothed her agitated mind temporarily as she recited them with the others. She relaxed slightly. However, when they reached the words '. . . but deliver us from evil . . .' there was a sudden noticeable drop in temperature, and her teeth started to chatter. If the others noticed, they gave no sign. She scanned the room, but couldn't see Roger anywhere. Would he put in an appearance, or would the vicar's words just make him disappear forever? Somehow the thought of that possibility made her want to cry out in anguish.

'. . . for thine is the kingdom, the power and the glory for ever and ever. Amen.' As Mr Brindle finished, the two candles were swiftly extinguished by a draught of air. The younger clergyman turned ashen and swallowed hard when the cold gust whooshed past his face.

The Reverend Brindle was made of sterner stuff and ignored the interruption. 'Free this place, O Lord, from all disturbances of demons and deliver it from evil. Spirits begone from this place, be banished for ever . . .'

The headache had grown to monumental proportions and Melissa cradled her head with her hands to ease the pounding.

'In the name of God the Father, God the Son, and God the Holy Spirit, I command you to leave here and proceed to that place beyond death which God has prepared for your reception and healing.'

The pain was agonising. Unbearable.

The priest repeated his command to the spirits of the house to leave, and as Melissa's eyes opened briefly she saw Mr Atwell staring towards the fireplace in stupefied terror. She turned to look at the familiar figure of Roger for the last time, but instead of his normal handsome self, her eyes encountered a horrifying sight. He was bleeding, battered and bruised, swaying as if he was having trouble staying upright. His face was contorted with pain and rage, and she could almost see the sparks flying from him. The air all around fairly crackled with his fury and frustration and in his hand he brandished his sword, as if defending himself from multiple attackers. Melissa drew in a shaky breath and looked at Dorothy. Could she see him, too? She thought she probably could, since the old lady's mouth was open in astonishment even though she remained calm.

The door to the hall slammed shut with such force that it shook the walls and a painting became dislodged. A crack appeared in the plaster next to the doorframe, zig-zagging its way up the wall. Mr Atwell gave a pitiful little moan and crumpled into a heap on the sofa in a dead faint. Everyone ignored him.

Eyeing the imposing spectre by the fireplace with determination, the Reverend Brindle raised his voice to repeat his command to the spirits for the third and last time.

'Free this place, O Lord, from all disturbances . . .'

'No! Hold! I haven't finished . . .'

Melissa's head was being torn apart by the wails of anguish. She was in real danger of being extremely sick right there on the carpet. She tried to will the voice to leave her alone, but there was no let-up. It was relentless, wearing her down. She just couldn't stand it.

'NO! Stop! Please, please, stop,' she screamed at the vicar, great sobs beginning to rack her body. She supported her head between her hands. 'We c-can't do this, I'm s-sorry,' she hiccoughed. 'It's wrong.'

Mr Brindle had been cut off in mid-sentence and it obviously wasn't something he was used to. He glared at her angrily.

'My dear Ms Grantham,' he hissed, 'I am a man of God and you are probably under the influence of the demons I've come to expel. I shall ignore you.'

'No, please, you have to stop. It's all wrong.'

Visibly controlling himself with an effort, he came over and put a large hand on the top of her head in a gesture of concern. 'My dear child, what makes you think it's wrong for a soul to take his rightful place beside God? Surely, that is as it should be?'

'No, not in this case. Not yet. He – that is the spirit – has something which binds him to earth, unfinished business. Until it's done, he can never rest in peace. Please believe me, I'm absolutely sure of this.' The tears continued to stream down her cheeks, but the ache behind her eyes was receding. 'I want you to leave now.'

'Very well.' Tight-lipped, he conceded defeat, although only temporarily as his next words confirmed. 'I shan't continue today, but I beg of you to reconsider your decision during the next few days. I'll be happy to come back another time when you are less distraught. There is no need for you to be present if you don't wish to be.' He clearly thought it was her own feelings at stake here, and Melissa saw no reason to enlighten him further. Let him think whatever he wanted. It made no difference. She had to find another way.

Mr Brindle packed up his things with jerky movements, indicating his impatience with such stupidity, but he couldn't continue without permission. Dragging the terrified, but slightly recovered, Mr Atwell with him, he disappeared after a curt, 'Goodbye.'

Completely drained, Melissa stayed in her chair as Dorothy saw the clergymen out. The angry shape by the fireplace had melted into the shadows as soon as Mr Brindle had stopped his incantation.

Melissa was alone. For now.

CHAPTER 30

'You've come to do what?'
Instead of Sibell's father, Roger was facing her eldest half-brother Henry, the dim-witted one. Apparently John of Ashleigh was out inspecting the fields so Roger had had to state his business to the heir instead. He tried to keep calm as he repeated his errand a second time, although it annoyed him that Simon had failed to mention his sire's absence. 'Is your father expected back soon? If not, I can return later.'

Henry stared at him with eyes that were dangerously close to popping out of their sockets. Roger regarded him warily in return. 'I've no idea,' Henry said. 'And what on earth makes you think he'd let Sibell wed a bastard, landless knight?'

'I am not landless,' Roger protested, keeping his voice level, despite the provocation. 'I stand to inherit some holdings from my maternal uncle, Roger of Langford the elder . . .' he began, but with a snarl of anger, Simon erupted from his seat on a nearby bench and came to jab his finger into Roger's middle.

'We don't care how many holdings your uncle

is giving you.' Simon spat vehemently on to the floor. 'Nor if the King himself gives you holdings. You're still an upstart nobody of no account, and we'll not have our sister associating with the likes of you.'

'But I–'

'You must know Sibell is to marry Sir Fulke of Thornby come September. Father has but recently returned from negotiating the contract. It's all settled.' He glanced at his other brothers. 'Now since you've not heeded our earlier warning, I think we'd best send you on your way with a reminder. What say you, Henry, Edmund?'

'Aye, Father did say he'd love for us to teach this son of a bitch a lesson,' Edmund smirked.

'Wait, you've not heard everything yet.' Roger strived to keep his voice even and stand his ground.

The fourth brother, Godwin, suddenly spoke up. He'd been sitting by one of the windows, staring out passively, but he rose now and walked over to join the group by the hearth. 'Let the man speak first,' he said.

'Stay out of this, Godwin. Lord, but you're such a runt,' Simon grumbled.

'I may be a runt, but at least I don't make ill-informed judgements,' Godwin retorted, glaring back. He turned back to Roger. 'Now what did you have to add, Sir Roger?'

'I was about to say that Sir Gilbert Presseille has agreed to acknowledge me as his natural son. He's backing my proposal.'

'A likely tale,' Edmund scoffed. 'And what difference does it make? As I said, Sibell is promised elsewhere.'

'Your father was keen for the connection with the Presseille family once before,' Roger reminded them.

'Well he isn't now he's got Sir Fulke instead. This changes nothing,' Simon spat again.

'Sir Gilbert has promised me some of his holdings as a wedding gift. He is very fond of your sister.' Roger glanced at Sibell, who had come sidling in during the conversation and now sat watching from a shadowed corner, obviously trying not to attract notice and thus make things worse. She shook her head slightly, as if to warn him not to draw attention to her presence, so he concentrated on the brothers instead.

'Perhaps we should at least inform Father and let him make the decision,' Godwin suggested, looking from Roger to the others. 'I'll go and fetch him if you have the time to wait?' Roger nodded his agreement and Godwin headed for the door. 'I'll be as quick as I can.'

'Yes, go, run to Father like you always do,' Simon sneered. As soon as they heard the front door close, he added, 'And in the meantime, we can have some sport.' He grinned at his brothers and unsheathed his sword. Henry chuckled and Edmund followed suit, a look of pure malice crossing his features.

'I'd say it was time to pay you back, Sir Knight.'

He laughed and in the next instant, the three of them attacked.

With grim determination, Roger pulled out his sword to defend himself.

Sibell screamed. Why had Roger come alone? she wondered. Why hadn't he brought his new-found father? Or, at the very least, Hugone. She could only think he must have been in such a hurry to see her again and tell her of his good fortune that he hadn't been thinking clearly. Her stomach muscles clenched in fear.

'For the love of God, stop this madness!' She forgot about staying unobtrusive and tried to throw herself into the fray.

'Stay out of this, woman.' Henry cuffed her so hard she flew backwards and tripped over a bench, hitting her head on the wall. She sank to the floor, the pain so strong it made her nauseous. Tears of frustration rolled down her cheeks as she realised she had no chance of helping her beloved. Nothing she could do would be of any use.

Roger fought like a man possessed. Time and again he held her brothers off, managing to turn just in time as they came at him from all sides. He had excellent reflexes and thrust his sword with lightning speed, wounding at least two of the brothers. Sibell knew he had bested four men once before, because he'd told her so. She prayed it hadn't been an idle boast and that he could do so again. As she watched the fight in mounting horror, however, Sibell began to think that perhaps there was one crucial difference – this time Roger wasn't dealing with honourable men.

Oh, Godwin, where are you? Hurry!

Terrified now, she made another attempt to join the fight, latching on to Simon's sword arm like an eagle holding on to its prey, but his strength was such that he managed to dislodge her with a single, impatient shake. Before she had time to try again, he gave her an almighty shove that thrust her into the wall once more. Her head swam and her vision became blurred.

Through a haze of pain, she saw Roger continue to fight valiantly. His breathing was becoming laboured, and sweat poured into his eyes. Impatiently he swiped at it with his sleeve. It was obviously more difficult by the minute to keep them all at bay. She saw him inch closer to the door, intending to make his escape, but someone was there before him, blocking his way.

Henry's sword had gone flying clean across the room, but instead of taking the time out to retrieve it, he had picked up a sturdy piece of wood from the pile next to the fire. The light of battle was in his eyes as he advanced on the man who had humiliated his brothers before the crowd at Idenhurst.

Just then, Godwin came into the room and took in the scene, his eyes widening in horror. He must have seen Henry's intent at the same time as Sibell, and launched himself in his brother's direction while shouting, 'Henry, no!' But it was too late.

Roger may have felt the stirring of the air before the heavy wood connected with the back of his skull, but he didn't have time to react. As his knees buckled, he looked up, his eyes connecting with Sibell's. She could only stare, horrified, as his lips formed her name, but no sound emerged.

Sibell screamed again. '*Nooooo!* Roger!' The drawn-out sound stopped her other brothers in their tracks and they froze, swords held in mid-strike. Slowly, they lowered their weapons and stared at each other as they took in what had happened

The room was suddenly eerily silent.

The nightmare struck without warning, even more frightening because of its intensity.

'*Melissa, Melissa!*' Several different voices were calling her, beckoning her towards . . . what? She didn't know, but she was afraid of it.

In the black void of darkness the voices were soft and silky at first, like a lover whispering endearments. They were persuasive, cajoling, but soon their tone changed subtly. She began to shake with fear and tried to say 'no'. Nothing happened. No sound was heard from her, but the voices continued, angrier now.

Suddenly faces appeared out of nowhere, swirling around her, luminous, translucent. She didn't know who they were or why they were there. Disembodied faces, nothing else. Some were happy, some sad. There were angry faces, threatening ones, too. She tried to shrink back, but they surrounded her on all sides, pursued her relentlessly. There was nowhere to hide.

A beautiful woman floated past. She reminded Melissa of herself, but the woman's icy glare startled her and froze her to the marrow. Then a man, breathtakingly handsome, smiled seductively as he sidled past, but when Melissa dared to relax even a fraction, his features turned angry, ugly and twisted. She gasped and her lungs constricted painfully.

'Melissa, you know you have to do it.' The voices were building to a crescendo, terrifying her into frozen immobility. The disembodied heads floated nearer, closing in on her, hemming her in on all sides. She had to get away.

She tried to scream, but as before nothing happened. Gathering her last ounces of strength she made one more attempt. A pitiful little whimper was all that came out, but it was enough.

It woke her up.

Someone put a cool hand on her brow. 'Relax, you're just dreaming, sweetheart.' Jake's arms enveloped her and she remembered that she was with him at Ashleigh Cottage. She tried to control her breathing so as to slow down her frantic heartbeat. She'd only meant to close her eyes for a moment, but must have dozed off. Although she knew it had only been a dream, she no longer felt safe there or anywhere else.

'I don't think so,' she whispered. 'It's all part of the same thing.'

'No, come on. It's only natural you should have nightmares, you've been through a lot recently. It will pass.'

'It won't, Jake. I was so sure the exorcism would end it, one way or another, but it's just made everything worse. Roger is even more determined now. I can feel it.'

The aborted exorcism had shaken her badly and she'd been so distraught, she had gone to see the local doctor for some advice. He had been quietly sympathetic and to her relief didn't ridicule her belief in the ghost.

'I'm not saying I believe in ghosts and the like, Ms Grantham,' he said kindly, 'but if you believe in them – and clearly you do – then you need to remove yourself from their vicinity before it's too late. The mind is a strange thing, and I think rest is the only cure for what ails you. You've been overdoing things lately.' He added as an after-thought, looking her straight in the eyes, 'Being pregnant often gives rise to strange fancies, as you probably know. It's certainly a drain on your energy. You must think of what's best for the baby, now.'

Having her pregnancy confirmed in such a stark manner made Melissa realise she couldn't ignore it any longer. A decision had to be made one way or another, but she knew she wasn't in a fit state at the moment. She had to escape from Ashleigh and Roger, if only for a short time, so that she could re-charge her batteries.

'Jake, I've got to get away for a while. I'm thinking of taking a holiday.'

'That might be a good idea.'

'Dorothy suggested a health farm. She said a friend of hers went and swears it did her a world of good.'

'I don't know. Sounds like a lot of money for not very much if you ask me. You really think mud packs are going to help?' The smile she could hear in Jake's voice calmed her slightly, but she knew it wasn't really a joking matter.

'Hmm, maybe not. I quite fancy somewhere warm actually.'

'You could perhaps find one of those last-minute holidays? Spain, Italy? Do you want me to come with you?'

'Would you be terribly offended if I said no? Only, I really think I need to go by myself. I have to do some serious thinking and if you come, you'll only distract me. In the nicest possible way, of course.'

She felt him stiffening slightly, then he sighed. 'Fine. I probably couldn't find a locum at such short notice anyway.' Jake pretended indifference, but Melissa could tell he was hurt. A part of her wanted to ask him to come in order to soothe his ruffled feathers, but she knew deep down she had to go by herself. She needed space.

In the end, she settled for Mallorca and Jolie persuaded her to take her and Amy as well. 'We won't be any trouble, I promise,' she cajoled. 'You can just rest as much as you want.'

Melissa had to smile at the vision conjured up by Jolie's words. Two angelic twelve-year-olds wasn't how she would have chosen to describe the pair normally. However, she would have felt guilty about leaving Jolie behind, so this was the best solution. She was lucky enough to find a holiday within her budget and Amy was given permission to go. Although Melissa sensed that Jake was still upset about not being asked to come, she pretended not to notice and breathed a sigh of relief as the plane took off from English soil.

At last, she would be free from Roger and any reminders of him, if only for a while.

The balmy gusts of wind were extremely welcome and Melissa closed her eyes to enjoy their cooling effect on her heated body. But lying on a lounge chair in the oppressive heat of a Mallorcan sun, she had far too much time to think, which wasn't what she was meant to be doing. She was supposed to relax and recover her strength. She concentrated on the soothing sound of waves splashing on the Mediterranean shore nearby.

Dorothy had warned her it would be too hot and Melissa was beginning to agree with her now. It really was burning. She shifted restlessly and debated whether to go for a swim, but she felt too lethargic. Finally, she couldn't stand the heat any more and walked over to the edge of the hotel pool. As she slid gratefully into the cooling water she breathed a sigh of pure pleasure. Jolie and Amy were diving at the other end, and there was noise and laughter all around her, but she ignored it. She leaned back to float slowly around, buoyed up by the wet cocoon. The water slapped gently over her stomach, which didn't as yet show much sign of the baby growing within. Why couldn't life always be this simple? she wondered.

The dream came unexpectedly after a respite of almost two weeks. Melissa sat up in her hotel bed, gasping for air and fighting the panic threatening to overwhelm her.

'Oh, God, not again,' she moaned. Her heart seemed to be trapped somewhere inside her chest, desperately beating on its prison bars.

Someone had screamed her name. No, not her name; Sibell's. She knew with terrifying certainty that it had been the scream of someone desperate. Someone in need of her help. The thought caused a tremor to shoot through her. She swallowed down the bile rising in her throat and exhaled slowly.

Roger. Even here in Mallorca, she couldn't escape him. He still wanted something from her, and he wasn't giving up. Hanging her head in defeat, Melissa climbed wearily out of bed and let herself out onto the balcony. She leaned on the balustrade, took deep breaths of the cool night air to calm her agitated nerves and listened to the lullaby played by the thousands of grasshoppers, the Spanish *cicadas*.

I was a fool to think I could get away. The problem wasn't going to disappear just because she went on holiday for a few weeks. Roger would be waiting for her at Ashleigh Manor, inexorably drawing her towards the end. *But the end of what?* If only she knew what he wanted. Was it something that would harm her or her baby? Dare she take the risk? Did she have a choice? So many questions and no answers.

'I can't help you if you don't tell me what to do, Roger,' she whispered, gripping the railing so hard her knuckles turned white. She felt a stirring in her mind as she said the last word, but it was so faint she couldn't be sure.

With a sigh she closed her eyes. It was almost time to go home, and it was past time for a reckoning. Melissa clenched her jaw in determination. She wouldn't break. She had to be strong. For herself and her baby; for Jake and Roger.

CHAPTER 31

Sibell watched in stunned disbelief as Roger slumped to the floor, her scream reverberating round her brain. For the life of her, she couldn't move, not so much as a finger. Her whole body was numb, her brain refusing to take in what she had just witnessed.

The entire room appeared frozen in time until her father arrived a moment later, slamming the door open and glaring at the occupants.

'What is going on here? Can I not leave the house for even a short time without . . .' He broke off in mid-sentence as he took in the scene. 'What the devil is the meaning of this?'

Sibell knew her father had never liked Roger and it was more than likely he'd told his sons to teach him a lesson after he had bested them at Idenhurst. She doubted her father had meant them to act on his words, however, at least not to this extent. He may even have been jesting while in his cups. Roger was, after all, attached to Sir Gilbert's household, in charge of training his men, and her father was well aware that Sir Gilbert wouldn't take too kindly to having any of his men beaten senseless.

She found her tongue at last and let out another ear-piercing scream of horror. Her father's expression mirrored her sentiments as they both stared at the lifeless form of Sir Roger, lying in a pool of blood on the floor near the door. The four brothers remained virtually motionless, three of them breathing hard, and still with the light of battle in their eyes. No one moved until Sibell staggered to her feet and ran over to Roger, throwing herself down on top of him, feeling for his pulse. Her feverish hands tried all the usual places, but without success.

'Jesu God, you've killed him!' Her eyes turned accusingly from one brother to the next, before she launched herself at the nearest one in a frenzy of rage. 'You foul swine, you have murdered him!'

'No, he's just unconscious,' Simon protested, although his voice didn't sound very convincing. He looked down at Sir Roger anxiously. 'We've only taught the man a lesson. It was long overdue.'

'He's not unconscious. He's dead! Dead, do you hear? *You . . . have . . . murdered . . . him.*' Sibell's small fists beat against his chest, punctuating her words, and her nails gouged at his face. Simon defended himself as best he could, but in the end he tired of the attack and cuffed her hard to stop her. She froze for an instant, then fell to the floor in a sobbing heap next to Roger.

Godwin glared at Henry in disgust. 'I told you

to stop, but as usual you wouldn't listen. You always have to go one step further than anyone else, you brainless clod.'

'Shut your mouth, runt. He got what he deserved,' Henry retorted, eyes narrowed in rage. He clenched his fists and looked ready to attack his brother next.

'You were three against one.' Godwin threw up his hands in exasperation. 'He was already beaten; there was no need to go so far. You should have let him leave, you fool.' The others looked at Godwin in surprise. It was seldom he was roused to make a speech of such length and vehemence.

Presently Sibell, who was still wailing and clutching at the body, saw her father's gaze return to the man on the floor and to her. 'Control yourself, girl,' he said brusquely. He pushed her out of the way and bent down to check Roger's pulse for himself. 'Surely, you didn't go that far?' he muttered and checked once more. Finding nothing, his anger returned with a vengeance. 'By all the saints, did I say anything about killing this man?' he hissed at his sons. 'You half-wits, you'll have to leave or you'll all hang for this.'

'But Father, you said to teach him a lesson', Henry protested, sounding petulant now the heat of the moment was giving way to more rational thought.

'I meant eject him from the house if he ever dared to show his face hereabouts. Knock him about a bit, yes, scare him a little, certainly, but I never said a word about killing. God's blood, what are we to do?' He began to pace the room, as if the motion would force his brain into action. 'We'll have to hide the body. If anyone asks, he was never here.' He pointed at his youngest son. 'You. Take his horse and set him loose somewhere far from here, and the rest of you,' he fixed his other sons with an icy glare, 'take care of the body. Then make yourselves scarce for a while, all of you.' He glanced at his distraught daughter. 'I'll see to her. If she knows what's good for her, she'll keep her mouth shut.'

Sibell turned cold eyes on him. 'Never!' she hissed. 'Do you hear me? You'll not get away with this. You'll have to kill me, too.'

'Don't try my patience too far, you little fool,' her father growled, clenching his fists, 'or I might just do that.'

'Hah! What do I care now whether I live or die? You're the fool here, Father. Didn't Godwin tell you? Your sons have just killed the only remaining son of Sir Gilbert Presseille . . . and my husband.' Her voice broke on another anguished sob.

'Husband?' Five pairs of eyes, widened in surprise, stared at her. Their owners looked as though they'd turned to stone.

Her father was the first to recover. 'What do you mean? Have you taken leave of your senses?' Sibell started to laugh hysterically. Grasping her by the shoulders in a vice-like grip he shook her violently to stop the horrible noise. 'Cease that! What nonsense are you spouting?'

'He came here to . . . tell you that Sir Gilbert . . . has acknowledged him at last,' she gasped, between fits of laughter. 'He wouldn't have asked for my hand formally otherwise. We were going to leave here anyway. We're already married.' The laughter turned into tears again, and she threw herself down on top of Roger's still warm body. 'Nooo!'

When her wailing rose to an alarming pitch, her father glanced at Henry. 'Do something,' he said.

Henry nodded. Without further ado he lifted Sibell forcibly off the corpse and drew back his arm. She didn't even try to deflect the blow, just watched it coming.

The uppercut had the desired effect, instantly cutting off the noise she was making. Henry let her body slump to the floor, where she sat staring at them all in shock and mute anguish.

Utter silence reigned while their father continued his pacing for a few minutes. 'Well, here's a mess and no mistake,' he said at last and turned on his sons once again. 'What are you waiting for? Do as I ordered, and be quick about it. If need be, we'll have to kill Sibell too, although I think there are other ways of assuring her silence. Go! Out of my sight. I'm sick to death of the lot of you. Fools, imbeciles . . .'

'I had nothing to do with this. Why should I go anywhere?' Godwin folded his arms across his chest and stood his ground for once. He glared at his brothers. 'It was their doing, let them sort this out.'

Their father went over to stand face to face with Godwin. 'I'm well aware of that, but we both know they don't have the brains between them to keep themselves safe. You must get them away from here, hidden from justice, and make sure they stay that way. And who'll believe you anyway? We'll all swear you were part of this if you don't do as I say.'

Godwin narrowed his eyes at his sire in a look of pure venom that seemed to shock even him, as he took a step back.

'Listen,' his father said, his tone slightly more placating, 'your brothers need you now. I need you. Are you going to let us down? And I'm sure once the hue and cry dies down, you'll be able to come back. Just keep everyone safe until I work out a way to solve this.'

'We'll be outlaws and if I go with them,' Godwin nodded at his brothers, 'it will be tantamount to admitting my own guilt.'

'If they don't find the body, no one can prove anything and I'll say you've all gone on a journey. Joined the King for a while or some such. In fact, that's not a bad idea. Go fight for your sovereign, then come back covered in glory. By then, this will all be forgotten.'

'And Sibell?'

'She's marrying Sir Fulke. Now her husband is dead, what's to stop the marriage taking place? I'll see to it.'

Sibell watched and listened as if in a dream, but

didn't protest. She didn't care what happened to her now. As far as she was concerned, her life was over.

Jake woke in a pool of sweat, tangled up in the thin sheet he'd been using as a cover. It was too warm even for that. He unwrapped it and sat up. 'Jesus!'

His breathing was laboured and he felt as if he'd run a marathon. Every muscle in his body screamed in agony. He flexed them all and tried to relax, but it was impossible. Everything hurt. He'd been dreaming again and as before, he remembered everything with shocking clarity.

There had been a fight. Three shadowy figures with menacing leers on their dark faces had stalked him before attacking all at once. They had come from every direction, and he had fought for his life. *And for his love.* The words came unbidden and echoed inside his head. A knot of grief formed in his stomach. *'I failed her!'*

The voice was inside his head, the agony of self-reproach unbearable. And the pain of remembrance was a red-hot poker in his cranium. *'I can't leave her to their mercy! I cannot!'* Jake put his hands over his ears, hoping to make the voice go away. He didn't want to hear this. Didn't want to know. Slowly the dream faded away, and the silence returned.

Feeling the back of his head gingerly, Jake was surprised to find a huge lump which was very sore to the touch. He flinched as his fingers found the centre of it, and cursed under his breath. He must have thrashed around so much he'd hit his head on the bedside table. 'Damn,' he whispered.

Out of the corner of his eye he saw something move on the other side of the room. Straightening up, he peered into the darkness. The bedroom was large, taking up half the top floor of the house, and it was some time before he could make out anything substantial. The next breath caught in his throat as a woman emerged from the shadows, wringing her hands and weeping quietly. *Melissa.*

Wide awake now, he sat rigidly in the middle of the bed and stared. Ice-cold tendrils of dread spread through him and he shivered violently before looking more closely at the figure. No, it wasn't Melissa. *Could it be . . . Sibell?* Jake shook his head. No, surely not. He was becoming as fanciful as Melissa. He continued to gaze at the woman. *God, but she's so much like Melissa.*

The woman was taking shape in front of him. She was wearing something white and diaphanous. It billowed around her legs in slow motion. Her hair was unbound and floated around her body as she moved. It was very long, longer than Melissa's. Feelings of tenderness and love welled up inside him, but somehow he knew those weren't his feelings for this woman. They were someone else's. It made no difference, though. At last he was beginning to understand what Melissa had meant about being attracted to two people. He could finally comprehend her confusion.

The woman was begging for something, but he couldn't make out her words.

'What do you want?' His voice sounded hoarse and much too loud as it reverberated around the bedroom, and a sudden feeling of fear washed over him. Was she trying to tell him something had happened to Melissa and the girls? *Oh, no. Please, no.*

Ignoring the apparition, he fumbled for the switch of the bedside light and a bright beam illuminated the darkness. He barely noticed the lady fading away. Quickly, he located a piece of paper with the number of the hotel in Mallorca where Melissa and the girls were staying, and dialled. It rang for a long time before a sleepy Spanish voice answered.

'*Buenas noches. Hotel Playa Grande.*'

'Do you speak English?' His voice was abrupt to the point of rudeness.

'*Si, señor.* How can I help you?' If he hadn't been sick with worry, Jake would have laughed at the voice, which sounded exactly the way Spanish people were always made to speak in films. Instead, he gritted his teeth.

'Put me through to room 1302, please.' The man hesitated, obviously debating the wisdom of waking one of his guests in the middle of the night. Reluctantly he said, 'Very well, *señor.* Just one moment.' After all, Jake thought, it was none of the porter's business if crazy English people wanted to wake each other at such a late hour.

He waited for another eternity.

'Hello?' Melissa sounded breathless, but not sleepy.

'Melissa, sweetheart, are you all right? And the girls?'

'We're fine, Jake. Is something the matter? It's three o'clock in the morning! Has something happened to Dorothy?' He could hear the threatening hysteria in her voice and hurried to reassure her.

'No, no. Everything's okay here, too. I was just worried about you.'

'Why?'

'I've had a visitor. And a dream.' He told her what had happened and for a while she didn't reply.

'Melissa, are you still there?'

'Yes. Yes, I . . . I just dreamed almost the same thing. Oh, Jake, I think something happened to Roger at Ashleigh. Something awful.' Her voice shook and Jake wished he could take her in his arms to soothe her fears.

'I think so, too,' he admitted finally. 'What I can't figure out is what he wants us to do about it. For God's sake, this happened, what, six hundred years ago? It's crazy. This whole thing is madness.'

'It can't be, Jake, or we wouldn't both be experiencing these things. You know, I'm really glad it's happened to you, too.'

'Yes, now I'm beginning to understand what you

388

meant about being attracted to two people.' He laughed wryly.

'Confusing, isn't it? Did, er . . . Sibell say anything?'

'I think she was trying to, but I couldn't make it out and then I started to panic, thinking something had happened to you or the girls.'

They were quiet for a while, each lost in thought. Finally Melissa said, 'I'll be home the day after tomorrow. We'll have to talk more about it then. Let's try and get some sleep now.'

'Yes, you're right.' Now that he knew she was okay, he felt calmer. Sibell had been trying to tell him something else. Perhaps if he turned off the light she would return. 'I'll pick you all up at the airport as planned. See you then.'

He stared into the darkness for ages, but by the time sleep eventually claimed him Sibell hadn't come back.

Melissa returned to Ashleigh with mixed feelings. On the one hand there was the exhilaration of coming home, which she felt every time she saw the house. On the other, there was an absolute certainty that soon she would have to face some kind of confrontation with Roger. She knew now it would be impossible to go on living in the manor house unless she solved the riddle of the ghost. One of them had to win, one way or another. In the past, all the red-headed girls of the family would have been married off and sent away, thereby leaving Roger's quest unresolved. But Melissa was here to stay.

And I'm not leaving, she vowed.

At first, there were no dreams, sensations or ghostly apparitions to disturb her. No voices and no unusual scents. Melissa began to relax and to her great relief Jake was more understanding since the night of his own dream and unearthly visitor.

'I still think that if we ignore Roger, he'll eventually give up,' he insisted, but he didn't press her for an answer to his proposal. This made Melissa feel much better, even if she was no further forward in her search for a solution to the problem.

She resumed her work with newfound enthusiasm. From time to time she managed to lose herself in her genealogical charts and research, and resolutely ignored the little voice at the back of her mind which insisted she had to tell Jake soon about the baby. *Not yet,* she told it. She wasn't ready.

It was amazing that he hadn't noticed for himself, Melissa thought. Her stomach wasn't as flat as it had been, but perhaps she only saw it because she knew. She hadn't suffered any morning sickness and there were no other outward signs, but she couldn't go on hiding her condition for much longer.

She often wondered how long the mad desire for Jake would last. She'd thought it would lessen with time, but if anything, it was growing stronger.

She wanted him by her side every night, and every minute they spent apart was agony. Yet she still didn't dare to trust that her feelings were genuine. Roger may be quiet for the moment, but she knew deep down he hadn't given up.

A week after her return, the phone rang. It was Jenny.

'So you're back then? All right for some, swanning off to warmer climes,' she joked.

'Doctor's orders, I'm afraid. And I really do think it did me some good. But never mind that, have you got any news for me?'

'Yes, as a matter of fact I do. Not the manor court roll yet, they're still working on it. Apparently it's like a minute jigsaw puzzle in the middle, or so Jeff tells me . . .'

'Jeff? Is there something you're not telling me?'

'Possibly, but never mind that now.' Jenny sounded coy, then turned serious again. 'Listen, I had another brainwave and I've found something that might interest you.'

'Go on, tell me then.'

Jenny giggled. 'Now, now, patience is a virtue and all that.'

'Come on, Jenny, put me out of my misery here.'

'Okay, okay. Well, it occurred to me that if Sibell's lover died she might have paid to have masses said for his body. At the time, everyone believed having lots of masses said helped a body to reach heaven faster, or something like that. Anyway, I happen to know one of the chaps at the Canterbury Cathedral Archives and as it's the nearest big church to you, I thought I'd give it a shot. And guess what? Bingo.'

'You mean she did? She had masses said for him?'

'Yup. The records say she paid for no less than fifty "for the soul of my beloved husband, Roger of Langford". Aren't I a genius?'

'Absolutely! Candidate for sainthood, too, at the very least. But Roger of Langford? So he wasn't a Presseille after all then, no wonder we couldn't find him. Wow, this is wonderful. Honestly, I don't know how to thank you enough, Jenny. And I can't believe they were married after all. You're sure it said husband?'

'Yes, no doubt about it. Great, isn't it? So do you think that's the end of your quest then? Apart from whatever the manor court roll might contain, of course.'

'I suppose so, although . . . somehow I don't think that's quite it. It doesn't feel like I'm finished.' Melissa shook her head with a frown. 'It's hard to explain, but something's still missing. Wish I knew what it was.'

'Hmm. Well, I'll let you know as soon as that roll is ready for inspection.'

'Okay, I'll try to see if I can find out anything about a place called Langford or any Roger with that surname.'

Melissa found several places of that name,

although most of them were prefixed with something like 'Little', 'Upper' or 'Lower'. Only one was called Langford on its own – a village in Bedfordshire, but she still couldn't be sure that was Roger's birthplace. Most of them had no records before the late sixteenth century, and despite an extensive search through the additional records of various counties, and a trawl through the notes about possible Roger's she'd made previously, she found no mention of him.

Her despair returned in full force. Was she never to be free of this?

CHAPTER 32

Sibell remained immobile while her brothers were galvanised into action by their father's ire and hurried to their tasks. The youngest rushed outside, presumably to saddle his own horse before collecting Snowflake on the way out of the stable. How he would manage Roger's fierce warhorse, Sibell had no idea. The huge animal normally took exception to being handled by anyone not known to him and he would know something was wrong, of that Sibell was sure. It was some time before she heard Edmund set off at a gallop in the opposite direction to Idenhurst. No doubt Snowflake would make his way home eventually, but she didn't think Edmund intended it to be any time soon.

The others, with Godwin a reluctant participant, wrapped Roger's lifeless body in a coarse blanket and set off before Sibell had another chance to protest. Not that it mattered. Having at last grasped the fact that nothing would bring Roger back to life, she was past caring what else they did to him for the moment.

'Be sure to bury him far away,' her father called

after their retreating backs. 'I don't want any corpses found anywhere near this manor.'

The word 'corpse' roused Sibell from her stupor and she lifted her eyes to stare at her father. 'Murderer,' she said quietly, fixing him with a look of hatred she hoped would pierce him to the bone. 'I'll see you hang for this, all of you.'

'Not I, it wasn't my doing.' He laughed mirthlessly. 'And how would you accomplish such a thing, anyway? I'll make sure you never set foot outside these walls again until you leave with your new husband. And never think he'll listen to your tales of woe. Why should he care? No doubt he's done worse deeds himself.'

Sibell shivered at the thought. For once she was sure her father was right.

He had obviously had enough of this conversation, because the next thing she knew, he hefted her onto his shoulder, knocking all the air out of her lungs, and set off towards the stairs leading up to her chamber. He threw her down onto her bed, and looked around for something to tie her up with, but this gave her the opportunity to wriggle out of his grasp. She tried to make a run for the stairs.

'Come back here, you little bitch.' He was after her in a flash, much faster than she would have thought possible for a man of his girth. He caught her at the bottom of the stairs and pushed her to the floor. A desperate fight ensued, with Sibell using every weapon at her disposal, including a nearby three-legged stool, but he won in the end and used the piece of rope he'd found upstairs to tie her hands behind her back. Breathing heavily, he went to fetch a gag, which he wasted no time in tying into place. Hardly able to breathe, Sibell was left in a heap by the bottom step.

Next, her father began the task of clearing away the evidence of the foul deed committed by his sons. The floor of the hall had only recently been covered with planking and he had great difficulty in mopping up the blood, which had soaked into the grain of the new wood. He wasn't used to such menial tasks and muttered under his breath all the while about being cursed with idiots for offspring. Sibell laughed behind her gag at his inefficient methods, which didn't help his temper in the least. Red in the face and heaving with the effort, he finally gave up and covered the spot with rushes. No sooner had he finished, however, than all hell broke loose.

The front door crashed open to admit Sir Gilbert and his men. They came swarming into the room and Sibell saw her father blanch before he apparently recollected that his neighbour couldn't possibly know what had just occurred at Ashleigh.

'What is the meaning of this?' he blustered, before being seized by the throat by Sir Gilbert, who shook him like a terrier with a rat. The smaller man was shoved up hard against the wall and had to stand on tip-toe to avoid being throttled altogether.

'What . . . have you done . . . to my son?' Sir Gilbert snarled, sparks of hatred shining in his eyes. 'Where is Roger?'

'I-I've no idea what you're talking about, my lord,' Sibell's father stuttered in a croaky voice. 'There is no one here but me.'

'I can see that, you lack-wit. But I have it on good authority that you have murdered my son, and by God I'll have the truth out of you!' His grip tightened and he shook the smaller man repeatedly until his teeth rattled.

'Put me down, I haven't done anything,' her father protested, gasping for breath. 'There've been no visitors today.' He was visibly quaking with fear, but still defiant in what he must have thought of as the sure knowledge there was no evidence against him.

'Hah! You lie. I have it from the mouth of your own serving woman, Ingirith Waite, my son was here this afternoon, and that he was foully murdered by your sons in this very house. She hastened to Idenhurst to inform me; says she witnessed the deed through a crack in the door. Now tell me where I can find him or I'll break every bone in your miserable body, so help me God . . .' Sir Gilbert was obviously in the grip of intense fury and was breathing hard. The veins on his neck stood out and his face was a blotchy red colour.

'My lord, Mistress Sibell . . .' One of Sir Gilbert's men had been trying to attract his attention to her sorry plight and finally managed to get a word in edge-wise. Gilbert rushed over and knelt by her side.

'Sibell, my dear . . .' He untied the gag, then ordered one of his men to fetch her some water.

'I'm . . . all right. Just . . . see to my father. Make him . . . pay. Roger, he . . . I . . . my brothers . . .' She couldn't continue. Her throat seized up and her entire body was shaking with the reaction to the shock.

Gilbert needed no further bidding and after asking one of his men to keep an eye on Sibell, he returned to question her father further.

'Where have your despicable offspring taken him? And why did they kill him in the first place, hmm? What had he ever done to you?' Each question was punctuated by a heavy blow to the solar plexus, and Sibell's father gasped for air, like a landed fish. 'Tell me, you scum.'

The smaller man only shook his head.

'Roger came here with honourable intentions. He didn't deserve to be treated badly, let alone killed. Why? Why did you do it? Was a son of mine not good enough for you this time? You must needs throw in your lot with the likes of Sir Fulke?'

The beating continued in time with each question. Blows rained over her father: to the stomach, the face, the nose. Sibell flinched as a sickening crunch told her his nose had been broken, but still the man remained stubbornly silent. She realised then that no amount of threats would make him admit what his sons had done. Safe in the knowledge they were by now far away, he knew the only way to save them was to keep quiet.

He held out against his assailants, despite a severe beating, and in the end Sir Gilbert was cheated of his revenge. Her father's heart, already abused by years of good living, gave up its fight. With a horrible gurgling noise, he slid to the floor clutching his chest, his features twisted in agony. 'Go . . . to . . . hell,' he gasped, before collapsing completely. Sir Gilbert looked at the contorted face without a trace of compassion, then turned away in disgust.

'Search this house, men, and bring anyone you find to me,' Sir Gilbert ordered. 'There must be someone here who knows where they've taken Roger.'

The search produced only a cook, a kitchen maid and a young boy, all quaking in their shoes. All the other servants were working out in the fields, helping with the harvest. Gilbert gave up on them and returned to question Sibell, who had watched everything in mounting despair.

'Can you tell me what happened, my dear?' he asked gently. He stared at the huge bruise on her swollen jaw and reached out to cup her cheek. Sibell rubbed her wrists and answered with difficulty, tears flowing freely down her pale cheeks.

'Y-yes. My brothers, well, three of them . . . killed Roger, my lord. I-I couldn't stop them. I tried to help, but Henry . . .' She shook her head, unable

399

to go on. She glanced over towards her father, who was lying on the floor. On unsteady legs she stood up and walked over to look down on him, nudging him with her foot. 'Is he really dead?'

'Yes, I'm sorry.'

'I'm not.' She aimed a vicious kick at the corpulent body and swore at him. 'It was all his fault, even if he didn't actually commit the deed. May he rot in hell.'

Sir Gilbert came and put his hands on her shoulders and shook her slightly to stop the rising hysteria. 'Sibell, I need your help. Where do you think they might have taken Roger? I want to find his body so we can give him a decent burial. Someone will pay for this, I swear, and locating him might lead us to their trail.'

Sibell looked into his blue eyes, eyes the same colour as Roger's, and saw the deep sadness in their depths. This reminder of what she had lost proved too much for her, and she threw herself onto his broad chest in a storm of weeping, unable to control herself. He said nothing, just held her close, stroking her back in a soothing motion.

Finally, she calmed slightly, and managed to speak. 'I don't think you'll find him. I didn't see which way they went. My brothers will be long gone by now and they'll make sure they have left no tracks.'

'Be that as it may, I have to try.' Sir Gilbert was still grimly determined. 'Will you be all right on your own here for a while? I'll send someone to fetch Maude to you.'

'Yes. Go, Sir Gilbert. Find him if you can.'

But she knew in her heart that he never would.

The storm broke without warning just after lunch-time, and claps of thunder shook the foundations of the house with frightening regularity. Melissa huddled in front of the fire in the sitting room, cradling a mug of tea. A storm was brewing inside her too, but there was no one around to help. She knew the time had come for her to face this particular tempest. Alone.

Dorothy had gone to visit a friend for the after-noon, taking Russ with her, and the two girls were at Ashleigh Cottage playing with a new Playstation game Amy had been given for her birthday a few days earlier. Melissa was glad, but scared at the same time. The feeling of foreboding had come back with a vengeance, and last night her sleep had been broken by nightmares again and again. As usual she remembered very little, there were only snatches of conversation and snap-shots of horrendous images. A tremor slithered up her spine.

The rain-soaked world outside the windows was dark and gloomy, and the dim interior of the sitting room was lit only by the light from the fire. The flames cast eerie shadows onto the walls, where they danced sinuously in an uneven rhythm. Concentrating on the white-hot, glowing cave in

401

the heart of the fire, Melissa took a fortifying sip of sweet tea, then tried to clear her mind. She narrowed her eyes and stared at the precise spot by the fire where Roger had appeared once before, willing him to return.

'Roger, if you're here, please show yourself.' The command sounded pitiful, and she almost laughed at herself, but this was no laughing matter. She needed to end this now, if she was to have any chance of happiness herself, and she was sure the key to the mystery was in this room. She squared her shoulders and took a deep breath.

'Roger, do you hear me? Show yourself!' she yelled, anger and frustration giving her vocal cords additional strength. 'If you want me to help you, then for God's sake come and tell me how. I'm sick and tired of your games.'

Nothing happened. For long minutes she sat and listened to the sound of the rain beating against the windows. Roger didn't materialise next to her, nor did he bang the door or even make the tiniest of draughts. Had she imagined it all? Was she really going crazy? Tears of helplessness poured slowly down her cheeks and she put her face in her hands.

'I can't live like this, Roger. Please, stop interfering with my life . . .' The tears ran more freely, accompanied by great hiccoughing sobs. She was so tired of this. So tired of waiting for an answer.

The light from the fire caught the emerald eyes of the little dragon on the ring she was wearing, making them twinkle at her. It felt warm to the touch and she held up her hand to look at the dragon's face. His lips were drawn back to show off the sharp teeth, but it looked more like a smile than a snarl to her.

'I don't know what you're smiling at, you were supposed to help me, he said,' she whispered mournfully. 'I wish you would.' But how could an inanimate piece of metal possibly help her? She laughed bitterly. The idea was ridiculous in the extreme. The emerald eyes gleamed once more with a fire in their green depths, and she thought she felt a strange jolting electric shock zig-zag up her arm.

'Ouch!' She scowled at it, then realised she was being silly. Pieces of jewellery didn't give people shocks. 'Is there no end to my imagination these days?' she wondered out loud, then closed her eyes with a resigned sigh.

'Sweeting, help me . . .'

Melissa jumped and twisted this way and that to see where the voice was coming from. 'Roger? Are you there?'

'Sweeting, help me . . .'

The words echoed around the dimly lit room with an intensity that was almost painful. Melissa wasn't sure whether anyone else could have heard them, or if they were just audible inside her head, but she was absolutely certain about one thing – they were driving her insane.

'Stop it, leave me alone. I can't help you if you don't tell me how,' she shouted. 'God knows I've tried . . .' She searched the room with narrowed eyes to locate her Nemesis, but there was no one there. She clenched her jaw in frustration. 'Show yourself, damn you. I know you're here.'

His reply was to taunt her with silence.

She could feel his presence now. A prickling sensation on the back of her neck alerted her to his possible whereabouts, but when she swivelled round to look behind her right shoulder, there was only thin air.

'Look, I can't take any more of this. Either explain what you want me to do, or go away. Otherwise I shall have to move out of here, and don't think you can stop me.' It was an empty threat and she knew it, but did he? She hoped not.

A cold invisible hand caressed her cheek as if mocking her defiance. *'Sweeting, help me . . .'* The voice was close this time, so close.

A violent shiver went through Melissa. She'd heard those words so many times over the last few months. As long as she remained in the house, there was no escape from them. Or him. She was enthralled, ensnared, enslaved – his prisoner and his only hope. *But hope of what?*

'If only you'd tell me!'

Rain attacked the windowpanes with a ferocity that made Melissa happy to be indoors, and the occasional drops found their way down the chimney to land with a hissing sound in the fire. The dying embers stirred and made a curious rustling noise as they swirled around the hearth. Melissa watched them and waited. Did they herald his appearance? she wondered. Unconsciously, she held her breath, but she remained the room's only visible occupant and the embers settled down once more.

She slumped in the chair, depression settling over her like a heavy cloak. The ultimatum she had issued was obviously useless. His hold over her was such that she knew she couldn't break free. And she'd come to love the manor house. It was all she could have wished for in a home and more, and she desperately wanted to stay. Was it really just a few short months since she had first set eyes on the place? It felt like an eternity.

Melissa had coped with a lot during the last two years, but the situation she now found herself in was completely beyond her scope. Desperation welled up inside her, choking her.

'Please, I beg you, tell me what to do and I'll be happy to help you.' She meant it. She would do anything for him, anything at all, if only he would stop tormenting her.

'Sweeting, help me . . .'

His voice rang out, strong and clear, circling the room as if projected in stereo surround sound. It came at her from all directions and shook her to the core. She squeezed her eyes shut and felt tears prick her eyelids.

'Please,' she whispered, 'please, no. Don't do this to me.'

But the words just kept echoing around the walls

and Melissa buried her face in her hands and cried.

Some time later, her crying bout at an end, Melissa had to admit defeat. Roger hadn't done anything except torment her, repeating those three words endlessly, and all hope had died inside her. She would have to resign herself to the fact that she'd never know the answers to her questions, and the only way she could stay sane would be to leave Ashleigh Manor. She had threatened him that she would, and somehow she'd find a way to do it. *If I don't have the strength to leave of my own accord, I'll get someone to take me away.*

As she leaned her weary head back, her eyelids felt heavy and she nodded off. At one point she opened her eyes and saw a tall, blond figure bending over her solicitously, his hand caressing her hair with infinite gentleness. But she thought he must be a part of a dream and the words he whispered into her ear didn't register until much later.

CHAPTER 33

Sir Gilbert returned after dark, entering the
hall at Ashleigh with a dejected stoop to his
shoulders. Sibell looked up from her position
by the fire, but said nothing. Instead, he was
greeted by Maude and Katherine, who had come
over to support her. Their expressions were grave
and changed to sorrow when he shook his head
in answer to their unspoken question. He sat down
in a carved chair and accepted a cup of wine from
Katherine.

'You found nothing at all?' Maude's question
was more a statement of fact.

'No.' The one word said it all, but he continued
stating the obvious anyway. 'Sibell's brothers have
vanished without a trace. Those whoresons probably took the body with them and have dumped
it somewhere along the road, perhaps in a river
or lake. We won't find it now.' He took a deep
draught of the wine. 'But John of Ashleigh is dead,
so at least we needn't worry about Sibell's safety.
I shall leave some men here to keep watch in case
any of her brothers return. You won't come to any
more harm, my dear.' He sighed, then clenched

his jaw as he added, 'And I'll see to it they're declared outlaws so that this manor will belong to you from now on. You've no other close male kin, have you?'

Sibell shook her head.

'Good. We have a reliable witness to say your brothers are all murderers. They'll never dare show their faces here again so they can't challenge your right to Ashleigh.'

'But Godwin . . .' Sibell began.

'Has sided with the others, whether he wanted to or not. He's made his bed and must lie in it.' It was a harsh verdict, but Sibell didn't have the strength to argue. And Sir Gilbert was right; Godwin should have remained firm and stayed out of it.

'Oh, Gilbert . . .' Maude came over to lay her arms round his neck and leaned her cheek against his. 'It is too much. To lose two sons in a year, and in such a manner. I can't bear it . . .' Her voice broke.

Sibell had returned to feeling numb, but Lady Maude's words made the tears prick her eyelids once more. She saw Katherine surreptitiously wipe a tear off her cheek with her sleeve and blink furiously.

Everyone sat in silence for a while, contemplating the events of the day. Finally, Sir Gilbert stood up and came to stand in front of Sibell.

'I'm so very sorry I was such a stubborn fool, denying Roger his rightful place until it was too late. He told me he was going to ask for your hand in marriage and you know I would have welcomed you as a daughter-in-law once again. Nothing would have pleased me more.'

'They were already married,' Maude interjected.

'What?'

Maude nodded forlornly. 'Yes. They've been married for nearly two months. Isn't that right, Sibell?'

'Yes.'

'But . . . How do you know that?'

'Katherine and I witnessed the plighting of their troth and signed the marriage contract. It is hidden, but I'll show it to you.'

'I don't know why I am surprised. You seem to be vastly more observant than I am.' He dry-washed his face with a tired sigh. 'I should have known Roger would make sure everything was done properly. He was a good man.' He paused before adding, 'A son to be proud of.' His voice hoarse, he fought for composure. 'A shame we had so little time together. What a waste. What a dreadful waste. And for what?'

The answer to his question hung unsaid in the room.

'Well, I suppose your marriage simplifies matters at least,' Gilbert continued when he had regained his equilibrium somewhat. 'You must come and live with us then, Sibell.'

'Thank you, but no. I want to stay here. If Ashleigh is mine now, it will be my child's after me. This is where he or she must be born.' She put a protective hand over her abdomen, where the bump was becoming more noticeable every day. She had yet to feel the first flutters of life, but knew the child inside her was thriving despite everything.

'Child? Oh, my dear!' Maude's eyes lit up with joy. 'Then all is not lost. A part of Roger remains and you must think of the babe now and be strong.'

'Yes, you're right,' Sibell replied, but she knew a part of her had died this day and although Roger's child could help ease the pain, she would never feel whole again.

The storm had abated slightly when Melissa woke up, but the rain continued to pound on the tiny windowpanes. The fire was nothing but a heap of smouldering ashes and the room was left in semi-darkness. She stretched to ease her cramped limbs, then stood up and walked purposefully towards the door. Whispered words were echoing around her brain, telling her what to do. Still a bit woozy with sleep, she felt compelled to obey them without question.

'Yes, yes, I will go out,' she muttered. There was something she had to do outside. Something important. As an afterthought she ran to her room to fetch the large torch.

Grabbing her Barbour and a rain hat, she quickly put them on before pulling on her rubber boots. The house was dark and still. It felt curiously empty. Melissa locked the door and set off towards the fields, urged on by the voice inside her head. Little rivulets of rain soon poured off her hat and dripped onto her shoulders, but she didn't notice them. Neither did her mind register the fact that her jeans were soaking wet within minutes. She was focusing on her task.

Jake had just returned from his afternoon surgery, and had barely had time to greet the two girls before the phone rang.

'Jake? This is Dorothy. Have you seen Melissa?'

'No, I don't think she's here. Hold on, I'll ask the girls.' He put a hand over the receiver and relayed the question to Jolie and Amy. 'No, Dorothy. Jolie says her mum was at home. She was feeling tired apparently. Why do you ask? Perhaps she's just gone shopping or something.'

'No, she did that this morning. She told me she was going to rest this afternoon, but when I came back from Anne's the house was in darkness and the front door locked. As far as I can see her rubber boots are gone and her jacket, but why would she go for a walk in this weather? And she should have been back by now, it's almost dark.' Jake could hear the worry in Dorothy's voice. It was unlike her, and a stab of fear shot through him.

'She didn't take the car?'

'No, it's still here.'

'All right. Let me just change quickly, and I'll

411

go out and look for her. Perhaps she decided to go for a short walk and slipped in the mud or something and sprained an ankle.'

'Do you want to take Russ? Perhaps he can help?'

Jake hesitated. 'No, it's not really fair to drag him out in weather like this, he'll get soaked. I'll try on my own first; I can always fetch him later. And I'll take my mobile with me and call if I need help.'

'Very well, thank you, Jake. I'll wait to hear from you. I daren't go myself.'

'No, no, don't even think of trying!'

The footpath was a sea of mud and Jake found himself struggling to keep his footing. His rubber boots were caked in the squelchy stuff, making every step a huge effort, and he was drenched within minutes. Impatiently he wiped the rain off his face for the hundredth time. Where the hell was Melissa? Was she even out here, or had she just gone to visit a friend and forgotten to leave a note? He swore silently as a wet branch slapped him on the cheek.

He walked all the way round the fields belonging to Ashleigh, where Melissa usually took her walks, but saw neither hide nor hair of anyone. Anxiously he scanned the ditches along the way, shining his torch under bushes and peering into thickets of bramble and rose-hip. Nothing.

'Melissa!' His shout was swallowed up by the wind. It was useless. He was only wasting his time. 'Come on, Jake, think,' he told himself. Leaning tiredly against a stile he closed his eyes and tried to imagine where he would go if for some insane reason he decided to go for a walk on a rainy afternoon.

The sound of running water jogged his memory. *The river?* She might have gone there, although it wasn't near any of the paths she usually took. Or had she taken it into her head to visit the ruins of Idenhurst again? She'd told him about going there with Colin. Well, it was worth a try, anyway.

Wearily he trudged off once again, his boots making a slopping noise for each step he took. Fear for Melissa's safety grew inside him and he stopped noticing the discomfort of wet clothes on cold skin. He had to find her. He just had to.

'I can't lose her now,' he muttered.

'*I failed her . . .*' Roger's agonised cry suddenly echoed inside his head, but he fought it down with calm determination.

'Well, I won't, damn you!' he yelled into the darkness.

The old bridge loomed ahead of her and Melissa could feel the sensations of panic beginning to swirl through her brain. She gritted her teeth. *It's only a stone structure, for heaven's sake.* There was nothing there that could hurt her. She strode on towards her goal.

She still had no idea why she had this urge to go to the bridge. It wasn't as if she couldn't go some other day. In daylight. She frowned. The whisper continued to run through her mind, egging her on, telling her the time was right. *Now. It has to be now.* The voice was insistent and utterly bewitching. She had no choice but to obey. She would have done anything for that voice.

The river was noisy, its water level higher than normal, and it rushed by at alarming speed. Melissa concentrated on keeping her footing so as not to slip into its murky depths. She shuddered as she looked down. The riverbank was steep and treacherous and in some places large chunks had caved in and fallen into the water.

As she came closer to the bridge she thought she glimpsed shadowy figures looking over the side, but when she reached the foot of it and looked up there was no one there.

'Hello?' Her tentative call received no reply. Perhaps they had been children playing in the rain. 'Never mind,' she muttered and concentrated on keeping the tentacles of fear at bay. She felt threatened, and as she took another step towards the bridge a huge gust of wind took her by surprise and knocked her off her feet.

Melissa landed on all fours in the mud and dropped her torch. It wasn't completely dark yet, but she had switched it on anyway as she walked along the quiet footpaths. The light comforted her, made her feel safer. Now the beam was shining into a tangle of bushes, the light slightly dimmed by a glob of mud. Standing up with an exclamation of disgust, Melissa wiped her sticky hands on her jeans and bent to retrieve it.

Her hand closed around the handle and the beam swung in a wide arc as she picked it up. Melissa stiffened and gasped, remaining motionless for several seconds before she found the courage to direct the torch back towards the base of the bridge. Close to the water's edge, the top of a human skull stuck out of the mud. Its hollow eye sockets seemed to be staring at the sky, as if in supplication. A scream rose in her throat and she flung away, retching into the nearest clump of grass.

'Dear God,' she mumbled, wiping her mouth with a shaking hand. 'Jesus Christ.'

Melissa heard laughter, an almost hysterical mirth carried by the wind swirling all around her. It was as if she had entered a lunatic asylum where all the inmates shared a joke at her expense. Looking about wildly, she still felt threatened and wasn't surprised when another gust of wind knocked her to the ground again. This time she sprawled face first in a puddle, struggling for breath. There was something heavy on her back, holding her down, as if someone was sitting on her to keep her there. The water began to invade her nose and mouth. She had to break free.

'*Sweeting . . .*'

Roger's voice seemed to ease the pressure on her back momentarily and with a superhuman effort she heaved herself onto all fours and screamed,

'HELP!' She thought she heard the evil laughter returning, before being pushed back down into the muddy water. Panic squeezed her insides and she fought to lift her face off the ground. It was becoming increasingly difficult, despite the extra strength gained from the sheer terror she was experiencing.

Roger, help me again, please! she cried inside her mind, and once more he seemed to come to her rescue, long enough for her to come up to breathe.

'Melissa? *Melissa!*' She vaguely heard the sound of her name being shouted, but wasn't sure where it was coming from. In the howling wind and with her face half-buried in a puddle, it was impossible to tell whether the sound had been uttered by a human or by something else. There was a sudden increase in the weight on her back, then unexpectedly the pressure disappeared. Melissa lifted her face and drew in a shuddering breath before stumbling to her feet unsteadily. She ran blindly, as fast as her legs could manage.

'*Melissa!*' She recognised the voice at last and headed in its direction.

'Jake, here. I'm here. Oh, thank God, thank God . . .'

'Melissa . . . ooof!' She catapulted into him and flung her arms round his neck, nearly sending him flying into the river. 'What's the matter? Have you been attacked?' He held her so tightly, she thought her ribs would break, but it felt good. Wonderful, in fact.

'No. I m-mean yes. But not . . . by anything h-human.' Violent tremors were making it difficult for her to speak. 'The bridge, Jake, th-the bridge!' His gaze followed her pointing finger.

'What? What about the bridge? It attacked you?' He stared at her as though he feared for her sanity. 'You know, this ghost business has really gone too far.'

'No, you don't understand. It's Roger. I-I found him.' With a moan she clung to him again. 'Oh, Jake, look under the bridge. He's there. I saw his head.'

Jake patiently disentangled her arms from around his neck. 'All right. Shhh, it's okay. I'll go take a look. Just stay there, darling, don't move.' Reluctantly she let him go, but disobeyed him and followed close behind. She tucked her hand into his and held on for dear life.

'Be careful,' she whispered. 'There's someone else there too.' Jake frowned and headed for the bridge.

The wind seemed to pick up and was howling all around them. They leaned into it and made it to the edge of the river. Melissa felt the air crackle with menace, but Jake gave no sign that he noticed. He shone his torch downwards, swinging it back and forth to locate the cause of Melissa's distress, and found it.

The skull wasn't the only thing emerging from the mud. The base of the bridge was in the process of collapsing, and a section of it had fallen into the water, forcing the river to change direction slightly. Where the stones had been, a gaping hole was revealed, and inside it was possible to make out a human shape draped inside some type of material. At the top, the skull stuck out with a few tufts of hair still attached to it. Long, pale strands of hair flapping in the wind and glinting in the sheen from his torch. Jake closed his eyes for a moment.

'Poor man. No wonder he's been haunting me.' Melissa stared down into the hole, numb with pain.

'Yes, poor man indeed. I'll have to call the police. If it isn't Roger, then someone has been murdered, although not recently, I think.'

'It is Roger, and he was murdered all right. He answered my plea and led me here, I'm sure of it. Thank you,' Melissa whispered, staring at the lifeless form.

'Yes, I believe you, but we can't deal with this ourselves. We need help.'

He reached for his phone.

CHAPTER 34

Sibell sat on her bed, cross-legged, and stared at her wedding ring. Slowly she slipped it off and ran a finger along the runes etched inside. The gold felt warm to the touch, the little emerald eyes winked at her.

'Roger said you would grant me a wish,' she whispered to the little dragon, caressing his head gently. 'But I doubt you have the power to wakethe dead, so I can't have what I most want. There is something else I would ask of you, though.' The gold began to pulsate with a stronger heat. The only thing left to her now was revenge. She was strangely calm and she knew what she had to do.

Holding the tiny dragon aloft, she smiled at him and told him her wish. 'Kill those who wished my husband dead, dragon. Kill them all!' she whispered fiercely. 'Take away their lives in retribution for the one they took so callously. Make sure they know why they are dying, and make them fear death. Then dispatch them to where they belong.'

The ring was so hot now, it was agony to hold it, but she laughed and held onto it for a while longer. Then she threw it onto the floor where it rolled out of sight under a chair.

'I hope you make them suffer for all eternity.' Her voice broke on a sob and the tears coursed down her cheeks once more. The dragon would see to it. It was her one and only wish and she knew he would grant it.

Six months later the solar at Ashleigh was as hot as a furnace. To Sibell, labouring endlessly in the huge four-poster bed, it felt as if all the fires of hell were already upon her.

She had taken over her father's room in the sure knowledge that her brothers wouldn't dare return, since they would be hanged for murder the minute they set foot in the neighbourhood. She had decided it would be fitting for her child to be born there, as he or she would be master or mistress of Ashleigh one day.

Lady Maude came over to wipe her sweating brow with a cool, damp cloth. 'There, there, dear, it will soon be over,' she soothed, but she didn't look Sibell in the eye.

Sibell's travail had already lasted for nearly two days and her strength was fading fast. Her body was racked with pain, but sheer stubbornness gave her the power to push one last time.

'That's it, mistress. Go on, you are nearly there, I can see the head.' Sibell didn't hear the midwife's encouragement, but pushed once more all the same. The white-hot agony slicing through her drowned out every sound.

'Aaaargh!' The scream came out as a hoarse whisper, so abused were her poor vocal chords, but at last the incessant pain left her. Sibell was dimly aware of an infant wailing, and then a bundle was placed next to her.

'It's a little girl, mistress. A beautiful girl.'

Sibell gazed in wonder at her daughter. 'Meriel,' she whispered. 'Sweeting.' There was just enough strength left in her weary body for her to bend and kiss her daughter's downy blonde head.

As she turned her head she saw someone coming towards her, someone she hadn't seen for many years. The other people in the room faded away into the background and instead she beheld her mother, waiting with open arms.

'Mother?' Her lips framed the word, but no sound came. A frown gathered on her forehead then, and her eyes darted around looking for the one she sought. The only one who should have been waiting for her.

'Roger?' She managed to whisper his name and saw the other occupants of the room smile. They obviously assumed she had found her love, and were happy for her. If anyone deserved some happiness, it was their mistress, she heard them murmur.

But where was Roger? She couldn't see him and panic assailed her. Without him, she wasn't going anywhere. Her mother came inexorably closer, beckoning her daughter, but Sibell resisted with all her might.

'No! I won't go without him. Leave me alone!' Her mother shook her head sadly and Sibell suddenly knew it was useless. It was time for her to leave, and she had to trust that she would meet up with Roger when she arrived at her destination. She began to pray feebly and clung to the hope that God would unite them. She had to believe in Him. He would make it all right.

'Roger,' she whispered hoarsely again, before surrendering. 'Roger, my love . . .'

The wheels of officialdom turned slowly, but on a cold day in March, Sir Roger of Langford was at last given a Christian burial in the little graveyard outside the village church. By special dispensation, Sibell's remains were disinterred and transferred to lie next to him, although the brass plaque in her honour remained inside the church. At Melissa's request, the ceremony was performed by Mr Atwell, who was very obviously relieved to be doing something he had been trained for and could cope with. Despite having only the few scant details about the deceased couple that Melissa had been able to provide him with, he managed an eloquent and very moving speech, for which Melissa was grateful.

Later, as she stood hand in hand with Jake, admiring the simple headstone in the shape of a cross, a sigh of contentment escaped her. She turned to smile at her new husband. 'Can you feel the peace, Jake? It's all around us.'

He smiled back and bent down for a kiss. He had to lean across the pouches they carried, each containing a tiny boy who were both, thankfully, asleep for the moment. He cradled the small, warm body of Roland Precy against his chest, as if not quite willing to entrust his son to the pouch's straps, even though they were perfectly safe.

'Yes, I hope they're as happy as we are,' he replied, and smiled again when he saw Melissa cradle little Roger in the same protective way. They stood in silence for a moment longer, before he added, 'I'm glad you don't have any brothers. Imagine being murdered by your own brothers-in-law.' He shook his head.

Jenny had finally faxed over the last part of the manor court roll and they now had the bare facts – Sibell's husband, Sir Gilbert's illegitimate son Roger, had been murdered by her brothers. The roll stated that they were hunted for the murder, but in the end they had evaded capture. Someone had brought word that they'd all died on a battle-field at Towton while fighting for the King, but whether this was true or not, no one knew. Apparently they were never seen again, though.

'Yes, a shame they weren't caught and punished, but I'm sure they received their just desserts one way or another. If they really fought at Towton, that battle raged during a snowstorm and a lot of the King's men drowned in a freezing cold river. Not a nice way to go.'

'Still too good for the likes of them,' Jake muttered. After another contemplative silence, he shook his head. 'So Roger of Langford was your ancestor, not mine. Weird, isn't it, when I'm the one who looks like him.'

'Yes, but don't forget you're descended from one of Sir Gilbert's brothers, so you share the same genes. It *is* strange to think you and I are related way back, but so many generations ago it doesn't matter now.' She sighed. 'You know, I almost miss the dreams when he talked to me, it was so real.'

Jake frowned. 'Well, I'm glad he's gone. I wouldn't want you to dream of other men now we're married.'

Melissa giggled. 'But how could you be sure it wasn't you I was dreaming of? After all, you're his spitting image or vice versa.' She smoothed away his frown with soft fingers. 'Don't worry, I know now you're the only one I love. I don't have Sibell's feelings running around inside me any longer, only my own.'

'Well, that's all right then.' He kissed her again and hugged Roland closer as the baby stirred in his sleep and whimpered slightly. 'Come on, let's get these two home before they catch cold. It must be feeding time soon, and anyway, we should all be sitting in front of the fire on a day like this. The girls and Dorothy will be waiting with tea by now.' Tactful as ever, Dorothy had kindly taken the girls home directly after the service, in order to give Melissa and Jake some time on their own.

Melissa felt the warmth of happiness spread inside her at his words. 'Yes, let's go home to Ashleigh. I'm glad you and Amy didn't mind moving in with us. It felt so right.'

'Why would we mind? It's a wonderful place to live.'

Melissa couldn't agree more.

Neither of them noticed the two shadowy figures hovering near the gravestone as they left. Entwined, as one, the wraiths sank slowly into the ground like mist on a summer morning and the birds in a nearby tree broke into song.